The
Tudor Secret

Also by C. W. Gortner

The Last Queen
The Confessions of Catherine de Medici

The
Tudor Secret

C. W. Gortner

St. Martin's Griffin
New York

This is a work of fiction. All of the characters, organizations, and events portrayed in this novel are either products of the author's imagination or are used fictitiously.

www.stmartins.com

Library of Congress Cataloging-in-Publication Data

Gortner, C. W.
    The Tudor secret : the Elizabeth I spymaster chronicles / C. W. Gortner.—1st ed.
        p. cm.
    ISBN 978-0-312-60390-8 (hardcover)
    ISBN 978-0-312-65850-2 (trade paperback)
    1. Elizabeth I, Queen of England, 1533–1603—Fiction.
2. Burghley, William Cecil, Baron, 1520–1598—Fiction.   3. Great Britain—History—Elizabeth, 1558–1603—Fiction.   4. Burghley, William Cecil, Baron, 1520–1598—Fiction.   5. Great Britain—History—Edward VI, 1547–1553—Fiction.   I. Title.
    PS3607.O78T83 2011
    813'.6—dc22

                                                        2010038846

First Edition: February 2011

10 9 8 7 6 5 4 3 2 1

For Linda, best friend

The
Tudor Secret

—◆◆◆—

Everyone has a secret.

Like the oyster with its grain of sand, we bury it deep within, coating it with opalescent layers, as if that could heal our mortal wound. Some of us devote our entire lives to keeping our secret hidden, safe from those who might pry it from us, hoarding it like the pearl, only to discover that it escapes us when we least expect it, revealed by a flash of fear in our eyes when caught unawares, by a sudden pain, a rage or hatred, or an all-consuming shame.

I know all about secrets. Secrets upon secrets, wielded like weapons, like tethers, like bedside endearments. The truth alone can never suffice. Secrets are the coin of our world, the currency upon which we construct our edifice of grandeur and lies. We need our secrets to serve as iron for our shields, brocade for our bodies, and veils for our fears: They delude and comfort, shielding us always from the fact that in the end we, too, must die.

"Write it all down," she tells me, "every last word."

We often sit like this in the winter of our lives, chronic insomniacs *in outdated finery, the chessboard or the game of cards neglected on the table, as her eyes—alert and ever-wary after all these years, still leonine in a face grown gaunt with age—turn inward to that place where none has ever trespassed, to her own secret, which I now know, have perhaps always known, she must take with her to her grave.*

"Write it down," she says, "so that when I am gone, you will remember."

As if I could ever forget . . .

Chapter One

Like everything important in life, it began with a journey—
the road to London, to be exact, my first excursion to that
most fascinating and sordid of cities.

We started out before daybreak, two men on horseback. I
had never been farther than Worcestershire, which made Master Shelton's arrival with my summons all the more unexpected.
I scarcely had time to pack my few belongings and bid farewell
to the servants (including sweet Annabel, who'd wept as if
her heart might break) before I was riding from Dudley Castle,
where I'd spent my entire life, unsure of when, or if, I would return again.

My excitement and apprehension should have been enough
to keep me awake. Yet I soon found myself nodding off to sleep,
lulled by the monotony of the passing countryside and my roan
Cinnabar's comfortable amble.

Master Shelton startled me awake. "Brendan, lad, wake up.
We're almost there."

I sat up in my saddle. Blinking away my catnap, I reached up
to straighten my cap and found only my unruly thatch of light

auburn hair. When he first arrived to fetch me, Master Shelton had frowned at its length, grumbling that Englishmen shouldn't go about unshorn like the French. He wouldn't be pleased by the loss of my cap, either.

"Oh, no." I looked at him.

He regarded me impassively. A puckered scar ran across his left cheek, marring his rugged features. Not that it mattered. Archie Shelton had never been a handsome man. Still, he had impressive stature and sat his steed with authority; his cloak, emblazoned with the ragged bear and staff, denoted his rank as the Dudley family steward. To anyone else, his granite stare would have inspired trepidation. But I had grown accustomed to his taciturn manner, as he had been overseeing my upkeep since his arrival in the Dudley household eight years ago.

"It fell off about a league back." He extended my cap to me. "Since my days in the Scottish wars, I've never seen anyone sleep so soundly on horseback. You'd think you'd been to London a hundred times before."

I heard rough mirth in his rebuke. It confirmed my suspicion that he was secretly pleased by this precipitous change in my fortune, though it wasn't in his nature to discuss his personal sentiments regarding anything the duke or Lady Dudley commanded.

"You can't go losing your cap about court," he said as I clapped the red cloth hat back on my head and peered toward where the sun-dappled road climbed over a hill. "A squire must be attentive at all times to his appearance." He eyed me. "My lord and lady expect much of their servants. I trust you can remember how to behave with your betters."

"Of course." I squared my shoulders, reciting in my most obsequious tone: "It's best to remain silent whenever possible and to always keep your eyes lowered when spoken to. If uncertain as to how to address someone, a simple 'my lord' or 'my lady' will suffice." I paused. "See? I haven't forgotten."

Master Shelton snorted. "See that you don't. You're to be a squire to his lordship's son, Lord Robert, and I'll not see you squander the opportunity. If you excel in this post, who knows? You could rise to chamberlain or even steward. The Dudleys are known to reward those who serve them well."

As soon he uttered these words, I thought I should have known.

When Lady Dudley joined her family year-round at court, she had sent Master Shelton twice a year to the castle where I remained with a small staff. He came ostensibly to oversee our upkeep, but whereas before my duties had been confined to the stables, he assigned me other household chores and paid me, for the first time, a modest sum. He even took in a local monk to tutor me—one of thousands who begged and bartered their way through England since old King Henry had abolished the monasteries. The staff at Dudley Castle had deemed her ladyship's steward unnatural, a cold and solitary man, unmarried and with no children of his own; but he had shown me unexpected kindness.

Now I knew why.

He wanted me to be his successor, once old age or infirmity demanded his retirement. It was hardly the role I aspired to, filled as it was with the tiresome domestic obligations that Lady Dudley had neither time nor inclination for. Though it was a far better future than someone in my shoes ought to expect, I thought that I'd rather remain a stable hand than become a privileged lackey dependent on Dudley sufferance. Horses, at least, I understood, whilst the duke and his wife were strangers to me, in every sense of the word.

Still, I mustn't appear ungrateful. I bowed my head and murmured, "I would be honored if I were one day deemed worthy of such a post."

A cragged smile, all the more startling because of its rarity, lightened Master Shelton's face. "Would you now? I thought as much. Well, then, we shall have to see, shan't we?"

I smiled in return. Serving as squire to Lord Robert would prove challenge enough without my worrying over a potential stewardship in the future. Though I'd not seen the duke's third-eldest son in years, he and I were close in age and had lived together during our childhood.

In truth, Robert Dudley had been my bane. Even as a boy, he'd been the most handsome and talented of the Dudley brood, favored in everything he undertook, be it archery, music, or dance. He also nursed an inflated sense of pride in his own superiority—a bully who delighted in leading his brothers in rousing games of "thrash-the-foundling."

No matter how hard I tried to hide or how fiercely I struggled when caught, Robert always managed to hunt me down. He directed his walloping gang of brothers to duck me into the scum-coated moat or dangle me over the courtyard well, until my shouts turned to sobs and my beloved Mistress Alice rushed out to rescue me. I spent the majority of my time scrambling up trees or hiding, terrified, in attics. Then Robert was sent to court to serve as a page to the young Prince Edward. Once his brothers were likewise dispatched to similar posts, I discovered a new-found and immensely welcome freedom from their tyranny.

I could hardly believe I was now on my way to serve Robert, at his mother's command, no less. But of course, noble families did not foster unfortunates like me for charity's sake. I had al-

ways known a day would come when I'd be called upon to pay
my debt.

My thoughts must have shown on my face, for Master Shelton cleared his throat and said awkwardly, "No need to worry.
You and Lord Robert are grown men now; you just mind your
manner and do as he bids, and all will go well for you, you'll see."
In another rare display of sensibility, he reached over to pat my
shoulder. "Mistress Alice would be proud of you. She always
thought you would amount to something."

I felt my chest tighten. I saw her in my mind's eye, wagging a
finger at me as her pot of herbs bubbled on the hearth and I sat
entranced, my mouth and hands sticky with fresh-made jam.
"You must always be ready for great things, Brendan Prescott,"
she would say. "We never know when we'll be called upon to rise
above our lot."

I averted my eyes, pretending to adjust my reins. The silence
lengthened, broken only by the steady *clip-clop* of hooves on the
cobblestone-and-baked-mud road.

Then Master Shelton said, "I hope your livery fits. You could
stand to put some meat on your bones, but you've good posture.
Been practicing with the quarterstaff like I taught you?"

"Every day," I replied. I forced myself to look up. Master Shelton had no idea of what else I'd been practicing these past few
years.

It was Mistress Alice who had first taught me my letters. She
had been a rarity, an educated daughter of merchants who'd
fallen on hard times; and while she'd taken a post in the Dudley
service in order to keep, as she liked to say, "my soul and flesh
together," she always told me the only limit on our minds is the
one we impose. After her death, I had vowed to pursue my studies

in her memory. I lavished the sour-breathed monk that Master Shelton had hired with such fawning enthusiasm that before he knew it, the monk was steering me through the intricacies of Plutarch. I often stayed up all night, reading books purloined from the Dudley library. The family had acquired shelves of tomes, mostly to show off their wealth, as the Dudley boys took more pride in their hunting prowess than any talent with the quill. But for me, learning became a passion. In those musty tomes I found a limitless world, where I could be whomever I wanted.

I repressed my smile. Master Shelton was literate, as well; he had to be in order to balance household accounts. But he made a point of saying he never presumed to more than his station in life and would not tolerate such presumption in others. In his opinion, no servant, no matter how assiduous, should aspire to be conversant on the humanist philosophies of Erasmus or essays of Thomas More, much less fluent in French and Latin. If he knew how much his tutor payments had bought for me in these past years, I doubt he'd be pleased.

We rode on in quiet, cresting the hill. As the road threaded through a treeless vale, the emptiness of the landscape caught my attention, used as I was to the unfettered Midlands. We weren't too far away, and yet I felt as if I entered a foreign domain.

Smoke smeared the sky like a thumbprint. I caught sight of twin hills, then the rise of massive walls surrounding a sprawl of tenements, spires, riverside manors, and endless latticed streets—all divided by the wide swath of the Thames.

"There she is," said Master Shelton. "The City of London. You'll miss the peace of the countryside soon enough, if the cutthroats or pestilence don't get to you first."

I could only stare. London was as dense and foreboding as I'd imagined it would be, with kites circling overhead as if the air contained carrion. Yet as we drew closer, abutting those serpentine walls I spied pasturelands dotted with livestock, herb patches, orchards, and prosperous hamlets. It seemed London still had a good degree of the rural to commend it.

We reached one of the seven city gates. I took in everything at once, enthralled by a group of overdressed merchants perched on an ox-drawn cart, a singing tinker carrying a clanging yoke of knives and armor, and a multitude of beggars, apprentices, officious guildsmen, butchers, tanners, and pilgrims. Voices collided in argument with the gatekeepers, who had called a halt to everyone's progress. As Master Shelton and I joined the queue, I lifted my gaze to the gate looming overhead, its massive turrets and fanged crenellations blackened by grime.

I froze. Mounted on poles, staring down through sightless sockets, was a collection of tar-boiled heads—a grisly feast for the ravens, which tore at the rancid flesh.

Beside me Master Shelton muttered, "Papists. His lordship ordered their heads displayed as a warning."

Papists were Catholics. They believed the pope in Rome, not our sovereign, was head of the Church. Mistress Alice had been a Catholic. Though she'd raised me in the Reformed Faith, according to the law, I'd watched her pray every night with the rosary.

In that instant, I was struck by how far I had come from the only place I had ever known as home. There, everyone turned a blind eye to the practices of others. No one cared to summon the local justices or the trouble these entailed. Yet here it seemed a man could lose his head for it.

An unkempt guard lumbered to us, wiping greasy hands on his tunic. "No one's allowed in," he barked. "Gates are hereby closed by his lordship's command!" He paused, catching sight of the badge on Master Shelton's cloak. "Northumberland's man, are you?"

"His lady wife's chief steward." Master Shelton withdrew a roll of papers from his saddlebag. "I have here safe conducts for me and the lad. We are due at court."

"Is that so?" The guard leered. "Well, every last miserable soul here says they're due somewhere. Rabble's in a fine fettle, what with these rumors of His Majesty's mortal illness and some nonsense of the Princess Elizabeth riding among us." He hawked a gob of spit into the dirt. "Idiots. They'd believe the moon was made of silk if enough swore to it." He didn't bother to check the papers. "I'd keep away from crowds if I were you," he said, waving us on.

We passed under the gatehouse. Behind us, I heard those who had been detained start to yell in protest. Master Shelton tucked the papers back into the saddlebag. The parting of his cloak revealed a broadsword strapped to his back. The glimpse of the weapon riveted me for a moment. I surreptitiously reached a hand to the sheathed knife at my belt, a gift from Master Shelton on my fourteenth year.

I ventured, "His Majesty King Edward . . . is he dying?"

"Of course not," retorted Master Shelton. "The king has been ill, is all, and the people blame the duke for it, as they blame him for just about everything that's wrong in England. Absolute power, lad, it comes with a price." His jaw clenched. "Now, keep an eye out. You never know when you'll run into some knave who'd just as soon cut your throat for the clothes on your back."

I could believe it. London was not at all what I had envisioned. Instead of the orderly avenues lined with shops, which populated my imagination, we traversed a veritable tangle of crooked lanes piled with refuse, with side alleys snaking off into pockets of sinister darkness. Overhead, rows of dilapidated buildings leaned against each other like fallen trees, their ramshackle galleries colliding together, blocking out the sunlight. It was eerily quiet, as though everyone had disappeared, and the silence was all the more disconcerting after the clamor at the gate we had left behind.

Suddenly, Master Shelton pulled to a halt. "Listen."

My every nerve went on alert. A muted sound reached me, seeming to come from everywhere at once. "Best hold on," warned Master Shelton, and I tightened my grip on Cinnabar, edging him aside moments before an onslaught of people came pouring into the street. Their appearance was so unexpected that despite my grip, Cinnabar started to rear. Fearing he would trample someone, I slid from the saddle to take hold of his bridle.

The crowd pressed around us. Deafening loud, motley, and smelling of sweat and sewer, they made me feel as though I were prey. I started to angle for the dagger at my belt before I noticed that no one was paying me any mind. I looked at Master Shelton, still mounted on his massive bay. He barked an indecipherable order. I craned my head, straining to hear him above the noise of the crowd.

"Get back on that horse," he shouted again, and I was almost knocked off my feet as the multitude surged forward. It was all I could do to scramble onto Cinnabar before we were propelled by the mob, careening among them down a narrow passage and spilling out onto a riverbank.

I yanked Cinnabar to a halt. Before me, algaed as liquid jasper, ran the Thames. In the distance downstream, rimmed in haze, a stone pile bullied the landscape.

The Tower.

I went still, unable to take my gaze from the infamous royal fortress. Master Shelton cantered up behind me. "Didn't I tell you to keep an eye open? Come. This is no time for sightseeing. The mob in London can turn cruel as a bear in a pit."

I forced myself to pull away and check my horse. Cinnabar's flanks quivered with a fine lather, his nostrils aflare, but he seemed unharmed. The crowd had rushed ahead toward a wide road, bordered by a line of tenement houses and swinging tavern signs. As we moved forth, I belatedly reached up to my brow. By some miracle, my cap remained in place.

The crowd came to a stop, an impoverished group of common folk. I watched, bemused, as barefoot urchins tiptoed among them, dogs skulking at their heels. Thieves, and not one over nine years old by the looks of them. It was hard to see them and not see myself, the wretch I might have been had the Dudleys not taken me in.

Master Shelton scowled. "They're blocking our passage. Go see if you can find out what this lot is gawking at. I'd rather we not force our way through if we can help it."

I handed over my reins, dismounted again, and wedged into the crowd, thankful for once for my slight build. I was cursed at, shoved, and elbowed, but I managed to push to the front. Standing on tiptoes to look past the craning heads, I made out the dirt thoroughfare, upon which rode an unremarkable cavalcade of people on horses. I was about to turn away when a portly woman beside me shoved her way forth, brandishing a wilted nosegay.

"God bless you, sweet Bess," she cried. "God bless Your Grace!"

She threw the flowers into the air. A hush fell. One of the men in the cavalcade heeled close to its center, as if to shield something—or someone—from view.

It was then I noticed the dappled charger hidden among the larger horses. I had a keen eye for horseflesh, and with its arched neck, lithe musculature, and prancing hooves I recognized it for a Spanish breed rarely seen in England, and more costly than the duke's entire stable.

Then I looked at its rider.

I knew at once it was a woman, though a hooded cloak concealed her features and leather gauntlets covered her hands. Contrary to custom, she was mounted astride, legs sheathed in riding boots displayed against the embossed sides of her saddle—a sliver of a girl, without apparent distinction, save for her horse, riding as if intent on reaching her destination.

Yet she knew we were watching her and she heard the woman's cry, for she turned her head. And to my astonishment, she pushed her hood back to reveal a long fine-boned face, framed by an aureole of coppery hair.

And she smiled.

Chapter Two

Everything around me receded. I recalled what the guard at the gate had said—*some nonsense of the Princess Elizabeth riding among us*—and I felt an actual pang in my heart as the cavalcade quickened down the thoroughfare and disappeared.

The crowd began to disperse, though one of the urchins did creep onto the road to retrieve the fallen nosegay. The woman who'd thrown it stood transfixed, hands at her breast, gazing after the vanished riders with the gleam of tears in her weary eyes. I reached out and lightly touched her arm. She turned to me with a dazed expression.

"Did you see her?" she whispered, and though she looked right at me, I had the impression she did not see me at all. "Did you see our Bess? She's come to us at last, God be praised. Only she can save us from that devil Northumberland's grip."

I stood immobile, grateful I carried my livery in my saddlebag. Was this how the people of London viewed John Dudley, Duke of Northumberland? I knew the duke now served as the king's chief minister, having assumed power following the fall of the king's former protector and uncle, Edward Seymour. Many in the land had cursed the Seymours for their avarice and ambition. Had the duke incurred the same hatred?

I turned from the woman. Master Shelton had ridden up behind me; he stared glowering from his bay. "You are a fool, woman," he rumbled, "Careful my lord the duke's men don't ever hear you, for they'll cut out your tongue sure as I'm sitting here."

She gaped at him. When she caught sight of the badge on his cloak, she staggered back. "The duke's man!" she gibbered. She stumbled away. Those who remained took up the cry as they, too, fled for the safety of the tangled alleys or the nearest tavern.

On the other side of the thoroughfare, a group of decidedly coarse-looking men paused to stare at us. As I saw the glint of blades being jerked from sleeves, my stomach somersaulted.

"Best mount now," said Master Shelton, without taking his eyes from the men. He did not need to tell me twice. I vaulted onto my saddle as Master Shelton swerved about, scanning the vicinity. The men started to cross the road, partially blocking the route the cavalcade had taken. I waited with my heart in my throat. We had two options. We could go back the way we'd come, which led to the riverbank and maze of streets, or plunge into what looked like an impenetrable row of decrepit timber-framed buildings. Master Shelton seemed to hesitate, whirling his bay back around on its hindquarters to gauge the approaching men.

Then his scarred face broke into a ferocious grin, and he dug his heels into his bay to vault forth—straight at them.

I kicked Cinnabar into swift action and followed at a breakneck pace. The men froze in midstep, eyes popping as they beheld the charge of solid muscle and hooves coming toward them. In unison, they flung themselves to either side like the clods of dirt our horses tore from the road; as we thundered past, I heard a gut-wrenching scream cut short. I glanced back.

One of the men lay facedown on the road, a pool of red seeping from his mangled head.

We plunged between the ramshackle edifices. All light extinguished. The miasmic smells of excrement, urine, and rotting food overpowered me like a mantle thrown over my face. Overhead, balconies formed a claustrophobic vault, festooned with dripping laundry and slabs of curing meat. Night soil splashed as our horses bolted through overflowing conduits that emptied the city's filth into the river. I held my breath and clenched my teeth, tasting bile in my throat as the torturous passage seemed to go on forever, until we burst, gasping, into open expanse.

I reined Cinnabar to a halt. Everything reeled about me, and I closed my eyes, breathing in deeply to catch my breath and steady the whirlwind in my head. I sensed sudden silence, smelled ripe grass and a tang of apple smoke on the air. I opened my eyes.

We had crossed into another world.

About us, looming oaks and beeches swayed. A meadow stretched as far as my eye could see. I marveled at the peculiarity of such an oasis in the midst of the city; turning to Master Shelton, I saw he was looking straight ahead, his face like weathered stone. I had never seen him behave as he had a moment ago, riding as if hell-bent over the body of a helpless man, as though he had sloughed aside the veneer of privileged chamberlain to reveal the mercenary underneath.

I took a moment to collect my thoughts. Then I said carefully, "That woman . . . she called her Bess. Was she . . . the king's sister, Princess Elizabeth?"

Master Shelton's voice was hard. "If she was, then she'll only bring trouble. It follows her wherever she goes, just as it did her whore of a mother."

I didn't dare say more. I knew about Anne Boleyn, of course. Who didn't? Like many in the land, I had grown up to the lurid tales of Henry VIII and his six wives by whom he had sired his son, our current king, Edward VI, and two daughters, the ladies Mary and Elizabeth. In order to marry Anne Boleyn, King Henry had cast aside his first wife, the Lady Mary's mother, Katherine of Aragon, who was a princess of Spain. He then made himself head of the Church. It was said that Anne Boleyn laughed when she was crowned; but she did not laugh for long. Reviled by the people as a heretic witch, who had spurred the king to upend the kingdom, only three years after she gave birth to Elizabeth, Anne was accused of incest and treason. She was beheaded, as were her brother and four other men. King Edward's mother, Jane Seymour, was betrothed to Henry the day after Anne died.

I knew that many people who had lived through Anne's rise and fall despised her, even after her tragic end. Katherine of Aragon still prevailed in the common heart, her stoic grace never forgotten, even as her life was torn apart. Nevertheless, I was unnerved by the vehemence in Master Shelton's voice. He spoke as if Elizabeth were to blame for her mother's deeds.

Even as I tried to make sense of it, he directed my attention to a silhouette etched like thorns against the darkening evening sky. "That's Whitehall," he said. "Come, it's getting late. We've had enough excitement for one day."

We rode across the vast open park, into streets that fronted walled manors and dark medieval churches. I saw a large stone cathedral standing like a sentinel on a slope and marveled at its stark splendor; as we neared Whitehall Palace itself, I was overcome by awe.

I had seen castles before. Indeed, the Dudley estate where I'd been raised was reckoned one of the most impressive in the realm. But Whitehall was unlike anything I'd seen. Nestled by a curve in the river, Henry VIII's royal residence rose before me—a multicolored hive of fantastical turrets, curved towers, and galleries sprawling like somnolent beasts. From what I could discern, two major thoroughfares dissected it, and every square foot teemed with activity.

We entered under the northern gate, cantering past a crowded forecourt into an inner courtyard crammed with jostling menials, officials, and courtiers. Taking our horses by the reins, we started to make our way on foot to what I assumed would be the stables, when a trim man in a crimson doublet walked purposefully toward us.

Master Shelton stopped, bowed stiffly. The man likewise inclined his head in greeting. His pale blue eyes assessed us, a spade-shaped russet beard complimenting his lively features. I had the impression of an ageless vitality about him, as well as a keen intelligence.

As I lowered my eyes in deference, I espied crescents of dried ink under his fingernails. I heard him say in a cool tone, "Master Shelton, her ladyship informed me you might be arriving today. I trust your travels were not too arduous."

Master Shelton said quietly, "No, my lord."

The man's gaze shifted to me. "And this is . . . ?"

"Brendan," I blurted, before I realized what I was doing. "Brendan Prescott. To serve you, Your Grace." On impulse I executed a bow that demonstrated hours of painstaking practice, though to him I must have seemed inept.

As if to confirm my thoughts, he let out a hearty laugh. "You must be Lord Robert's new squire." His smile widened. "Your master may require such lofty address from you in private, but I am content with a mere 'Master Secretary Cecil' or 'my lord,' if you do not mind."

I felt heat rush into my cheeks. "Yes, of course," I said. "Forgive me, my lord."

"The lad is tired, is all," Master Shelton muttered. "If you would inform her ladyship of our arrival, we'll not trouble you further."

Master Secretary Cecil arched a brow. "I'm afraid her ladyship is not here at the moment. She and her daughters have moved to Durham House on the Strand, in order to free up room for the nobles and their retinues. As you see, his lordship has a full house this evening."

Master Shelton stiffened. My gaze darted from him to Master Secretary Cecil's unrevealing smile and back again. In that moment I saw that Master Shelton had not known, and had just been put in his place. Despite Cecil's friendly demeanor, equals these men were not.

Cecil continued: "Lady Dudley did leave word that she has need of your services, and you are to proceed to Durham forthwith. I can provide you with an escort, if you like."

In the background, pages raced about with torches, lighting iron sconces mounted on the walls. Dusk slipped over the courtyard and Master Shelton's face. "I know the way," he said, and he motioned to me. "Come, lad. Durham's not far."

I made a move to follow. Cecil reached out. The pressure of his fingers on my sleeve was unexpected—light but commanding. "I believe our new squire will lodge here with Lord Robert, also at her ladyship's command." He smiled again at me. "I will take you to his rooms."

I hadn't counted on being left on my own so soon, and for a

paralyzed moment I felt like a lost child. I hoped Master Shelton would insist I accompany him to report in person to Lady Dudley. But he only said, "Go, boy. You've your duty to attend to. I'll look in on you later." Without giving Cecil another glance, he strode off, leading his bay back to the gate. Taking Cinnabar by the reins, I started after Cecil.

As I passed under an archway, I looked over my shoulder.

Master Shelton was gone.

I barely had time to gawk at the immensity of the hammer-beamed stables, populated by a multitude of steeds and hounds. Entrusting Cinnabar to a young dark-haired groom with an avid palm for a coin, I shouldered my saddlebag and hastened after Secretary Cecil, who led me across another inner courtyard, through a side door, and up a staircase into a series of interconnecting rooms hung with enormous tapestries.

Thickly woven carpets muffled our footsteps. The air was redolent of wax and musk, sweat, and musty fabric. Candles dripped from the eaves, studded on iron candelabra. The strains of a disembodied lute wavered from an unseen place as courtiers drifted past us, the glitter of jewels on damasks and velvets catching the light like iridescent butterfly wings.

None glanced at me, but I could not have been less at ease than if they'd stopped to ask my name. I wondered how I would ever manage to find my way about this maze, much less steer a clear route to and from Lord Robert's rooms.

"It seems overwhelming at first," Cecil said, as if he could read my thoughts, "but you'll adjust to it in time. We all do."

I let out an uneasy chuckle, eyeing him. He'd seemed prepossessing in the courtyard, but here in the gallery's length, dwarfed as we were by the surrounding grandeur, I thought he resembled one of the middle-class merchants who came to sell their wares at the Dudley Castle; men who'd carved out a comfortable niche for themselves, having learned to weather life's vicissitudes with good humor and a careful eye to the future.

"You have a certain look," Cecil went on. "I find it refreshing." He smiled. "It won't last long. The novelty fades quickly. Before you know it, you'll be complaining about how cramped everything is, and how you'd give anything for some fresh air."

A cluster of laughing women in dazzling headdresses glided toward us, aromatic pomanders clanking from their cinched waists. I gaped. I had never seen such artifice before, and when one of them glanced at me with seductive eyes, I returned her invitation, so entranced by her exquisite pallor I completely forgot myself. She smiled, wickedly, and turned away as if I had ceased to exist. I stared after her. At my side, I heard Cecil laugh under his breath as we rounded the corner into another gallery, empty of people.

Mustering my nerve, I said, "How long have you lived here?" As I spoke, I wondered if he might think me too forward, and reasoned that even if he did, I could hardly be expected to learn anything if I did not ask. He was, after all, still a servant. Regardless of his rank over Master Shelton, Lady Dudley had given him orders.

Again, I received his curious smile. "I don't live here. I have my own house nearby. Rooms at court, such as they are, are reserved for those who can afford them. If you seek my business, I will tell you that I am master secretary to his lordship the duke and the council. So, in a manner of speaking, we all eat from the same hand."

"Oh." I tried to sound nonchalant. "I see. I didn't mean to offend, my lord."

"As I said, Master Cecil will suffice. There's ceremony enough here, without us adding to it." A mischievous gleam lit his pale eyes. "And you needn't be so humble about it. It's not often a courtier has the privilege of conversing with someone untainted by pretense."

I kept quiet as we mounted a flight of steps. The corridor we entered was narrower than the galleries, devoid of tapestries and carpets, revealing functional plaster walls and plank floor.

He came to a stop before one of several identical doors. "These are the apartments of the duke's sons. I'm not certain who is in at the moment, if anyone. They each have their duties. In any event, I must leave you here." He sighed. "A secretary's work never ends, I fear."

"Thank you, Master Cecil." I bowed with less effect due to the saddlebag in my hand, though I was grateful for his kindness. I sensed he had gone out of his way to make me feel less uncomfortable.

"You are welcome." He paused, regarding me in pensive silence. "Prescott," he mused, "your surname has Latin roots. Has it been in your family long?"

His question caught me off guard. For a second, I plunged into panic, unsure as to how, or if, I should answer. Would it be better to brazen an outright lie or to take a chance on a possibly newfound friend?

I decided on the latter. Something about Cecil invited confidence, but even more compelling was the possibility that he already knew. He was aware I'd been brought to court to serve Lord Robert. It stood to reason that Lady Dudley, or perhaps the duke himself, had shared other, less palatable truths about me. It wasn't as if I was worthy of their discretion. And, if I spoke an outright falsehood to one who held their trust, it could ruin any chance I had of furthering myself at court.

I met his placid stare. "Prescott," I said, "is not my real name."

"Oh?" His brow lifted.

Another wave of hesitation engulfed me. There was still time. I could still offer an explanation that would not stray too far from reality. I had no idea why I didn't, why I felt the almost overpowering need to speak the truth. I had never willingly imparted the mystery of my birth to anyone. From the time I had discovered that what I lacked made me the brunt of taunts and cruel suppositions, I decided that whenever asked I would admit only what was necessary. No need to offer details that no one cared to hear or to invite speculation.

Yet as I stood there, I perceived a quiet thoughtfulness in his regard that made me think he would understand, perhaps even sympathize. Mistress Alice had often looked at me like that, with a comprehension that never balked at admitting the most diffi-cult of truths. I had learned to trust that quality in others.

I took a deep breath. "I am a foundling. Mistress Alice, the woman who raised me, gave me my name. In olden times, those called Prescott lived by the priest's cottage. That's where I was found—in the former priest's cottage near Dudley Castle."

"And your first name?" he asked. "Was that Mistress Alice's doing, as well?"

"Yes. She was from Ireland. She had a deep reverence for Saint Brendan."

A laden moment ensued. The Irish were despised in England for their rebelliousness, but until now my name had not roused undue curiosity. As I waited for Cecil's response, I began to fear I'd made a mistake. Illegitimacy was a handicap an industrious man could turn to his favor. Lack of any lineage, on the other hand, was a liability few could afford. It usually sentenced one to a lifetime of anonymous servitude at best, and beggardom at worst.

Then Cecil said, "When you say 'foundling,' I assume you mean you were abandoned?"

"Yes. I was a week old, at best." Despite my attempt to seem unaffected, I could hear the old strain in my voice, the weight of my own sense of helplessness. "Mistress Alice had to hire a local woman to nurse me. As fate would have it, a woman in town had just lost her child; otherwise, I might not have survived."

He nodded. Before another uncomfortable silence could descend, I found myself rushing to fill it, as if I'd lost control of my own tongue. "Mistress Alice used to say the monks were lucky I wasn't dropped on their doorstep. I'd have eaten their larders dry, and what would they have had then to withstand the storm old Henry brewed for them?"

I started to laugh before I realized my error. I'd just brought up the subject of religion, surely not a safe subject at court. Mistress Alice, I almost added, had also said my appetite was exceeded only by the size of my mouth.

Cecil did not speak. I began to think I'd done myself in with my indiscretion, when he murmured, "How dreadful for you."

The sentiment failed to match the scrutiny of his eyes, which remained fixed on me as if he sought to engrave my face in memory. "This Mistress Alice, might she have known whom your parents were? Such matters are usually local in origin. An unwed girl got in the family way, too ashamed to tell anyone—it occurs frequently, I'm afraid."

"Mistress Alice is dead." My voice was flat. Despite my previous honesty, some hurts I could not willingly reveal. "She was beset by thieves while on the road from Stratford. If she knew anything about my parents, she took it with her to her grave."

Cecil lowered his eyes. "I'm sorry to hear it. Every man, no matter how humble, should know from whence he came." He suddenly inclined to me. "You mustn't let that dissuade you. Even foundlings may rise high in our new England. Fortune often smiles on those least favored."

He stepped back. "It's been a pleasure, Squire Prescott. Please, do not hesitate to call upon me should you require anything. I'm easily found."

He gave me another of his cryptic smiles, turned heel, and walked away.

Chapter Three

I watched Master Cecil disappear down the gallery before I sucked in a deep breath and turned to the door. I knocked. There was no reply. After another knock, I tried the latch. The door opened.

Stepping in, I found that the apartments, as Cecil had called them, consisted of an undersized chamber dominated by a bed with a sagging tester. Scarred wainscoting adorned the lower half of the walls, and the lone small window was glazed with greenish glass. A lit candle stub floated in oil in a dish on the table. Across the floor were strewn matted rushes, soiled articles of clothing, and assorted utensils and dishes. The smell was nauseating, a mixture of rancid leftover food and dirty garments.

I dropped my saddlebag on the threshold. Evidently, some things never changed. Rooms at court or not, the Dudley boys still lived like hogs in a sty.

I heard snores coming from the bed. I edged to it, my heels crunching on slivers of meat-bones embedded in the rushes. I avoided a pool of vomit by the bedside as I grabbed hold of the tester curtain and tugged it aside. The rungs rattled. I leapt back, half expecting the entire howling Dudley clan to lunge out at me, brandishing fists as they used to do in my childhood.

Instead, I saw a lone figure sprawled on the bed, clad in wrinkled hose and shirt, his tangled hair the color of dirty wheat. He exuded the unmistakable stench of cheap beer: Guilford, the fair babe of the tribe, all of seventeen years old and in a drunken stupor.

I pinched the hand dangling over the bedside. When all I roused was another guttural snore, I grabbed his shoulder and shook it.

He swung out his arms, rearing a sheet-lined face. "Pox on you," he slurred.

"Good eve to you as well, my Lord Guilford," I replied. I took a prudent step back, just in case. Though he was the youngest of the five Dudley sons, against whom I'd won more battles than lost, I was not about to risk a thrashing my first hour at court.

He gaped at me, his saturated brain trying to match identity to face. When he did, Guilford scoffed. "Why, it's the bastard orphan. What are you—" He choked, doubled over to spew on the floor. Groaning, he fell back across the bed. "I hate her. I'll make her pay for this. I swear I will, that righteous bitch."

"Did she spike your ale?" I asked innocently.

He glared, forced himself up to clamber out of bed. He had the Dudley height, and I knew that if he hadn't consumed his weight in ale he'd have pounced on me like a cub with a boil. Instinctively, I slid my hand to the sheathed dagger. Not that I could dare brandish it. A commoner could be put to death for so much as verbally threatening a noble. Still, the feel of its worn hilt against my fingers was reassuring.

"Yes, she spiked my ale." Guilford swayed. "Just because she's kin to the king, she thinks she can snub her nose at me. I'll show her who's master here. As soon as we're wed, I'll thrash her till she bleeds, the miserable—"

A voice lashed across the room. "Shut your miserable trap, Guilford."

Guilford blanched. I turned about.

Standing in the doorway was none other than my new master, Robert Dudley.

In spite of my apprehension at our reunion after ten years, he was a sight to behold. I had always secretly envied him. While mine was an unremarkable face, so commonplace it was as easily forgotten as rain, Robert was a superlative specimen of breeding at its best; impressive in stature, broad of chest and muscular of shank like his father, with his mother's chiseled nose, thick black hair, and long-lashed, dusky eyes that had certainly made more than a few maidens melt at his feet. He possessed everything I did not, including years of service at court and, upon King Edward's ascension, prestigious appointments leading up to a distinguished, if brief, campaign against the Scots, and the wedding and bedding, or vice versa, of a damsel of means.

Yes, Lord Robert Dudley had everything a man like me could want. And he was everything a man like me should fear.

He kicked the door shut with his booted foot. "Look at you, drunk as a priest. You disgust me. You have piss for blood in your veins."

"I was"—Guilford had turned white as canvas—"I was only saying . . ."

"Don't." Robert spoke as if he hadn't seen me standing there. He swerved, his eyes narrowed. "I see the stable whelp has made it here intact."

I bowed. Our association, it seemed, was to take up where

we'd left off, unless I could prove I had more to offer him than a hapless body he could pummel.

"I have, my lord," I replied in my finest diction. "I am honored to serve as your squire."

"Is that so?" He flashed a brilliant smile. "Well, you should be. It certainly wasn't my idea. Mother decided you should start earning your upkeep, though if it were up to me I'd have let you loose in the streets, where you came from. But seeing as you were not"—he flung out an arm—"you can start by cleaning this mess. Then you can dress me for the banquet." He paused. "On second thought, just clean. Unless you learned how to tie a gentleman's points while mucking out horseshit in Worcestershire." He let out a high laugh, finding, as ever, great pleasure in his own wit. "Never mind, I can dress myself. I've been doing it for years. Help Guilford, instead. Father expects us in the hall within the hour."

I guarded my expression as I bowed again. "My lord."

Robert guffawed. "Such a gentleman you've become. With those fancy manners of yours, I'll wager you'll find a wench or two willing to overlook your lack of blood."

He turned back to his brother, stabbed a finger circled by a silver ring at him. "And you keep your mouth shut. She's but a wife, man. Bridle her, ride her, and put her to pasture as I did mine. And, for mercy's sake, do something about your breath." Robert gave me a tight smile. "I'll see you in the hall, as well, Prescott. Bring him to the south entrance. We wouldn't want him to spew all over our exalted guests."

With a callous laugh, he turned and strode out. Guilford stuck out his tongue at the departing form, and, to my disgust, promptly vomited again.

It took every last bit of patience I had to accomplish my first assignment in the time allotted. Most of the discarded clothing needed a good soaking in vinegar to remove whatever detritus clung to it, yet seeing as I was no laundress I hid the nasty stuff from view and then went in search of water, finding an urn at the end of the passage.

I returned and ordered Guilford to strip. The water ran brown off his flaccid skin, the raw bites on his thighs and arms indicating he shared his bed with mites and fleas. He stood scowling, naked and shivering, cleaner than he'd probably been since he first arrived at court.

Unearthing a relatively unstained chemise, hose, doublet, and damask sleeves from the clothing press, I extended these to him. "Shall I help my lord dress?"

He ripped the clothes from my hands. Leaving him to wrestle with his garments, I went to my saddlebag and removed my one extra pair of hose, new gray wool doublet, and good shoes.

As I held these, I had an unbidden memory of Mistress Alice smoothing animal fat into the leather, "to make them shine like stars," she'd said winking. She had brought me the shoes from one of her annual trips to the Stratford Fair. Two sizes too large at the time, to accommodate a still-growing boy, I'd proudly sloshed around in them, until one dark day months after her death, I tried them on and found they fit. Before I'd left Dudley Castle, I'd rubbed fat into the leather, as she would have. I'd taken it from the same jar, with the same wooden spoon. . . .

My throat knotted. While I had lived in the castle I could pretend she was still with me, a benevolent unseen presence. The mornings spent in the kitchen that were her domain, the fields where I'd ridden Cinnabar in the afternoon, the turret library where I'd read the Dudleys' forgotten books: It always felt as if she were about to come upon me at any moment, remonstrating that it was time I eat something.

But here, she was as far away as if I'd set sail for the New World. For the first time in my life, I had the post and means to build a better future, and I was skittish as a babe at a baptism.

Recalling this favorite saying of hers, I felt a surge of confidence. She had always said I could do anything I set my mind to. Out of respect for her memory, I must do more than survive. I must thrive. After all, who knew what my future held? Ludicrous as it might seem at this moment, it wasn't inconceivable that one day I could earn my freedom from servitude. As Cecil had remarked, even foundlings could rise high in our new England.

I slipped off my soiled clothes, careful to keep my back to Guilford as I washed with the last of the water and quickly dressed. When I turned about, I found Guilford entangled in his doublet, shirt askew, and crumpled hose about his knees.

Without needing to be told, I went to assist him.

Chapter Four

Though Guilford had been at court for over three years, presumably engaged in more than the satiation of his vices, he got us lost within a matter of seconds. I imagined being discovered centuries later, two skeletons with my hands locked about his throat, and took it upon myself to ask directions. With the aid of a gold coin secured from a grumbling Guilford, a page brought us to the hall's south entrance, where the duke's sons waited in their ostentatious finery. Only the eldest, Jack, was absent.

"Finally," declared Ambrose Dudley, the second eldest. "We'd begun to think Brendan had hog-tied you to the bed to get you dressed."

Guilford curled his lip. "Not bloody likely."

The brothers laughed. I noticed Robert's laughter didn't reach his eyes, which kept shifting to the hall, as though in anticipation of something.

Henry Dudley, the shortest and least comely of the brothers, and therefore the meanest tempered, clapped my shoulder as if we were the best of friends. I was pleased to discover that I now stood a head taller than he.

"How fare you, orphan?" he jibed. "You look as if you haven't grown an inch."

"Not where you can see," I said, with a tight smile. Matters could be worse. I could be serving Henry Dudley, who as a boy had enjoyed drowning kittens just to hear them mewl.

"No," spat Henry. "But even a dog can tell who its mother was. Can you?"

He eyed me, eager for a tussle. His attacks on me had always been edged with more than derision, but he wasn't saying anything I hadn't been subjected to before, or indeed even contemplated myself, in the loneliness of the night. I refused to rise to his bait.

"Given the chance, I rather hope I could."

"No doubt," sneered Guilford. "I'd say the same if I were you. Thank God I'm not."

Robert glared at his brothers as they again burst into raucous laughter. "God's teeth, you sound like a gaggle of women. Who cares about him? If I were you, I'd be more concerned about what's happening around us. Just look at the council, hovering about the dais like crows."

I followed his stare to where a group of somber men stood close together, the black of their robes blending together like ink. They were indeed gathered before a dais draped in cloth of gold. Upon it sat a large velvet-upholstered throne; overhead, hung a canopy embroidered with the Tudor Rose. It suddenly occurred to me that I might see the king himself tonight, and I felt excitement bubble up in me as I looked into the hall itself.

It was luminescent, its painted ceiling offset by a black-and-white tile floor over which nobles moved as though on an immense chessboard. In the gallery, minstrels strummed a refrain, while lesser courtiers streamed through the open doors, some moving to trestle tables laden with victuals, subtleties, and decanters; others assembled in small groups to whisper, preen, and stare.

If intrigue had a smell, Whitehall would reek of it.

I heard a footstep behind us. Turning about, I had a fleeting glance of a tall, lean figure in iron-colored satin before I bowed as low as I could.

John Dudley, Duke of Northumberland, said in a quiet voice, "Ah, I see you are all here. Good. Ambrose, Henry, go attend to the council. They look in dire need of drink. Robert, I've just received word there is need for someone of authority to see to an urgent matter at the Tower. Pray, go and attend to it."

Even with my head bowed I heard incredulity in Robert's reply. "The Tower? But, I was there only this afternoon and all seemed well in order. There must be a mistake. Begging your leave, my lord father, but might I see to it later?"

"I'm afraid not," said the duke. "As I said, the matter is urgent. We've imposed an early curfew tonight, and nothing can occur that might unsettle the populace."

I could almost feel the fury emanating from Robert. With a curt bow, he said tersely, "My lord," before he strode off.

The duke addressed his remaining son. "Guilford, find a chair by the hearth and stay there. When Their Graces of Suffolk arrive, attend to them as befits your rank. And may I suggest you be a little more circumspect tonight with your intake of wine?"

Guilford skulked off. With a pensive sigh, the duke turned his passionless black eyes to me. "Squire Prescott, rise. It's been some time since I last saw you. How was your trip?"

I had to crane my head to meet Northumberland's gaze.

I had been in his presence only a handful of times, his service to the king having kept him at court for most of my life, and I was struck by his imposing figure. John Dudley had retained the lean build instilled by a lifetime of military discipline, his height complimented by his knee-length brocade surcoat and tailored doublet. A thick gold chain slung across his shoulders bore testament to his wealth and success. No one would have mistaken this man for anyone other than a man of great power; few in fact would have looked beyond that to the hint of insomnia under his deep-set eyes, or the careworn lines wiring his mouth in its cropped goatee.

Recalling what Master Shelton had said about the price of absolute power, I said carefully, "My trip was uneventful, my lord. I thank you for the opportunity to be of service."

Northumberland was looking distractedly toward the hall, as if he barely registered my words. "Well, it is not me you should thank," he said. "I did not bring you to court. That was my lady wife's doing, though I hardly think Robert merits the luxury of a private body servant." He sighed, returning his gaze to me. "How old are you again?"

"I believe twenty, my lord. Or, it's been twenty years since I came to live in your house."

"Indeed." His cold smile barely creased his mouth. "Perhaps that explains my wife's persistence. You are a man now and should be allowed to prove yourself in our service." He motioned. "Go. Attend to my son and do as he says. These are perilous times. Those who demonstrate their loyalty to us will not go unrewarded."

I bowed low again, about to slip away when I heard the duke murmur, "We won't forget those who betray us, either." He didn't look at me as he spoke. Turning away he stepped into the hall, where a palpable hush greeted his entrance.

Unnerved by his words, I moved in the direction Robert had taken, my mind in a tumult. Master Shelton had also said the Dudleys would reward my loyalty. At the time I had thought he meant they'd accept me as Shelton's eventual successor. Now I could not shake the sudden sense that I'd been plunged into a nest of serpents, where one false step could spell my ruin. The more I considered it, the more I began to question the true reason for my summons. Unlike her husband the duke, Lady Dudley had been part of my childhood—an aloof presence I'd avoided at any cost. She'd always treated me with disdain, when she deigned to notice me at all. She never interfered even when her sons tormented me, and I always suspected she only allowed Mistress Alice to care for me because she did not want it said she'd let a founding child perish on her grounds. So why did she want me at court now, serving her son, in the midst of what seemed to be an exacting time for her family?

I was so distracted by my thoughts I did not heed my surroundings. Halfway through a corridor, an arm shot out and grabbed me about the throat. I was hauled into a closed, fetid room. The fecal-spattered hole and stomach-churning smell demonstrated the room's function. As I staggered against a wall, I thrust out a hand to avoid fouling my clothes, reaching with my other hand to the dagger I'd stashed under my doublet.

"I could cut off your hand with my sword before you release that paltry blade."

I turned about. A shadow stepped forth. Lord Robert seemed overwhelmingly large in the confined space. "Well?" he said. "What did my father say to you?"

I kept my voice calm. "He said I should attend to you, and do as you bid."

He took another step forward. "And?"

"That's all."

Robert stepped so close, the smell of his expensive musk filled my nostrils. "You'd best be telling me the truth. If you're not, then you'd best pray I don't find out." He regarded me intently. "He made no mention of Elizabeth?"

"No." I said immediately, and then I paused as I realized whom he spoke of.

He snorted, "I don't know why Mother bothers with you. What would you know, a simple fool from the country brought here to clean my boots?" He stepped away. I heard a flint being struck. Moments later, a taper flared in his hand. He set it on the floor. "I'll give you this much: You haven't learned to lie yet." He looked at me over the wavering flame, as misshapen shadows splashed across his face. "So, my father said nothing about her?"

I recalled what I heard as we entered London, and as if a bell went off inside me I decided to feign ignorance. Looking down to my feet, I murmured, "If he had, I would tell you."

He guffawed. "Aren't you the meek one? I'd forgotten how good you were at fading into the background, never seeing or hearing what didn't concern you. I understand now why Mother was so set on bringing you here. You're truly someone who doesn't exist."

His sharp burst of laughter ended as abruptly as it had appeared. "Yes," he breathed, as if to himself, "the squire who doesn't exist. It's perfect."

I stayed very still. I did not like the look creeping over his face, the slow calculated malice. He rocked back on his heels. "So, tell me, what would you say if I asked you to do an errand for me tonight that could earn you your fortune?"

The thick air in the room felt like a noose about my throat, cutting off my breath.

"What?" Robert's smile showed a hint of perfect white teeth. "Have you nothing to say? How odd—a weasel like you. I'm offering you the opportunity of a lifetime, the chance to earn your way out of service and become your own man. It is what you dream of, is it not? You don't want to be nobody forever? Not you, not the clever little foundling. Why, I think you must be fully literate by now, what with that old monk Shelton hired. I bet he taught you Latin with one hand while buggering you with the other. Well, am I right? Can you read and write?"

I met his eyes. I nodded.

His smile turned cruel. "I thought as much. I always knew you weren't as stupid as you'd have us think." His tone lowered, adopting a sinister intimacy. "And I know our proud Bess will come here tonight, though my lord father pretends to know nothing."

At these words, I could not stop the rush of excitement that went through me. So, it *was* true. Elizabeth Tudor was here, in London. I had witnessed her arrival.

Then I saw Robert's expression darken. When he next spoke, his voice was tainted by a furious heat, as if I had in fact faded to nothing, an invisible being before who he needn't measure his words. "My father promised me that when the time came, I would not be neglected. He said none was more worthy than I. But now it seems he prefers to heap honors on Guilford, and put me to do his dirty work instead. By God, I've done everything he asked; I even married that insipid sheep Amy Robsart because he thought it best. What more can he want from me? When will it be my turn to take what *I* deserve?"

I'd never heard any of the Dudley boys express anything other than conformity with their father's wishes. It was the way of the nobility: Fathers sent their sons away to serve in influential posts and assist the family. Dudley's sons had no will other than his, and in turn, they would reap his fortune. As far as I was concerned, Robert had no cause for complaint. He'd never known a day of hunger or want in his life; he probably never would. I had no reason to pity him; but in that moment I saw that like so many sons who feel helpless, Robert Dudley had begun to chafe against the paternal tether binding him.

"Enough!" He hit his fist into his palm. "It's time I showed my mettle. And you, you worm—you are going to help me." He thrust his face at me. "Unless you'd rather I sent you back to the stables for the rest of your miserable days?"

I did not speak. I knew I should prefer the stables, where life was at least predictable, but I did not. I met Robert's stare and said, "Perhaps my lord should explain what he expects of me."

He seemed taken aback. He glanced over his shoulder before he looked back at me. He gnawed at his lower lip, as if he had sudden doubt. Then he menaced, "If you fail me or do me wrong, I swear there isn't a place in all England where you can hide. Do you understand me? I will find you, Prescott. And I will kill you with my bare hands."

I did not react. Such a threat was to be expected. He had to intimidate me, ensure that I feared him enough to not betray his trust. It made me all the more curious. What did he want so desperately?

"Very well," he said at length. "The first thing you need to know is that she's apt to surprise you when you least expect it. I've known her since she was a girl, and I tell you, she likes nothing more than to set everyone around her to wondering. She delights in confusion."

The guarded note that crept into his voice alerted me to an unspoken undercurrent. This sounded more than just a son's bravura against his father.

"Take her arrival today, for example," he continued. "She steals into the city without prior warning, and only once she's reached her manor does she send word requesting leave as to when she may visit her brother, as her sister, the Lady Mary, did a few months past." He let out a staccato laugh. "Now, there's pure connivance, if ever I saw it. God forbid she should put herself at our mercy or that her papist sister should outdo her. And she knows we dare not refuse her, for just as she planned, rumors of her arrival run like wildfire through the city. She wants us to know no Dudley is more powerful than her."

He spoke as if it were an elaborate game, when it was clear Elizabeth must have come to London because she'd heard rumors of her brother's impending death. Once again I fought back the near-overwhelming sensation that I should be doing everything possible to escape this errand. Why put myself in harm's way? Why risk becoming Lord Robert's victim again? Inviting as it was, freedom from servitude seemed a rather remote possibility at this particular moment.

I drew in a steadying breath. "Why would she even heed me? We've never met."

"She'll heed you because I am her friend, whom she's never had cause to doubt. She knows I am not my father. I will not play her false." He fished under his gauntlet, tossed a ring at me. "Give her this. She will understand. But do it in private; I don't want that busybody matron of hers, that Mistress Ashley, knowing my business. Tell her I've been delayed but I will send word soon, by the usual route, so we can meet alone. Tell her I will have what I was promised."

He took a menacing step toward me. "And don't let her out of your sight, not even if she dismisses you. I want a full accounting of her actions, from the time she enters the palace until she leaves." He unhooked a pouch from his belt and dropped it by the taper, which was melting onto the floor. "There'll be more if you succeed. Who knows? You could end up a rich man, Prescott. The water gate lies straight ahead. After you've done as I ask, feel free to enjoy yourself. Elizabeth always retires early. Find yourself a cunt. Drink. Eat till you puke. Only don't breathe a word to anyone, and be in my chamber by the stroke of nine tomorrow."

He unlatched the door. When I heard his footsteps fade away, I grabbed the pouch and fled from the room. As I stood gulping air in the corridor, I untied the pouch with quivering fingers. It contained more than I could imagine. A few more like this and I could buy my way to the New World, if need be.

All I had to do was deliver Lord Robert's ring.

Chapter Five

I trekked down a series of corridors, passing from the palace into sudden night.

Torches mounted on the walls converted Whitehall's mullioned bays into opaque eyes. A near-full moon rode in the sky, rimming the knot garden before me in a tarnished glow. There were copses of willows and fragrant herb patches, edged by a waist-high yew hedge that lined the path to moss-licked river steps and a private landing quay. Three guards swathed in wool stood near the quay; a lit iron brazier beside them cast fiery reflections onto the river.

There was no one else in sight.

The soughing of water reached me. I might have enjoyed the unexpected tranquility and the balm of the night, had I not the dilemma of what to do next. I didn't know when the princess would arrive and I couldn't simply approach and state my desire to speak with her. No guard worth his salt would be amenable to a stranger lacking proof of identity, save for the badge on my sleeve, which could be stolen, and a ring I couldn't show.

The opportunity would have to present itself. I tarried under the palace shadow, listening to water shred against stone. When I discerned a distinct, more rhythmic splash, I readied myself.

A canopied barge glided into view.

The guards formed rank. From within the garden, a trim figure suddenly materialized. A jolt went through me when I recognized Master Cecil. Another man dressed entirely in black emerged to stand beside him. My nape prickled. How many others lurked in the shadows?

The barge was secured. I inched closer to the quay, my creeping steps sounding impossibly loud in my ears as I tiptoed through pools of darkness and crouched low behind the ornamental hedge. I was almost at the river's edge.

Three cloaked figures emerged from the barge and mounted the steps to the quay. She was at the forefront, leading a thin silver-colored hound by a chain. As her tapered hand cast aside her hood, I glimpsed fiery tresses caught in silver filigree, framing an angular face.

Cecil and the stranger in black bowed. I edged closer, taking advantage of the hedge's shadows. They were a pebble's throw away, and the silence enhanced their voices. I heard Cecil's first, imbued with urgency.

"Your Grace, I must beg you to reconsider. The court is not safe for you at this time."

"My sentiments precisely," interposed an officious voice. It came from the shorter of the princess's two attendants, a stout matron who spoke with impudence. This must be the woman Robert had mentioned—Mistress Ashley. Behind her, the other, slightly taller attendant remained silent, muffled in a cloak of tawny velvet.

"I told Her Grace the same not an hour ago," said the matron, "but would she heed me? Of course not. Who am I, after all, except the woman who raised her?"

The princess spoke, her voice crisp with impatience. "Ash Kat, don't talk about me as if I weren't here." She stared at the matron, who, to my surprise, stared right back. Elizabeth turned her attention to Cecil. "As I have informed Mistress Ashley, you both worry too much. This court was never safe for me, yet I'm still alive to walk its halls, am I not?"

"Of course," said Cecil. "No one questions your capacity for survival, my lady. But I do wish you'd consulted me before leaving Hatfield. In coming to London as you have, you risk his lordship the duke's displeasure."

Her reply carried a hint of asperity. "I hardly see why. I'm as entitled as my sister Mary was to see my brother, and he received her well enough." She yanked at her cloak. "Now, if there's nothing else, I must get to the hall. Edward will be expecting me."

I had to scramble behind the hedge after them, dreading the thought that at any moment my foot might crunch down on a stray twig and betray my presence. Fortunately, my soft leather soles made no discernible sound on the lawn, but I was acutely aware that I'd just eavesdropped on a conversation not meant for my ears, entrusted with a message that more and more seemed like a ruse. Robert might say he'd never play the princess false, but Cecil clearly believed the duke might. What if delivering my master's missive and ring caused more trouble than I knew?

"Your Grace, please." Cecil hustled after her, for despite her delicate appearance, she had an athletic stride. "I must implore you. You must understand the risk you run. Otherwise, you would not have refused his lordship's offer of rooms in the palace."

So, Robert had been right! The duke did know she was coming: He had even offered her rooms in the palace. Why was he misleading his own son?

She stopped. "Not that I need to explain myself, but I 're-fused,' as you say, to lodge in the palace because there are far too many people at court and my constitution is such that I cannot afford to contract an illness." She held up a hand. "And I will not be dissuaded. I have waited long enough. I mean to see my brother tonight. No one, not even his lordship the duke of North-umberland, can stop me."

Cecil's reluctant incline of head showed that he recognized the futility of further argument. "At least, let Master Walsing-ham accompany you. He's well trained and can give you proper protection should—"

"Absolutely not. I've no need for Master Walsingham's or anyone else's protection. By the rood, am I not the king's sister? What need I fear from being at his court?" She didn't wait for an answer. She continued toward the palace, her dog in perfect pace at her side. Then all of a sudden it paused. With a low growl, it turned its baleful eyes to the hedge. I froze; it had smelled me. She yanked at its chain. The dog did not budge, its growl be-coming louder, turning into a menacing snarl.

I heard her say, "Who goes there?" and knew I had no other choice.

To the hound's bloodcurdling bark, I stood and shifted through an opening in the hedge. I swiftly knelt, removed my cap. The moonlight sliced across my face. She went still. The dog snarled again. Cecil snapped his fingers. The guards were at me, swords scything in release. In a second, I was surrounded by blades. If I so much as moved a muscle, I would impale myself.

The dog strained at its chain, snout drawn back and fangs bared. She patted its sleek head. "Hush, Urian," I heard her say. "Be still." The hound sat on its haunches, its strange green-toned eyes fixed on me.

Cecil said, "I believe I know this youth, Your Grace. I assure you, he is quite harmless."

One of her thin red-gold brows arched. "I don't doubt it, seeing as he thought to hide from us in the yew, of all places. Who is he?"

"Robert Dudley's squire."

I glanced up in time to catch the quick look Cecil cast in my direction. I couldn't tell whether he was displeased or amused.

The princess motioned. The guards shifted back. I stayed on one knee.

There are moments that define our existence, moments that, if we recognize them, become pivotal turning points in our life. Like pearls on a strand, the accumulation of such moments will in time become the essence of our life, providing solace when our end draws near.

For me, meeting Elizabeth Tudor was one of those moments.

The first thing I noticed was that she was not beautiful. Her chin was too narrow for the oval of her face, her long thin nose emphasizing the high curve of her cheeks and proud brow. Her mouth was disproportionately wide and her lips too thin, as if she savored secrets. And she was too pale and slim, like a fey creature of indeterminate sex.

· Then I met her stare. Her eyes were fathomless, overwide pupils limning her gold irises, like twin suns in eclipse. I had seen eyes like hers before, years ago, when a traveling menagerie entertained us at Dudley Castle. Then, too, I had been captured by their dormant power.

She had the eyes of a lion.

"Lord Robert's squire?" she said to Cecil. "How can it be? I've never seen him before."

"I'm new to court, Your Grace," I answered. "Your dog is foreign, is he not?"

She shot me a terse look; she'd not given me leave to speak. "He is Italian. You are familiar with the breed?"

"I had occasion to learn many things during my time in the Dudley stables."

"Is that so?" She tilted her head. "Hold out your hand."

I hesitated for a moment before warily extending my wrist. She loosened her grip on the chain. The hound thrust his muzzle at me. I almost recoiled as I felt his breath on my skin. He sniffed. To my relief, he licked my skin and retreated.

"You have a way with animals," Elizabeth said. "Urian rarely takes to strangers." She motioned me to my feet. "What is your name?"

"Brendan Prescott, Your Grace."

"You're a bold fellow, Brendan Prescott. State your purpose."

I suddenly realized I was trembling and recited in a voice that sounded far too rushed to my ears: "My lord asks that I convey his regret that he could not be here to receive Your Grace. He was called away on urgent business."

It was as far as I dared go. I had promised to deliver the ring in private and had the uncanny certainty that she would not like her association with Robert Dudley bandied about in public. As it stood, she was looking at me with an intensity that made me think of tales I'd heard of her late father, whom it was said had such a piercing stare, he could see through a man's skin to his veins and judge for himself how true the blood ran.

Then she arched her throat and released a gust of husky laughter. "Urgent business, you say? That much, I do not doubt. Lord Robert has a father to obey, does he not?"

I felt my smile emerge, lopsided. "He certainly does."

"Yes, and I know better than most how demanding fathers can be." With the laughter still on her lips, she handed Urian's chain to Cecil and motioned to me with long fingers. "Walk with me, squire. You've given me cause for amusement tonight, and it's a quality I value greatly." She cast a pointed look at those behind her. "Seeing how little of it I find around me these days."

Elation rushed from my head all the way to my feet. Master Shelton had warned me that trouble followed her wherever she went.

But in that moment, I did not care.

I moved after her into the palace, taking care not to overtake her. At the first opportunity, Mistress Ashley shouldered past me to the princess's side, muttering something inaudible. I heard Elizabeth reply, "No. I said I would walk with him, and walk I will. Alone."

Mistress Ashley retorted, "I forbid it. It will incite talk."

"I hardly think a simple walk can incite anything, Ash Kat," said Elizabeth dryly. "And you're far too short to forbid me anything anymore."

The matron glowered. Cecil interposed, "Mistress Ashley, the lad will do no harm."

"We'll see about that," said Mistress Ashley. "He serves the Dudleys, doesn't he?" With a glare at me, she reluctantly retreated.

I nodded gratefully at Cecil. He must have realized that I had been sent here by Robert and was trying to facilitate my first official duty, yet to my discomfiture, he avoided my gaze, slowing his pace to fall behind us. Equally discomfiting was the stranger in black named Walsingham, who moved with the soundless stealth of a cat, his long features a study in stony indifference.

I was surrounded by mistrustful strangers; I could almost feel their protectiveness toward the princess boring into my back.

The only person whose face I had not yet seen was Elizabeth's other attendant, though I assumed she too must view my presence as unwelcome; as I thought this, I glanced over at her and caught a glimpse of bold brown eyes looking back at me from within her hood.

Elizabeth interrupted my thoughts. "I said walk with me, squire, not dawdle at my heels."

I hastened to her side. When she next spoke, her words were both rapid and hushed. "We've little time before we reach the hall. I would know the true reason for Robin's absence."

"Robin, Your Grace?" I said, drawing a momentary blank.

"Do you serve another Lord Robert, perchance?" She gave a terse laugh. "Urgent business, indeed; I'd have thought nothing save imprisonment would keep him away this night." Her mirth faded. "Where is he? He well knows how much I've risked by coming here."

"I . . ." My tongue felt like leather in my mouth. "I . . . I cannot say, Your Grace."

"Meaning you do not know." She turned into a gallery. I quickened my step.

"Meaning he didn't tell me. But he asked me to give you this." I reached to my doublet, forgetting in my haste to appease her that Robert had specified I deliver the ring in private.

Her hand shot out, gripping my wrist. Though her fingers were cold, her touch seared like flame. "God's teeth, you are new to court. Not here! What is it? Tell me."

"A ring, Your Grace, silver with an onyx stone. My master took it off his own finger."

She nearly came to a halt. Even in the dimly lit passageway, I saw color flare in her white cheeks. For a second, the regal mask slipped, revealing the flush of a maiden who cannot hide her pleasure. I was so flustered by its revelation that I plunged on, reckless in my zeal to fulfill my orders.

"He said Your Grace would understand, and that he will soon arrange a time for you to meet alone, so he can have what he was promised."

Dead silence followed my words. To my dismay, her entire person stiffened. This time, she did come to a stop. She turned to me, regarding me as if from a height I could not possibly hope to scale. "You may tell your master that I understand perfectly. And as usual, he thinks far too much of himself—and far too little of me."

I froze. From ahead came muffled music and voices, signaling our proximity to the hall.

"My lady," I finally said, "I'm afraid my lord was most insistent that you accept proof of his constancy."

"Insist!" she exclaimed, with mortifying shrillness. She paused, lowering her voice to a taut whisper. "I will not be compromised by your master or any other man. Tell Robert he goes too far. Too far, by God." She turned pointedly away from me, and Mistress Ashley hustled forth, shoving me aside so she could remove Elizabeth's cloak.

I was dismissed. As I stepped back, Elizabeth's other attendant moved past me, pulling back her own hood. I stared at her. She was lovely and young, her vivacious features complimented by a knowing gleam in her large eyes. She gave me a quick smile and I averted my gaze, stung by what I saw as her delight in my humiliation.

When I looked about, I noticed that Walsingham had slipped away. Cecil bowed before Elizabeth. "Master Walsingham asked me to offer his apologies; he had business to attend to. By your leave, I'll see Urian to his kennel." He kissed her extended hand, started to turn away.

"Cecil," she said, and he paused. "I must do this, for Edward. I cannot let them think that I'll cower in my house and wait for their summons."

He gave her a sad smile. "I know. I only hope you'll come to no harm because of it." He walked away, the hound at his side.

I watched Elizabeth turn toward the hall entrance. Her women flanked her; she suddenly looked small, vulnerable, even as she lifted her chin with regal poise to descend the steps. When she entered that crowded space, the music in the gallery sputtered, twanging discordantly before it ceased. Silence fell, so profound I could hear her footsteps on the painted wood floor. I inched forward, slipping past the shadows by the doors, blending into the crowd to watch as the duke strode to her through bowing courtiers.

"My lord of Northumberland, this is an honor," said Elizabeth. She held out her hand. The duke bowed, his bearded lips lingering on her fingers even as his eyes lifted to hers.

"The honor is mine, Your Grace. I welcome you to court."

"Do you?" She smiled with dazzling candor. "I confess I'd begun to think you would deny me the pleasure of this court indefinitely. How long has it been since my sister Mary came to visit? Four months? Five? Yet not one invitation did you extend to me in all that time."

"Ah, you see I waited for an opportune time." The duke righted himself, standing a head taller than her. "As you are aware, His Majesty has been ill."

"Yes. I am aware. I trust Edward is on his way to a full recovery?"

"Indeed, and he has asked for you several times. Did you not get his letters?"

"I did, yes. I . . . I am relieved." I saw her soften; she even managed to toss her head with a touch of flirtatiousness as she set her hand on the duke's arm and allowed him to guide her into the hall. Amid the incandescent flames and sheen of mirrors, the colored satins, and extravagant jewels, as courtiers sank into obeisance like overdressed heaps, she stood out like alabaster. A chill slithered up my spine. It was as if I were seeing everything for the first time, my senses attuned to this forest of treachery and deceit, populated by well-fed predators who circled the princess much as wolves circle their prey.

I had to remind myself that my antiquated notions of chivalry, nurtured on childhood tales of knights of lore, were getting the best of me. Delicate in appearance as she may be, Elizabeth Tudor was not a helpless fawn. She'd been breathing this venomous air from the very hour of her birth. If anyone knew how to survive at court, it was she. Instead of worrying about her, I'd do better to focus on my own troubles. I had yet to deliver the ring, and Robert had made it clear what I could expect if I failed. I saw others like me in the hall, liveried shadows behind their masters, carrying goblet and napkin. Perhaps I too could become invisible, until I found the opportunity to approach her again.

I searched the crowd. Elizabeth drifted in and out of my vision, pausing to tap a shoulder here, offer a smile there. When she reached an enormous hearth near the dais, she paused. Sitting on upholstered chairs were persons of obvious importance. All rose to offer obeisance. I thought it must be difficult to command such deference, to know she'd always be set apart by rank and blood. And then I saw my chance.

Lurking at a sideboard not far from that noble company was Master Shelton.

Chapter Six

I stepped into a surge of incoming courtiers, evading an on-slaught of servitors carrying platters as I navigated toward a cluster of ladies in mammoth gowns, who blocked my way.

Someone hauled me by my sleeve.

"What are you doing here?" hissed Master Shelton. I smelled wine on his breath as he pulled me to the sideboard. He had a foul frown, the same one he wore when the household accounts failed to add up or he'd discovered one of the gamekeepers poaching Dudley livestock.

"Well?" he said. "Aren't you going to answer? Where is your master Lord Robert?"

I decided that the less I said, the better. "His lordship the duke sent him to the Tower on an errand. He asked me to meet him here." As I spoke, I was distracted by a shift in the ebb and flow of the crowd, through which I caught sight of the princess, standing by the chairs.

"Then you should have gone with him," said Shelton. "A squire must never be far from his master's side."

Elizabeth was talking to a diminutive girl seated in one of

those grand chairs. The girl wore simple garb that resembled Elizabeth's, as did her copper-tinted hair and pale skin, only hers was freckled. Sprawled in a chair at her side, flushed from wine, was Guilford Dudley.

"Stop staring!" barked Master Shelton, but his face was set like mortar, his own eyes focused on Elizabeth, who smiled at something the girl was saying. He seemed to have trouble looking away, his big hand fumbling as he reached for his cup. As he quaffed its contents, I remembered that I had never seen him drink while on duty. But perhaps he wasn't on duty tonight. Perhaps Lady Dudley had given him the night to himself. Somehow, I doubted it. For as long as I had known him, Master Shelton had always been on duty.

"Who is that?" I asked, thinking I might as well draw him into conversation while I debated how best to deliver the ring hidden in my pocket.

He frowned. "Who else would it be? Are you blind? That's Lord Guilford, of course."

"I mean the lady sitting next to Lord Guilford."

He went silent. Then he muttered, "Lady Jane Grey," and I thought I heard a pained timbre in his voice. "She's the eldest daughter of Her Grace the Duchess of Suffolk."

"Suffolk?" I echoed, and he added impatiently, "Yes. Jane Grey's mother is the daughter of the late French queen, Mary, younger sister of our King Henry the Eighth. Jane is now betrothed to Lord Guilford." He took another sip of wine. "Not that it has any concern for you."

That tiny slip of a girl was the she-bitch who'd allegedly given Guilford sour ale? I found that amusing and was about to probe further when another figure caught my attention.

Elizabeth's other attendant had discarded her cloak somewhere and now moved confidently through the crowd, dressed in a tawny velvet gown that matched the umber in her hair, which tumbled, loose, under her crescent-shaped headdress. She was quite striking, a vivid contrast to the painted creatures around her, with natural radiance to her skin and easy grace to her movements. I thought she must be seeking out an admirer—a girl like her must have many—but then I saw that she seemed intent on avoiding the gallants who eyed her, sauntering instead past the immense white hearth and nearing the noble company. She must be returning to attend the princess, I started to think, but then I saw Elizabeth make a pointed turn, acting as though she did not recognize her own attendant.

I stared. I may not have been at court long but I knew theatrics when I saw them. It looked to me as if the girl was eavesdropping on her betters' conversation, and Elizabeth, her mistress, was fully aware of it. As if she sensed my scrutiny, the girl paused, looked up. Her gaze met mine. In her regard, I read defiance, arrogance—and definite challenge.

I smiled. Besides her evident attractions, she offered the perfect solution to my dilemma. She'd seen me speaking with Elizabeth; she may have even guessed that I sought to convey a private message, which, in different circumstances, Elizabeth might be inclined to accept. Surely so trusted a servant would be amenable to facilitating her mistress's desires?

All of a sudden, I felt the urgent need to act, get the errand done with. I wanted to deliver my part of the bargain, make my excuses, and go to bed. Whether or not I could retrace my steps to the Dudley chambers remained to be seen, but at least I could rest easy knowing I'd done as ordered. After a good night's sleep, I'd be in a better frame of mind to ascertain how best to navigate any future role I might have in Robert Dudley's schemes.

I continued to watch the girl for an appropriate time to approach, following her with my gaze as she turned to a group of passing women. Before I knew what was happening, she'd blended into their midst. As they sauntered past, she cast a smile over her shoulder. It was an invitation only a fool would pass up.

Master Shelton chortled. "There's a comely wench. Why not see what she has to offer?" He gave me a pat on the back. "Go on. If Lord Robert comes looking for you, I'll tell him I sent you away, the hall being no place for a squire alone."

I was momentarily flummoxed. I might have been mistaken, but I had the distinct impression he wanted to get rid of me, which suited me fine. Forcing out a smile, I squared my shoulders and strolled off. When I looked back over my shoulder, I saw he had turned to the wine decanter behind him.

I trailed the girl at a distance, admiring her confident air and that lustrous hair rippling like a banner down her back. I wasn't inexperienced when it came to women, and I thought her far more enticing than any primped or powdered court lady. But I had so taken to her pursuit, I didn't pause to consider she might have another end in mind than facilitating our acquaintance.

She made an abrupt maneuver, and, like smoke, vanished into the crowd. I turned, searching, turned again, and came to a stop.

I couldn't believe it. I'd never seen anyone disappear thus. It was as if she'd taken flight.

Only then did I take stock of my surroundings and realize with a belated curse that she had, in fact, brought me around the hall to the other side. Now I stood closer than before to the royal dais, the company of nobles, and the princess.

I sought to make myself small. Close up, they were an intimidating group: privileged and glossy, with the air of unassailable primacy that characterized the nobility. Elizabeth had left Jane Grey and sat, bemused, listening to the person opposite her. All I could see of this person was a gross, ringed hand clutching a cane.

I began to sidle backward, wary as a cat, praying the princess would not catch sight of me. All I needed was for her to single me out and cast the remainder of my already doubtful future into ruin.

So intent was I on my retreat that I almost failed to see the person bearing down upon me. When I did, I froze in my tracks. It was Lady Dudley, Duchess of Northumberland.

The sight of her was like cold water flung in my face. Lady Dudley, Lord Robert's mother. Could it get any worse? Of all the people I might have come across, why her? In her world, lackeys always knew their proper place. And mine was certainly not lurking in this hall.

She was like marble, her austere beauty enhanced by an exquisite garnet velvet gown. As I stood there, paralyzed to my spot, I was plunged back to a day, years ago, when she'd come upon me smuggling a book out of the Dudley Castle library.

I'd turned thirteen and was grief-stricken over the sudden loss of Mistress Alice. The book was one of French psalms, a favorite of Alice's, bound in calfskin, with a French dedication on its frontispiece: *A mon amie de votre amie, Marie.*

Lady Dudley had taken it from my hands, told me to remove myself to the stables. An hour later, Master Shelton arrived with a whip. He had been in the Dudley service less than a year; he scarcely knew me and thus delivered the punishing strokes uncertainly, causing more humiliation than pain. But until Lady Dudley departed for court, I never went near the library again. Even after she left, it took weeks before the books lured me back, and I only went at night, returning each book to its shelf the moment I was done with it, as if she might somehow spy my transgression from afar.

As for the volume of psalms, it was the only thing that didn't belong to me that I'd taken when I left the castle. I wrapped it in cloth and hid it in my saddlebag. I could not leave it behind.

Caustic laughter came from the person in the chair opposite Elizabeth, jolting me to attention. Lady Dudley hadn't seen me yet. Left with no other alternative, I started to inch my way toward the group, sweat soaking me under my doublet. I was so focused on evading Lady Dudley's notice, I didn't watch where I was going until I'd stumbled against Jane Grey's chair.

She shifted about, startled. In her gray-blue eyes, I glimpsed haunting resignation. Then she tensed her thin shoulders. In a tremulous voice she said, "Who are you?"

I felt my entire existence come crashing down around me.

At her side Guilford exclaimed, "What, you again!" He sprang to his feet, an accusatory finger pointed at me. "Prescott, you intrude on your betters."

I had made a fine mess of things. I should never have come so close. I should never have followed that girl. Come to think of it, I should have just stayed put in Worcestershire.

"Prescott?" Jane Grey looked at Guilford in confusion. "You know him?"

"Yes, and he's supposed to be serving my brother Robert," Guilford snarled. "Prescott, you'd best have a reason for this."

I opened my mouth. No sound came out. Jane Grey was staring at me. In a jerking motion, I removed my cap and bowed. "My lady, please forgive me if I have disturbed you."

Glancing up through the tangle of hair falling across my

eyes, I saw faint color blotch her cheeks. "You look familiar," she said, her voice halting, hesitant. "Have we met before?"

"I don't believe so, my lady," I said softly. "I would remember it."

"Well, you obviously haven't remembered your manners," snapped Guilford. "Go find something to serve us this instant, before I have you flogged."

As I feared, his belligerence alerted the others. Elizabeth rose from her chair and retreated to the hearth. Her disdain was secondary, however, to Lady Dudley's inexorable passage. My chest constricted. I had no excuse to offer, save that I searched for Robert, which sounded contrived even to me. As I bowed low, I feared it was the end of whatever illusions I had of furthering myself in the Dudley service.

"Is something amiss, my dear?" Lady Dudley asked Jane. I imagined her chill green-blue eyes passing over me in utter disregard. "I trust this manservant of ours isn't troubling you. He's obviously misinformed as to his proper place."

"Yes," said Guilford gleefully. "Mother, see to it he doesn't disturb us again."

I peeked up, saw Jane's gaze shift from Guilford to her soon-to-be mother-in-law, and back again. She gnawed her lip. I had the distinct impression she wanted nothing more than to disappear.

"He, he . . ."

"Yes?" prompted Lady Dudley. "Speak up, dear."

Jane crumpled. Darting an apologetic look in my direction she muttered, "I thought I knew him. I was mistaken. Forgive me."

"There's nothing to forgive. Your eyes must be tired from all that reading you do. You really must try to study less. It can't be good for you. Now please excuse me a moment."

I almost gasped aloud as I felt Lady Dudley's fingers like

blades, digging into my sleeve. She steered me a short distance away. Without a slip of that rigid smile, she said, "Where, pray tell, is Robert?"

My mouth went dry as bone. "I thought Lord Robert might . . ."

It was useless. I could barely talk to her, much less lie. It had always been like this. I often wondered why she'd taken me in, when it was clear she couldn't abide me. I lowered my gaze, bracing for an ignominious end to my short-lived career at court. She'd not forgive my breach of etiquette. I'd be lucky if I spent the rest of my days scrubbing her kennels.

Before she could speak, a strident voice boomed, "Why the fuss over there?" And the ringed hand gripping the cane banged it twice, hard, on the floor. "I would know this instant!"

I recoiled. Lady Dudley went perfectly still. Then a peculiar smile tilted her lips. She motioned to me. "Well, then. It seems Her Grace of Suffolk would meet you."

Chapter Seven

With a knot in my throat, I followed her. As we neared, Elizabeth glanced at me from her stance at the hearth. There wasn't a hint of recognition in her cool amber gaze.

"Kneel," Lady Dudley hissed in my ear. "The duchess of Suffolk is of royal blood, daughter of the younger sister of our late King Henry the Eighth. You must show her your respect."

I dropped to one knee. I caught a glimpse of a spaniel huddled on a massive lap, its red leather collar encrusted in diamonds. The dog yipped.

I slowly lifted my gaze. Ensconced on a mound of cushions, constrained by a gem-encrusted bodice and galleon-sail nectarine skirts, was a monster.

"Her Grace Frances Brandon, Duchess of Suffolk," lilted Lady Dudley. "Your Grace, may I present Squire Prescott? He's newly come to court to serve as a squire to my son."

"Squire?" The civility in the duchess's high voice was brittle as piecrust. "Well, I can't see the churl bowed over like that. On your feet, boy. Let us have a look at you."

I did as she bade. Metallic eyes bore into me. She must have been handsome once, before inactivity and overindulgence at the table had taken their toll. The phantom of a once-robust beauty could still be discerned in the tarnished auburn hair coiled under her enormous jeweled headdress, in the strong line of her aquiline nose, and in the pampered translucence of her skin, which was taut and white, without blemish or wrinkle.

But it was her eyes that transfixed me; cruel, appraising, and appallingly shrewd, those eyes belied the indifference of her expression, tyrannical as only those born to privilege can be.

I couldn't hold her stare for long and dropped my discomfited gaze to her hem. I saw that her left foot, squashed into a ludicrously delicate slipper, twisted inward, grossly misshapen.

I heard her chuckle. "I was an expert rider in my youth. Are you? A rider, that is?"

My reply was low, cautious. "I am, Your Grace. I was raised among horses."

"He was raised at our manor," interposed Lady Dudley, a perverse challenge in her voice. "He came to us by chance twenty years ago. Our housekeeper at the time found him—"

A terse wave of the duchess's ringed fingers cut her off. "What? Have you no family?"

I glanced at Lady Dudley, though I knew she'd give me no succor. Her lips parted, showing teeth. With a sudden drop of my stomach, I wondered if I was about to be cast off. It happened. Masters transferred or exchanged servants for favors, to pay off debts, or to simply dispose of those who ceased to please. Was this why she'd brought me to court? Had all my aspirations been mere fanciful notions?

"No, Your Grace." I couldn't keep the quaver from my voice. "I am an orphan."

"A shame." The duchess's tone indicated she'd heard enough.

She said briskly to Lady Dudley, "Madam, your charity is to be commended. I trust the boy proves worthy of it." Her hand flicked at me. "You may go."

Overcome by relief, I bowed, remembering not to turn my back on a person of the blood royal. Just as I took a step backward, praying I wouldn't bump into another chair, Lady Dudley leaned to the duchess and said: "*Il porte la marque de la rose.*"

She couldn't realize I understood her words, unaware I'd studied French with the aid of one of Robert's discarded lesson books. The duchess sat as if petrified, her ferocious gaze fixed on me. I froze in my tracks. What I saw in her narrowed eyes chilled my blood.

He bears the mark of the rose.

I felt sick. Lady Dudley stepped back from the chair, offered the duchess a brief curtsy. The duchess seemed unable to move. Behind her, lurking at the fringe of the group, I caught a tawny flicker. I blinked, looked again. It was gone.

A heavy hand came down on my shoulder. I wheeled about to find fury etched on Master Shelton's scarred face. He hauled me to the sideboard. "I thought I'd seen you off with that wench. Instead, here you are getting yourself into trouble again! Is this to be my reward, eh? Is this how you repay me for everything I've done for you?"

His reprimand fell on me like rain. My mind whirled, though I had the forethought not to give voice to my tumult, even when he stabbed his finger at my chest and said, "Don't dare move. I've something to do; and when I get back, I expect you to be here."

He strode off. I caught my breath, my mouth dry as bone. With almost painful trepidation I slid my hand to the top of my hose. Further down, near my hip, where points held my codpiece in place, I could feel it. It took all my strength not to strip away my clothing, to reassure myself it couldn't be possible.

The rose—Mistress Alice had called it that. She said it meant I was blessed. But how did Lady Dudley know? How could she have discovered something so intimate, which I'd thought belonged to a lonely boy and a laughing, red-cheeked woman, his only friend in a hostile world? And why would she have wielded it like a weapon upon someone who had no reason to care?

Anger flared in me. Mistress Alice was gone. I couldn't stop mourning her; but in that instant, God help me, I almost hated her for wrecking our memories, for violating our trust. It did not matter that no doubt Lady Dudley had seen my birthmark when I was a babe; all I could think was that she'd been granted a confidence I believed was mine and Mistress Alice's alone.

I closed my eyes, removed my hand from my hose to press it to my pounding heart. As I felt the ring tucked there in my inner pocket, I suddenly realized I was in serious peril, hurled into a situation I had no means to survive. Something was happening, something terrible. I didn't know what it was but somehow I had a part in it, and so, it seemed, did the princess. The Dudleys meant to do us both harm. And if I could find a way to warn her, then maybe—

A blast of horns came from the gallery, and the duke marched to the dais. The hall went silent. I peered to the hearth, where Elizabeth stood motionless. The duchess of Suffolk had risen, as well; as her eyes met mine, fear stabbed through me and I shifted sideways, seeking the camouflage of the crowd.

The duke's speech carried into the hall. "His Majesty wishes to extend his gratitude to all those who've expressed concern over his health. It is at his request that I make this announcement." He scoured the courtiers with his stare. "His Majesty is a benevolent prince, but he is most displeased by the rumors that have come to his attention. Contrary to those who dare speculate, he is well on his way to recovery. Indeed, at his physicians' advice, he has retired to his palace at Greenwich, where he can hasten his cure. As a sign of his improvement, he also wishes it be known he's given gracious consent to the marriage of my youngest son, Guilford Dudley, to his beloved cousin, Lady Jane Grey. Said union will be celebrated tomorrow night with festivities at Greenwich, where His Majesty himself will bless the couple. His Majesty commands we toast this joyous occasion."

A page hastened forth to hand the duke a goblet. He brandished it in the air. "To His Majesty's health; may he long reign over us. God save King Edward the Sixth!"

As if on cue servitors entered with platters of goblets. Courtiers rushed to snatch these, thrusting them upward. "To His Majesty!" they cried in unison.

Northumberland gulped down his wine and abandoned the dais, proceeding from the hall with the lords of the council behind him, like dark leaves in his wake. From where I hid, I saw Lady Dudley follow, as well, but at a distance, accompanied by the glowering duchess of Suffolk. The duchess's daughter, Jane Grey, was behind her mother, one tiny hand lost in Guilford's as he strutted proudly, his father's chosen link to the Tudor royal blood.

The moment they exited, courtier turned to courtier like fishwives in a market, and I glanced in sudden painful understanding at the hearth. Ashen disbelief spread over Elizabeth's face. Her goblet fell from her hand. Wine splashed across the floor, spattering her hem. Without warning, she whirled about and stalked out the nearest side door.

The next minutes passed like years as I stood waiting to see if anyone would follow. The courtiers began to take their leave. No one seemed to notice that Elizabeth had left. I started to move to the door when I espied the princess's attendant sidling up to a stark figure I failed to recognize at first. When I did, my heart lurched. It was Walsingham, Cecil's associate. He and the girl exchanged a few words before they parted, Walsingham turning pointedly away. Neither showed any intention of following the princess.

I slipped to the door. I didn't see Master Shelton before he suddenly blocked my way. "I thought I told you to stay put. Or haven't you found enough trouble for one night?"

I met his bloodshot stare. He'd never given me cause to mistrust him. Yet he answered to Lady Dudley for everything he did; and in that moment all I saw was a reminder of the powerlessness I had felt all of my life. "Since you seem to know more about this so-called trouble than I do," I retorted, "maybe you can explain it to me."

His voice turned ugly. "You ungrateful whelp, I don't need to explain anything to you. But I'll tell you this much: If you value your skin you'll stay far from Elizabeth. She's poison, just like her mother. No good ever came of the Boleyn witch, and none will come of the daughter."

He flung the words at me like filth. It was a warning I knew I should heed, but at that moment all I wanted was to get away from him and the Dudleys, no matter the cost.

"Be that as it may, I have my master's bidding to fulfill."

"If you go after her," he said, "I'll not be responsible for it. I'll not protect you from the consequences. Do you understand? If you go, you're on your own."

"Perfectly." I inclined my head and walked around him. I did not look back, though I could feel his eyes boring into me. I had the uncanny sensation that despite his threats, he understood what I was about to do, that somehow, in a distant past, he'd felt the same compulsion, and was, in his belligerent way, trying to save me from myself.

Then all thought of him left my mind as I hurried into the passage in search of Elizabeth.

Chapter Eight

I thought I was too late, for she seemed to have vanished into the labyrinth of halls and galleries. My heels struck hollow echoes on the floors as I dashed down one corridor, paused, and turned into another. I was following my instinct, avoiding the line of sputtering sconces spaced unevenly on the walls, braving the darker twists and turns in the blind hope that she would not take so easy a route.

I nearly sighed aloud when I finally came upon her, standing in an archway that led into an inner courtyard, bunching handfuls of her gown. She'd removed her filigree net; her hair coiled loose, like fire, over her taut shoulders. Hearing my approach before she saw me, she spun about. "Ash Kat, get word to Cecil at once. We must—"

She stopped, staring. "By God, you *are* bold." She looked past me. Panic colored her voice. "Where are my women? Where are Mistress Ashley and Mistress Stafford?"

I bowed low. "I haven't seen Mistress Ashley," I said, using the tone I'd learned to wield when dealing with a volatile foal.

"If by Mistress Stafford, you refer to your other lady, she didn't follow you out. In fact, I saw her go in the opposite direction."

"She must have gone to ready my barge." Elizabeth paused. Her eyes were unblinking, riveted on me as if she might truly divine my purpose under my skin. She abruptly gestured, moving on swift steps into the courtyard, where the shadows lay thick. Glancing back to the doorway, she said, "Why are you still following me?"

My hand went to my doublet. "I'm afraid I still have my master's orders to complete."

Her face hardened. "Then uncompleted those orders will remain. I believe I've suffered enough humiliation from the Dudleys for one night." In the open air, her indignation echoed a decibel higher than it should. She looked translucent, almost wraithlike. She had come to court to see her brother, only to be disdained, informed in public that the king, no doubt by the duke's command, had departed for Greenwich. Now here I was skulking after her, a nuisance determined to win favor at any cost. Disgust swept through me. What was I doing? Let Robert and his ring be damned! I'd concoct some excuse as to why I'd failed in my assignment. If I was beaten or dismissed, so be it. I was literate, able. With any luck, I wouldn't starve.

"Forgive me." I bowed. "I did not intend to cause Your Grace any distress."

"I'm far more concerned by the distress the duke has caused me." She fixed the full force of her eyes on me. "You're their servant. Do you know what he plans?"

I went still. Master Shelton's words spilled in my mind: *She's poison. Poison to the core.*

Even as I considered it, I knew I wouldn't turn away, wouldn't evade or flee her question, even though it might end up costing me everything. I'd reached that inevitable crossroads that comes in every man's life—the crucial moment when, if we're fortunate enough to recognize it, we can make a choice that will forever alter our fate. Elizabeth was the catalyst I'd sought without ever knowing it; poisonous or benign, she offered me the key to a new existence.

"I do not," I replied. "If I did know, I would tell you. But I have eyes and ears; I saw what happened tonight, and I fear that whatever he plans, it will not bode well for Your Grace."

She tilted her head. "You've an able tongue. But before you go any further, let me warn you, I've dealt with abler in my time. Be careful where you tread, squire."

I did not flinch. "I state what I see. I learned early in life to look beyond the obvious."

A faint smile creased her lips. "It seems we have something in common." She paused again, and the silence restored that invisible divide between royal and commoner. "So, you have my attention. Tell me what you saw to make you think I may be in danger?"

I didn't disregard the underlying threat in her voice. This was treacherous ground, not some fable in which I might play the knight. This was the court, where the sole coinage was power. She'd grown up among its quicksands, tasted its brine since she'd been old enough to learn the truth of her mother's death. But whether she cared to admit it or not, she knew we were both now pawns in some Dudley game. It was the primary reason I couldn't walk away; in truth, there *was* no walking away.

"I saw that you did not anticipate being denied His Majesty's presence. You expected him to be in the hall to greet you, as he surely would have, were he truly on the mend from his illness.

Now you are afraid, because you do not know how he is or what the duke has done."

She was silent, so still she might have been a statue. Then she said, "You are indeed perceptive. Eyes such as yours could take you far. But if you can see so much, then God spare me from those with even keener sight, for it's clear that travesty in the hall was meant as a warning that John Dudley, Duke of Northumberland now rules this realm."

I fought the urge to look over my shoulder, half expecting to see the duke padding up to us, his black-robed council at his heels with warrants for our arrest.

"Does Robin know of your suspicions?" she asked.

I swallowed. It was on the tip of my tongue to tell her what I suspected about Robert, and of the mysterious exchange between Lady Dudley, the duchess of Suffolk, and me. But all I had were, in fact, suspicions, and something instinctual kept me quiet. Whatever the Dudleys had planned for *me* was not her concern—not yet.

"Your Grace," I said at length, "I do not know if Lord Robert can be trusted or not. But if you so command it, I will try to find out."

Without warning, a burst of laughter broke from her lips, wild and uninhibited, and then it vanished as soon as it appeared. "I do believe you would do exactly as you say. For better or worse, their corruption has not yet touched you." She smiled, in sudden sadness. "What is it you want of me, my gallant squire? Don't deny it; I can see it on you. I am no stranger to longing."

And as if I'd known the answer all along, never knowing when or if this moment would come, I said, "I want to help Your Grace, wherever it may lead."

She clasped her hands, glancing down. Dry wine stains soiled her hem. "I hadn't expected to make a friend tonight." She lifted her gaze to me. "Much as I appreciate the offer, I must decline. It would complicate your standing with your master, which seems to me none too firm. I would, however, accept an escort to my barge. My ladies must be waiting for me."

Resisting sudden emptiness, I bowed low. She reached out, touched my sleeve. "An escort," she said softly, "to see me safe. I'll lead the way."

Without another word she took me through the courtyard and back into a maze of silent galleries hung with tapestries, past casements shuttered by velvet drapes and embrasures that offered moon-drenched glimpses of patios and gardens. I wondered what she felt, being in this place built by her father for her mother, a monument to a passion that had consumed England and ended on the scaffold. I saw nothing in her expression to indicate she felt anything.

We emerged where we had started, in the mist-threaded garden leading to the quay. Standing there in anxious vigil were her women. Mistress Ashley bustled forth, the princess's cloak in her hands. Elizabeth raised a hand to detain the matron's advance. Her other attendant, the one called Mistress Stafford, remained where she stood, enveloped in her tawny cape.

I feared Elizabeth might nurse a serpent in her midst. She turned to me. "A wise man would look to his safety now. The Dudleys brew a storm that could rend this realm apart, and if there is any justice, they will pay for it. I'd not wish to be associated with their name, then, not when men have lost their heads for far less." She drew back. "Fare you well, squire. I don't think we'll have occasion to meet again."

She strode to her barge. Her cloak was thrown over her shoulders. Flanked by her women, she moved down the steps.

A few moments later, I heard the boatman's oars strike the water as the craft plied the rising tide, sweeping her away from White-hall, from court. From me.

In the wake of her departure, I sought reassurance. She had said no to my help, but only because she cared. Much as it hurt, I hoped she left London while she still could. This court, I thought, echoing Master Cecil's pronouncement only hours ago in this garden, was not safe. Not for her.

Not for any of us.

I passed a hand over my doublet, feeling the ring in my pocket. I had failed in my first, and probably last, task for Robert Dudley. I should indeed see to my own safety now.

I started back into the palace. After what seemed like hours of aimless wandering, I stumbled upon the stables, where the dogs greeted me with lazy barks, drowsy eyed amid slumbering horses in their painted stalls. After checking on Cinnabar, whom I found well stabled, with plenty of oats, I located a coarse blan-ket in a corner. Divesting myself of doublet and boots, I bur-rowed into a pile of straw, drawing the blanket around me as if it were linen.

It was warm and cozy, and it smelled like home.

Chapter Nine

I awoke disorientated, thinking I was back in Dudley Castle having once again fallen to sleep in the stables with a stolen book. I drowsily searched by my side for the book, before I recalled with a start the events of the past day and night.

I had to smile. *Not the most auspicious way to start a career at court,* I thought, as I righted myself on my elbows and reached for my boots.

I paused.

Crouched at the edge of the hay, wrist-deep in my doublet, was a young groom.

I smiled. "If you're looking for this"—I held up the pouch— "I never go to sleep without it."

The youth jumped to his feet, his mop of disheveled black curls and wide indignant eyes making him look like a startled seraph. I recognized him. He was the same lad I'd entrusted Cinnabar to yesterday, the one with the eager palm. Upon closer inspection I also noted that under his uniform of flax and hide, he was spare as a blade, implying firsthand experience with hunger. A lowly stable hand, perhaps an orphan, as well. London must teem with them, and where else could a parentless, penni-less lad seek employment than in the machinery of court?

I pulled on my boots. "Are you going to explain why you were about to steal from me, or shall I summon your Master of Horses?"

"I wasn't going to steal! I only wanted . . ." The boy's protest faded. I could see on his face that he'd not stopped to concoct a believable excuse in the remote chance he was caught.

I repressed a smile. "You were saying?"

He thrust out his chin. "You owe me money. You paid me to feed your horse, didn't you? Well, if you want it fed and brushed again this morning, you need to pay again. By the looks of it, you're not noble. And only nobles have the right to board their animals for free here."

"Indeed?" I opened up my pouch, taking great delight in the fact that I now had the ability to actually toss out a coin, never mind it might be the last trove I ever saw.

The boy caught it. His curious green-flecked eyes narrowed. "Is this a real gold angel?"

"I think so." I retrieved my rumpled doublet. "I certainly hope so, after all the trouble I went through last night to earn it."

As I slid my arms into the sleeves, I watched the boy bite the coin. With a satisfied nod that would do a moneylender justice, he pocketed it. I had the suspicion I'd just paid for an entire month of boarding and feed. It didn't matter. I knew how it felt to labor without financial reward. Besides, I had an idea. I'd been a boy like this not too long ago, canny as a street cur and as care-ful to keep from being trampled. Boys like us, we saw and heard more than we realized.

"There's no need for anyone to know about this," I said. "Oh, I'm Brendan. Brendan Prescott. And you are . . . ?"

"The name's Peregrine." He perched on a nearby barrel, removing two crabapples from his jerkin. He pitched one at me. "Like the hunting bird."

"Interesting name. Do you have another to go with it?" I grimaced as I bit into the apple. I was famished, seeing as I hadn't eaten since yesterday morning, but the apple was terribly sour.

"No," he retorted, defensively. "Why would I need a surname?"

"No reason. At least, it's simple to remember. How old are you, Peregrine?"

"Twelve. You?"

"I'm twenty," I said, and I almost added, *or so, I think.*

"Oh." He tossed the apple core into Cinnabar's stall. My roan snorted and began to munch. "You look younger," he added, echoing my thoughts. "I thought you were closer to Edward's age. He's fifteen."

"Edward." I paused. "Do you mean, Edward as in His Majesty the king?"

Peregrine frowned. "You're strange. You're not from here, are you?"

This time, I had to grin. Oh, he was an orphan all right. Only someone who'd spent the majority of their life fending for themselves had that quick a reflex. Deflect the question with another. I hadn't thought to encounter such an unvarnished soul in Whitehall.

And, of course, the fact that he had not answered me meant I was right. He knew the king.

"No, I'm not," I said. "I'm from Worcestershire."

"Never been there. Never been anywhere outside Temple Bar."

I nodded, brushing sprigs of straw from my hose. "Do you know His Majesty well?"

He shrugged. "As well as you can know any prince. He used to come here a lot. He loves his animals and hates being stuck indoors all day. His lordship the duke always had him—" He stopped, scowling. "That's not fair."

"I only asked you a question." I smiled. "Besides, who am I going to tell? I'm not anyone important, remember? I'm just curious as to how a stable boy got to meet the king."

"I'm not just a stable boy. I can do other things." He pursed his lips, regarding me as if he wasn't sure if I was worth the effort. But underneath the stance I could see he was also eager to share; like me, he had grown up lonely.

"You were saying the king doesn't like to be indoors?" I prompted.

"Yes, Edward—I mean, the king—he always has to study or write or meet people he doesn't care about, so sometimes he steals away to visit me. Or rather, his dogs and horses. I care for them. He loves his animals."

"I see." I thought of Elizabeth, of the fear on her face as she heard the duke's pronouncements in the hall, and I had to restrain the urge to hurl questions at this boy. He had seen the king, perhaps recently. Conversed with him. What else might he know?

"And does he often come here, to the stables?" I said, thinking that if he were exaggerating his association with the king, it would show.

He didn't look abashed at all. He shrugged again, with the nonchalance of one who knows not to pay much mind to the comings and goings of his betters. "He used to come more but he hasn't been back in a while. The duke probably made him stop. Edward once told me his lordship reprimanded him for befriending menials. Or maybe he's got too sick. He coughed up some blood the last time he was here. I had to fetch him some water. But at least he has that old nurse of his to take care of him."

"Nurse?" For no apparent reason, the hair on my nape prickled.

"Yes. She came here once with a signed order from his lordship, to fetch one of Edward's spaniels. An old woman with a bad limp. She smelled sweet, though, like some kind of herb."

Though I stood on firm ground, for a second the stable swayed around me, as if it were a galleon in a storm. "Herb?" I heard myself say. "Which one?"

"How would I know?" He rolled his eyes. "I'm not a spit boy who turns the roast. Maybe she's an herbalist or some such thing. I suppose when you're the king and you get sick, you get one of those along with the doctors and leeches."

I had to consciously remind myself to breathe, to not give in to the irrational urge to grab the lad by his collar. Everything that had transpired since I'd arrived had addled my wits. Plenty of women dabbled in herb lore, and besides, he'd said she was old, with a limp. I was jumping at shadows. Much good I'd be to anyone in this sorry state.

"Did this woman say who she was?" I managed to ask. Considering the circumstances, I could only hope my expression didn't betray my chagrin at my own foolishness.

"No. She took the dog and left."

I realized I should stop but I couldn't help myself. "And you didn't question her?"

Peregrine stared at me. "Now why would I do that? She knew the dog was Edward's. Why else would she have come? In case you haven't noticed, I mostly do as I'm told. Ask too many questions and you're asking for trouble. I don't want no trouble."

"Of course." I forced out a smile. I should cultivate this scamp. It certainly couldn't hurt.

Peregrine leapt off the barrel. "Well, I have to get back to work. The Master of Nags is due back at any moment and he'll have my hide if I don't get the beasts fed and saddled. Everyone's leaving for Greenwich today. I even have to crate Her Grace's hound for transport. She's like Edward, loves her animals. A pretty lady and nice, too, not like some people around here. She actually pays me."

I gaped at him. "Her Grace the Princess Elizabeth? She . . . she was here?"

Peregrine laughed. "In the stables? You really did drink too much last night, didn't you? No, Brendan Prescott from Worcestershire, her friend Secretary Cecil paid me last night to see to Urian. Hope you find your way back to wherever it is you belong."

I scrambled in the straw for my cap. "Wait." Searching my pouch for the largest coin I could find, I threw it to Peregrine. "I'm afraid I did overindulge last night. I was lucky to make it here. I don't think I could find my way back by myself, and I should be in my master's chamber already. Can you show me the way?"

He grinned, fingers clamped on the coin. "Only to the gardens; I have my work to do."

The sun struggled to break through a pall of cloud. Wind nipped at my face, sharp as teeth, shredding flowerbeds and showering the air with petals. As Peregrine led me to a tree-lined pathway, he asked, "Is that the duke's badge on your sleeve?"

"It is. I serve his son Lord Robert."

"Oh." He pointed down the path toward the bulk of the palace in the distance, rooftops and turrets and gateways digging into the sky. "Through there and to your left. Once you reach the first courtyard, you'll have to ask someone for directions. I've never been inside."

I bowed. "Thank you, Master Peregrine. I hope we meet again."

His smile lit up his face. In that instant he appeared very much his age, reminding me again, with a pang, of myself—precocious and striving for attention in a hostile world. "If Lord Robert ever has need of another page," he said, "or just someone to help out with the odd chore, I'm your man. I can do more than feed horses, you know."

"I'll keep it in mind," I said, and I started down the path, wind-tossed leaves at my feet.

I glanced over my shoulder. Peregrine had disappeared. I frowned, and then, out of the corner of my eye, I saw two figures emerge from the trees on either side of me, daggers in hand. I spun about to bolt back the way I'd come.

The men pounced. Shouting, flailing with my arms, I succeeded in landing a kick in a groin before a massive fist crunched my jaw and sent me to the ground. As everything about me overturned, I heard a cold voice say, "That's enough. I don't want him bloodied."

The men eased back, one of them clutching his groin and letting loose an obscenity. Despite the pain in my head and jaw, I mustered a chuckle. "Too late," I said, to the unseen man who'd called off the attack. "I think he broke a tooth."

"You'll recover." My cap was tossed at me. "Get up. Slowly."

He stepped into view, a cloak hanging from emaciated shoulders: Walsingham, looking even more austere in the dawn than he had under moonlight. He couldn't have been much older than me, judging by the timbre of his voice and unlined sallow skin, yet he seemed ancient, like someone who had never known a moment of spontaneity. At least I knew now what his training was. Evidently, Walsingham was an expert henchman.

"You might have asked to speak with me," I said.

He ignored me. "I suggest you not attempt to flee or otherwise resist. My men can yet break a tooth, or other things." He motioned. The ruffians flanked me. There was no way to extract my dagger from my boot.

One of the men grasped my arm, hard. As I spun about to fend off his attack, the other thrust a sackcloth over my head and bound my hands with rope. Blinded and restrained, I was forced off the path, in a direction I assumed led away from the palace.

They marched me at an unflagging pace through the hunting park and into winding streets, where the clatter of wheels vied with heels on stone, vendors shouting, and the hawking cries of beggars. I smelled the Thames, rank with rot; and then I was shoved through a door, protesting, for which I earned another ear-ringing clout.

Pushed down a passageway and through another door, I staggered into a sudden silent space, filled with the scent of oranges. I'd eaten an orange once, years ago. I had never forgotten it. Oranges were imported from Spain. Those who could afford them had luxurious tastes and the wherewithal to indulge them.

The rope about my wrists was undone. The door shut behind me. I tore off the hood. A familiar figure rose from a desk set before a casement window that offered a sweeping view of a riverside garden, willow trees bending over wrought-iron benches and boxwood hedges.

I stared. "You," I breathed.

Chapter Ten

𝔍'm afraid so," said Master Secretary Cecil. "I apologize if you were mishandled. Walsingham thought it best if we gave you no other choice than to accept my invitation."

I knew without asking that Walsingham stood outside the door, preventing any attempt I might make to escape. I clamped back a retort, watching Cecil move to an oak sideboard, upon which sat a platter of victuals, the basket of oranges, and a flagon. I was fairly certain this alleged invitation of his had something to do with last night, which made my curiosity a little stronger than my trepidation—but only a little.

"Have you broken your fast?" asked Cecil.

I wiped at the blood on the side of my mouth. "I lost my appetite."

Cecil smiled. "You'll recover it soon enough—a young man like you, with no gristle on his bones. When I was your age, I ate at all hours. I gather by your tone, however, that you are displeased with me. I did apologize."

"For what? Dragging me here by force?" I asked, before I could stop myself. I clenched my jaw, hearing the anger in my voice.

This was not a man to reveal myself to. He must want something from me, if he'd gone to the trouble of tracking me to the stables and having me abducted. And if last night was an indication, he held the princess's trust. That he also served the duke only complicated an already complex situation.

In the final say, a man can only have one master. Which one did Cecil serve?

He busied himself at the sideboard. "I'm not Her Grace's enemy, if that's what you're thinking. Indeed, I regret to say I may be her only friend, or at least the only one with any influence. Please, sit." He motioned to an upholstered chair before the desk, as if he were receiving a guest. I sat. Handing me a plate and goblet, which I deliberately left untouched, he returned to his desk, an assured presence in his black breeches and doublet. "I believe Her Grace is in danger," he began, without preamble. "But then, I think you already know that."

I hid my mounting apprehension. I wouldn't be cajoled, graciously or otherwise, into admitting my thoughts about the princess's situation.

Cecil reclined in his high-backed chair. "I find your reticence curious. You were listening in the garden last night, were you not?" He raised his hand. "There's no need to deny it. Eavesdropping is a time-honored rite of passage at court. We've all done it at one time or another. Only, sometimes what we overhear can be misinterpreted. Particularly when we fail to get the details."

A bead of sweat trickled between my shoulder blades. What an incompetent I was. What on earth had possessed me to creep so close? Of course Cecil had known I was there. I'd probably made enough noise to alert the entire palace guard. Had I overheard more than was good for me?

Cecil was looking at me. I had to say something. "I . . . I was sent there by my master." I sounded hoarse, my voice barely making it past the knot in my throat. I could die today. This man took the business of protecting Elizabeth seriously. He could have me killed, and no one would ever know. Squires who failed their masters must disappear often enough.

"Oh, I do not doubt it. Lord Robert always has an agenda, and he doesn't care who he uses to accomplish it." Cecil sighed. "A squire new at court, with everything you owe the Dudleys: What else could you do? And I must admit, you exceeded yourself. Gaining Her Grace's confidence without rousing her suspicion is no easy feat. I hope Lord Robert paid you well. You certainly earned it."

It occurred to me that Cecil might wish to know about the message I carried. If so, then feigning ignorance could convince him I posed no threat. I'd best play the part for all it was worth, at least until he revealed his hand; for a hand he most certainly had to play.

"I'm afraid I don't understand," I said.

"No. Why would you?" He had a stack of ledgers to his left, an inkwell rimmed in jewels to his right. "I, on the other hand, am in a position to know a great many things. And what I don't know, my intelligencers find out for me. You'd be astonished at what can be bought for the price of a meal these days." He met my stare. "Does my candor surprise you?"

Play the fool. Play it for all it is worth.

"I'm wondering what any of this has to do with me."

He chuckled. "I should think a clever boy like you will figure it out. It's not every day you gain Elizabeth Tudor's notice. Indeed, I look for those with your unique talents."

I absorbed this in silence. Just when I thought matters

couldn't get any worse, here I was about to get another offer of employment. No use acting the bewildered rube now.

"What exactly are you saying?"

"Put simply? I wish to hire you. It's a lucrative offer, I can assure you. I require someone fresh, outwardly ingenuous, and somewhat forgettable, at least to the undiscerning eye, yet capable of engendering trust even in those as skeptical as the princess. You did offer to help her last night? She told me so herself. If you agree to work for me, then you will be helping her, in more ways than you can imagine."

The tightening in my stomach forewarned me not to show my sudden, burning interest. However I proceeded, I'd best do it very carefully. This could be a trick. It probably was a trick. How could it be anything else? As talented as I might be, I was certainly no spy.

"Why me? I don't have any training as an . . . intelligencer."

"No. But what you don't know, you can learn. It's your instinct that cannot be taught. I should know. I possess it myself. Believe me, it's more valuable than you realize."

"And on a more practical note, I serve Robert Dudley," I said. "Who trusted me enough to give me a private message for the princess, yes?"

"Indeed. I need to know what he wants from her. Her life may depend on it."

"Her life?"

"Yes. I have reason to think the duke plots against her, and that Lord Robert, your master, is a part of his scheme. It wouldn't be the first time they've pretended to be at odds while secretly working in conjunction to bring down an opponent."

It *was* a trick. I wasn't here for my hidden talents: I was here because I served Lord Robert. Elizabeth had not revealed my message. That was why Cecil had me dragged here with a sack over my head. He wanted my message, and the moment I confessed it I would be silenced.

Forever.

"I regret to hear that," I managed to say, resisting the urge to start shouting, thinking it would be better to die fighting than accept whatever demise Cecil prepared for me. "But as my lord secretary must know, a servant who betrays his master risks having his ears and tongue cut off." I forced out a weak laugh. "And I'm fond of mine."

"You've already betrayed him. You just don't know it."

It was a statement, brisk and impersonal. Though nothing overt changed in his manner, he abruptly exuded a calm menace. "Regardless of how you choose to act, your days as a Dudley servant are numbered. Or do you think they'll keep you after they obtain what they want? Lord Robert used you as his errand boy, and his father and mother despise loose ends."

He bears the mark of the rose.

I saw again the duchess of Suffolk, her metallic eyes staring through me, into me.

"Are you saying they'll kill me?" I asked.

"I am, though of course I have no concrete proof of it."

"And you can offer me assurance that if I leave their service for yours, I'll be safe?"

"Not exactly." He folded his hands at his bearded chin. "Are you interested?"

I met his regard. "You certainly have my attention."

He inclined his head. "Let me start by saying that the duke and his family are in a precarious situation. They were not prepared for Her Grace to appear at court. None of us were, in truth. Yet there she was, determined to see her brother, and so she must be dealt with. She took precautions by letting news of her presence leak out to the people, which will provide her some measure of protection, at least in the short term. But she makes a grave mistake in assuming the duke will do her no harm. She's so incensed by what she sees as his refusal to let her speak with her brother the king, now she insists on proceeding to Greenwich and ascertaining His Majesty's recovery for herself."

Cecil gave a regretful smile. It looked unsettling on his face, as if he didn't quite ever feel surprised by anything Elizabeth Tudor did. "She's not easily dissuaded once she sets her mind to something, and Northumberland has been thorough. Edward's absence last night roused her deepest suspicions and her anger, as he no doubt hoped it would. She is a devoted sister. Too devoted, some might say. She will never stop until she finds out the truth. And that is what I fear: You see, though we may seek it, the truth is rarely what we hope for."

I found myself perched on the edge of my chair. "You think the duke has . . . ?" I couldn't say the rest aloud. I saw in my mind the inscrutable look in Northumberland's eyes and heard his strange murmur, which suddenly adopted a more sinister overtone.

We won't forget those who betray us.

"I wish I knew," said Cecil. "When Edward suffered a relapse, the duke ordered him sequestered, with all access to his person denied. Who can say what has happened? At the very least, I do suspect he is far more ill than any of us know. Why else would Northumberland have taken such pains to announce his recovery, even as he sent Lord Robert to oversee the munitions in the Tower and the manning of every gate in and out of London? Even if Her Grace could be persuaded to return to Hatfield, she'd find her way barred. Not that she will. She believes the duke is holding her brother against his will. If that is true, there is, I fear, very little we can do for the king. My main concern is that she not be lured into the same trap."

It was the first time since Mistress Alice's death that someone had spoken to me as an equal, and the trust it implied went a long way to easing my doubts. I had to remind myself that duplicity at court was endemic. Not even Cecil could be immune.

"Have you told her of your concerns?" I asked, and as I spoke I recalled her stinging admonishments last night. Clearly, Elizabeth wasn't one to take his caution to heart.

He sighed. "Repeatedly, to no avail. She must see Edward, she says, if it's the last thing she does. That's why I need you. I must have irrefutable proof the Dudleys work against her."

My hands tightened in my lap. All of a sudden I didn't want to hear anymore. I didn't want to be forced across a threshold that only last night, in her presence, I'd willingly have crossed. The danger he described was beyond anything I felt I could contend with. To risk myself like this would be to ensure my own death.

Yet even as I prepared my defense and refusal, a part of me could no longer be denied. I felt a transformation taking place, quite against my better nature. I was no longer an anonymous squire, determined to better my lot. I wanted more, to be a part of something bigger than my own self. It was inexplicable, disconcerting, even terrifying, but there was no escaping it.

"Her Grace means everything to me," Cecil added, and I heard in his voice that he, too, had felt her power. "But more importantly, she means everything to England. She is our last hope. Edward became a king too young and has been under the thrall of his so-called protectors ever since. Now, he might be dying. Should Her Grace fall into the duke's hands, it will destroy what those of us who love England have strived for—a

united nation, invincible against the depredations of France
and Spain. The duke knows this; he knows how important she
is. And if he is to survive, he must have her under his control.
But what can he offer her that will guarantee her participation
in whatever he plans?"

He paused, his pale blue eyes focused on me.

I had to stop my hand from moving to my doublet. The ring.
Robert had given me his ring. He said he would have what he'd
been promised.

"It's . . . it is not possible," I said in a whisper. "Lord Robert
already has a wife."

Cecil smiled. "My dear boy, one need only look to Henry the
Eighth to see how easily wives can be disposed of. Robert's marriage to Amy Robsart was a mistake he must have come to regret almost as much as his father did. She's a country squire's
daughter, and the duke would have higher rewards for his sons.
If he could persuade the council to approve Guilford's union
with Jane Grey, why not Robert's to the princess? It would be
the ultimate coup, the feather in the collective Dudley cap,
not to mention the means to secure his rule. For, make no mistake, the duke rules England. He has ever since he saw the Lord
Protector beheaded and gained control of Edward's person."

The ring in my pocket felt twice its weight. The very thought
was insane, and yet it fit with everything I'd expect of the
Dudleys. What had Robert said? *Give her this. She will understand.* Had she understood? Was that why she refused to take it?
Because she knew what it represented? Or did she, in a secret
place in her heart not even she dared admit, *fear* it? I had seen
the look on her face; she had said she was no stranger to longing. She had a depth of passion no one had yet plumbed. Maybe
she wanted Robert Dudley as much as he wanted her.

I made myself breathe. This was happening too quickly. I had to concentrate on what I knew and what I had heard. "But Her Grace and the king—they have an elder half sister, the Lady Mary. She is heir to the throne. If Her Grace were to wed Lord Robert, she still couldn't be queen unless . . ."

My voice faded into silence. I heard a fly buzzing over the platter of neglected fruit on the sideboard. I could barely contemplate where my own words had led.

"Now, do you see?" said Cecil softly. "You can learn, and quickly. Yes, the Lady Mary is next in line to the throne. But she is also an avowed Catholic, who has resisted every attempt to persuade her to convert, and England will never stomach Rome in our business again. Her Grace, on the other hand, was born and raised in the Reformed Faith. She is also seventeen years younger than Mary and can most certainly produce a male heir. The people would rather see her on the throne than her papist sister. And that, my boy, is what the duke can offer her: England itself. It's a temptation very few can resist."

I reached for my goblet, took a long draught. Religion. The eternal bone of contention. People died for it. I'd seen their heads displayed on the gates of London at the duke's command.

Was he capable of doing the same to a princess? For that was what Cecil implied. In order for Elizabeth to inherit, Mary must be dead. I couldn't pretend to know the inner workings of a man I'd seen a half dozen times at most, whose values were far removed from my own. Was he capable of it? I wouldn't think he'd shy away, if it came to his own survival. Still, something here troubled me, an assumption it took me a few seconds to disentangle and put into words. Once I did, I stated it bluntly, with conviction.

"Her Grace would never condone it, not if it meant the murder of her own sister."

"No," said Cecil, to my relief. "She and Mary have never been close, but you are right. She'd never let herself become embroiled in treason, at least not willingly. It is, I hope, the one fatal flaw in the duke's plan. He underestimates her. He always has. She would have the throne, but only when, or if, her time comes."

So, it was treason. The Dudleys plotted treason—against the king and his two sisters. I heard Elizabeth as though her lips were at my ear.

I'd not wish to be associated with their name, then, not when men have lost their heads for far less.

She had warned me. She wasn't leaving London to return to her country manor, because she had divined what the duke intended and she didn't want lives endangered for her sake. She'd come to court fully aware of what she risked.

I took out the ring. "Robert wanted me to deliver this. She wouldn't take it. He doesn't know yet."

Cecil let out a long breath. "Thank God." His smile had no warmth in it. "Your master has overstepped himself. I'm quite sure his father would not have wanted quite so blatant a gesture. This must be in part why Her Grace has insisted on staying. Now that she knows Robert's ploy, she will try to exploit it to reach her brother." He regarded me. "I wish you had more time to consider, but as you can surmise, time is the one commodity we lack. We may have only a few days remaining in which to save her."

I glanced toward the window. I saw a woman enter the garden, leading a limping child by the hand. She smiled as the boy pointed to something I couldn't see on the river, perhaps a passing boat or flock of swans. She bent over to kiss his cheek, tucking a stray curl under his cap.

Desolation opened in me. I was reminded in that moment of

Mistress Alice and, less tenderly, of Master Shelton. The steward would never forgive me for what he could only deem as a betrayal of the family that had kept me alive. But Alice would have understood. Of all the lessons she had instilled in me, the one closest to my heart was being true to one's self.

But I'd never had the opportunity to exercise that truth. A foundling and probable bastard, a servant with nothing to my name, I had spent my life struggling to survive. I had never looked beyond the demands of the day, except when it came to studying, and that was just so I could get better at surviving. Still, I couldn't deny that I craved the freedom to make my own destiny, to become the man I wanted to be, not the one my birth condemned me to.

I returned my gaze to Cecil. "What is it you want of me?"

He smiled. "Perhaps the question should be: What do you want? I should think that at the least you'll expect to be paid."

I knew what I wanted. What I didn't know was whether I should trust him with it, even if the situation told me I couldn't trust anyone else. The question burned inside me unspoken, demanding an answer I wasn't sure I should seek. What had he said?

The truth is rarely what we hope for. . . .

I wondered if he was right.

"You needn't decide right now," Cecil said. "For now, I can promise you freedom from drudgery for the rest of your days, as well as a permanent post in my service." He reached for a ledger. A brief silence ensued. Then he said with uncanny insight, "In my experience, however, men usually hunger for more than material appeasement. Do you? Hunger, that is?"

He looked up. I wondered if he saw my hesitation. I recalled again the words that had passed between Lady Dudley and the duchess of Suffolk. There was a truth there, tangled and twisted.

But I found I couldn't speak of it. I couldn't entrust everything to this man. In the final say, he was still a stranger to me.

When he next spoke, his voice was low. "I make it my duty to study those who cross my path, and you are someone who carries a secret. You hide it well, but I can see it. And if I can, so will others. Take care to guard yourself, lest one day it's used against you when you least expect it."

He paused. "I should also tell you that my role in this matter must remain anonymous," he added. "The princess's safety must come first, above all else. It goes without saying that you must also follow my orders without deviation or question. Do you understand? Any change you make could put you, and consequently our plan, in danger. You are not the only one working to save her. You will have to learn to trust even those whom you do not like or know."

I took a deep breath. "I understand."

"Good. For now, you will continue to attend Lord Robert. Watch everything he says and does. You will be advised of how to report your information when the time comes, as well as any changes in our plans." From his stack of ledgers he took a folder. He opened it before me. "Herein is a scaled map of Greenwich. Memorize it. I'm not certain when, but I believe that at some time during the festivities for Guilford and Lady Jane's wedding, the duke will make his move. Before he does, we must get the princess away."

I nodded and leaned in, surveying the map as Cecil explained my assignment.

Chapter Eleven

I left the Thames-side manor in a daze. The sounds and sights of the city assaulted me, reminding me I was late for my appointment with Robert. I quickened my pace. Cecil had assured me the palace wasn't too far away. He even offered an escort, which I politely refused. The less I saw of Walsingham and his rough men, the better.

The sun drew random fingers of light over the river. An oppressive humidity hung in the air. The day promised to be sweltering, once the freshness of the morning dissipated, and merchants and vendors were already hurrying about their business.

No one seemed to mark me as I passed, and still I pulled my cap lower on my brow. I was all too aware of the badge on my sleeve, announcing my affiliation, and it required strength of will not to rip it off. I'd have to learn to conceal my revulsion for the Dudleys if I was to convince Robert of my continuing devotion.

A spy: I was going to spy for Master Cecil, to help Princess Elizabeth. It wasn't a role I could ever have envisioned for myself, even in my wildest moments. Only yesterday I had been riding into London, a callow lad pondering how best to adapt to my new post. One day later, I was returning to my master with treachery in my heart. I found it difficult to sort out my feelings about my own duplicity, until I thought of that frightened young woman standing alone in a corridor in her wine-spattered gown.

What is it you want of me, my gallant squire?

I had traversed several crowded, noisy blocks when I realized I was being followed. Once or twice, I caught a glimpse of the shadow behind me and had to resist the impulse to wheel about to confront it. I set my hand on my dagger, now at my hip. With a taut smile I continued, avoiding the dense undergrowth and trees of the hunting park. Rounding into King Street, which passed under a gateway through Whitehall, I paused to adjust my cap. When I felt the shadow draw close, I said, "Some fool courts a knife in his belly."

A stricken pause followed. I glanced over my shoulder. "Why are you dodging me?" I asked, and flush-faced Peregrine replied, "You . . . because you needed my protection."

"I see. So you witnessed the attack." I hooked my hands in my belt. "You might have called for help. Or, better yet, gone and fetched some. Or didn't I pay you enough?"

"I was going to, at first," he said in a rush, "but I decided to follow you instead, in case they hit you over the head and threw you in the river. I used to fish out corpses for a living. You're lucky I did, too, because I wasn't alone."

"Oh?" I raised my eyes to scan the vicinity. "Someone fished out corpses with you?"

"No." He sidled up to me, his voice lowering to an urgent whisper. "Someone else is following you. I saw him come out of the trees in the park after you were taken. He crept around the manor while you were inside, peeking in windows and—Ouch!"

Peregrine yelped as I grabbed him by his jerkin, thrusting him into a side alley.

He struggled. I clamped a hand to his mouth. "Be still, coxcomb. Whoever you saw back there could be watching at this very moment. Do you want us both to end up in the river?"

His eyes widened. Removing my hand, keeping one eye on the alley's entrance, I said, "Do you know who he is?"

He nodded, and wormed out from inside his jerkin a pocket dagger. I had to grin. I'd had one just like it when I was a boy, good for slicing apples and hunting squirrel. "Does he know you?"

"No. Or, at least, not by name. He came to the stables a few days ago, but I didn't attend him. He had two horses stalled. He's wearing a hood and cloak today, but I recognized him. When he left the stables, he kicked one of the yard mutts. It was just wagging its tail, hoping to be petted, and he kicked it." Peregrine grimaced. "I hate anyone who kicks a dog."

"Me, too." I took off my cap, wiped cold sweat from my brow. Our mystery man hadn't accosted us, though the alleyway, snaking as it did to a dead end littered with refuse, presented the ideal spot for an ambush. Either he wasn't willing to reveal himself or he wasn't yet ready to risk a confrontation. Neither offered consolation.

I opened my pouch to ladle coins into Peregrine's palm. "Listen closely. I can't afford to play right now, much as I'd like to. I assume your work can be neglected, seeing as you followed me here, so can you find out where he goes without getting into trouble?"

"I've been tiptoeing around him all morning. I'll find out everything you need to know. Trust me. I can be sly as a snake when I want to."

"Oh, I'm sure. Here's what we'll do." I explained quickly, then clapped a hand on the boy's shoulder and hauled him back to the street, where I threw him from my side.

"And don't let me see the likes of you again! Next time, I'll feed you to my pigs, you thieving knave!"

Peregrine scampered off. Several passersby paused to wag their heads at this evidence of roguery in their midst. I searched my doublet in visible anger, slapped on my cap, and tramped onward, scowling like a man who's narrowly escaped having his hard-earned wages filched.

I was relieved to reach Whitehall. The main courtyard was full of servants and chamberlains, and I discreetly asked one for directions to the Dudley chamber.

Despite my determination to help the princess and despite Cecil's explicit trust, I hadn't been convinced I could look Lord Robert in the face and not give myself away. It was one thing to despise him for using me, quite another to know I had to show an impenetrable front to keep him from achieving his ends. And knowing I was being followed had only added fear to my already extreme case of nerves. If whoever it was had discovered my meeting with Cecil, I thought it safe to assume the intent was not benevolent. Not only was Elizabeth's safety and that of her sister, Princess Mary, at stake, but my own life could hinge on my ability to complete this task. All I needed to do for the moment, I kept telling myself, was to convince Robert his cause was not lost, only delayed by feminine caprice. As for what came after, given recent events, I thought it best not to look too far ahead.

Inhaling a deep breath, I threw open the chamber door, my excuse ready on my lips.

The room was empty. Only the stripped bed frame and

scarred central table remained. On this table were thrown my saddlebag and cloak.

"Finally," a voice said from behind me. I spun about.

Resplendent in scarlet brocade, his slashed breeches cut short to reveal his muscular thighs and to enhance the protruding splendor of his curled and patterned codpiece, Lord Robert Dudley swaggered into the room.

I bowed low. "My lord, forgive my tardiness. I got lost and—"

"No, no." He waved a gloved hand, perfuming the air with a distinct scent of musk. "Your first night at court, all that free wine and food, a wench or two—how could you resist?"

His grin was brazen, displaying strong teeth. Not a pleasant grin, but appealing all the same. Much as I hated to admit it, I could see why women responded to him. The grin also indicated to my relief that he wasn't inclined to see me grovel.

He arched a brow. "You missed the packing, however, not to mention my good news."

"My lord?" Of course. That was why he looked so smug. He had news.

His dusky eyes glittered. "Yes. I've received word from my father that Her Grace has decided to stay to celebrate Guilford's nuptials. It seems she can't resist me. And I owe it all to you." He let out a guffaw, slinging an arm about my shoulders. "Who could have guessed you had such a sweet tongue? We should consider sending you abroad as an ambassador."

I forced out a grin. "Indeed, my lord. Thus may you take heed of how to woo a lady."

"Bah!" He thumped my back. "You are a live one, I'll grant you, but you've a ways to go before you're fit to woo anything other than a tavern slut. I, on the other hand, will soon pay suit to a princess of the blood royal."

Naturally, he assumed the princess was going to Greenwich because of her interest in him. But at least I had something to report to Cecil. By Robert's own admission, he confirmed his intent. I could scarcely look at his face, thinking that under that enviable facade lay the soul of a villain.

"Does my lord think she'll . . . ?" I let my insinuation linger.

"Oblige me?" He played with the fringe of his gauntlets. "How could she not? She may be a princess, but she's also Nan Boleyn's daughter. And Nan always had an eye for the gentlemen. But, like her mother, she'll make me wait. It's the Boleyn way. She'll make me beg before I am deemed worthy, just as Nan did to Henry. No matter. It gives us all the more time to bait my snare."

I detested him in that instant, overcome by the urge to wipe that insufferable superiority off his face. Instead, I found considerable pleasure in removing the ring from my doublet. I extended it. "I certainly hope so, my lord, because she wouldn't take this from me."

His self-indulgent expression froze. He stared at the ring in my palm. "Did she say why?" he asked in a flat voice.

"She said you thought too much of yourself. Or too little of her." I realized I shouldn't be saying this. I was supposed to encourage his delusions, not crush them. But I couldn't help myself. Lord Robert Dudley deserved to be yanked down a notch or two.

His jaw clenched. For a moment, I thought he would knock my hand aside. Then he gave a terse laugh. "Well, well. So, she refused my token. Of course, she did. The royal virgin—always presuming on her chastity. It's her favorite role. We'll let her have her fun for now, eh?"

The icy mirth in his tone crept down my spine. Then he

gestured magnanimously, all charm and ease once more. "Keep the ring. I'll put a finer one on her finger yet."

Cuffing my shoulder, he sauntered to the door. "Gather up your things. We're going to Greenwich, but not by barge. Leave the river to weaklings and women. We'll ride our steeds over good English soil, like comrades and friends."

Friends. He thought we were friends now, accomplices in a sordid game of deceit. I bowed, turning to the table. "My lord," I said in a low voice.

He chuckled. "That's right, I forgot. I'll leave you to change. Don't take too long." He paused. "Come to think of it, you always were particular as a maiden when it came to undressing," he mused, and my heart leapt against my ribs. He shrugged. "It's not as if you've anything I haven't seen before."

He strolled out, closing the door behind him. I waited until I was certain he wouldn't return before I furtively divested myself of my rumpled new doublet and good shoes.

I stood in chemise and hose. I had to look. Hooking my hand in my hose, I lowered it to my groin. The large maroon discoloration spilled across my left hip, its edges like wilted petals.

It had been there since birth. Though not uncommon, such blemishes were often dubbed "demon bites" or "Lucifer's pawprints" by the ignorant and superstitious. I'd learned early to conceal it from prying eyes, particularly those of the Dudley boys, who'd have tormented me all the more. Never had any of them seen me naked.

Mistress Alice had said it was a rose left by the kiss of an angel while I was still in the womb. A fanciful tale, which I'd almost believed. But as I matured, it had been the touch of a real woman, like the maid at the castle who introduced me to pleasure and eased its stigma, that taught me that not everyone was as sensitive to its significance as I was.

La marque de la rose . . .

I shuddered, yanking up my hose and reaching for my leather jerkin. Rolling up the doublets, I stuffed them into my saddlebag. I'd not told Cecil, not yet, but I would. As soon as I fulfilled my obligations I would ask him to help me discover the truth of my birth, no matter the cost. For now, being Robert Dudley's new friend was a fine enough start. A friend was trusted, relied upon, confided in—someone we turn to in times of need. And wherever Robert went, there his new friend would be, like a shadow.

I had no doubt that the shadow trailing me wouldn't be far behind.

Chapter Twelve

Greenwich Palace materialized in a multitude of turrets and pointed blue slate rooftops, fronted by the southeastern swath of the Thames. From the slope where Robert and I halted to rest our mounts, I thought it a more graceful sight than Whitehall's colossal sprawl, a secluded palace nestled amid woodlands, removed from the grit and chaos of London. It was difficult to conceive of any menace lurking there. Yet Cecil believed it was in Greenwich that the duke had sequestered the king, and here he would make his move against Elizabeth.

"She was born in Greenwich," Robert said, breaking into my thoughts. "September 7, 1533." He chuckled. "It was quite the occasion. King Henry had been striding about for months, crashing heads, and cutting off not a few, declaring to all who cared to listen that his beloved queen would bear him a son. But when Anne Boleyn took to her bed, all she brought mewling into the world was, as Henry himself put it, 'a worthless daughter.'"

I glanced at him. "A beautiful place to be born, my lord. She must be fond of it."

"She is. She even had her own apartments as a babe, at

Queen Anne's insistence. Anne wanted her daughter close to her, regardless of how Henry felt." Robert straightened in his saddle. "I wonder if she's arrived yet. It would be just like her to keep us waiting."

I hoped she did. The longer she delayed, the more time I'd have to appraise the situation. Cecil had said it was likely Edward had been lodged in the palace itself, perhaps in the so-called Secret Lodgings, a series of guarded chambers connected to a long gallery, designed to afford the monarch privacy and seclusion. The more I found out about Edward's exact whereabouts, the more Cecil might discern about the duke's impending plans. I also had to join up with Peregrine and find out who was following me and why.

"Let us be off," cried Robert. "Last one there has to feed the horses."

With a spirited laugh, he set spurs to his bay. Cinnabar leapt at my nudge, reveling in the opportunity to display prowess. Habituated to long daily rides outside Dudley Castle, my roan was not used to too many hours in the stable. With the wind against my face and Cinnabar's flanks propelling me forth, I surrendered to the moment, reminded of the days when I'd rode bareback in the fields as a boy, feeling for a brief time as though I hadn't a care in the world.

The palace sprang up before me, faced in red brick riddled with plaster grotesques, octagonal chimneys emitting roast smoke and knot gardens breathing a confection of perfumes from herbs and perennials. Waving his hand imperiously, using his horse as a wedge, Robert steered us through the courtiers amassed outside the main gatehouse. We rode past a ward into a cobblestone courtyard, around which were assembled edifices painted in Tudor green and white.

Grooms led lathered horses into these stables, while noble-men in leather cloaks peeled off gauntlets as they stalked into the palace.

Robert leapt from his saddle. Unhooking his bags, he said, "I won the wager. You see to the horses. I've a room off the inner court. Wait for me there. I have to report to my father." He strode off, leaving me with the horses panting in my ears, oblivi-ous that I'd curbed Cinnabar's enthusiasm so I might deliberately lag behind.

I led the horses into a stable. Harried grooms were accom-modating a multitude of roans, geldings, and palfreys, divesting them of saddles, brushing them down, and stabling them with armloads of fresh oats and hay.

None took notice of another servant among them. I recog-nized the duke's own sleek Barbary in a far stall removed from the others, beside an exit gate with a view of a vast hunting park. I brought the horses to it. Like his son, Northumberland had disdained travel by river. I couldn't say I blamed them: I was not enamored of running water myself, a childhood fear I had never fully conquered.

I clicked my tongue at the Barbary, who pricked its ears as I stabled Robert's steed and Cinnabar nearby. "Enjoy it," I told Cinnabar. "There's no predicting where we might lodge next." He nuzzled me, grateful for the run.

A liveried groom approached. "Will you be requiring feed?"

I nodded, reaching into my jerkin for a coin. "Yes, please, and—" I stopped. Stared. "Where in God's name did you get that green coat? Or should I say, steal it?"

Peregrine grinned. "I borrowed it. These Greenwich stable

grooms are so easily bribed. They'd strip naked for the mere glint of gold."

"Is that so?" I returned to the horses, lowering my voice. "Did you find him?"

Taking my cue, Peregrine busied himself spreading hay on the floor. "Yes. He's here."

I paused. "In the palace?"

"Yes. After I left you, I followed him to a tavern where he'd tethered his horse. He didn't even stop for a drink. He took to the road and got caught up in the servant transport from Whitehall, which gave me time to hop a cart. He rode beside us but stayed apart, as if he smelled better, though there were ale and songs aplenty. When he arrived, he went to the queen's apartments. The guards didn't check his papers at the gatehouse. He must have distinction."

"The queen's apartments?" I frowned. "His Majesty isn't married."

Peregrine shook his head, as if I were hopeless. "That's just what they're called. Old Henry's wives used to reside there. Guess who's lodged there now? Jane Grey and her mother, the duchess of Suffolk: I think our man is a Suffolk hireling."

I suppressed my disquiet. Had the duchess set one of her men to trail me? If so, she was probably learning at this moment about my enforced visit to Cecil's manor house.

"What does he look like? Is he big or small? Tall or short?"

"He's taller than you," said Peregrine, "but not by much. He has a pointy face, like a ferret."

"A ferret." I gave him a wry smile. "I'll remember that. Excellent work, Peregrine. I'm sorry I can't repay you the coins you used to get that coat, but maybe later, eh?" I ruffled his hair, about to turn away when I heard him scoff.

"I don't want your money. I can earn extra coins whenever I like. There are plenty of lords and ladies willing to pay for information. What I want is to work for you. I've had enough of mucking out stables. I think you'd make a good master."

I was taken aback, though of course I should have seen it coming. The boy had clung to me like a clam since we'd met. Regardless of how I might view my circumstances, to him I was worth impressing—the personal squire to the duke's son, in his debt for saving me from a potentially lethal stalker, with money to throw his way.

Then I thought of another possibility.

I smiled. "I'm flattered, but I can't afford you."

"Why not? I don't cost much, and you must earn a decent wage. Secretary Cecil always pays his men well, and— Stop that!" He yanked away from my pinch to his ear.

I glanced about the stables. The grooms were too busy to pay us any mind, and the stalls partially concealed us in any event. Still, someone could be nearby, listening.

I pulled Peregrine close. "I never said *who* was paying me," I hissed.

He recoiled. "You didn't? I . . . I must have thought . . ." He chewed his lower lip. I could practically see his agile mind conjuring up lies out of thin air. "You were taken to his house." He stopped. That didn't sound convincing, and he knew it.

I regarded him without visible reaction. His stare shifted to the stall gate. In the second before he bolted, I registered panic on his face. Jerking forward, I snatched him by the collar. He was stronger than he looked, being little more than gristle and bone, but I got a firm enough grip to hold him dangling off the floor, like an errant pup.

"I think," I said, "it's time you told me who you work for."

"No one!"

I tightened my grip, making an overt move for my dagger with my other hand. He sang out in a shrill treble, "I can't say. He threatened to kill me if I did."

That sounded better. I slackened my grip, letting a moment pass before I let him go. To his credit, Peregrine didn't make a run for it.

"I'm disappointed. I thought you were my friend."

"I am your friend," he retorted, with an impressive indignation, all things considered. "I helped you, didn't I? I warned you about being followed, and I followed that Suffolk man here. No one paid me to do that."

"Oh? If memory serves, I believe I paid you. Four times, I might add."

"I still risked my life." He puffed out his chest. "And for what? Maybe I was wrong. Maybe you'd not make such a good master, after all."

I smiled coldly. "It was Walsingham, wasn't it? He told you to guide me to that path so I could be overtaken. You didn't *happen* to see my abduction. You knew about it beforehand. Did he also tell you to make sure I caught you pretending to try to rob me, or did you think about that yourself? That was a nice touch, actually—disarming, yet it engendered contact and rapport."

Peregrine shuffled his feet in the straw and lowered his eyes, a portrait of abject misery, which I was not buying for a second.

"Then you came after me," I went on, "and, according to you, happened to chance upon this Suffolk man dodging us. Does he actually exist? Or is Walsingham setting me up for more trickery?"

That got his attention. He reared his face up, furious. "Of course he exists! And why would Walsingham want to trick you? You both work for Cecil."

"Perhaps, but then I never thought *you'd* trick me, either."

"I haven't!" His protest resounded into the stables, causing the horses to stomp their hooves and grooms to look up. Abashed, he dropped his voice. "I didn't trick you," he repeated. "I'm not Walsingham's lackey. Yes, he came and ordered me to see you to that path. He knew you were asleep in the hay pile. Don't ask me how. But I don't work for him, and he didn't pay me. He said either I did as he told me, or else. I figured you'd fallen into serious trouble when his men took you, so I decided to follow you, in case."

"In case what? You could fish out my corpse from the river and steal my pouch?"

He glared. "In case you needed me. I . . . I like you."

I heard an unwilling ring of truth in his avowal. Had I been in his place, I would have done the same. I knew what it felt like to be scared and have everything to lose. Moreover, Walsingham wasn't one to tolerate no for an answer, particularly from some urchin he'd just as soon kick as look at.

"Let's say for argument's sake that I believe you," I said at length. "I still can't hire you. I don't have a treasury to draw upon, and who's to say what'll happen the next time someone offers you a few coins?"

"I'll work for free, then, to prove myself. I'm not afraid of anything. I'll go anywhere you want me to, find out anything you need to know. All you have to do is tell me."

I softened my tone. "I'm sorry, but the answer is no. This task I'm entrusted with . . . it could be very dangerous. I'll not put you at risk."

"I've been at risk all of my life. I can take care of myself."

"I realize that. But I can't allow it."

"Why not? You obviously need someone to help you. You can't possibly hope to save the princess without—" Choking on his own words, Peregrine leapt back from me into Cinnabar's rump. He was lucky that my horse was a tolerant creature, unlikely to kick unless provoked.

I rounded on him. "How do you know about that? And don't you dare lie to me this time, or you'll rue the day we met."

"I overheard it. At Cecil's house. The window . . . it was ajar."

"And you were there the entire time, listening?"

"Yes. Our man almost saw me. He crept right past the hedge where I was hiding. I could have reached out and grabbed his cloak."

I went still. "He also heard? Everything?"

"I don't know. I don't think so, or at least not all of it. He wasn't there long enough. When Cecil's wife and son came into the garden, they scared him off."

"Cecil's wife and son?" I almost rolled my eyes. "You knew who they were? You *are* the little snake, aren't you?"

He let out a nervous laugh. "Yes! Yes, I am. See? This little snake can be of use to you."

"Not so fast. What else do you know? Best tell me now. I hate surprises."

"Nothing. I swear it on my mother's soul, may she rest in peace, whoever she was."

Whoever she was . . .

I paused. I should order him back to Whitehall, back to his life of anonymity and opportunism. It would be safer than whatever awaited here.

But I knew I wouldn't. I saw myself in him, the child I had been. He deserved a chance. I just hoped neither of us would have reason to regret it.

"I expect you to earn your keep," I said. "And to obey me in all things, no matter what."

He sketched a clumsy bow. "Say no more, master. I'll do anything you require."

I couldn't contain my smile. "And don't call me that. My name will suit fine."

Peregrine's smile was so fulsome it warmed my heart. It was certainly an odd way to go about making a friend, but a friend I had made, nevertheless.

Chapter Thirteen

It turned out that my new friend was also extraordinarily well versed on the layout of Greenwich, having been here on several occasions and in various capacities, including as a scullion. He'd ridden transport barges with animals from London, brought the creatures to their various owners, and was thus able to answer most of my questions concerning the palace, including the fact that Greenwich, like most abodes beautified by the Tudors, had been built upon the remnants of an older medieval edifice. I asked about the Secret Lodgings and how we might access them.

"The privy gentlemen watch over those rooms," Peregrine explained as we entered an inner ward. "They're charged with guarding the gallery to the royal chamber and preventing anyone from intruding. Of course, they can be bribed, but it's risky. A privy gentleman who betrays the king's trust can lose his post, and his head, if His Majesty gets mad enough."

"Do you know any of Edward's privy gentlemen?"

"You do. Your master Lord Robert is one of them."

"I mean, one we can trust."

He considered. "There's Barnaby Fitzpatrick. He's the King's childhood friend. Sometimes he'd accompany Edward to the stables. He never said much, just stood and watched Edward like a bull. I don't know if he's here, though. I heard that most of Edward's attendants were banished after he fell ill. Something about exposing His Majesty to contagion, though he looked well enough to me until the duke got hold of him."

"Peregrine, you're a veritable mine of information." I donned my cap. "If you ever do choose to betray me, I won't stand a chance."

He gave me a sour look. "Do you want me to look for Barnaby? He might know a way to get into the Secret Lodgings, if that's what you're after."

I glanced over my shoulder. As I did, I realized scouting the vicinity was becoming second nature to me. "Keep your voice down. Yes, he might be useful. Look for him but don't tell him anything. I don't know where I'll be, but . . ."

"I'll find you. I've done it before. Greenwich is not that big."

I nodded. "Good luck, then. Whatever you do, please do stay out of trouble."

Clad in his stable clothes, having discarded the groom's coat, Peregrine dashed across the ward and up a staircase. With a whispered prayer for his safety, I went the opposite way, into the wing that housed the nobility. I'd decided to leave my saddlebag hidden in the straw near Cinnabar, where no one could steal it without getting their guts kicked in. My horse was tolerant but hardly amenable to searches in his stall by strangers. I'd removed only my dagger, which I kept in my boot, and so I moved easily, without visible burden.

The corridors were quiet. I faced a passage lined with identical doors, some shut, others ajar, all indistinguishable. I should have asked Robert exactly which room was his, I thought, as I began trying latches and peeking into chambers. They were similar in layout, containing a leather or faded cloth curtain separating a small front room from a much smaller bedchamber, some of which had primitive privies. As in Whitehall, the walls were uniformly whitewashed, the wood floors unadorned. What few furnishings the rooms had—a stool or bench, table, battered bed or pallet on rickety legs—were strictly utilitarian. Not luxurious by court standards, but at least they appeared free of fleas, rodents, and the ubiquitous smelly rushes.

It took a few tries before I located Robert's room at the far end, recognizable because of his saddlebags tossed beside a leather coffer brought from Whitehall. His mud-spattered riding cloak was flung across a chair, as if he'd discarded it in a hurry.

He was gone, presumably to report to his father. I debated what to do next. Perhaps I could take advantage of this spare time to search his saddlebags for clues.

I froze in my tracks. There were footsteps coming. Bolting past the curtain into the bedchamber, with my breath lodged in my chest, I crouched down and put my eye to a frayed moth hole in the worn fabric.

I waited. A cloaked figure appeared in the doorway. For a paralyzing second I feared my shadow had found me. I forced myself to look, relief overwhelming me when I realized that despite the hooded cloak and scuffed boots, this person was shorter than me, smaller in build. Unless Peregrine had made a mistake, it couldn't be our mystery man.

The figure glanced about the room. Then it withdrew a folded parchment from within its cloak and set it on the table, shifting the pewter candlesticks so as to make it plain to whomever entered. It didn't linger after that, leaving as quickly as it had appeared.

I counted to ten under my breath before I slipped forth. The parchment was fine, of an obvious expensive grain. But it was the seal which captured my attention: That filigreed wax 𝔈 encircled by vine tendrils could belong to no one else. I had to stop myself from tearing it open. There could be something in it I needed to know, something that would affect the course of my mission. But I couldn't just break the seal on a letter from the princess intended for Robert. Not unless . . .

I scratched the edge of the seal with my fingernail. It was still tacky, easily lifted. With my heart hammering in my ears, I unfolded the parchment. Two brief lines were inscribed there in an aristocratic hand, followed by an unmistakable initial.

My lord, it seems there is a matter of some urgency we must discuss. If it suits your discretion, pray reply in kind by the established route, and we shall meet tonight, after the stroke of twelve, in the pavilion. E

I stood, breathless. I almost failed to hear the staccato footsteps marching down the passage outside, until they were suddenly at the door, sending me diving once more into hiding.

This time, Robert strode in, still in his riding gear, his features contorted. "Why must I always be the one to do his dirty work?" He yanked off his gauntlets, flung them aside.

Behind him, poised and immaculate, was his mother, Lady Dudley.

My throat tightened, even as my fingers quickly resealed the note. She clicked the door shut. "Robert, stop this. You're not a boy anymore. I'll not countenance a tantrum. Your father can request obedience, but I demand it."

"You have it! You've always had it. I even wed that stupid Robsart wench because you and Father thought it best. Everything you've ever asked of me, I've done."

"No one said you weren't an exemplary son."

He laughed harshly. "Excuse me if I beg to differ. In my experience, exemplary sons aren't sent off on fool's errands."

"It is not a fool's errand." There was something eerie about the bland inflection in her tone. "On the contrary, what we ask implies significant trust in your abilities."

"What ability? To ride off at a moment's notice to arrest some old maid, which any idiot with half an escort could do? It's not as if she'll put up a fight. I'll wager she has no more than a dozen retainers with her, if that." `

"Indeed." I was relieved to hear Lady Dudley's voice revert to its familiar cold severity. "And yet that same old maid could be our undoing." Her eyes fixed on him. "Mary has demanded a full accounting of her brother the king's condition. Otherwise, she threatens to take matters into her own hands. I need not tell you that this can only mean she's receiving information from someone here at court."

"No doubt. She's not stupid. And there are still enough papists about to wish her well."

"Yes," she replied, "and the last thing we need is for one of those papists to help her flee the country so she can throw herself on her cousin the emperor's mercy. Mary must be captured and silenced, and you're the only one we dare send. None of your brothers has your training. You've ridden in battle; you know how to command men to your will. The soldiers will not question your orders when it comes time to take her."

I clenched my teeth. They were talking about Princess Mary, the king's older sister. I recalled what Cecil had said about her, about her staunch Catholicism and how she threatened the duke. I leaned closer to the curtain, slipping the missive into my jerkin. It did not escape me that I was, at this very moment, indulging in the very rite of passage of the court Cecil had mentioned, for the second time. Only if I were caught, I could forget getting out of here alive.

"I understand all that." As Robert raked a hand through his tangled hair, he resembled an uncertain youth, caught between his own compulsive desires and the iron will of his parents. "I know how much we stand to lose. But Father and I had agreed that for now Mary posed no immediate threat. She has no army, no nobles willing to support her, and no money. She might suspect but she's not in a position to do anything about it. Elizabeth, on the other hand, is here, in Greenwich. She's a survivor, above all else. I know she'll recognize the advantages of our proposition. Once we have her agreement, there'll be more than enough time to hunt down her meddlesome sister."

I did not move a muscle. I barely drew breath as I awaited Lady Dudley's response.

"My son," she said, and there was a subtle waver in her voice, as if she sought to repress an emotion that threatened to overwhelm her. "Your father doesn't confide in me these days. But I know he faces tremendous odds. He has overseen this realm since Lord Protector Seymour went to the scaffold and hasn't gained in popularity because of it. If he was seen as the Lord Protector's right hand before, now he's seen as the hand that struck his master's head off. Though I agree that your proposal is sound, we still must contend with both the Suffolks and the council. They are only asking questions, for now. But soon they will demand answers."

"Once we have Elizabeth, we can answer them. That's what I tried to tell Father, but he wouldn't listen. She is the key to everything. She'll get us whatever we require."

"You're impatient," she rebuked. "Without council approval, you cannot hope to have your marriage to Amy Robsart annulled. And until you're free of her, you cannot hope for anything more than a friendship with Elizabeth Tudor."

Robert's face drained of color. "Father promised," he said in a fierce whisper. "He promised me that neither the Suffolks nor the council would stand in our way. He said the annulment wouldn't be an issue, that he'd force them to sign it at sword point if need be."

"Circumstances change." She sighed. "Your father can't force further concessions at this juncture. There's too much at stake. Elizabeth should never have come to London. By doing so, she's put our feet to the flames. If she takes it into her head to petition the council to see her brother, or, God forbid, demand it of us in public . . ." She paused, the unspoken consequences of this calamitous possibility hovering between them.

Then she said, "Your father needs time, Robert. If he's decided it's best to not approach her yet, you must trust in his judgment. He never does anything without a purpose."

As she spoke, I saw her eyes lift a fraction, past Robert to the curtain. My blood froze in my veins when I spied the coiled malice in her gaze. It made me think of how she'd looked when she'd brought me before the duchess of Suffolk, and I knew in that instant she was lying, right through her teeth. She misled her own son.

"He hasn't forsaken you," she continued, softly now. "He simply thinks it wiser to attend to Mary first. After all, who can predict what she'll do? You say she has no money or support, but someone at court is obviously feeding her information, and the Spanish ambassador has money, if she needs it. The situation is too precarious. She must be disposed of, before she does us some irreparable damage."

My belly knotted. Why was she mixing lies with truth? Why would she want Robert sent away from here, from Elizabeth? What could she possibly hope to gain from having her most capable son, the one with an intimate link to the princess, gone at a time of peril for the family?

Robert was staring at his mother as if he'd never seen her before. It was clear that he too sensed the betrayal but was at a loss as to how to decipher it. His hesitation cut like a blade between them before he let out a derisive chuckle.

"The only damage Mary can do is to make an ass of herself. She should have been married off years ago—to a Lutheran who'd beat some sense into that obstinate Catholic head of hers."

"Be that as it may," countered Lady Dudley, "you must admit she does represent a hindrance. She's free to roam the countryside and rouse sympathy. The rabble loves a lost cause. I for one would sleep easier knowing she's in the Tower. A day or two of hard riding, a few hours of unpleasantness, and it will be done. Then you can return to court and Elizabeth. Surely, she won't spoil in the meantime."

I observed the conflicting emotions on Robert's face as his mother spoke and wasn't surprised when at length he nodded, albeit in poor humor, and muttered, "Of course not. She's stubborn as a mule, that one, just like her sister. She'll stay put until all her questions are satisfied. I suppose that if I must see Mary to prison in order to get that idiot council to heed reason, then I will. I'll bring her in chains to London."

Lady Dudley inclined her head. "I am relieved to hear it. I will go tell your father. He's deliberating with Lord Arundel. They'll want to send trustworthy men with you, naturally. Once the preparations are done, you'll be informed. Why not rest till then? You look tired." The hand she set on his cheek should have invoked tenderness. It did not.

"You are our most gifted child," she murmured. "Patience. Your time will come."

Then she turned and, with a swish of skirts, departed the room.

As soon as the door shut Robert grabbed one of the candlesticks and flung it against the wall. Plaster sprayed. In the ensuing silence, his panting was like a cornered beast's.

Fighting back the sinking sensation in the pit of my stomach, I passed a hand quickly through my hair, ruffling it, undid my jerkin laces, and emerged blinking from behind the curtain. He whirled about. "You! You were here? You . . . you heard?"

"Given the situation," I said, "I thought it best if I remained out of sight, my lord."

His eyes narrowed. "Fuck you, you eavesdropping dog."

I dropped my gaze. "Forgive me but I was so tired. All that free wine last night, the ride here . . . I fell asleep on my lord's bed. I beg your forgiveness. It won't happen again."

He eyed me. Then he strode to me and struck me hard, across the face. I rocked back on my heels. He stared at me for a long moment. Then he said tersely, "Asleep, were you? You'd best learn to hold your wine then. Or drink less." He paused again.

I held my breath, my face smarting. It was a plausible excuse, if not a very convincing one, but it did save him embarrassment, and he might just be arrogant enough to assume I'd barely understood what had been said. After all, he'd never rated my intelligence highly, and I'd never expressed an ambition beyond serving his family. But there was the possibility that if he decided I posed a liability, he would kill me. I could only pray he actually saw me as a dog that would never turn on the hand that fed it.

To my relief, Robert kicked the candlestick aside and stalked to the table. "To the devil with my father. Just when I had matters in hand. I'm beginning to think he deliberately wants to thwart me. First he sends me off to the Tower on some stupid errand while he invites her to court, and now, once again, he's found a reason to delay his promise."

I made a sympathetic sound, trying to piece together what I'd learned.

First of all, the much-vaunted Dudley familial unity appeared to be crumbling. Lady Dudley had said her husband no longer confided in her, though she'd always been his mainstay, the iron behind his silk. Whatever plans the duke had in store for Elizabeth now excluded Robert, despite the repeated mention of a promise made to him. I could hazard a guess as to what this promise had entailed.

Moreover, Lady Dudley had mentioned the Suffolks, the new in-laws to the Dudleys. Could it be they, as royal kin, were opposed to this royal union for Guilford? Jane Grey was a grandniece of Henry the Eighth's: She had Tudor blood in her veins through her mother, the daughter of King Henry's younger sister. That might explain why the duke had elected to send Robert after Mary. Putting the heir to the throne in the Tower would prove a persuasive counter to the Suffolks' objections. Or was there an even more sinister motive to these machinations?

I wanted to delve deeper, particularly where the Suffolks were concerned. They had an important role here. The duchess, in particular, was someone whose intentions I needed to discover. Elizabeth's safety, and my own, could depend on it. But a servant who hadn't overheard anything shouldn't ask clarifying questions.

I finally ventured to say, "Initiative like my lord's should be appreciated."

It was a tepid attempt, but like most people with a hurt to avenge, Robert seized on it. "Yes, you'd think it should. But my father apparently thinks otherwise. And my mother—God's teeth, I know well the only one she's ever cared about is Guilford. She'd see the rest of us dead in an instant if it came to his life or ours."

I let the moment pass. "I've heard it said mothers love their children equally, regardless."

"Did yours," he retorted, "when she left you to die in that cottage by our castle?"

The question was rhetorical; it didn't require an answer. I stood silent as he went on.

"She doesn't give a fig about me. Guilford's always been her favorite because he's the one she can control. She pushed to see him wed to Jane Grey. Father said she even went up against Jane's mother when the duchess refused to consider it, citing that her daughter had the blood of kings in her veins, while we were upstarts with only the king's favor to commend us. Somehow, she got the duchess to change her mind. Knowing my mother, she probably put a knife to that old cunt's throat."

His words jolted me to my sinews. A knife at the duchess's throat: Suddenly I felt as if I were snared in a dark tangled web, where I had no chance of escape.

Robert undid his doublet, threw it onto the bench. "Well, foul on her! Foul on all of them, I say. I've my own plans now, and I'm not about to give them up just because she says I must. Let her go after Mary herself if she thinks that papist is a threat. I'm not some lackey to be ordered about at will." He scoured the room. "Is there nothing to drink in this godforsaken hole?"

"I'll fetch wine, my lord." I went immediately to the door. I had no idea where to find it, but at least I could take some time to compose my reeling thoughts.

Robert stopped me. "No, forget the wine. Help me undress. No use muddling my wits. I'm going to find a way to see Elizabeth, whether my father approves or not. I'll see her and get her consent, and once I do, he'll have to agree. He can do nothing else."

I divested Robert of his breeches, chemise, and boots. From his saddlebag, I extracted a cloth and dried the sweat from his torso.

"They'll have no idea of what hit them," he expounded. "Guilford and my mother, especially: I can't wait to see the looks on their faces when I tell them the news." He guffawed, spread his legs as I untied his points and peeled off his hose. "What? Have you nothing to say?"

Folding his undergarments and setting them on the coffer, I said, "I'm content to serve as my lord deems best."

He laughed. "Brash courage, Prescott—that's what it takes to survive this cesspit we call life. Not that you would know." He turned naked to the bedchamber. "Do as you like this afternoon. Just make sure you're back in time to dress me for tonight. And don't you get lost this time. I'll need to look my best."

"My lord." On sudden impulse, I reached to my jerkin. The

die was cast. It would not do to have her messenger return to inquire why Lord Robert had failed to reply. "I found this on the table when I first came in." I extended the paper. "Forgive me. I forgot I had it."

Robert snatched it from my fingers. "Clever boy. It wouldn't do for my mother to have seen this. It's a good thing you took a nap when you did." He tore the letter open. Triumph flooded his face. "What did I tell you? She can't resist me! She says she'll see me tonight, in the old pavilion, no less. She has a macabre sense of humor, our Bess. It's said her mother spent her last night of freedom in that pavilion, waiting in vain for Henry to come to her."

"Then, it is good news?" There was a vile taste in my mouth.

"Good news? It's the best bloody news I've had yet. Don't stand there like a simpleton. Fetch the ink and paper from my bag. I must send an answer before she changes her mind."

He scrawled his reply, sanding it and sealing the paper with his signet. "Deliver this to her. She arrived hours ago, demanding apartments overlooking the garden. Take the corridor to the ward, cross to the stairs, and climb them to the gallery. You won't see her in person. She has a penchant for afternoon naps. Her women should be about, though, including that morsel Kate Stafford, who has her trust." He guffawed. "Whatever you do, don't give it to the dragon Ashley. She hates me as if I were Lucifer himself."

I slid the paper into my jerkin. "I'll do my best, my lord."

He gave me a cruel smile. "See that you do. For if all goes as planned, you could soon be squire to the next king of England."

Chapter Fourteen

As soon as I got out of the room and ran down the hallway, I turned a corner and stopped to examine the seal on Lord Robert's reply. I cursed. The wax was still wet. I'd destroy the paper if I tried to undo it. Thinking I could tarry until it dried sufficiently, I moved into the ward.

I reminded myself not to act precipitously. Anything I did could turn against me. Still, I couldn't deliver Robert's reply and simply wait for whatever happened next. The hunt had begun. If I was right, Elizabeth would become the first of the two royal sisters to end up in the Tower, especially when Robert learned she'd never consent to a plot that hinged on both her siblings' deaths. I desperately wanted to see Cecil, but I had no idea of how to reach the secretary, nor had he offered, which didn't say much for my fledgling skills as a spy.

I would have to warn Elizabeth myself, while I delivered the letter.

Which meant I had to somehow see her in person.

I crossed the ward and entered a short passage leading to the stairs Robert had mentioned. I turned my attention back to the seal, about to worry it a bit when a sudden movement caught my eye. For a second I couldn't move. Then I bent to my boot and took my dagger from its sheath. I shifted toward a nearby doorway. The door was ajar. I'd seen a figure slip past it.

I inched forth, my dagger in my fist. I drew short stifled breaths through my nose, but even this sounded too loud to my ears. Whoever waited for me could at this moment be drawing a far more lethal weapon than the blade I brandished, readying to cleave my skull the moment I inched over the threshold. Or perhaps it wasn't my death he sought. He had stalked me through the streets of London and not taken me when he'd had the chance. He had come to Greenwich, presumably after me. Now he was lurking in this room.

I came to a halt. Cold sweat beaded my brow; as a drop slid down my temple I found to my horror that I couldn't take the final step that would bring me inside. I couldn't reach out and throw the door open, announcing my presence.

Coward. Get in there. Face the bastard and be done with it.

I reached out, every finger stretched taut. I grazed wood. With a simultaneous uplifting of my blade and savage push at the door, I leapt into the room, a half cry on my lips.

A skeletal man stood there, dressed in black.

I exhaled in fury. "Christ. I could have killed you."

Walsingham returned my stare. "I doubt it. Shut that door. I'd rather we weren't seen."

I closed the door with a kick of my heel. He was the last person I'd expected to see.

The slight tilt to his lips might have passed for a smile. "I'm here for your report."

"Report? What report?"

"For our mutual employer, of course. Unless you've returned

your dubious loyalties to that pack of scheming traitors who reared you."

I returned his stare. "I don't answer to you."

"Oh? I believe you do. Indeed, our employer has entrusted me with your welfare. Henceforth, you take your instructions from me." He paused, with marked intent. "That means that whatever you have to report, you will report directly to me."

In the starkness of the chamber he looked taller and so gaunt the light seemed to pierce his skin and skim the angles of his cadaverous face. His eyes were sunken, black and dull as cinders, the eyes of a man who has seen and done things I could not imagine.

I made myself sheathe my dagger. I didn't trust him. He had an air of immorality about him, a corruption he wore like a second skin. He was probably capable of doing anything to suit his purpose, without thinking about it twice. But he still had to answer to Cecil, and in my current straits, I had to oblige him. To a point.

With my other hand still clenched about Robert's note, I said: "I only just arrived. I have nothing to report."

"You're lying." His stare bore into me. "I do not relish the antics of callow boys, nor am I in favor of employing them. But I will accommodate our employer's misguided trust in you, for now. Therefore, I'll ask once more. What do you have to report?"

I debated, prolonging the moment just enough to see his jaw edge. Then, with deliberate reluctance, I opened my hand to reveal the crushed missive. "Well, there is this."

He took it from me. He had peculiarly feminine hands, soft and white and no doubt icy to the touch. He slid a long nail under the seal. With expert precision, he unglued it from the paper. After reading the missive he refolded it, pressing the damp seal back in place.

"An ideal place for a rendezvous," he said, handing the paper to me. "Secluded, unfrequented, yet close to a postern gate. Her Grace plays this game well."

The note of chill admiration in his otherwise passionless voice surprised me. "You approve? But I thought . . ." I paused. I didn't know what I thought. I had been instructed to retain Robert's confidence, to listen and report, and to facilitate, if instructed, the princess's escape. I suddenly realized no one had hired me to think, and I felt exactly like what he had called me—a callow fool, my strings yanked by some unseen puppeteer.

Walsingham regarded me. "Did you think we had days in which to fine-tune our plan? Proof enough of how unsuitable you are. In matters such as these, success depends on initiative. It is something an experienced intelligencer would understand."

"Look here," I replied, and I couldn't ease an infuriating tremor from my voice. "I didn't ask to get involved in this. You forced me into it, remember? Neither you nor Cecil gave me a choice. If I hadn't agreed to help, no doubt I'd be at the bottom of the river by now."

"We always have a choice. You just took the one that you think will give you the most advantage, as does every man. Anything else you care to remonstrate about?"

Again, he took me off guard. I couldn't think of anyone I'd less prefer to give my information to. But withholding wouldn't help Elizabeth.

"I overheard Lady Dudley and Lord Robert talking." I kept my tone impersonal. "His lordship will send Lord Robert to capture the Lady Mary. He also refused Robert's request to see Her

Grace and present what my master calls his 'proposal.' You should tell Cecil the duke may have another purpose in mind for her than the one we think."

I paused. Walsingham remained expressionless.

"It stands to reason it must be something he doesn't want his son to know about," I added. "Why else would he send Robert away?"

Walsingham did not speak.

"Did you hear me? Whatever the duke plans, it can't be good for the princess. You just said success depends on initiative. Here's our chance. We should get Her Grace as far from here, and from the Dudleys, as soon as we can."

Had I not known better, I'd have thought he couldn't have cared less. Then I detected a surreptitious gleam in his hooded eyes, a near indiscernible tightening of his mouth. What I had relayed was important. He didn't want me to know it.

"I'll convey your concerns," he said at length. "In the meanwhile, this note must be delivered, lest your master suspect our interference. After you do, return to Lord Robert. If your services are required again, you'll be advised."

I stared at him. "What about Her Grace? Aren't you going to warn her?"

"That is not something you need concern yourself with. You were told to follow orders."

To my disbelief, he turned to the door. I burst out, "If you don't warn her, I will."

He paused, looked at me. "Are you threatening me? If you are, let me remind you that squires who inform on their masters are not irreplaceable."

I met his eyes, held them for a long moment before I slipped the note back into my jerkin. Then I heard a soft thud at my feet.

"For your services," he said. "I suggest you be prudent where you spend it. Servants eager to flaunt ill-gotten wealth end up at the bottom of the river almost as often as disloyal squires." Without another word, he strode out. I didn't want to touch the purse he'd flung on the floor but I did anyway, pocketing it without examining its contents.

I edged back out the door. There was no sign of Walsingham. Turning into the passage, I made for the stairs.

If I had had any doubts before, my mind was made up. I must warn the princess. Robert couldn't be trusted, and I was beginning to think that neither could anyone else. The purse in my hand might be small but it surely contained enough to buy my silence. Walsingham was Cecil's creature, and I had no idea what the Secretary's ultimate purpose might be. I suspected this matter was more complex than I'd been led to believe. I found it difficult to believe Cecil would harm the princess, but perhaps Walsingham himself played a false hand. I wouldn't put it past him. I also had no idea if she would willingly see me, but if I refused to budge she'd have to. I'd leave her no other choice.

I climbed the staircase, resolved.

A gallery stretched before me, its width leading to a pair of imposing doors, the lintel boasting carved cherubim. To the right, recessed embrasures overlooked a garden. The panes were cracked open to admit the afternoon breeze.

Standing halfway between the far doors and me were three men in court velvets.

I didn't know them. Nor did I have much time to look, for as I started to take a step back a voice came at me from behind: "By the cross, where do you think you're going this time?" I swiveled about as a familiar figure swept up to me to wag her finger in my face.

It was Elizabeth's attendant, the one I'd seen at Whitehall—Kate Stafford.

"Haven't I told you already the kitchens are not in this wing, you oaf?" she declared. Up close, her curious yellow-hued eyes were alive with an intelligence that belied her careless air. She exuded a heady scent, like crisp apples and gillyflowers. I didn't know whether to laugh or flee, until I noted the warning in her gaze when it met mine.

"My—my lady, forgive me?" I stammered. "I got lost, again."

"Lost?" She turned from me in a whirl of tawny skirts to the man who approached. "Horses may lose their way but only mules are likely to return time and time again to the same empty stall. Don't you agree, Master Stokes?"

"I do." Master Stokes was of medium height, slim, his face too sly to be called handsome, with elegant cheekbones accentuated by light brown hair slicked back from his brow. On his hands were displayed various gemstone rings; from his left ear dangled a glittering ruby pendant. It caught my attention. I had never seen a man wearing an earring before, though I would later learn it was more a fashion abroad than in England.

"Speaking of which, is this servant bothering you?" His voice was languid. "Shall I teach him not to trouble our pretty damsels, Mistress Stafford?"

Stokes's insolent stare dropped to her cleavage as he spoke. She flipped her hand, a trill of laughter reeling from her lips. "Bothering me? Hardly. He's just a servant new to court, who seems to think we keep the kitchens under Her Grace's duvet."

His corresponding laugh was equally high-pitched, almost effeminate. "If it will cure her headaches," he said. "As far as our mule is concerned . . ." His stare rose over her head to fix on me. "Perhaps I can set him on his way."

Mistress Stafford turned to him. Though she had her back to me, I could imagine the provocative look she treated him to. "Why waste your time on hired help? Let me see the boy back to the stairs, yes? I'll be a moment."

"If you promise," said Stokes. For no discernible reason, the finger he drew down her exposed throat filled me with dread.

He turned heel on his elegant boots and returned to where the other men stood grinning. Linking her arm in mine, Kate Stafford drew me back into the passage.

The instant we were out of sight, she pulled me into a recessed window bay. All semblance of indulgent coquetry vanished. "What do you think you are doing?"

Seeing as she'd foregone the pretense, I saw no reason why I shouldn't follow her example. "I was going to see Her Grace. I bring important news she must hear at once."

She thrust out her hand. "Give me the missive, whoever you are."

"You know who I am." I paused. "I didn't say I had a missive."

She stepped close, her apple-blossom scent taunting me. "I assumed you did, under the circumstances. You are Lord Robert's squire."

"Ah, so you remember me." I too leaned close, so that our noses almost touched. "Not to mention that you must also be expecting a reply to the missive you just delivered."

She drew back. "I'm sure I don't understand."

"Oh? That wasn't you in my master's chambers earlier? There is another lady at court who wears boots under her gown?"

She went still. I smiled as I saw her inch the betraying foot back under her hem.

"I was behind the curtain," I explained. "Now, I must deliver my lord's reply." I started to turn away. She gripped my arm again, with astonishing strength for so small a person.

"Are you mad?" she hissed. "You mustn't be seen anywhere near her. You are his servant. Their meeting is supposed to be a secret." She glanced to the gallery entrance before returning her eyes to me. "Give me his reply. I'll see that she reads it, have no fear."

I pretended to consider. Then I removed the paper from my jerkin. As she made a move to take it, I shifted my hand behind my back. "I must say, this is rather convenient—you being here at the precise moment I arrive."

Her fingers closed on air. Her chin lifted. "What is that supposed to mean?"

"Well, for one, that I saw you at Whitehall."

"Yes, and . . . ?"

"And you didn't look too concerned for your mistress when she left the hall, though she was clearly in distress. In fact, I saw you speak to Master Walsingham. So, before I hand over my master's missive, I think I need some answers."

She tossed her head. "I've no time for this. Keep your master's reply. I know his answer." She started to step past me.

I blocked her way. "I'm afraid I must insist."

"I could scream," she said. "I am the princess's lady. Those gentlemen would be here in a few seconds, and that would not bode well for you."

"You could. But you won't. You don't want your admirer back there to know you're doing more than showing me to the kitchens." I drew myself to full height. "Now, who told you I was coming? Walsingham? Are you his doxy? If so, Her Grace won't enjoy discovering that her own lady-in-waiting, whom she entrusts with personal correspondence, is being paid to spy on her."

She burst out laughing, then clapped a hand to her mouth. "You really are too inexperienced for this sort of thing," she said in a low voice. "I should send you on your way and not tell you a thing. But in the interest of time, no, I am not Walsingham's doxy. I simply know him because of Her Grace's acquaintance with Master Cecil. Or rather, I know *of* him. He's a professional informant—and if rumors are true, trained in Italy as an assassin."

"Hence his gallant manner."

Her smile was tart. "Exactly. He happened to be near me as Her Grace left the hall. I assure you, we exchanged only the required niceties."

"I suppose you weren't listening in on her conversations, either?" I said dryly.

"No, that I *was* doing. She calls me her ears. I'm the reason she need not resort to outright gossip, which would be unbecoming in one of her rank. Before you ask, I also tried to hear your presentation to the duchess of Suffolk. I reasoned Her Grace must have been curious as to why you were brought before her cousin."

She paused, searching my face. All of a sudden, her expression softened. Her look of compassion startled me with its sincerity. "I realize you have no reason to trust me, but I would never betray her. Her aunt Mary Boleyn, sister to her mother Queen Anne, was my mother's benefactor. Though we are not related, I couldn't love her more than if we shared blood."

"Relatives don't always love each other," I said, but I was no longer suspicious. "In fact, most often the opposite seems to be the case." My voice quavered. To my mortification, all of a sudden I couldn't control myself. "God help me, I don't know who or what to believe anymore."

She was silent. Then she said, "Trust Her Grace. That is why you are here, is it not? She told me you had offered to help her and she refused. Do you know why?"

I nodded. "Yes. She would not see me harmed for her sake." I hesitated another moment before I handed her the missive. She tucked it into her bodice.

Footsteps came toward us. She went still. There was no time, or place, to hide. Without warning, she flung herself at me, taking my astonished face in her hands to press her lips to mine. As she did, I managed to catch a fleeting glimpse of the figure who stalked past us, followed by the three men, none of whom paused to make comment at what we were doing.

For a paralyzing moment I thought I must have imagined it.

Kate Stafford melded her body to me; she breathed into my mouth, "Don't move."

I didn't. Only after the echoes of booted feet faded away did she draw back. "He's left her. I must go." She paused. Her expression was somber. "You mustn't say a word to anyone. Not even Cecil. If you do, you could place her in more danger than she already is."

I hadn't imagined it. "That was the duke. He was with her. Why? What does he want?"

"I don't know. He arrived before you did, demanding admittance. She was abed, resting. She let him into her audience room and sent us all away."

I didn't like the sound of this. "Then I must speak with her."

"No. It's not safe. He could return; someone could see you. We can't risk it. We cannot be exposed. If anyone should know—"

"Know?" I exploded under my breath. "Know, what? *What* in hell is going on?"

"You will discover all in time. Now I must go."

She turned away. I followed her to the gallery entranceway. As she made to enter, I touched her shoulder. "Tell her this, from me. Tell her there's a plot afoot to arrest her sister. She must not meet my master. She must leave now, before it is too late."

From the gallery came a ringing: "Kate? Kate, are you there?"

The voice immobilized us. Kate pushed me from the entrance, but not before I saw Elizabeth silhouetted against those magnificent far doors, her hand clasping the collar of her crimson robe, her hair unbound. "Kate!" she called out again, and I heard the fear in her voice.

"I'm here, Your Grace! I'm coming," Kate cried back. "I'll be right there."

"Hurry up," said the princess tremulously. "I've need of you."

She moved forward. Though I had the perfect opportunity at that moment to go to Elizabeth, something held me back. I said, "You will tell her?"

"She won't listen." Kate met my stare. "She loves him, you see. She has always loved him. Nothing we say or do will stop her." She smiled. "Gallant squire, if you truly wish to help her, be at the pavilion tonight with your master."

She left me standing there, incredulous.

I didn't want to believe it, though it made perfect sense. This was why she had stayed at court despite every apparent threat to her safety.

She loved him. Elizabeth loved Robert Dudley.

Chapter Fifteen

I needed time to sort out my turmoil before I could return to Lord Robert. The palace was eerily still. I saw only menials going about their business, none returning my wan greeting as I wandered Greenwich's unfamiliar labyrinth of corridors. All the courtiers had retired to their respective quarters or gone to stroll in the formal gardens, it seemed.

I was adrift in a shadowy world.

Brooding engulfed me. I tried to tell myself that despite being the daughter of a king, Elizabeth was still flesh and blood. She was fallible. She did not know him as I did; she did not see the depths of avarice and shallow ambition that ruled his heart. But then, she herself had admitted as much to me. She said only last night in Whitehall that she'd never had cause to mistrust him.

Yet anything less than the truth would bring about her doom.

I reached a grand hall, where servants were laying out carpets, setting up tables, hanging silk garlands over a dais in preparation for the festivities. Those few that paid notice looked at me once and turned away. I stopped, suddenly knowing what I must do.

Shortly thereafter I emerged onto a tree-lined promenade leading into the formal gardens that stretched to a loamy hill. Daylight faded from the sky, scalloping the clouds in scarlet. It looked as if rain were on the way. I took Cecil's miniature map from my pocket, ascertaining my location. To my disappointment, the map didn't detail the gardens, and I didn't have much time before I had to make my way back.

Like most palace gardens, however, these must follow an established pattern. Spacious yet laid out for the court to amble and enjoy without getting lost, wide avenues bordered with topiaries wound past herb patches and flowerbeds before threading off in various directions.

I took one of these narrower paths.

Thunder rumbled overhead. Drizzle began to fall. I stashed the map in my pocket, pulling my cap low on my brow as I looked about. In the distance, I glimpsed what looked like an artificial lake girdling a stone structure.

My heart leapt. That must be the pavilion.

It was farther than it appeared. I found myself traversing the length of a forested mall into a wild, strangely haunting parkland. Glancing over my shoulder, I spied fresh-lit candles in the palace windows. I wondered if Elizabeth herself gazed out from one of them at this moment, deliberating on her encounter with the duke. Or was she thinking only of tonight, of what her rendezvous with Robert would bring? I'd never been in love myself, but from what I knew, lovers pined for each other when apart. Did Elizabeth? Did she long for Robert Dudley?

I regretted I'd not taken the opportunity to tell her what I knew. I might not have relished the deliberate destruction of her romantic notions, but at least she'd arrive at her rendezvous to-night forewarned as to just how high my master aspired.

The rain grew stronger. Turning away from the palace, I quickened my pace.

The lake surrounded the pavilion on three sides. A set of crumbling steps led up to it from the unkempt pathway where I stood. It must have been a lovely spot once, idyllic for dalli-ances, before years of neglect had rendered it lichen stained and near-forgotten.

Exploring the area nearby, I located, as Walsingham had said, an old postern gate in an ivy-covered wall, leading to a dirt road and the sloping hills of Kent. This gave me pause. Horses could be tethered here out of sight and hearing, if properly muzzled and their hooves bound up in cloth. Had the princess selected this place less out of a sense of irony and more because of its value as an escape route? The possibility lightened my spirits, until a less-appealing prospect occurred to me.

What if this was Cecil's plan? He may have decided to take advantage of her intention to lure Robert here, a place from which she could quickly, by force, be spirited away. No matter what else the secretary might be doing, it couldn't serve him to let Elizabeth fall prey to the Dudleys. She was, as he had said, the kingdom's last hope.

I paused, considering. Now that I was alone, out of the pal-ace and with enough space around me to feel as though I could actually breathe, I realized I had been led about like the prover-bial blind man, by my nose. I had accepted Cecil's proposition, delivered my master's reply, reported to Walsingham. But I did not know any of these men, not really. Had I become another pawn to be discarded? What if there was more to this elaborate subterfuge than met the eye, more lies twisted within lies? I felt compelled to recall every word that had passed between Cecil and me, to search our verbiage for clues. Somewhere in our conversation lay the answer to this riddle. And I'd best find it.

I froze.

The tip of a dagger pressed into my back, just below my ribs.

A nasal voice intoned, "I wouldn't resist if I were you. Take off your jerkin."

I slowly removed my outer garment, thinking of the map folded in my pocket as I let it drop at my feet. My assailant's blade felt very sharp against my thin chemise.

"Now, the dagger in your boot. Carefully."

I reached to the hilt and pulled my knife from its sheath. A gauntleted hand reached around to take it from me. Then the voice, which I now recognized, said, "Turn around."

He wore a hooded cape, his features were concealed.

"You have me at a disadvantage," I said. "I hardly call that fair play."

With an effete laugh, he cast aside his cowl. He had a face too sly to be deemed handsome, with prominent cheekbones and in one earlobe, a ruby. His sloe-eyed look pierced me where I stood. How had I not recognized him as the man Peregrine had described?

He's taller than you, but not by much. He has a pointy face, like a ferret.

"We meet again," I said, just before a burly henchman emerged from the shadows and hit me in the face.

I could barely make out the way before me, my left eye throbbing, my jaw aching from the blow, as I was marched with arms twisted behind my back past crumpled structures and through a ruined cloister into a dank passageway. Rusted iron gates hung like dislocated shoulders from doorways. We descended a steep staircase into another passage, descended yet again. The passage we now entered was so narrow two men could not walk abreast. A lone pitch torch crackled in a peeling holder on the wall.

The air smelled fermented. I had to breathe deep of it, reminding myself not to give in to panic. I must concentrate, observe, and listen, find some way to prolong my survival.

We came before a thick door. "I hope you'll find your accommodations agreeable," said Stokes as he slid back the bolt. The door swung outward. "We want only the best for you."

Inside was a small circular cell.

His ruffian shoved me inside. Slime coated the uneven flagstone floor. Skating on my boots, hands splayed before me, I skidded into the far wall. The smell in here was rank; a sticky, moldering substance on the wall adhered to me like crushed entrails.

Stokes laughed. He stood under the flickering light of the torch, his cloak parted to display his stylish garb. I saw a gem-studded stiletto on a thin silver chain at his waist. I'd never seen anyone wear the Italian weapon before. Unlike the earring, I assumed it was not for display.

He clucked his tongue. "I daresay no one would recognize you now, Squire Prescott."

As my shoulder throbbed from where I'd hit the wall, I felt fury rush through me. I righted myself, surprised by my own outward composure. "You know my name. Again, not fair play. Who are you? What do you want with me?"

"Aren't you the nosy one? No wonder Cecil likes you."

I hoped my jolt of fear didn't show. "I don't know any Cecil."

"Yes, you do. You earned his interest in a record span of time, too. And as far as I know, bedding boys isn't his taste. I wouldn't say the same for Walsingham."

I lunged. Stokes flung up his arm, unsheathing and aiming the stiletto at my chest in one elegant movement. "If I miss," he said, with a quivering laugh, "which is most unlikely, my man outside will disembowel you like a spring calf."

Breathing hard, I moved back. What had gotten into me? I knew better. "You wouldn't be so confident if we were evenly matched," I told him.

His face darkened. "We'll never be evenly matched, you miserable imposter."

Imposter. Did he mean spy? I went cold. *He* was the Suffolk hireling, my mystery stalker. I was certain of it. How much had he overheard of my meeting with Cecil? If he'd learned enough to unmask the secretary, then whatever Cecil planned could flounder, fail.

"I'm Robert Dudley's squire," I ventured. "I have no idea why you think I know this Cecil or why I'd pretend to be anything else."

"Oh, I do hope you're not going to play the innocent when she gets here. That will not do. No, not at all. False modesty never impressed Her Grace. She knows all too well why you were brought to court and why Cecil shows such interest in you. And she's not pleased. She does have the Tudor temper, after all. But you'll learn that soon enough."

With theatrical flair, he waved his hand at me. "Don't go anywhere." He yanked the door shut. A bolt outside it shot into place. Pitch darkness plunged over the cell.

In all my life, I had never been so afraid.

Chapter Sixteen

I closed my eyes, drew in slow even breaths. I let my eyes adjust to the gloom. Gradually the darkness lightened, shadows peeling from shadows. Judging from the chill, I determined I was underground. I could also discern the murmur of water nearby. Was I near the river?

I crept around the cell. I didn't like what I found. Despite the wet algae on the floor and walls and the overall unpleasantness of the place, there were no droppings or other signs of rodents, though rats must infest Greenwich as they did every place where food could be found. There was a wide barred grate at the base of one wall by the floor; crouching down to look beyond that black hole I found a miasmic stench and clearly heard the gurgling water. I also discovered that although I could scratch clumps of mortar from the grate's crevices, it was solid.

I must be under the ruins of the old medieval palace, perhaps in an ancient dungeon. But we'd come a distance from the lake, and not enough rain had fallen to explain this palpable moisture. Greenwich had been built after the age of feudal warfare. It had no ramparts or defensive moats, as independent-minded lords with armies of vassals were allegedly no longer a threat. Yet the slimy floor and moldering air indicated this cell had been flooded recently.

None of which eased my anxiety.

After circling the cell twice, I thought I knew how a caged lion must feel. Stamping my feet to stir the blood in my legs, I squatted back by the grate. My attempts confirmed that I could not dig or break it out from the wall. Even if the mortar around it could be dug out, the grate loosened or broken, I had no way to do so without a pick of some sort.

I was trapped, while in the hall the festivities for Jane Grey and Guilford Dudley's wedding would soon commence, and the hour of Robert's meeting with Elizabeth neared.

I sank to my haunches. I couldn't have said how long I sat there, waiting. At one point I slipped into exhausted sleep and awoke, gasping, thinking I was drowning in a viscous sea. Only then did I realize that the smell permeating my skin was of river water, and that a muted clamor approached.

I came stiffly to my feet. An exasperated voice declared, "By the rood, Stokes, was there no other place to lock the wretch in?"

"Your Grace," said Stokes. The bolt slid back. "I assure you this was the only place I could find on short notice that proved suitable to our needs."

The door opened. Torchlight flooded the cell, blinding me. Seeing only shadows in the doorway, I brought up a hand to shield my eyes. A bulk pushed inside, swatting about with a cane. Then it went still, peering. "Bring in that torch!"

Stokes squeezed in behind the bulk. The torch he carried illuminated what first looked to me like a mastiff swathed in carnelian, a ludicrous pearl-dotted coif perched on its oversized head. I blinked repeatedly, forcing my one eye to focus. The swollen one had completely shut.

Frances Brandon, Duchess of Suffolk, glared back at me. "He looks smaller. Are you certain it's him? It could be someone else. Cecil is wily. He'd substitute his own mother if it would further his cause."

"Your Grace," said Stokes, "it's him. Let my man handle this. It's not safe."

"No! I am not some lily-livered girl. If he so much as looks at me the wrong way, I'll bash in his skull and be done with it." She blared at me, brandishing her stout silver-handled cane, "You! Come closer."

I advanced as calmly as I could, making certain to stop far enough away to evade an unanticipated swipe at my head. "Your Grace," I began, "I'm afraid there's been a misunderstanding. I assure you, I have no idea how I've offended."

The end of her cane stabbed out, missing me by an inch. She guffawed. "Well, well. He has no idea. Did you hear that, Stokes? He's no idea of how he's offended."

"I heard, Your Grace," twittered Stokes. "An actor he most certainly is not."

The cane slammed down. "Enough!" She lumbered to me. I had to stop from flinching. During my wandering through Whitehall the night after Elizabeth left, I had come across a portrait of Henry VIII, his gross ringed hands on his hips, bulging legs apart. Standing face-to-face now with the late king's niece, I found the resemblance daunting.

"Who are you?" she asked.

I met her vicious stare. "Begging Your Grace's pardon, I believe we were introduced. I am Brendan Prescott, squire to Robert Dudley."

I choked on a cry. With savage accuracy, her cane slammed up between my legs. I doubled over as white-hot pain seared off my breath. Another whack brought me gasping to my knees, my groin pulsating in agony.

She stood over me. "There, that's better. You will kneel when I address you. You are before a Tudor, daughter of Henry the Eighth's beloved sister Mary, late duchess of Suffolk and dowager queen of France. By all that is royal in my blood, you *will* show me respect." She jabbed my concaved shoulders with her cane. "Again, who are you?"

I gazed up at her contorted visage. Her mouth turned inward, like a venomous bloom. "Seize him." Stokes's henchman, who was broad as a wall and twice my height, lumbered in. He hauled me up, pinioning my arms. I didn't have the strength to struggle, limp from the pain of her blow to my genitals.

Stokes asked, "Shall we start with kicks to his ribs? That tends to loosen the tongue."

"No." She didn't take her eyes off me. "He has too much to lose, and Cecil has no doubt paid him well for his silence. I don't need him to say anything. I have eyes. I can see. Some things cannot be forged." She stabbed her hand at me. "Strip him."

Stokes handed her the torch and tore off my chemise. "He has very white skin," he purred.

"Get out of my way." She shoved Stokes aside, thrusting the torch at me. I tried to recoil, but the henchman's grip manacled my wrists. Her eyes scoured me. "Nothing," she said, "not a mark. It's not him. I knew it. Lady Dudley has deceived me. That she-bitch forced me to surrender my claim to the throne for nothing. By God, she'll pay for this. How dare she set her drunkard of a son and my own mealy-mouthed daughter above me?"

My blood congealed.

"Perhaps we should be thorough," Stokes suggested. He instructed his man, "Turn him around." The henchman started to pivot me. As he did, to my horror, I felt my breeches slip a notch, over my hip.

Silence fell. Then a hiss escaped her. "Stop." She thrust the torch at me again. I clamped down on a cry as the flame singed my skin.

"Where did you get that?" she said haltingly, as if she couldn't trust her own sight. I hesitated. Pain speared through my shoulders and across my chest as the henchman yanked up my arms farther.

"Her Grace asked you a question," Stokes said. "If I were you, I'd answer."

"I—I was . . . born with it," I whispered.

"Born with it?" She reared her face at me, so close I could see tiny broken veins threading her nose under her powder. "You were *born* with it, you say?"

I nodded, helplessly.

She met my eyes. "I don't believe you."

Stokes peered. "Your Grace, it does look like—"

"Yes, I'm certain. It's not him. It cannot be." She handed Stokes the torch, grabbed back her cane. "If you want to save that pretty white skin," she said, her fist clenching about the silver handle, "you'd best tell me the truth. Who are you, and what has Cecil paid you to do?"

I felt nauseous. I had no idea what to say. Should I spill out the truth, as I knew it, or pretend to know something I didn't? Which was more likely to keep me alive?

"I am a foundling," I said. "I . . . I was raised in the Dudley household, brought here to serve Lord Robert. That is all."

I sounded like I was lying: I heard in my own voice the terrified justification of a man caught in an illicit deed. She of course knew it. It was why I was here. Whomever she believed I was had frightened her enough to have me followed, abducted, and, if I didn't find a way out of this nightmare soon, killed.

Nevertheless, I'd caught her attention. "A foundling?" she repeated. "Tell me this, were you truly left in the priest's cottage near Dudley Castle?"

Without taking my gaze from hers I nodded, a shard in my throat.

"Do you know who left you there? Do you know who found you?"

I swallowed. A dull roar filled my head, like an ocean in my brain. I heard myself say as if from across a vast distance, "I don't know. . . . Mistress Alice, the Dudleys' housekeeper and herbalist, she—she found me. She took me in."

I gleaned something in her eyes. "An herbalist?" Her stare was a physical instrument, a probing device in my sinews. "A small woman with a merry laugh?"

I began to tremble. She knew. She knew Mistress Alice. "Yes," I whispered.

The duchess of Suffolk took a jerking step back. "It can't be. You . . . you are an imposter, tutored by Cecil, paid for by the Dudleys." Her next words issued in a scalding torrent. "Because of you, they forced me to hand over my daughter in marriage to their weakling son. Because of you, I am humiliated in my God-given right!"

She paused, her voice horrifying in its resolve. "But I am not so easily fooled. I'll see this kingdom destroyed before I let that Dudley woman and her spoiled brat triumph over me."

And as I hung there by my arms, all of a sudden it made perfect, dreadful sense.

Stokes let out a gleeful twitter. "Why, Your Grace, I do believe he speaks the truth. He truly has no idea of what they're doing with him. He doesn't know who he is."

"That remains to be seen," she snapped. She angled her cane level with my face, clicked the handle. A sliver slid from its bottom tip—a concealed blade, thin enough to pop an eye out.

"See how fine it is? I can slide it between two sheaves of paper without leaving a mark. Or I can cut through boiled leather." She angled the cane down until it grazed my groin.

I heard Stokes giggle. I met her stare. I had one last chance. Ignorance might save me.

"I do not know of what Your Grace speaks. I swear it to you."

For a moment, doubt blurred her expression. Then the savage cunning returned, and I knew it was over.

"They've taught you well: You play the innocent to perfection. Maybe you are what you say, a wretched unfortunate trained to be used against me. Cecil could have told Lady Dudley the story, seeded the idea that would give her the weapon she needed." The duchess's chuckle rattled in her chest. "He's capable of that, and much, much more. It's a devious game they play, each to their own end. They'll die for it by the time I'm through with them. They'll regret having ever crossed my path and made a fool of me."

She went still. The expression that came over her was unlike any I'd seen—a dark mask lacking empathy or compassion. "As for you, it doesn't matter who you are." She swerved to Stokes. "I've wasted enough time. When will it be done?"

"As soon as the tide rises. The court will be on the gallery watching the fireworks." He snickered. "Not that they'd know. No one's been down here in years. It reeks of papist vice."

I saw it then, in all its clarity, each thread a part of the whole. While the festivities in honor of Guilford and Jane Grey's nuptials distracted the court, Robert—deprived by his father of what he believed was his right to win a royal bride—would meet with Elizabeth. Deluded and misled, blinded by his overwhelming ambition, he had only empty words to offer her.

The duke had no intention of letting him wed the princess. Jane Grey was his weapon now, a perfect pawn of Tudor blood, bride of his malleable youngest son. Two hapless adolescents were to be England's next sovereigns, while Elizabeth and her sister Mary were slated for the scaffold.

The henchman swung out his arm, delivering a clout that sprawled me onto the floor.

"No more of that," said the duchess. "It must look as if he wandered off by himself. No wounds, no bruises that can't be part of his death. I want no indication of foul play."

"Yes, Your Grace," Stokes said, as I crawled from them. My cheek was cut, the blood spurting hot on my bruised face. Through a blur I saw her swerve about and lumber to the door.

"Your Grace," I called out. She stopped. "I . . . I would know the reason for my death."

She glanced at me. "You were never meant to live. You are an abomination."

She trudged out, the henchman behind her. Stokes tripped to the door. Before he closed it he said, "Don't hold your breath. You'll die much faster—or so I'm told."

The door slammed shut. The bolt clanked over it.

Alone in the darkness, I began to shout.

Chapter Seventeen

Ishouted until I had no voice left. I couldn't believe I would end like this. It was unthinkable. I wanted to roar the walls down into rubble, dig my way out with my bare hands, knowing now how a slaughterhouse animal must feel, waiting for its executioner.

Without realizing what I was doing, I started to pace. It was astounding how much had fallen into place—astounding and appalling. My arrival at court must have been premeditated, orchestrated by Lady Dudley to force the duchess into relinquishing her place in the succession. And if this was true, then Lady Dudley knew something about me. She'd taken me into her care *because* of it. The woman who disdained and humiliated me, set me to cleaning her stables, ordered me flogged when I sought to read a book—she held the secret to my past.

Il porte la marque de la rose. . . .

A wave of desperation overcame me. I fought not to give in, reminding myself that everything could be an illusion, a manipulation. In my pain and anger, as I sought to make sense of the senseless, I didn't pay heed to the subtle changes in the air around me, to the mounting gurgle that signaled the beginning of the end, until I heard water seeping across stone, felt its cold touch swirl about my feet.

And I reeled around to see a black torrent gushing in through the wall grate.

I stood, petrified. The flow grew stronger, faster, bringing a smell of rot and sea, gushing in with unstoppable force as the flooding tide funneled through underground conduits into the small cell. In a matter of minutes, the entire floor was awash.

I backed to the door. There was no latch or keyhole; several furious kicks confirmed that breaking it down was not an option. Fear tightened about my chest. The overflow from the river would keep pouring through that grate until it filled the room to the ceiling.

I was going to drown unless I found a way out.

For an instant, my body refused to move. Then I jerked forward and sloshed through a death trap rapidly vanishing under liquid. I acted on instinct. I bent by the grate, maneuvering past the torrent. Mustering every last bit of strength, I grabbed hold of it and pulled, resisting the burning tear of muscles and the fact that I was kneeling in water that now reached my waist.

I pulled. Nothing. Tightening my grip, I pulled again. Rusted shards scraped my fingers.

"Move," I whispered. "Move. *Move!*"

With a crumbling crack, the grate gave way. My arms flew up to shield my head as I plunged into the pool. Gasping, spitting out a slimy mouthful, I clambered to my feet. The grate had twisted outward, a toothy maw. I had no way of squeezing out.

The water continued to rise.

I still couldn't believe I would die.

Scenes from my brief time at court drifted past me, so that I saw again the bedlam of London, the maze of Whitehall, the faces of those I'd met, who had become the architects of my demise. I thought Peregrine; of all of them, he might mourn, and just as I could abide no more, I recalled Kate Stafford's face as she kissed me. And I beheld the twin suns in Elizabeth's eyes.

Elizabeth.

Molten blood pumped through my limbs. I could feel the water creeping upward, an implacable presence whose clammy fingers swam about my chest. As I imagined that taste of death and silt filling my lungs, I swirled about and started hammering on the visible top of the door with all my might. My cries erupted from me like a feral howl. I didn't care if anyone answered. I refused to drown in silence.

As if from across a chasm I heard a faint call. *"Brendaaan!"*

I paused, pressed against the door, straining.

"Brendan! Brendan, are you there?"

"I'm here! Here!" I banged again on the door, scraping my knuckles raw. "Here! I'm here!" My knees started to buckle when the muffled splashing footsteps grew louder, running toward me. "Open it! Open it!" Unseen hands seized hold of the bolt, yanking it back.

"Be careful," I shouted. "The room's flooded. Get back before—"

I was knocked off my feet. Propelled out on a wave, I crashed against the opposite wall and slid to the floor, a boneless sodden rag.

In the dripping hush, a frightened voice asked, "Are you alive?"

"If I'm not, then you must be dead," I muttered. Arms like blocks of marble hauled me up. Before me stood two figures; one was Peregrine. The other, massive, carrottopped, square jawed and his face marred by pimples, was a stranger.

Peregrine said, "What happened to you? You look awful."

"You would, too, if you'd been used as bear bait." I looked at the stranger. "Thank you."

He nodded, his freckled hands hanging big as bread panders at his side. I said to Peregrine, "How did you find me?"

"This." He lifted my crumpled jerkin. "We found it by the entrance. We started searching for you when Barnaby saw a man running away."

"These old cloisters and cells," added Barnaby, "belonged to the Grey Friars until King Henry kicked them out. They've been abandoned for years. If someone comes here, most likely it's for no good purpose. The moment I saw that man, I knew something was amiss."

I put on the jerkin, grateful for something dry. I was chilled to my bones.

"We didn't get a good look at him," Peregrine said, with excitement in his voice, now that he realized they'd just saved my life. "It was too dark and he wore black. But he caught Barnaby's attention—he's got eyes like a falcon, this one. Lucky for you, he did. If we hadn't happened to find your jerkin, we'd never have thought to look down here." He paused, regarding me with a newfound awe. "Someone must really want you dead."

"Indeed. There was no one else with this man?" I asked,

though I didn't need to hear more. I knew who the man in black had been.

Barnaby shook his head. "He was alone. Strange thing—it was if he wanted us to see him. He could have gone any number of ways besides right within our eyesight."

This gave me pause. I passed a hand over my hair, which was plastered with silt, then accorded the muscular youth a bow. "You must be Master Fitzpatrick, King Edward's friend. Allow me to introduce myself. I am Brendan Prescott. I owe you my life."

He couldn't have been more than eighteen. Tall and built like a barbican, not uncomely despite his blemished complexion, with a shock of wiry red hair springing out from under his cap, he was not someone to disregard. Judging by the size of those hands and his drenched doublet, he must have been the one who unbolted and yanked open the cell door.

Barnaby said matter-of-factly, "Peregrine told me who you are. You're a Dudley servant. He also tells me you're a friend to Her Grace. She's like a sister to me, which is why I agreed to help you. But I must warn you, if you intend her any harm"—he shook his massive fist—"you won't like the results."

I nodded. "Trust me, I intend her no harm. I would explain more, if we had the time. Unfortunately, we must make haste. She is in danger." I reached up to wrench the crackling torch from the bracket. Peregrine piped, "His Majesty is here, in the Secret Lodgings. Barnaby says he's been here for weeks. See? I told you I'd find out anything you asked."

My gaze shifted to Barnaby over the tarry, smoky flame. His stare conveyed grim resolution. We started down the passage, sloshing through ankle-deep pools, toward the steep staircase. I ventured, "Is His Majesty very ill, Master Fitzpatrick?"

Barnaby's voice caught. "Edward is dying."

I was silent. Then I said, "I am sorry to hear it. Not only for his sake, but because Her Grace hoped to see him again. Now I fear she never will. I can only pray she'll heed me."

"She'll heed *me*," Barnaby said, with a certainty I found comforting in the extreme. "Her Grace, His Majesty, and I were raised together. She and I shared Edward's lessons. In fact, we first taught Edward how to ride." He smiled briefly. "Old King Henry would laugh out loud whenever Edward's tutors went running to him, squawking that we must be punished for putting His Highness at risk."

He shifted his dark blue stare to me. His smile became a taut grimace. "She knows I would never leave Edward's side unless I was forced to. And she knows that even in exile, I'd find a way to watch over him. She'll heed me, especially once I tell her about the duke."

We reached the gardens. I'd never been more grateful for fresh air in my life. Above the palace, fiery jettisons and wheels careened and exploded, showering multicolored glitter over rapt figures crammed together on balconies lining the hall windows.

I started to attention. "The fireworks! Quick, which way to the pavilion?"

Peregrine sprinted to the left. Crossing an overgrown thicket of hedges and topiaries, I saw the pavilion ahead. The lake's still waters reflected the artificial spectacle, so it seemed bathed in glittery fire. As we approached, I spied a silhouette in black standing at the balustrade. Another figure stood paces away, looking into the gardens.

"Give me a moment with her," I said to Barnaby. "I don't want to overwhelm her at first." He nodded, and he and Peregrine crouched down as I walked forth into the splashes of moonlight and counterfeit fire.

The figure in black turned to me. I came before her, bowing. At her side, Kate gave a startled gasp. I hadn't stopped to consider that besides my considerably soiled clothing, I must look a mess of bruises and cuts, blood caked on my face.

To her credit, Elizabeth did not comment, though her concern was plain. "Squire Prescott, please rise." She paused. "Isn't it rather late in the day for swimming?"

I smiled. "An accident, Your Grace. It looks worse than it is."

"Thank God for that." Her eyes gleamed. Her hair was seeded with pearls, coiled at her nape. She looked disarmingly young, the severity of her black gown with its banded ruff and lace cuffs emphasizing her willowy figure. Only her hands gave her away, those exquisite ringed fingers twisting and untwisting a handkerchief.

"Well?" she said. "Will you speak? Has an accident also detained your master?"

"Your Grace, I'm afraid I bring news of His Majesty your brother. And of your cousin, Lady Jane." I paused, wet my parched lips. In that moment, I realized how fantastic, even ludicrous, my tale would sound, let alone lacking in any proof. I also had the disquieting sensation she knew exactly what I was about to say.

"I'm listening," she said.

"His Majesty your brother is dying," I said quietly. "The duke keeps his illness a secret so that he can set Lady Jane and his son Guilford on the throne. He plans to capture you and your sister the Lady Mary, put you both in the Tower. If you stay in Greenwich, no one will be able to vouch for your safety."

I went silent. Without taking her eyes from me, Elizabeth said, "Kate, is this true?"

Kate Stafford stepped to us. "I fear so."

"And you knew about it? Cecil . . . knew?"

"Not everything." Kate didn't avoid my stare, though she had just confirmed she did report to Cecil. "But I do not doubt Squire Prescott's word. It would appear he has good reason for saying this."

Elizabeth nodded. "I don't doubt it, not for a second. I've suspected something of this nature was afoot from the moment Northumberland refused my request to visit Edward. I suppose I should consider myself fortunate I haven't been arrested yet." She paused, her gaze still on me. "Do you know why I haven't been arrested?"

"I believe his lordship does not dare risk it," I replied, "lest word of it gets to your sister and prompts her to flee the country. It would explain why he ordered my master Lord Robert to capture her first. Someone at court, they say, is feeding her information."

"I'm sure someone is," said Elizabeth. "We're talking about John Dudley, after all. By now he's made more enemies than Mary ever could."

"Then we mustn't press your luck further. I've friends nearby who can help us get you away. Even His Majesty's close companion Master Fitzpatrick is—"

"No."

For a moment, the last of the fireworks popping in the distance seemed to pause.

"No?" I echoed, thinking I must have heard wrong.

"No." Her face set. "I'm not leaving Greenwich. Not yet."

Kate said quickly, "Your Grace cannot mean to stay after what we've just heard. It would be madness. We promised Master Cecil you would—"

"I know what we promised. I said I would consider his advice. Consider, Kate, not comply. Now, I must see this through. I couldn't live with myself if I did not."

"My lady," I ventured and I received the full force of her stare. "I beg you to reconsider. You cannot change the duke's course, no matter what you do, nor can you hope to save His Majesty. Under the circumstances, you must now save yourself, for England."

Her mouth pursed. "That's Cecil speaking and I like it not. Be yourself, Prescott. I prefer you that way—impudent, rash, and determined to do whatever it takes."

I might have smiled, had the matter not been so serious. "Then, impudent as I am, I must emphasize how dangerous it would be to keep your appointment with my master. Lord Robert aims higher than Your Grace knows. He will deceive you in any way he can. He has refused to go after your sister because he believes you will accept his proposal of marriage."

Her expression underwent a change. It was almost imperceptible, but I saw it, the tightening of the sensitive skin about her mouth, a flash of something livid in her eyes.

"And I," she said softly, "know best how to deal with him." She raised her chin. "Besides, it's too late. Here he comes now."

I spun about. Kate grabbed me, pulled me back. "Go," she hissed. "Hide!"

I scrambled over the balustrade, dropping with what sounded like a deafening crash into the hawthorn bushes. "Graceful," muttered Peregrine. He and Barnaby had crept up unheard, each armed with daggers. Peregrine handed me one. I remembered my old dagger, which Master Shelton had given me. Stokes owed me, if only for stealing my knife. As for my cap, it seemed I had finally lost it for good.

Through the leaves, I watched Robert swagger down the pathway. He had asked me to make sure to return to help him dress tonight. Despite my absence, he'd done well enough, resplendent in a doublet of gold brocade studded with opals that must have cost an estate. He paused, removing his jeweled and feathered cap as he stepped up the stairs into the pavilion, his legs sheathed to his thighs in cordovan boots with gold spurs.

He dropped to one knee before Elizabeth. "I'm overwhelmed to find Your Grace safe and in good health." Even in the openness of the pavilion, his musk perfume was overpowering, like the breath of a magnificent beast in its prime.

She did not extend her hand to him, nor give him leave to rise. Slipping her handkerchief into her cuff she said, "I can't complain about my health. As for my safety, that remains to be seen. This court was never a place of refuge for me."

He glanced up. She'd spoken lightly, almost offhandedly, but even he could not have mistaken her tone. He reacted as if he had, however, replying huskily, "If you let me, I will make this court and all the realm places of refuge and glory for you."

"Yes." She smiled. "You would do so much for me, wouldn't you, my sweet Robin? Since we were children, you have always promised me the sun and the stars."

"I still do. You can have anything you desire. Ask for it and it shall be yours."

"Very well." She stared at him. "I wish to see my brother before he dies, without fearing for my life."

Robert stiffened. Still relegated to his knees, he took longer than expected before he managed to say, "I . . . I dare not speak of that. And neither must you."

"Oh?" She tilted her head. "Why? Surely friends have nothing to hide?"

"We do not," he said. "But it is treason to speculate on such a matter, as you know."

Her laughter rang out. "I'm relieved to hear someone in your family still has a conscience! And that, apparently, my brother still lives. It would no longer be treason to speculate if he did not." She paused. "I thought you said I could have anything I desired. Would you fail me now in my hour of need?"

"You toy with me." He sprang to his feet, overpoweringly robust against her slimness. "I did not come to play games. I came to warn you that your right to the throne is in danger."

"I have no right," she retorted swiftly, but I detected a weakening in her voice, a supple yielding. "My sister Mary is heir, not I. Thus, if you must warn someone, let it be her."

Robert reached for her hand. "Come now. We're not children anymore. We needn't see who can outwit whom. You know as well as I that the people will not have your sister for their queen. She represents Rome and the past, everything they've come to detest."

"And yet she is their rightful—their *only*—heir," said Elizabeth. She yanked her hand from him. "Besides, who's to say? Mary could change her faith, as so many these days are apt to do. She's a Tudor, when all is said and done, and we're not ones to let religion stand in our way."

Robert regarded her with a discomfiting familiarity. I hadn't thought about how much history can be collected in a mere twenty years, how much two children reared on a diet of intrigue and deception can come to rely upon each other.

"Do you take me for a fool?" he said. "You know Mary would defend her faith to the grave if need be. You know it, the council knows it, your brother the king knows it, and—"

"Your father knows it best of all," said Elizabeth. "You might say, he anticipates it." She eyed him with calculating intimacy that made him look like an amateur. "Is that why you wished to see me? Have we danced around each other these past two days for you to tell me that my sister mustn't take the throne because she reveres the faith in which she was raised?"

"God's blood! I came to tell you that in the eyes of the people, you—and only you—have the right to be queen. You are the princess they revere; you are the one they await. They would rise in arms to uphold you, if you would say the word. They'd die in your defense."

"Would they?" Her voice was a cruel caress. "There was a time when they would have done the same for Mary's mother. At that time, it was Katherine of Aragon who was the rightful queen and my mother the hated usurper. Would you have me step into a dead woman's shoes?"

The air between them was charged, the tension so palpable it set my teeth on edge. There was indeed history between them, and far too much emotion. It was my first glimpse into a passion so deep, so volatile, that were it unleashed it would destroy everything before it.

"Why must you always banter with me?" Robert's voice quavered. "You fear Mary taking the throne as much I do. You know it would mean the end of the Church your father built so he could wed your mother; the ruin of any hope for peace or prosperity. She'll set the Inquisition upon us within the year. But not you; you have no desire to persecute. That is why you have the people on your side and most of the nobility. And me. Anyone who dared question your right will suffer my sword."

She regarded him in silence. From my hiding place I could see her hesitation, her terrified understanding of all that was at stake and all she might gain by it. My legs tensed like an animal's about to spring, imagining her struggle to justify a past smeared by her mother's spilt blood. Then she spoke. "My right, you say? Is it my right, truly? Or do you mean, *ours*?"

"It's one and the same," he said quickly. "I live to serve you."

"Inspiring words. They might stir me, had I not heard similar ones before."

It was the first time in my life I had seen Robert Dudley struck speechless.

"Do you want to know from whom?" Elizabeth added. "It was your father. Yes, my sweet Robin—your father offered me much the same this afternoon. He even used the same arguments, offered the same enticement."

Robert stood petrified to his spot.

"You can ask Mistress Stafford if you don't believe me," said Elizabeth. "She saw him leave my rooms. He barged in—while I was abed—to declare he would make me queen if I consented to marry him. He promised to get rid of his wife, your mother, for me—or rather, for my crown. For of course I would have to make him king. Not king-consort, but king in his own right, so that should I die before him, say in childbed, as so many do, he could continue to rule after me and bequeath the throne to his heirs, regardless of whether they are my issue or not."

She smiled, graceful and unforgiving. "So you must excuse me if I don't react with the enthusiasm you hoped for. I'm fresh out of enthusiasm where Dudleys are concerned."

Her performance was mesmerizing. She hadn't breathed a word of this, though it explained why Northumberland had chosen to set Jane Grey on the throne. An experienced courtier, he had a contingency plan, in case his first choice fell through. His declaration at Whitehall on the night of Elizabeth's arrival—it had been his warning that he was willing to proceed against her if she stood in his way. And she had done just that, refusing him and everything he contrived to obtain for her and in return issuing her own declaration of war.

As Cecil surmised, the duke had underestimated her.

The disbelief on Robert's face drained his sun-bronzed skin to a chalky hue. I actually felt sorry for him as he said in a faltering voice, "My father . . . he offered . . . to marry you?"

"You sound surprised. I don't see why. The seed is the same as the apple it came from, or so they tell me."

He stepped to her with such fury that without thinking, I started to lunge. Barnaby's viselike grasp on my shoulder detained me, coupled with a lightning warning glance from the otherwise motionless Kate. I closed my fist about my dagger hilt. As I did, I saw Kate slip a hand into her cloak, for something no doubt equally sharp. It reassured me that in this instance, at least, she demonstrated her loyalty.

Robert gripped Elizabeth by the arm with such brutality her hair unraveled and cascaded like flame over her shoulders, pearls scattering across the pavilion floor.

"You lie! You lie and play with me, like a bitch in heat—and still, God help me, I want you." He crushed her mouth against his. She reared back; with a stinging retort that echoed in the electrified air, she raised her hand and struck him hard across the face. Her rings cut into his skin, lacerating his lip.

"Unhand me this instant," she said, "or by God I'll never let you near me again."

Her words were more blistering than her blow. Robert stood stunned, his cut lip bleeding, before he backed away. They faced each other like combatants, their breath audible, heavy. Then the aggression crumbled from his face and he gazed at her with something akin to grief.

"You're not considering it? You'd not wed him to spite me?"

"If you think that, you are more deluded than he is," she said, but her voice was trembling now, as though she fought back uncertainty that threatened to undo her. "As if I, a princess born and bred, would ever let some lowborn Dudley rut in my bed. I'd die first."

He flinched. His face set like stone. It was a terrible moment, sounding the death knell on years of childhood trust. No woman had humiliated Robert Dudley; any woman he'd wanted, he'd had. But despite all his guile, all his vanity and pretense, he desired only one woman, and she had just rejected him with a callous resolve aimed like a spear at his heart.

He drew himself erect. "Is that your final word?"

"It is my only word. King or commoner, I will be no man's victim."

"What if that man should declare his love for you?"

She let out a chuckle. "If this is a man's love, I pray God to spare me any more of it."

He exploded. "So be it! You will lose it all—country, crown: everything! They'll take it all from you and leave you with nothing but your infernal pride. I love you. I have always loved you, but seeing as you'll have nothing to do with it, you leave me with no other choice but to do as my father commands. I will go and arrest your sister, see her to the Tower. And as God is my witness, Elizabeth, when he next sends me out at the head of soldiers, I cannot promise it will not be to come knocking at your door in Hatfield."

She lifted her chin. "Should that come to pass, then I'll be grateful for a familiar face."

Robert bowed furiously and stormed back down the steps toward the palace. The night swallowed him. The moment he was gone, Elizabeth swayed. Kate hurried to her.

"God help me," I heard her whisper. "What have I done?"

"What you had to," Kate said. "What Your Grace's dignity required."

Elizabeth stared at her. A quivering laugh escaped her. "Squire Prescott!"

I rose, brushing dead leaves from my damp breeches as I came before her. In her eyes I glimpsed an anguish she'd never admit to. "You told me I was in danger of my life. It seems you were right. What shall we do now?"

"Leave, Your Grace," I said, "before Lord Robert confesses to his father. Once he does, they will have to take you. You already know too much."

"Strange," she replied, as Kate removed her cloak from the balustrade and draped it about her thin shoulders. "It seems you do not know him as much as you should, for boys that were raised together. Robert will never go to his father with this. I've hurt him in the one place he'll not forgive or forget, but he'll not seek revenge through the duke. No, he hates Northumberland now even more than me. He may do as he's bid and take Mary down like a prize doe, for his pride of manhood demands it, but he'll never set his father's hounds on me willingly."

"Whatever the case, we can't wait to find out." I turned to Kate. A lesser woman might have flinched at the tone in my voice. "Any instructions from Cecil we should know about?"

She met my stare. "I am to take Her Grace through the postern gate. There is transport waiting for us on the road. But, you aren't supposed to be here."

Elizabeth said, "I am overwhelmed by the concern, and the effort expended on my behalf, but I've no desire to leave my Arabian, Cantila, here for the duke's use. He's too valuable a friend." Her lips curled. "Speaking of which, didn't you say you had friends nearby?"

In answer to her query, Peregrine bounded up out of hiding. "I'll fetch Your Grace's horse!" Behind him Barnaby offered stiff genuflection, shreds of leaves in his hair. "My lady," he said with the warmth of years of familiarity.

"Barnaby Fitzpatrick," she breathed, "I am glad of you." She leaned to Peregrine with a wry smile. "Don't you work in the stables at Whitehall? Where is my dog?"

Peregrine gazed at her in unabashed adoration. "Urian is safe. He is here, stabled with Cantila. I'll fetch him, too, if you like. Anything you need. It would be my honor."

"He means it," I added. I glanced at Peregrine. "My horse Cinnabar is also here, my friend, in case you'd forgotten. And my saddlebag is under the straw."

Peregrine nodded, flustered. Elizabeth said briskly, "Then it's settled. Our friend here will fetch my dog and the horses, and meet us at the gate. I've a friend of my own outside Greenwich, where we can seek refuge lest the duke sends troops after us. I don't think it wise to return to Hatfield quite yet." She paused. A chill went through me as I saw her tense. Even though I anticipated her words, they still took me off guard.

"But before we go anywhere, I must see Edward."

Chapter Eighteen

A deafening hush followed her declaration. I marveled that I should feel any shock; it wasn't as if she behaved in an unexpected fashion. I also wondered why I tried to convince her otherwise, even as I said: "That's impossible. We can't get inside. And even if we could, His Majesty's rooms are too well guarded. We'll never get out again."

Elizabeth regarded me stonily. "Perhaps before we give up, we should ask Master Fitzpatrick, who's slept at the foot of my brother's bed these many years. He will know how impossible it is." She turned to Barnaby. "Is there a way for us to get into Edward's apartments without being caught?"

To my disbelief, Barnaby assented. "There's a secret passage to the bedchamber. In times past, His Majesty your late father used it. Last time I checked, the duke hadn't set a guard there. But I must warn you, if he does, the only way out is through the apartments, and they're infested with his minions."

"I'll take my chances." Elizabeth returned her gaze to me. "Don't try to detain me. If you wish to help me, do so. If not, you can meet me at the gatehouse. But I must do this. I must see my brother before it is too late." She paused. "I . . . I have to say good-bye."

Her words tugged at my soul. This, I understood.

Barnaby stepped forth. "I will take Your Grace." He shot me a look. "I'll see her to His Majesty and back to the gatehouse safely."

"Thank you, Barnaby." She didn't take her eyes from me. I finally conceded defeat with a sigh, lifting my own gaze past her to the palace and rows of glowing windows. The fireworks display had ended. Furtive storm clouds leaked fragrant humidity. The festivities would reach their apex soon, with the court imbuing free wine and dancing in feverish delight in front of the morose couple ensconced on the dais. The duke would be obligated to stand attendance, keep close watch on the nobles, seeing as the king had not made his promised appearance to bless the nuptials. If ever there was a time to sneak into royal apartments, this was it. Why, then, did I feel a terrible presentiment?

"Ash Kat has sent word to the hall that I'm indisposed," said Elizabeth, misinterpreting the reason for my silence. "My assorted stomach complaints and headaches are notorious, as is my temper when disturbed. In addition, the duke knows what he said to me this afternoon and he'll not wish to push his luck. I didn't tell Robert as much, naturally, but I did not refuse Northumberland completely. I merely said I needed some time to contemplate his offer."

She smiled coldly. "Of course, that time will soon run out, but unless they decide to break down my bedchamber door, for now, no one will dare intrude on me."

"Or not while His Majesty lives," I said. "Once he is gone, you can't expect mercy."

"I never would," she replied. "You are bold, nonetheless, to remind me."

I looked to Barnaby. "Are you sure it's safe to use that passage?"

"Providing it isn't guarded and someone stands watch while we're inside, yes. Only the king's favorite, Harry Sidney, is with Edward now. He'll not raise warning against us."

"I'll stand guard." Kate withdrew a dagger from her cloak. I repressed immediate protest. We weren't so many that I could afford to disdain help; and we did need someone to watch.

"Fine. Peregrine will come with us. If it looks safe, he can go to the stables. Your Grace does realize your visit with your brother must be brief?"

She pulled up her hood. "Yes."

With Kate and Peregrine flanking her, I motioned to Barnaby and we edged past the facade of the palace, a stalwart company of five, avoiding the taper light spilling from the loggias and windows. Laughter, uninhibited, slightly frenetic, tumbled from open panes; the revelry in the hall was in full sway.

I wondered if the duke had been obliged at the last minute to let more courtiers into the palace than he'd have preferred. I hoped so. The more distractions he had to contend with, the more time it would give us to get in and out of Edward's rooms. Elizabeth's absence from the nuptial celebration had surely been noted; Northumberland might even have decided that some incentive was required to facilitate her contemplation of his offer and had set guards at her doors at this very moment. Much as I disliked the thought, we had to be ready for every eventuality.

I stole a glimpse at Barnaby. If I ever found myself in a brawl, he was someone I'd want on my side. "Barnaby," I said in a low voice. "Will you promise me something?"

"Depends on what it is."

"If something goes wrong, will you do whatever you must to see her safe?"

His bared teeth gleamed. "Did you think I'd leave her to that pack of wolves? I'll see her safe all right. Or die trying. Either way, they'll never get hold of her."

We passed into an enclosed ward, fronted by the palace. An odd derelict-looking tower rose at one end. I smelled the aroma of the river nearby.

Barnaby halted. "The entrance is in that tower." He went still. I likewise came to a halt, an unspoken curse on my lips. The others also paused. In the silence, I heard Elizabeth draw a sharp breath between her teeth. "Sentries," she whispered.

There were two of them before the tower, which squatted among Greenwich's soaring tiers like a medieval toadstool. The guards, sharing a wineskin and conversing, were not keeping an eye toward whoever might approach. They probably didn't expect anyone on a night like this, with the duke's son's wedding afoot. It explained why they were probably half drunk and surly, lounging by the wall. They'd been left in the cold to watch over a doorway few knew about, while the court fattened itself inside on roast meat and frolic.

"I thought you said it was safe," I said to Barnaby.

He grunted. "It usually is. I guess our lord the duke isn't taking any more chances. He never had that entrance watched before."

I glanced at Elizabeth. Inside the hood of her cloak, her face was like a pale icon, the toll of her encounter with Robert hidden in her eyes. "There are only two," she said in response to my

unvoiced question. How could I have thought she'd say anything else? "We'll have to find a way to distract them."

Before I could reply, Kate shifted to me. Her apple-tinged
fragrance made me acutely aware of how much she had begun to
affect me, much as I wanted to deny it.

"I have an idea. Her Grace and I have played similar games
before, albeit with a different caliber of gentlemen. But men are
still men, and these two have drunk more than their share. If
you and Barnaby are amenable, I believe we can accomplish this
task with a minimum of effort."

I stared, speechless. Barnaby grinned. "Now, there's a lass
after my own heart." Even as I struggled for a reasonable refusal,
Elizabeth tugged her hood farther over her head, concealing her
face. I reached for her arm. "Your Grace!" I ignored her barbed
glance at my fingers. "Please, think before you do this." I shot a
look at Kate. "You could both be arrested."

"I have thought of it." Elizabeth reached down and pried my
hand from her sleeve. "It is all I have thought about since I came
to court. I told you, I must do this. Are you willing to see it
through or not?"

I met her stare and nodded. Kate muttered instructions, such
as they were, then flipped back her hood to expose her face.
With a deliberate sway of her hips, she sauntered over to the two
men as they passed the wineskin between them.

"Time to fly, my friend," I said, and Peregrine fled into the
darkness.

I gripped my blade, watching with my heart in my throat as
Kate and Elizabeth neared the men. The sentries had come to
their feet, startled but not suspicious. The random light cast by
the waning moon and reflections of candles in the palace's upper windows were enough to show the intruders were women,

who had wandered into the gardens. And women who wandered into gardens at night were, by the very act, not considered ladies.

The larger of the two men lumbered forth, a lascivious grin on his face. Kate was in the lead. Elizabeth lingered a few paces behind, her elegant stature made more pronounced by her hooded cloak. I doubted the sentries would bother to notice that the cloak's velvet was costly, but should her face be revealed by some mishap, I had no illusions as to whether or not she'd be recognized. There wasn't another face like hers in all of England.

"Be on the ready," I said to Barnaby. He grunted in response.

The guard's voice carried into the night. "And what are these pretty damsels doing here?" He was already reaching a grubby paw to Kate, and my fist closed convulsively over my dagger hilt. Barnaby murmured, "Easy, lad. Give her a moment."

Kate effortlessly evaded the man's grope. Cocking her hip and head in a disingenuous display, her right hand hidden within the folds of her cloak, where I knew she'd stashed her own blade, she said, "My lady and I had thought to escape the air of the palace. It's so loud and hot inside. We were told there's a pavilion nearby, but alas, we seem to have lost our way."

She paused. Though I couldn't see it, I was certain she was gracing the man with one of her artful smiles. Peril notwithstanding, her audacity made my unwitting admiration of her only increase. She had the heart of a lioness. No wonder Elizabeth trusted her.

"A pavilion?" The guard glanced at his companion, who stood, gazing warily. The less drunk of the two and therefore the one to watch. "Did you hear that, Rog? These ladies were looking for a pavilion. Ever heard of the like 'round here?"

The one called Rog didn't answer. I saw Elizabeth tense under her cloak, her shoulders involuntarily squaring. It wasn't so much the gesture that alerted the man as the manner in which it was done. With that one movement, she exposed herself as someone of import, unaccustomed to being questioned, and Rog reacted. He strode to Kate, chin thrust forward in the universally belligerent display of men who think they have some power.

"There's no pavilion in these parts that I'm aware of. I must ask you ladies to give us your names. This is no time to be out alone." He cast a pointed stare at Elizabeth. "I would see you returned to the palace and the hall, my lady."

Kate laughed. "Surely this palace poses no danger, what with all these celebrations going on. But I see we were misled. We would welcome an escort, if you would be so kind."

It wasn't the plan, but she was improvising as she could, trying to dissuade further questioning and secure us the cover we needed. And it would work, if she could lure them to the wall where Barnaby and I lurked at the ready. The thick shadows cast by the tower would serve almost as well as its interior.

Rog wasn't taking the bait. He'd not removed his suspicious stare from Elizabeth; and just as I felt the situation becoming too strained and that Barnaby and I would have to act, with a thrust of hand as swift as it was inescapable, Rog yanked back the princess's hood.

Dead quiet fell. Elizabeth's pale skin and fiery tresses glowed. The larger guard let out a strangled gasp. "God's bones, it's—she—"

He didn't finish. Kate threw herself at him, her knife raised in a scything arc. Barnaby and I rushed forward, fleet as hounds. I hadn't thought we might have to murder these two men, but in the heat of the moment, with my own knife ready, I understood it was exactly what our survival might require.

I reached Kate as she grappled with the guard, his fist closed about hers, fending off her knife and guffawing as he did it. Grabbing her by the shoulder, I whirled her away and slammed my own fist as hard as I could into the man's face. I felt my knuckles connect with bone. The guard went down with an audible smash onto the cobblestones.

I spun around to see Barnaby dodging the sword Rog had yanked from his scabbard. Even as I realized Barnaby's dagger was no match for the sword and it was only a matter of moments before Rog delivered a lethal blow, I caught sight of a blur of movement, a swish of dark cloak.

A long white hand came up.

I heard a wet crack. Rog stood perfectly still. His sword wavered, dropped clattering. He swayed, half turning in disbelief to his attacker. A thin line of blood seeped down his forehead.

Then he fell, face forward.

I met Elizabeth's eyes. The stone she held dropped from her fingers. A speck of blood spattered their tapered length. Kate ran to where the princess stood. "Your Grace, are you hurt?"

"No. I'll wager this one, however, will wake with a headache he won't soon forget." Elizabeth looked almost in disbelief at the man sprawled at her feet. She lifted her eyes to me. As I stepped to her, Barnaby bent over Rog to check his pulse.

"He lives," Barnaby pronounced.

Elizabeth exhaled. "Merciful God. They were only doing their duty."

Kate pushed disheveled hair from her brow, her color high in her cheeks. "What a pair of louts! Can Northumberland find no better than these to do his work?"

"Let us hope not." Barnaby took Rog by his wrists and started hauling him toward the tower doorway. I gestured to Kate. "Come, help me."

Urgency overcame us. With Kate and Elizabeth lending assistance, we dragged the larger guard through the door into a small round room, such as might be used for storage. A rickety set of stairs spiraled up toward a concave ceiling.

We lay the guards side by side. I went back to retrieve the sword. When I returned, Barnaby was using his belt to bind each of the inert men's wrists together, palms facing. He took the handkerchief Elizabeth gave him, ripping it in half and stuffing the pieces of cloth into the men's mouths. "Not much of a hindrance if they really want out," he said, "but it should hold them otherwise."

"I'll see they don't stir." Kate took the sword from me. "If they so much as breathe too loud, I'll skewer them like a Mayfair swan."

Elizabeth had moved to the staircase. Barnaby stopped her, "No, this way." He walked around the stairs to the seemingly solid wall. He reached down to lift a flagstone. I watched, amazed, as he pressed a concealed lever with his foot.

The wall opened outward, revealing an archway. Beyond, another narrow staircase wound upward into cobwebbed gloom. Elizabeth glanced from Barnaby to me. "It's very dark."

"We can't risk any light," said Barnaby. She nodded, went to the stairs.

I motioned Barnaby to follow. "I'll be right behind you." Then I turned to Kate. "Are you sure you want to stay here?" I tried to keep my tone neutral, unwilling to admit the personal concern I felt for her, which only a few minutes earlier had driven me at the guard with the intent to kill. I didn't want to leave her here alone. And I did not like that. I did not want to feel anything for her, not at this juncture.

She gave me a knowing smile. "Still suspicious, are we?" Before I could respond, she set a finger on my lips. "Be quiet. I know I owe you an explanation, but for now rest assured that I can use a blade for more than peeling apples."

I had no doubt she could, but no matter how well she might wield a weapon, she'd be no match for these two should they decide to break their bonds.

"Don't fight them." I looked her in the eye. "They're the duke's men. The punishment would be . . . severe. If it comes to it, make your escape. Find Peregrine and meet us on the road. We'll find another way to get her out." I paused. "Promise me."

"I'm moved that you would worry," she replied, still with that ironic smile. "But this is hardly the time to start doubting your allies. Go. You've more important things to worry about."

I did not argue. Turning away, I stepped into suffocating darkness.

The passage containing the secret staircase was impossibly narrow, the ceiling angled low, barely high enough to accommodate a man. With my knees bent and shoulders hunched, my hair brushing cold stone, I wondered how enormous Henry the Eighth had ever navigated it. An unwitting gasp escaped me as the sense of space behind me was cut off.

Kate had depressed the lever and closed the false wall.

It was like moving up a tunnel. My eyes gradually adjusted. Rats perched on the steps, eyeing me without fear. Elizabeth and Barnaby climbed ahead, single file; I lost sight of them at each turn in the pike. The clammy air was wringing sweat from my brow.

Suddenly the staircase ended at a wooden door. Barnaby paused. "Before we go in," he said, "Your Grace should know that Edward . . . he isn't the prince we knew. The illness and the treatments have taken a terrible toll on him."

She edged closer to me as Barnaby rapped on the door. In the hush, I heard her draw in a quivering breath. Barnaby rapped again. I gripped my dagger.

The door cracked open. A sliver of light cut across our feet.

"Who goes there?" said a man's low, frightened voice.

"Sidney, it's me," whispered Barnaby. "Quick. Open up."

The door swung inward, a covert entry masked by the wainscoting of a small but well-appointed chamber. The first thing that struck me was the heat. It was stifling, emanating from scented braziers set in the corners, from a fire burning in the recessed hearth, and from the tripod of candelabra illuminating the scarlet and gold upholstery of the chairs, the curtains at the alcove, and the damask hangings shrouding a tester bed.

A young man with lank blond hair faced Barnaby, his fine features haggard. "What are you doing here? You know his lordship ordered you away. You must not . . ." His voice faded. His blue eyes widened. Elizabeth stepped around Barnaby, cast back her cowl.

I stood behind her. Beyond the breath-quenching heat I began to detect another smell in the air—something very faint but also fetid, barely masked by the herb fumes from the brazier.

Elizabeth noticed it, too. "God's teeth," she murmured, as Sidney dropped to his knees before her. She stepped past him. "There's no time for that," she said faintly, moving toward the bed. On a crosshatch a falcon watched, its ankle tethered to its gilded post; candle flames reflected in its opaque pupils.

"Edward?" she whispered. She reached out to the bed hangings. "Edward, it's me, Elizabeth." She drew back the hangings. She gasped, staggered back.

I rushed to her side. When I saw what she stared at, I went still.

The stench in the room came from a shrunken figure supine on the bed, the flesh of his emaciated legs and arms blackened, festering. Propped on the pillows like a decaying marionette, only the rise and fall of his chest indicated the young king's heart still beat. I could not believe anyone in such a state could be conscious. I prayed he wasn't.

Then Edward VI's gray-blue eyes opened, and his anguished gaze, as it rested on us, showed he was fully aware of his torment and that his sister stood before him. He opened caked lips, struggled to mouth unintelligible words.

Sidney hastened to his side. "He can't speak," he told Elizabeth. She had not moved, her face pared to an alarming transparency.

"What . . . what is he trying to say?" she whispered.

Sidney leaned close to the king's mouth. Edward's talonlike fingers gripped his wrist. Sidney looked up sorrowfully. "He begs your forgiveness."

"My forgiveness?" Her hand crept to her throat. "Blessed Jesus, it is I who should beg for his. I wasn't here. I wasn't here to stop them from doing this . . . this horror to him."

"He is beyond such concerns. He needs you to forgive him. He had no power to gainsay the duke. I know. I have seen everything that has transpired between them, from the day Northumberland began to poison him."

"Poison him?" Her voice turned hard, cold. I thought I would never want to be the recipient of the look she now cast. "What are you saying?"

"I'm talking of the choice, Your Grace, the terrible choice they forced on him. He was ill with fevers; he coughed up blood.

Everyone knew that he could not live; he too knew his end was near and he'd made his peace with it. He'd also made his decision about who must succeed him. Then the duke transferred him here and ordered his physicians dismissed. He brought in the herbalist, who began treating him with some mixture of arsenic. He was told it would help him, and it did—for a little while. But then it got much worse."

Sidney glanced at Edward, who lay there with his eyes distended in his appalling, skeletal face. "He began to rot from within. The pain became an unending torment. Northumberland was at him night and day, without respite. He signed in desperation, because he could take no more, because they had promised him relief and he was burning in a never-ending hell."

"He . . . he was forced . . . to sign . . . something?" Elizabeth had trouble speaking; I could see the veins in her temples. "What was it? What did they make him sign?"

Sidney averted his eyes. "A device naming Jane Grey as his heir. The duke made him disavow your and the Lady Mary's claims to the throne. He made him"—his voice lowered to a whisper—"declare you both illegitimate."

Elizabeth stood perfectly still. I watched her countenance darken. Then she whirled about, took a furious step toward the apartments' main door.

"Your Grace," I said.

She paused. "Don't," she said to me. "Don't say it."

"Listen." I moved in front of her.

A dragging sound grew steadily louder, coming closer and closer.

"It's the herbalist," Sidney said, as if surprised; and as Barnaby leapt to the wall by the door, I drew Elizabeth behind the alcove curtains. I shielded her with my body, the dagger in my hand feeling insignificant as a toy. I tightened my hold, watching the apartment door open.

A stunted woman limped in. Her ankles contorted inward, displaying livid scars.

She paused in the center of the room.

"I told you, it's the herbalist," Sidney said again. Barnaby sagged with relief against the wall.

I looked closer. My entire world keeled.

Slowly, I stepped out of hiding. I knew it without needing to say a single thing, like a nail driven in my heart. All the blood in my veins seemed to empty. I saw no recognition in the withered face framed by an old-fashioned wimple—a leathery face, almost unrecognizable, scored by suffering. Even as I paused, all of a sudden, beset by a horrible, almost hopeful doubt, the scent of rosemary, of childhood, overcame me. I remembered what Peregrine had said:

He has that old nurse of his to take care of him. . . . She came here once . . . to fetch one of Edward's spaniels.

I looked at her for an endless moment. Her eyes were bovine, dull in their resignation. I raised a trembling hand to her cheek, my fingers poised over her desiccated flesh. I was terrified of touching her, as if she were a mirage that might turn to dust. My heart pounded in my ears. If I hadn't known it was true, that I was seeing her, here, in front of me, I would never have believed this was happening.

Not after all these haunted, grief-stricken years.

Behind me Elizabeth said, "You know her."

And I heard myself reply, "Yes. Her name is Mistress Alice. She cared for me when I was a child. I was told she was dead."

Silence ensued. Barnaby shut the door, planted himself in front of it.

I couldn't take my eyes from her, couldn't reconcile this brittle, ancient figure with the quick-witted woman enshrined in my memory. She'd always been spry, fleet of word and gesture; her eyes had been discerning, bright and keen, not these sunken hollow orbs.

She had left on a trip to Stratford, as she did every year. A few days to come and go, she'd said. *Don't fret, my pet. I'll be back before you know it.* But she didn't come back. Thieves had beset her on the road: That's what Master Shelton told me. I didn't weep, didn't ask to see her body or where she was buried. The pain was too intense. It hadn't mattered. All that mattered was that she was gone. She was gone and she would never return to me. That's what I'd been told. That's what I believed. I was twelve years old and bereft of the one person in the world who had loved me. Her loss became an incurable wound that I hid deep within.

Now the question boiled inside me, with the force of an eruption.

Why? Why did you leave me?

But as I took in her appearance, I knew.

The scars on her ankles—I'd seen the same on mules condemned by unfeeling masters to a lifetime of hobbling about manacled, forced to turn the churning wheels of mills. I let my hand trail to her jaw, as I might soothe a frightened mare. Like a mare she understood. She opened her lips. Her mouth was dark inside. Defiled.

They had cut out her tongue.

A scream curdled in my throat. I choked it back as I heard Elizabeth utter, "Is this the woman who has been poisoning my brother?"

From the bed Sidney replied, "Yes. Lady Dudley brought her

here . . . She gave her instructions, to make the treatments. But . . . she . . . she . . ."

"What?" Elizabeth snapped. "Spit it out!"

"Mistress Alice is a master herbalist," I said. "She cured me of many illnesses in my childhood. She would never have done this willingly."

Elizabeth pointed at her brother. "You can say that after what she's done?"

Mistress Alice's misshapen hand tugged at my jerkin. I looked into her eyes. The lump in my chest turned molten. Barnaby acknowledged my warning glance as I turned to where Elizabeth stood. "She'd never do this to any living being, much less to a man—not unless she was forced to," I said. "She has been hurt, tortured. The duke ordered this done."

"Why?" Elizabeth's voice caught. "Dear God in heaven, why do this to him?"

"To keep him alive. To gain time," was my grim reply.

Elizabeth stared at me. "I can't leave him here. We must get him out of that bed."

"We can't," I said, and she took one look at my face and stiffened. "We must go. Now."

She glanced at Barnaby. "I don't hear anything," she said.

I answered, "Neither do I. But Mistress Alice does. Look at her."

Elizabeth did. Mistress Alice had shuffled to the secret door and was motioning to us with unmistakable agitation. Her hands were unbearably twisted, those of a hundred-year-old crone. What they had done to her had stolen years from her life. She was not yet fifty.

I had to fight back my rage, and returned to Elizabeth. She

met my stare defiantly and then turned away and made for the door without a backward glance.

Barnaby followed. Sidney bolted to a coffer, flung open the lid. He yanked out a jewel-hilted sword sheathed in leather and tossed it to me. "Edward has no need of it anymore. It's of Toledo steel, a gift from the imperial ambassador. I'll try and delay them while you get away."

I knew instantly from the feel that it had been fashioned for someone light of build, like me. Only I could never have afforded such a sword on my own.

Mistress Alice shuffled purposefully to the bed. "See that Her Grace gets out safely," I ordered Barnaby, and I kicked the secret door shut in his face. Sidney was at the main door. He froze, gaping at me. "Where are you going? They're almost here!"

I moved to where Mistress Alice stood at the bedside table, rummaging through a wooden chest—her medicine chest, which she'd stashed on the kitchen shelf, out of my reach. I felt a cold shock as I realized I'd never even noticed it was missing, though she never took it with her when she traveled. Whenever I'd tried to peek inside it, she'd said,

Nothing in there for a big-eyed curious lad; no secrets for him to see. . . .

She turned, gazing at me as if she saw me for the first time. Tears leapt in my eyes as she took my hand. With quivering gnarled fingers, she set something wrapped in oiled cloth in my palm. She folded my fingers over it. I was captivated by the look that came over her face then, as if she had finally found redemption.

Then the door opened. Sidney was thrust back.

With her gift in one fist and the sword in the other, I pivoted to meet my past.

Chapter Nineteen

She wore a gown the color of armor. Of all those who might have entered through that door, she was the last person I expected to see—though it made perfect sense it should be her. Behind her was Archie Shelton, his scarred face impassive. At the sight of him, I had to stop myself from vaulting forward in fury.

I heard voices in the antechamber. "Wait until I call for you," she said over her shoulder, and Master Shelton came in and closed the door. I registered Sidney's retreat out of the corner of my eye. At my back I felt Mistress Alice go still. I outstretched an arm to shield her, even as I recognized the futility of it. Though she must have been surprised to see me, Lady Dudley's expression was imperturbable.

"I see you've failed to heed the one unbreakable rule of every loyal servant," she said. "You failed to recognize your proper place." She glanced at the panel in the wainscoting concealing the secret door. "But, I do give you credit for finding that entrance." Her voice hardened. "Where is she?"

Knowing Barnaby and Kate must be rushing Elizabeth to

the gate where Peregrine waited with the horses at that very moment, I said, "I am alone. I wanted to find out for myself."

"You're not a very good liar," she replied. "She'll never get away, no matter what you think you can do. She's going to lose that feckless head of hers, just like her whore of a mother."

I ignored her threat. "Why have you done this?"

She arched one thin eyebrow. "I'm surprised you have to ask." She motioned. "Move away from the bed. Oh, and drop that . . . sword, is it?" She smiled. "My son Henry and our retainers are outside, eager for better sport than toasting Guilford's fortune between Jane Grey's thighs. One word from me and they'll flay you alive."

I threw the sword onto the rug between us. I didn't deign Master Shelton a glance. The steward stood in front of the door, in the same stance Barnaby had affected, powerful arms folded across his barrel chest.

Bastard. I hated him as I'd never hated anyone in my life, as if it were venom in my blood. I wanted to kill him with my bare hands.

Lady Dudley said, "Mistress Alice, please mix His Majesty's draught now."

From the chest, Mistress Alice removed a pouch and sprinkled white powder into a goblet.

I found it almost impossible to maintain my stance. *She* had done this, all of it. She had mutilated Mistress Alice, set her to poison the king. She'd always been efficient, whether she was organizing her household or ordering the autumn slaughter of the pigs. Why should this have been any different? Understanding now what had been hidden from me all these years, I marveled at how I'd missed it, how I had failed to sense the deception.

It had been Lady Dudley who had plotted to provide an

alternative heir to the two princesses. Implacable, she had aimed at exalting her favorite son, used everything she had at her disposal. She'd even divined a weakness in the duchess of Suffolk's past and made a devil's pact to one end and one end only—preserving the family power.

But her husband the duke had repaid her in false coin. He'd gone along with her plans, even as he contrived to take Elizabeth for himself. Somehow, Lady Dudley had found out. She had discovered the truth.

What else did she know? What else had she kept secret?

As if she could read my thoughts, her bloodless lips curved. "Twenty years. That's how long it's been since you came into our lives. You were always clever, too clever by far. Alice used to say she'd never seen a child so eager to grasp the world. Perhaps I should keep you alive a bit longer, in case our angry duchess reneges on her promise. She thinks you're dead, but I still need her compliance until we have Jane declared queen. I could use you again."

I felt sweat on my brow and in my fist clutching the cloth. Without betraying my spiraling fear, I replied, "I might prove more useful if your ladyship told me everything."

"Everything?" She regarded me with a hint of mirth in her cold gray eyes.

"Yes." My chest tightened, as if I were short of breath. "I was brought here for a purpose, wasn't I? At Whitehall, your ladyship told the duchess about my . . . my birthmark."

"So, you understood that. I wondered if you counted a fluency in French among your many hidden talents. How fascinating; you certainly have been busy."

The sweat trickled down my face, pooled in the hollow of my throat. The salt stung the bruises on my cheeks. "I taught myself," I said. "I am clever, yes. And if I knew who it is the duchess thinks I am, I could help you. I'm amenable to an arrangement that will serve us both."

It was a pathetic deceit, born of desperation, and she responded with startling laughter.

"Would you, indeed? Then you're not as clever as I'd supposed. Do you think I'd be stupid enough to trust you, now that I know you protect that Boleyn whore? However, you have solved my dilemma. Shelton, watch him while I see to His Majesty."

She glided to the bed. I stealthily tucked the cloth into my jerkin pocket, pushing it down against the inside seam as I braved a glance at Master Shelton. He avoided all eye contact, his gaze fixed ahead, but I knew that if I made any move to escape he would leap into action. He had the reflexes of a soldier—which is why I found it disconcerting that he didn't seem to notice Sidney shifting away from the alcove where he'd retreated.

In Sidney's wake, the curtains stirred.

I turned my attention to the bed. Mistress Alice had finished mixing the powder in the goblet. Edward didn't stir or protest as Lady Dudley reached down to smooth his coverlets and rearrange his pillows. He stared fixedly at her through his pain-laced eyes when she took the goblet from Mistress Alice and, placing one hand under his head, propped him up.

"Drink," she said, and Edward did. She smiled. "Now rest. Rest and dream of angels."

His eyes closed. He seemed to melt into his pillows. Turning away, Lady Dudley set the goblet on the table and reached into the medicine chest. She brought up something, made a sudden movement. Steel slashed. There was no sound. A gush of scarlet sprayed from Mistress Alice's throat, splattering the carpet and the bed. Before my horrified eyes, she fell to her knees, looking straight at me, then crumpled onto the floor.

"NOOO!" My wail erupted from me like a wounded howl. I sprang forth. Master Shelton rushed at me, seizing my left arm to yank it behind my back. My cry was cut short, the pain searing through my torn shoulder muscles.

"I told you not to meddle," he hissed in my ear. "Be still. You cannot stop this."

I panted with helpless rage, watching Lady Dudley drop the bloodied knife and step over Mistress Alice's convulsing body. Blood pumped out from under her, darkening the carpet.

"Kill him," she told Master Shelton.

I kicked back with all my strength. I felt my heel slam into the steward's shin, rammed my elbow simultaneously into his chest. It was like hitting granite; yet with a surprised grunt, Master Shelton released me.

Sidney scooped up the sword and thrust it at me as I dove for the alcove, where a draft now blew through the curtains. I heard Lady Dudley cry out, heard the door open, heard furious shouting; but I didn't pause to see how many were entering the room to come after me.

Something whined and popped. I ducked as the ball flew past and embedded itself in the wall. Someone, perhaps one of the Dudley retainers with Henry, had a firearm. Such weapons were lethal but difficult to manage at close range. I knew it would take a good minute to reload and ignite the matchlock. It was all the time I had.

I leapt onto the windowsill, squeezing through the open window. With sword in hand, and my heart in my throat, I dropped into the night.

I hit the stone leads of the story below with teeth-rattling impact. The sword flew from my hand, clattering off the edge into the courtyard below. Sprawled, my head reeling, the agony was so intense I thought I had shattered both my legs. Then I realized I could move, despite the pain, and glanced up to the window through which I'd just leapt in time to see a long-nosed hand-pistol belch smoke.

I rolled. A ball struck the spot where I'd lain and ricocheted against the palace wall.

"A pox on it," I heard Henry Dudley curse. "I missed him. Don't worry. I'll get him."

The pistol disappeared for reloading. I forced myself upright. Standing as flat against the wall as I could, I looked to either side with a sickening drop in my bowels. The leads weren't leads at all. Instead of a walkway there was an extended parapet with a decorative balustrade, punctuated by stucco nymphs and running parallel with an indoor gallery. At the far end I could see a mullioned casement and the turrets of a water gate. At any moment someone above me would realize the same and race downstairs to finish me off.

I had no escape.

Think. Don't panic. Breathe. Forget everything else. Forget Mistress Alice. Forget her blood seeping into the floor. . . .

To the left rose the moldering roof of the tower housing the secret staircase. To the right stood the gate. I began edging in that direction, away from the light spilling from the window above. I didn't know that much about firearms but Master Shelton did, for he had served in the Scottish wars. He once remarked to me that guns were a primitive weapon, infamous for not igniting when lit, missing targets despite perfect aim, or backfiring due to poorly packed powder. It was too much to hope that Henry might blow his own face off, and instinct urged me to put as much distance between me and that window as I could.

Instinct proved correct. I froze as the pistol fired again. This time Henry displayed remarkably improved marksmanship, the ball spraying grotesquerie right above my shoulder. Tiny shards of plaster flew into my face. It wasn't until I felt the warm trickle of blood that I realized the ball had grazed me, as well.

"You got him!" Henry guffawed. Someone else had fired the shot. I continued my precarious advance. My escape must have addled their wits. I was surprised that whoever had the gun hadn't realized they could far more effectively shoot at me from the gallery.

The pistol pulled back. I quickened my step, nearing a casement. I hoped there wouldn't be shutters, locks, small leaded panes I couldn't smash. Between the pain in my legs and the throbbing in my shoulder, I was feeling faint. Another pop came, the ball razing the air above my head.

I struggled forward, flat with the wall.

The casement swung open. I halted when I saw a figure step onto the parapet with feline stealth. It paused. Another shot rang out, sending plaster flying. It turned. In the moonlight, I caught the gleam of dark eyes.

Then the figure started moving. Toward me.

My entire being clamored an urgent warning, even as I stood transfixed by the sight of the man approaching me in complete disregard for his own safety.

Two distinct impressions went through me in those crucial seconds. The first was that he moved as if he'd been tripping over rooftops all his life. The second was that either he'd come to finish the job for the Dudleys or he sought to rescue me.

When I spied the curved blade in his gloved hand, I realized

I shouldn't wait to find out. Hopefully I had come close enough to the water gate. If not, I wasn't likely to regret my error.

I sprang forth with all the strength I had left.

And leapt out into nothingness.

Chapter Twenty

I plunged feetfirst into the river. I had kept my body pointed like a blade, knowing that if I hit the surface any other way I would certainly die. Still, it was like falling into slate, the impact yanking all air from my lungs with terrifying suddenness. I gasped, flailed to the surface. The brackish taste of salt mixed with dregs and mud clogged my nostrils, my throat, my ears. I coughed it out, trying to gain control of my floundering body.

The river flowed all around me, a swift current flooded by the tidal influx, its inky back littered with branches and leaves. A bloated corpse of something bobbed nearby, sank briefly, and resurfaced. Caught in the current, the corpse and I were like flotsam, dragged along while I, at least, struggled to stay above water.

My left shoulder had gone numb, as had my arm. Gazing back toward the dwindling palace, I envisioned my would-be assassin staring down in disbelief. I also understood just how far a jump it had been. It was amazing I had survived at all.

And once again I was going to drown.

I struggled to swim sideways against the current, toward a

distant cluster of trees on a shore, evading the putrid corpse. I couldn't ignore how dire my situation had become. I'd been shot, or at least skimmed by a ball, and must be losing blood. The cold had also begun to affect my lungs, making it difficult to breathe and move at the same time. Even while my heart and head roared, somewhere deep within, in that dark place where nothing has consequence, I wanted to stop, go still, drift, and let it all pass.

The shore wavered like a desert mirage. Submerged in an icy, suffocating cocoon, I stared toward it with faltering eyes, my arms inexorably ceasing their futile movements. In a rush of panic, I thrashed my legs, seeking to quicken my blood. Nothing moved. Or I didn't feel anything move. I kicked again, in desperation. There was something twined about my ankles.

"No," I heard myself whisper. "Not like this. Please, God. No."

An eternity passed. I tried to bring my legs up to my unfeeling hands and untangle whatever had wrapped about me. I was feeling better. Strange warmth welled under my skin. The cold had ceased its stinging assault.

I sighed. It was just a skein of riverweed or an old rope. . . .

That was the last thing I thought before the water closed over my head.

Rain, intermixed with what sounded like fistfuls of gravel being flung against a rooftop, was the first thing I heard, the first sound that told me I was miraculously still alive.

Cracking open a grit-sealed eye, I tried to raise my head. The pounding in my temples and a wave of nausea told me I'd best stay put.

After the spinning in my head waned, I tentatively lifted the sheet covering me. I appeared intact, though my torso was a mass of contusions. I wore a linen undergarment—not my own—and my bruised chest was bare. When I tried to move my left arm, sharp pain coursed through my bandaged shoulder. I looked up. The room was unfamiliar; sprawled in slumber across the rushes near the door was a silver dog.

"Some watchdog," I muttered.

As I drifted back to sleep I thought the dog looked remarkably like Elizabeth's.

When I next awoke, delicate sunlight drifted in shafts throughout the room. The dog was gone. I also found, to my relief, that I was both less stiff and less sensitive, and I could sit up, albeit with much clumsy maneuvering. Easing a pillow under my head, I reclined against the daub wall and prodded my wounded shoulder. It was tender to the touch. Oily salve seeped through the bandage. In addition to tending to my obvious bodily functions, someone had taken the time to dress and treat my injury.

Lying on the bed as afternoon faded into dusk, I glanced from the door to the half-shuttered window. I heard water dripping from gutters. The slant in the ceiling led me to deduce I was lodged in a garret. I wondered when whoever had brought me here would make his or her appearance. I could still remember plummeting through seemingly endless abyss, crashing into black water. I even had a faint recollection of trying to stay afloat, swimming for a time against a sweeping current. After that, nothing. I had no idea how I had been rescued or ended up here.

My eyelids started to droop. I blinked. I couldn't be certain what I'd find upon awakening. Despite my efforts, I slipped off again, only to be jolted awake by the creaking of the door. I struggled upright. When I saw her walk in, bearing a tray, I stared in disbelief.

"I'm pleased to see you awake." She pulled up a stool by the bed and set the tray beside it. She wore a russet gown laced over a chemise. Tendrils of lustrous hair curled about her face. I couldn't believe how, given my state, my loins could react to her proximity. But they did.

She uncovered the tray, releasing the aroma of hot bread and soup.

Water flooded my mouth. "God," I said, in a hoarse voice I didn't recognize, "I'm starving."

"You should be." Kate unfolded a napkin, leaned over to tie it about my neck. "You've been lying here for four days. We were afraid you might never wake up."

Four days . . .

I averted my eyes. I wasn't ready to remember everything.

"And you've been here," I ventured, "all this time . . . caring for me?"

She broke the bread in chunks over the soup, ladled a spoon, and cooled it with her breath before lifting it to my lips. "Yes, but don't worry. You look like any other naked man."

Was I so bruised that the birthmark on my hip had gone unnoticed? Or was she being tactful? A closer look at her didn't reveal anything, and I was too flustered at the moment to ask.

"This soup is delicious," I said.

"Don't change the subject." She narrowed her eyes. "What on earth possessed you to stay behind in that room, when you should have followed Her Grace and Barnaby? I'll have you know, we risked our lives waiting for you at the gate. Her Grace refused to budge. She kept saying you'd arrive at any moment, that you knew the woman attending His Majesty and had tarried to question her. It was only when we heard gunshots and saw the duke's retainers coming out from every doorway that she agreed to leave. She wasn't happy about it, though. She said it was nothing less than cowardly of us to abandon you."

"But she did go? She's safe now, at her manor?"

Kate refilled the spoon. "Safe is a relative term. Yes, it's been given out that she's at Hatfield, where she's taken to her bed with fever. Illness can be a useful deterrent at times like these, as she well knows. Of course, so can the cellars of numerous neighboring houses in Hatfield's vicinity, any one of which would gladly shelter a princess should the duke's men be spotted on the road."

"And you?" I asked. "Why are you not with her?"

"I stayed with Peregrine, of course. He insisted that we look for you."

"Peregrine found me?"

"He did, on the riverbank. He told us he used to fish the Thames for bodies." She paused. A slight tremor crept into her voice. "He said we had to keep searching, that in the end everything washes up. He was right. You'd been swept upstream by the tide and appeared near where the river bends. You were soaked through, wounded and delirious. But alive."

"And you nursed me back to health." I heard the sullen gratitude in my voice. It had become second nature for me to doubt even my good fortune. "Why? You lied to me about not working for Cecil. Why care if I lived or died, as long as you did your master's bidding?"

She set down the spoon, dabbed my mouth and chin clean with the napkin. When she finally spoke, her voice was composed.

"I apologize that I didn't tell you the entire truth. I never meant to put you in danger. My loyalty has always been to Her Grace, though she can be too headstrong and often needs protection from herself, whether or not she cares to admit it. When Walsingham told me that Master Cecil felt it best if we got her away from Greenwich, I agreed to help. I didn't tell you because he said you had your own orders. He said you had been hired and paid."

She paused. "I didn't expect you. But I am glad of it. I . . . I am glad you are here."

I observed her face as she talked. I saw what she meant. But as the events of the past days began to seep in, pain and anger arose in me. I didn't want complications; I didn't want vulnerabilities or heartache. Feeling something for her would bring me all those things.

"Walsingham gave me instructions, yes," I replied. "And I was paid. But I also knew that allowing Her Grace to go ahead with her plan to meet with Lord Robert would put her in more danger than she'd incurred already. I'm surprised no one else shared my concern."

"What would you have had us do?" If she'd detected the deliberate harshness in my manner, she didn't let it show. "She insisted on questioning Robert about her brother and wouldn't hear anything to the contrary. None of us could have known that the duke intended to woo her himself or put Jane Grey on the throne if she refused him."

That made sense. I should rest my suspicions, at least as far as Kate was concerned. She'd not been involved in any plot against Elizabeth.

As if she had read my thoughts, she smiled gently. She knew how to pluck a chord in me, much as a hand knows a lute. In my inept attempt to hide my discomfort, I said the first thing that came into my head: "It's not fair to test a man who doesn't have his clothes on."

She laughed. "You've managed well enough thus far."

I wanted to weep. In some indefinable way, she reminded me of Mistress Alice, of the garnet-cheeked honest girl that Alice must have been in her youth. And as I thought of this, I saw again the triumphant look in Alice's eyes when she turned to me by the king's bed. She had been trying to tell me something, but I would never know now.

I met Kate's gaze. "I thought I was going to die. . . ." I faltered. Conflict surged again in me, without warning, inundating me in darkness. "Where are we?" I asked in a taut whisper.

"In a manor not far from Greenwich town. Why?"

"Whose manor? Who is here with us?"

She frowned. "Her Grace owns the deed, privately; the house is leased to a friend. Besides Peregrine, you, and me, Walsingham comes and goes. He was here earlier in fact, wanting to know how you— Brendan, what is it? What is wrong?"

I hadn't realized I had recoiled until I saw the alarm on her face. "That's who I saw on the leads. Walsingham. He had a dagger. It's why I jumped. I remember now. Cecil arranged Her Grace's escape, but he wanted me dead. He sent Walsingham to kill me."

"No," she said quietly. "You have it wrong. Walsingham was there to help you. We would never have known where to look had he not told us he'd seen you leap into the river. He even fetched your sword from where it had fallen into the courtyard."

"Maybe he had no other choice! The sword was evidence I'd been in Edward's presence. I might survive the fall, as I did."

"But you still wouldn't have been found, not in that current.

You had a wounded shoulder. There were rope and riverweeds wrapped about your legs. By all rights, you should have drowned." She paused. "Cecil entrusted Walsingham with your welfare. He's been watching over you the entire time. That's why he was on those leads. When we failed to show up at the postern gate, he followed our trail."

I let out a harsh chuckle. "I wonder where he was when the duchess of Suffolk and her henchman locked me in an underground cell and left me to drown." Yet even as I spoke I thought of my jerkin, which I'd left by the pavilion and which had inexplicably materialized near the ruined cloister entrance, where Peregrine found it. What had the boy said?

If we hadn't happened to find your jerkin, we'd never have thought to look . . .

"Peregrine told us about that," said Kate. "At the time you were taken, Walsingham was readying the horses we never took. Surely, you can't fault him?"

"Not unless you take into account that everyone I've met at court, not to mention everyone I've known since childhood, has proven false," I retorted. The instant the words were out, I regretted it. Kate bit her lip. "I'm sorry," she murmured. She stood.

I caught hold of her hand. "No. I'm the one who must apologize. I . . . I didn't mean it."

She looked down at our twined hands, lifted her gaze to me. "Yes, you did." She unhooked her fingers. "I understand. That woman . . . Barnaby said she was an herbalist brought by the Dudleys to poison His Majesty. He said you knew her, that they lied to you about her death. How could you not be angry?"

My throat knotted. I looked away, tears burning in my eyes. I didn't see Kate reach into her pocket, only felt her set something in my hand. When I saw what it was, I went still.

"I found this in your jerkin pocket. I took the liberty of polishing it. It's a strange thing, but pretty." She took up the tray, went to the door. "I'll be back in a few hours with your supper. Try to get some rest."

The door clicked shut.

I gazed at the gift that Alice had given me. It was a delicate gold petal, its jagged edge indicating it had once formed part of a larger jewel. On its tip, like a perfect dewdrop, was a ruby. I had never seen anything like it. It was the last thing I'd have expected her to possess.

I enclosed it in my hand as dusk faded into night.

When grief finally came to claim me, I did not fight it.

Chapter Twenty-one

Kate returned with a bundle of clothes and her tray heaped with meat on trenchers and sauced vegetables. Peregrine was with her, grinning. He carried a folded table. After he set it up, he returned with my saddlebag, and, to my surprise, the king's sheathed sword, which I'd last seen clattering off the leads at Greenwich. I opened the bag to examine its jumbled contents. I sighed in relief when I found the stolen psalm book, still wrapped in its protective cloth.

I turned to Kate. She'd changed into a rose velvet gown that enhanced the muted gold in her hair. As she busied herself lighting candles about the room, I acknowledged my desire to draw her into my arms and caress away the last of my mistrust. But Peregrine demanded my attention, dancing about like a precocious imp, Elizabeth's silver hound at his heels.

"You look rather pleased with yourself," I said as he helped me to my feet and into a robe. "And isn't that Her Grace's hound? Have you been thieving again?"

"I have not," he replied. "Her Grace left Urian here with us, so we could track you. He's the best tracker in her kennels, she said. She knows her beasts. He was the first to smell you on the riverbank." He paused, his nose crimping. "What is it with you and water? You've done nothing but get wet since we met."

I burst out laughing. It felt wonderful. I took Peregrine's hand, made my slow but steady way to the dinner table. "Unrepentant as always," I said, easing onto a stool. "I'm glad of you, my friend." I looked at Kate. "And you. I thank God for both of you. You saved my life. It's a debt I can never repay."

The sheen in Kate's eyes might have been tears. She brushed them aside with her sleeve, and Peregrine perched next to me as she started to serve.

"I'm not helpless," I said, as Peregrine handed me my plate. "I can feed myself."

Kate wagged her finger. "He's not here to feed you. You've had quite enough pampering. Peregrine, either you tell that dog to get its paws off the table or you can both go eat in the kitchen."

Amid laughter and candlelight, we dined and spoke of innocuous matters. Only after we'd wiped up the last of the sauce with our bread and Peregrine had recounted for the hundredth time how he and Barnaby employed Urian's olfactory skills to track me did I breach our camaraderie. Leaning back in my chair, I said as casually as I could, "And where is Fitzpatrick?"

The rustle of Kate's skirts as she stood broke the sudden silence. She began stacking the empty platters. Peregrine reached down to caress Urian.

"The king is dead, isn't he?" I said.

Kate paused. Peregrine nodded sadly. "It's not been officially announced, but Master Walsingham told us he died yesterday. Barnaby returned to court as soon as we found you, to be at his side. It's said that at the hour of Edward's death, heaven wept."

The rain. I had heard it.

As the memory of that youth rotting away in a fetid room surfaced in me, my gaze went to the sword on the bed. My voice tightened. "And the herbalist? Did Walsingham say anything about her?"

Kate said quickly, "Brendan, please, let it be. It's too soon. You're still weak."

"No. I want to know. I . . . I need to know."

"Then I will tell you." She sat at my side. "She is dead. Sidney told Walsingham. Someone took her body away. No one knows where. The Dudleys threatened to kill Sidney for helping you, but by then word had gotten out that Elizabeth had escaped and the palace was in an uproar. Brendan, no. Sit down. You cannot—"

I came to my feet. Resisting the dizziness that came over me, I paced to the window to stare into the night. My stalwart Alice was dead. She was gone forever this time. Lady Dudley had slashed her throat as if she'd been some barnyard beast, and left her to bleed to death.

I couldn't think of it. I couldn't. It would drive me insane.

"What about Jane Grey?" I said quietly. "Has she been declared queen?"

"Not yet. But the duke removed her and Guilford to London. And there are rumors he will send men after the Lady Mary."

"I thought he already had. I thought he sent Lord Robert after her."

"It seems he had to delay. We think that after he discovered Elizabeth had fled Greenwich, he wanted to first get Lady Jane somewhere safe. She is all he has now."

I nodded. "Peregrine," I said. "Can you leave us, please?"

The boy rose and left, Urian padding behind. Kate and I faced each other from across the room. Then she stood and turned to pick up the tray. "We can talk tomorrow."

I stepped to her. "I agree. Only . . . don't leave." My voice broke. "Please."

She came to where I stood helpless and put her hand on my bearded cheek. "It's so red," she said. "And thick. I wouldn't have thought you'd have such a thick beard."

"And I," I whispered, "never thought you'd care."

She regarded me steadily. "Neither did I. But there you have it."

I brought her to me, held her close, as though I might meld her to me forever.

"I've never done this before," I said.

"Never?" She raised her eyes to me in genuine surprise.

"No," I said. "I only ever loved one woman. . . ." I stroked her cheek. "And you?"

She smiled. "Suitors have been begging for my hand since I was a babe, of course."

"Then add my name to the list." The words did not discon-cert me as much as I had supposed. I had never fallen in love before; now it seemed the most natural thing in the world.

She looked into my eyes. "Must we wait that long?" She took my hands, guided them to her bodice. I undid the laces. The bod-ice slipped from her shoulders. Moments later, she was stepping out of her skirts, shrugging off her chemise until she stood naked, pat-terned in candlelight and slivers of moon, desirable as no woman I'd ever seen.

I gathered her up, burying my face in her breasts. She gasped involuntarily as I carried her to the bed, where she reclined and watched me cast off my robe before she sat up on her knees to help me pull my shift over my head. My shoulder ached. She frowned at the fresh spotting of blood on the bandage. "I should change that," she said.

"It can wait," I replied against her lips. As I drew back, her gaze traveled down my torso, resting for a moment on the blemish on my hip. Then she brought her gaze lower.

I lay down beside her. Her experienced air did not deceive me. Under my hand I could feel her pulse racing, and I knew that if she had explored the ways of the flesh to a certain extent, in the end, like so many girls of breeding, she'd remained shy of the consummation.

But I soon discovered that I too was innocent, in every way a man can be. As I pressed her length against me and we tasted each other with fervor, I realized I could not hope to compare this luxury to my rambunctious couplings with the castle maids and damsels at the fairs. I worshipped as I might at a temple, until the desire in Kate's eyes turned to flame and she was shuddering beneath me, rising to meet my ardor. Only once did she cry out, but softly.

After we were spent and she cradled in my arms, I whispered, "Did I hurt you?"

She laughed shakily. "If that was pain, I never want to know anything else." She spread her hands over my chest, resting her fingers on my heart. "All I want is here."

I smiled. "Be that as it may, I would still make an honest woman of you."

"For your information," she said, "I am eighteen. I can make my own decisions. And I'm not sure I want to be an honest woman quite yet."

I chuckled. "Well, when you do decide, let me know. I should at least request Her Grace's blessing; you are her lady. And your mother, I'm sure she too will want to be asked."

She sighed. "My mother is dead. But I think she would have liked you."

I detected an old pain in her voice. "I'm sorry. When did she pass away?"

"When I was five." She smiled. "She was so young when she bore me: just fourteen."

"And your father . . . was he also young?"

She gave me a curious look. "I'm a bastard. And no, he wasn't. Not as young as her."

"I see." I did not look away. "Do you want to tell me?"

She was quiet for a moment. Then she said, "It wasn't a love affair. My mother was born of servants who served the Carey household; they died in the sweating sickness outbreak that killed Mary Boleyn's first husband. When she remarried and became Mistress Stafford, my mother served her. Mistress Stafford wasn't rich; her new husband Will Stafford was a common soldier but she had two children by her first marriage, a stipend, and her late husband had left her a house. She also liked my mother, so she offered her a post as her maid."

"This Mary Stafford," I said, "is she the same who was sister to Anne Boleyn?"

"Yes, but she had none of her sister's pride, God rest her soul. When my mother became pregnant, the morning sickness gave her away. She was terrified; but Mistress Stafford did not utter a word of reproach. She knew the hardship women can suffer, so she bundled my mother up and sent her to live under Lady Mildred Cecil's care. I was born in the Cecil household."

So, this explained Kate's connection to Cecil. She had lived under his roof.

"Did Mistress Stafford know who your father was?" I asked.

"She must have suspected. My mother never said his name aloud, but there weren't that many men of age in her household who would have taken the liberty. It must have hurt her deeply.

Mary had been married to him less than a year, risked her family's displeasure and exile from court to be with him." Kate sat up, pushing her hair aside. "He's still alive. I saw him at Mistress Stafford's funeral. We have the same eyes."

I was quiet, struck by the similarities—and crucial differences—between us.

"Of course, Mistress Stafford would have understood," she added. "After all, she'd been Henry the Eighth's mistress before her sister Anne caught his eye; she knew fidelity is not a man's best asset, and no woman invites misfortune willingly. But she let my mother keep her secret and raise me herself, without interference. She also left us with the Cecils. I think she wanted to keep my mother safe and away from her husband."

She paused. "I owe her everything. Because of her kindness, my mother wasn't turned out to beg. We lived well; I had a good childhood. I received an education. Lady Mildred saw to it, being an educated woman herself. I'm one of the few ladies in Her Grace's service who is literate. That's why she trusts me. If a message needs to be destroyed, I can memorize it."

"I can see why she would trust you," I said. "How did your mother die?"

"She caught a fever. It was quick, painless. I saw Mistress Stafford a few times after my mother passed; she was always gracious. She died three years later."

"And the man you believe is your father . . . ?" I ventured.

"He has remarried. He has children. I don't fault him. I think he took my mother as men do, in a moment of lust, without thought for the consequences. If he knows about me, he's never shown it. I've lived all of my life without him. But I use his surname. It's the least he can do," she said, with a mischievous smile. "It's not as if there aren't hundreds of Staffords in England."

She poked my chest with her finger. "Your turn. I want to make an honest man out of you." It was out before she even realized what she'd said. She took one look at my face and flinched. "Forgive me. I sometimes speak before I think. If you don't want to talk, I understand."

I cupped her chin. "No, I don't want secrets between us." I paused. "The truth is I don't know who my mother is. I was abandoned as a babe. Mistress Alice raised me."

"You were abandoned?" she echoed. I nodded, waiting for her to collect her thoughts. "Then Mistress Alice . . . *she* was the woman in the king's room?"

"Yes. She saved me." As I uttered these words, I felt an overpowering need to tell someone, to leave the memory in someone other than myself, so she'd never be forgotten. "I was left in the priest's cottage near Dudley Castle, presumably to die. I was later told it happens more than we think—unwanted babies dropped off on noble thresholds—in the hope the rich will take pity on what the poor can't afford. I would have none of it; according to Mistress Alice, I made enough fuss to wake the dead. She heard me wailing all the way from the slop pit, where she was dumping leavings, so she went to investigate."

My voice caught. I steadied it, focusing on Kate's eyes for strength. "She was like the mother I never knew. When she died—or rather, when I was *told* she died—I couldn't forgive her for leaving me without saying good-bye."

"That is why you agreed to help Her Grace. You knew she needed to say good-bye."

"Yes. I couldn't let her suffer what I had. I know what it is like to lose someone unexpectedly. I believed Mistress Alice was dead. Peregrine mentioned a woman caring for the king when I first met him, and for a moment I felt . . . But I never truly thought it was her. I couldn't. Even when I saw her . . ." I paused again. My voice trembled. "They cut out her tongue, did something to her legs to hobble her. Master Shelton, their steward, whom I'd looked up to, who had told me of her death—he stood there and did nothing when Lady Dudley stabbed her. She bled to death and he did nothing."

The recollection was like shards in my gut. I had been a fool to ever think Master Shelton would choose me over duty. To be a loyal servant, in everything it entailed, was what he knew. I might have pitied him for his stolid, meaningless life, had I not burned for vengeance.

There was a long silence. Kate's hair draped like a curtain about her. She lifted tear-filled eyes. "Forgive me for how I spoke of her death. It was selfish. I . . . I didn't want you to hurt."

I kissed her. "My brave Kate, you couldn't have prevented my pain. It happened long before I met you. I lost Alice on that day they took her from me. The woman I met in His Majesty's chamber wasn't the woman I knew. Now I know the truth. I know she didn't abandon me. Lady Dudley must have ordered her taken on the road, and Shelton was her accomplice."

"But why would they do such a terrible thing? It happened long before the King fell ill, yes? Why did they want you to believe she was dead?"

I smiled grimly. "I've been asking myself the same thing. I think it's because of what she knew. I'm certain of it. Mistress Alice knew who I am."

She stared at me. "Does this have something to do with that piece of jewelry?"

In response, I rose, padded naked from the bed to my crumpled robe. From the pocket I withdrew the jewel. The ruby caught the moonlight filtering through the window as I handed it to her. "I think it's a piece of my past," I said. A shudder ran through me. "Mistress Alice gave it to me, and I think it's because in that moment she recognized me. I don't think she knew me before; she'd suffered too much. But she kept that gold petal with her for a reason. It means something. It has to."

Kate gazed upon it. "Yes, but what?"

I took it back from her, ran my fingertips over the fragile veined gold. "Mistress Alice never had much use for anything save her herbs. She didn't covet material things. She used to say things took up too much room. Yet she kept this object hidden in her medicine chest for God only knows how many years. I went through her chest many times; she used to scold me, saying I'd intoxicate myself with some herb. But I never found it. She hid it in some compartment. She must have. I have a feeling that not even Lady Dudley knew she had it."

I looked past her to the window. "Lady Dudley is the key to all this. She used me to force the duchess to agree to wed her daughter Jane Grey to Guilford. The duchess said as much when she held me in that cell. Whatever this petal represents, it must be powerful enough to have warranted my death. It might even be the weapon I need to stop the Dudleys—for good."

She crossed her arms over her breasts, as if she felt a chill. "You'll seek revenge for what they did to her."

I returned my gaze to her. "How can I not? She was everything I had in the world, and they destroyed her. Yes, I seek revenge. But even more than that, I seek the truth." I leaned to her. "Kate, I need to know who I am."

"I know. It's just that I'm afraid for you. For us. This secret can't be good if the duchess of Suffolk wants to kill you to keep it quiet. And if the Dudleys used it against her, they must know what it is."

"Not every Dudley. Only Lady Dudley knows. I don't think she ever told the duke. She must have suspected he would betray her. She wasn't about to entrust him with the only weapon she had— her ability to coerce the duchess. Without her coercion, without this secret, I believe the duchess would never have agreed to give her daughter to a—"

"Lowborn Dudley," Kate mused. She regarded me thoughtfully. "Why don't you tell Master Cecil about this? He knows important people. Maybe he could help you."

"No." I grasped her hands. "Promise you'll not breathe a word of this to anyone, not even the princess—especially not her. Northumberland still holds power, perhaps now more than ever, and she may still need our help. It's best that I carry this burden on my own for now."

I silently asked forgiveness for my lie. I couldn't risk exposing her to that frozen hatred I'd seen in Lady Dudley's eyes, nor did I want murderous Stokes stalking her on the duchess's behalf. I would become a hunted man once it was discovered I was still alive. Whatever happened, Kate must be kept safe. Still, what I must ask of her next would hurt.

"I need you to do something for me. I need you to promise you'll return to Hatfield."

She bit her lip. "And if I refuse?"

"Then I'll remind you that Elizabeth still needs you. None of her servants have your skills, which she may require in the days to come. You know it as well as me. Just as you know, but haven't yet said, that Cecil has an assignment for me. It's why Walsingham has been coming and going, inquiring after my health. He's not that solicitous."

"I don't care," she whispered. She thumped the mattress with her fist. "Let them find someone else. You've risked enough. Not even Her Grace would ask more of you."

"Yet I would do more. So would you. How can you not? You love her."

"And you?" she asked, haltingly. "Do you . . . love her?"

I pulled her to me. "Only as my princess. She deserves that much, I think."

Wrapped in my embrace, Kate murmured, "They say her mother was cursed. Sometimes I wonder if Elizabeth carries it in her blood. Robert Dudley threw himself at her feet; so did his father. Yet when she denied them, they turned on her like wolves. Can it be that the spell she weaves can just as easily turn men to hatred as it can to love?"

"For her sake, I pray not." I let the moment pass. "Will you go?"

She sighed. "Not now."

Chapter Twenty-two

When I awoke the next morning, it was to an empty bed. I was taken aback. Then I chuckled, passing a hand over my tousled hair. The trestle table had been dismantled, the stools set in a row against the wall. Folded in a pile by the bed were the clothes she'd brought me. Otherwise, it was as if Kate hadn't been here at all.

I started to slide out of bed when the door opened. She appeared with towel, basin, and a small coffer—once again in her russet gown, her hair braided, neat as if she'd spent an uneventful night. I hugged her as she set the articles down, drowning out her feigned protest with my mouth. She clung to me for a moment before she pushed me away.

"Enough." She went to retrieve a tray. "Walsingham is downstairs. He wants to see you as soon as you break your fast."

"That's what I was trying to do." I reached out to grab her again.

She pranced away, elusive as dandelion seed. "You'll have to content yourself with last night, for that's all I plan to give until you put a roof over my head." She tossed the towel at me.

I laughed. "This from the wanton who assured me she had all she wanted last night."

"A woman can always change her mind. Now, behave yourself whilst I wash you."

I affected a penitent stance, though it took concentration as she cleaned me from head to foot, lathering and rinsing without discrimination. Only when she undid my bandage to replace it did I wince. "Does it hurt?" she asked.

"A bit." I glanced at the wound. It was as ugly as I expected. "Corrupted?"

"It was. But you're fortunate. The ball shredded and took a few layers of skin, nothing more." From the coffer she extracted a jar and proceeded to swab green salve over my shoulder. I stood immobile. Like Mistress Alice, she was an herbalist.

"It's a French recipe," she explained, "rosemary, turpentine, and rose oil. It hastens healing." With expert fingers she applied a fresh bandage, tucking it under my armpit. "It'll have to suffice. It's uncomfortable, but I'm assuming a few more days in bed are out of the question."

I pecked the tip of her nose. "You know me too well."

She helped me into my clothes—shirt, new leather jerkin, breeches, and a belt with a pouch. I was surprised when she produced soft kid boots in almost my exact size.

"Peregrine bought them at the local market. He got himself a cap and cloak, as well. He says he's going to be your manservant once you get rich."

"He's got a long wait." I turned about. "Presentable?"

"A prince." She served me bread and cheese and dark ale, which we consumed in companionable silence, though I could sense her anxiety.

"Is it bad news?" I finally said.

"With Walsingham, it usually is. But I've no idea what he wants. He didn't say anything other than that I fetch you." She grimaced. "Now that I'm no longer required, I've reverted to being another ignorant woman in his eyes. Never mind that I'm as able as any hooligan he could hire, or can pick locks and intrigue with the best of them."

"Not to mention, you've a temper. If I were him, I'd watch my step."

"You're the one who needs to watch his step." Kate faced me as she'd done that afternoon—it seemed ages ago—in the gallery at Greenwich. "Whatever he wants of you, you can rest assured it won't be safe."

"I thought he helped save my life," I reminded her.

"He did. That doesn't mean I trust him with it. He's a serpent, out for his own advantage. I don't think even Cecil can control him." Her voice wavered. "Promise me you'll not agree to anything dangerous. I said I'll go to Hatfield and I will, but I don't want to spend all my time sick with worry over you."

I nodded solemnly. "I promise. Now, show me the way."

She pointed to the door. "Down the stairs and to your right. He's in the study off the hall." She turned away. "I'll be in the garden, hanging sheets."

The image brought a smile to my face as I took the stairs to the ground floor and moved through the country house, which was sparsely furnished, a refreshing change after the spiked opulence of court. Outside the hall I paused before a door and took a deep breath.

I pulled it open. Like Kate, I likened Walsingham to a serpentine presence. His alleged contribution to my survival had done nothing to change this impression. Rather, it was unnerving to know that the man had been ghosting me since Whitehall, watching but not interfering, until that night on the leads. I wasn't convinced of his motives but hid my discomfort at the sight of his gaunt figure seated at the desk, Urian's head resting on his thigh.

"Squire Prescott." His spidery hand caressed Urian with hypnotic repetition. "You've recovered with alacrity, I see. The vigor of youth, and of a woman's care, are indeed a marvel."

His tone indicated he knew more of said care than I preferred. I had to force myself not to order Urian away, appalled by the dog's lack of discernment.

"I was told you wanted to see me?"

"Ever to the point." His bloodless lips twitched. "Why waste time on the superfluous?"

"I hope you weren't expecting a friendly chat."

"I never expect anything." His hand paused in its stroking of the dog's ears. "That's what makes life so interesting. People never fail to surprise." He gestured to a stool opposite his. "Pray, sit. All I require is your attention."

Because my shoulder was starting to pain me, I obliged. I had that vague feeling of unease I now recognized. Cecil and his men seemed to exude it like disease.

"Jane Grey and Guilford Dudley have been taken to the Tower," he said without warning.

I bolted upright on my chair. "Arrested?"

"No. It's traditional for a sovereign to lodge there before the coronation." He eyed me.

"I see." My voice tightened. "So, they're going to do it. They're going to force the crown on that innocent girl's head, regardless."

"That innocent girl, as you call her, is a traitor. She usurps another woman's throne and now awaits her coronation with all

the dignitaries of the court at her side. Thus far, the only com-
punction she's shown is her continued refusal to allow her husband to be crowned alongside her—to the collective Dudley
fury."

I contained my revulsion. Of course Walsingham would
brand Jane Grey a traitor. It was always easier to view the world
through the prism of his convenience.

"By 'another woman,'" I said, "I assume you mean the Lady
Mary."

"Of course. Any change in the succession would require the
sanction of Parliament. I doubt our proud duke has gone so far
as to request official approval of his treason. So, by law, and
Henry the Eighth's will of succession, Lady Mary is our rightful
queen."

I paused, deliberating. "But the council has agreed to uphold
Jane as queen? Northumberland doesn't act alone?" I was thinking of the duchess, of her threats to bring down the Dudleys. If
she raised protest against this usurpation of *her* rights, it could
buy both princesses the time they needed.

Again I received his unblinking stare. "What exactly do you
ask, squire?"

"Nothing. I just want to clarify the situation." I watched him
fold his hands at his chin. Deprived of his caresses, Urian lay
down on the floor with a dejected sigh.

"The council members would agree to anything to save their
skins," continued Walsingham. "The duke has badgered them
into submission with threats that he has enough ammunition in
the Tower to crush any revolt in Mary's name. He's also garrisoned the surrounding castles. Still, our sources indicate not a
few of his so-called associates would as quickly see him hang as
give him further rein over England. He's made more enemies

than is safe for any man. He may also soon face significant opposition from the Lady Mary herself."

It was the longest speech I had heard from him, and it held a few unexpected surprises.

"Significant?" I said carefully. "I understood her Catholicism and doubtful legitimacy made her anything but."

"It would be wiser not to discredit her quite yet."

"I see. What is it you want of me?"

"The duke has not yet officially announced Edward's death; however, with Jane Grey in the Tower awaiting coronation, it can't be long in coming. Mary has let it be known she's at her manor of Hoddesdon, from where she continues to issue demands for information. We suspect someone at court has warned her to stay away. She has no resources to draw upon, however, and few will risk themselves for a princess whose own father and brother declared her a bastard and whose faith is at odds with their own. There is the possibility she'll flee the country, but we think it more likely she'll head for the northern border and her Catholic noble strongholds."

As if it were the most ordinary circumstance between us, Walsingham withdrew an envelope from his sleeve. "We want you to deliver this."

I didn't take it. "I assume that isn't a safe conduct to Spain."

"Its contents," he replied, "are of no concern to you."

I stood. "I beg to differ. Its contents could be my death, judging from past events. I'm as loyal as the next man, but even I have my limits. I need to know what it says before I agree to anything. And if you are not authorized to tell me," I added pointedly, "I suggest you tell Cecil to come here instead."

He deliberated for a moment. "Very well." He gave me a slight incline of his head. "It's from a few select lords on the council, an explanation of their predicament, if you will. It offers Mary their support, should she choose to fight for her throne. They would prefer she not abandon England, an absent queen being even less desirable than an illegal one."

"Hedging our bets, are we? She must have become quite significant, indeed."

"Accept the job or decline. It makes no difference to me. I can hire a dozen couriers."

Cecil was behind this, naturally; he had seen the way the matter could go. I had no illusions as to whether he wanted the duke's daughter-in-law or the Catholic heir on the throne, and so I took my time, smiling and patting my knee, enticing Urian to my side.

Walsingham's black eyes turned stony.

After enough time had elapsed to establish I was no longer his for the taking, I said, "Since our last engagement, my rate has gone up."

It pleased me to note that he visibly relished the introduction of money. It put us squarely in his terrain, where everything was open to negotiation. He removed a leather pouch from his doublet. "We are willing to double your fee, half in advance. If you do not deliver the letter or if Mary is captured, you forfeit the second half. Would you like me to put it in writing?"

I took the pouch and the letter. "That won't be necessary. I can always take care of any misunderstandings when I next see Cecil." I walked to the door and paused. "Anything else?"

He stared at me. "Yes. As you may know, time is of the essence. You must get to her before the duke's men. We also don't think it's wise for you to use your real name. You are now Daniel Beecham, son of Lincolnshire gentry. The persona is real enough; Cecil patronized the family before its demise. Daniel's mother died in childbed, his father died in Scotland. The boy himself was under Cecil's care until his own death years ago. Your beard should help with the disguise, so don't shave it. Master Beecham would be two years older than you if he were alive."

"So, I'm finally a dead man. My enemies will be pleased."

"It's for your protection," he said humorlessly.

I smiled. "Yes, I've been told how protective you are. I heard about your ill-timed venture to the stables while I was otherwise engaged, and of your aborted intervention on the leads. I can't help but wonder about the time before, when I was trapped in the monk's cell. It was you who found my jerkin by the lake, wasn't it? You dropped it at the entrance to alert Peregrine and Barnaby. A rather passive attempt, but I suppose I shouldn't complain." I reached for the door latch, resisting the jab in my shoulder. "Am I free to go?"

"In a minute." Walsingham's eyes flicked to Urian, who stood attentively by me. "Henry Dudley didn't fire the shot that hit you."

I didn't move.

"The steward Master Shelton held the pistol. I saw him take aim from the window. I thought you should know. He is, I believe, someone you trust?"

"Not anymore," I said, and I strode out.

In the hall, a scullery girl emptied the hearth of cinders. With a shy smile she indicated the way to the garden, which I found enclosed by walls and windswept with the scent of lavender.

Kate was doing as she said—hanging sheets on a line to dry. I crept up behind her, wrapped my arms about her waist. "Did you scrub them yourself?" I breathed in her ear. With a gasp, she let a pillowcase fly from her hand. Urian barked in delight, jumping up to seize it in midair. He trotted off with his trophy, tail held high.

Kate turned on me. "I'll have you know Holland cloth doesn't come cheap. Unless you indeed plan on getting rich, we've a household to economize for."

"I'll buy you a hundred pillowcases in Egyptian silk, if you like." I pressed the pouch in her hand. As she felt its weight, her eyes widened. She searched my face. Before she could voice the question that hung between us, I pulled her to me.

In my arms, she whispered, "When?"

I replied softly, "As soon as I can let go of you."

That night, as I finished packing my saddlebag for the trip, a knock came at my door. I suspected before I went to answer it who it was; neither Kate nor Peregrine would have requested admittance, and Walsingham would never climb stairs to see a hireling.

She stood in the passageway, cloaked head to toe in black velvet. Kate paused on the landing of the staircase behind her, a flickering candle in hand. As she met my eyes, I nodded. She turned away, but not before I saw her troubled expression.

I stepped aside. As Elizabeth moved into the room, I felt again that magnetic lure she seemed to exude like a scent. She pulled down her hood; it crumpled in soft waves about her long throat. She wore no jewelry, her fiery hair caught in a braided net. There were, I noticed, dark circles about her expressive eyes, as if she had spent a sleepless night.

I bowed low. "Your Grace, this is an unexpected honor."

She nodded absently, looking about. "So, this is where you

recovered? I trust you were well cared for." There was no hidden emphasis in her tone, no indication she had any idea of my involvement with Kate. I decided it would be better to leave it that way, at least for now. Kate would tell Elizabeth in her own time.

"Yes, very well cared for," I replied. "I believe I owe you my gratitude."

"You do?" One of her thin eyebrows arched.

"Yes. This is your house, is it not?"

She flicked her hand dismissively. "That's hardly reason for gratitude. It's but a house, after all. I have several, most of which stand empty." She paused. Her eyes met mine. "Rather, it is I, Master Prescott, who should be giving you thanks. What you did for me at Greenwich . . . I will never forget it."

"You had to know the truth. I understand that."

"Yes, apparently you do. Better than most." She smiled tremulously. It felt strange to be alone in this room with her, where I sweated out my feverish delirium, learned the terrible final fate of Mistress Alice, and discovered my love for Kate. I had forgotten how powerful a presence Elizabeth could be, how unique she was to her own environment. She did not seem to belong in this rustic room, her very essence too large for such a confined space. It did not escape me that she had also put herself at considerable risk to come here.

As if she read my thoughts, she said, "Do not worry, Cecil knows I am here. I insisted, and so he sent some men to escort me. They are downstairs, waiting. They'll take me back to Hatfield tomorrow." Her lips curled in disdain. "It seems henceforth I must get used to having these men about me at all times when away from my manor at Hatfield, at least until they bring Northumberland down."

There it was—spoken out loud, at long last.

"Is that what Cecil plans?" I said quietly.

She gave me a curious look. "Of course. Why else would they be sending you to my sister Mary? If she flees the country, she'll leave England wide open to the duke. Who knows what would happen to any of us, then? They'd rather a Catholic spinster took the throne than a Dudley. My poor sister." She let out a tart laugh. "Mary has always been either feared or disdained. Her lot is never easy. And now she faces the fight of her life. If the duke's henchmen get to her first . . ."

"They won't." I stepped to her. "I will not let them."

She regarded me in silence. Up close, I saw again the amber flecks in her irises that had so mesmerized me that first night, at the water gate of Whitehall; I recognized once more the dormant power lurking in the depths of her regard, which I now understood very few were capable of resisting. I had been ready to throw myself at her feet that night, to do almost anything to ensure her favor. I found it interesting that while I still felt the pull of her, I no longer was enslaved by it. I preferred it this way: I preferred being able to look the princess in the eye and recognize our shared humanity.

"Yes," she murmured, "I believe you will do just that. Cecil is right: You'll do anything to keep the Dudleys from winning. But, you do have a choice. You've paid your dues, as far as I am concerned. Even if you decided not to go on this errand, you'll have a place in my service."

I inclined my head with a smile, made myself take a small step back.

"What?" she said. "Does the choice not please? You did ask this of me once, at Whitehall, if I recall correctly: You said you wanted to serve me. Has Cecil made you a better offer, perhaps?"

"Not at all." I raised my gaze to her. "I am honored and grate-ful. But, that is not why Your Grace has come all this way. You already know I will serve you, no matter what."

She went still. Then she said, "Am I so obvious, then?"

"Only to those who care to look." I felt a hollow open inside me, as I considered everything she was, everything she stood for, and everything she might lose if she ever gave in to her own conflicted heart—that magnificent heart, which had propelled her to me tonight despite the peril to her own person.

"I . . . I do not want him harmed," she said, haltingly. "Rob-ert is not to blame . . . He did as he was bade, and he—he did try to warn me. I've known him since we were children and there is much good in him. It's only that, like so many of us born to this world, he has never been taught the value of truth. But he is not unredeemable. Even he can atone for his sins."

I let the silence between us absorb her confession. I would not denigrate it with my own opinions nor commit it to a promise we both knew I might not be able to keep.

She bit her lower lip; her fingers, so startling in their un-adorned length, plucked at her gown. Then she said abruptly, "You will take care of yourself, for Kate's sake?"

I nodded. So she did know. We shared this, too, in common.

She turned to the door, where she paused, her hand on the latch. "Be careful with Mary," she said. "I love my sister, but she is not a trusting woman. Life has made her that way. She has always believed the worst of people, never the best. Some say it is the Spaniard in her. But I say it is our father."

I met her eyes as she looked over her shoulder. "You will take Kate with you?" I said. "I want her safe, or as safe as we can be under the circumstances."

"You have my word." She pulled open the door. "Guard yourself against dragons, Brendan Prescott," she added, and I heard a hint of wry mirth in her voice, "And whatever you do, steer clear of water. It obviously is not your element."

I stood listening to her footsteps fade down the stairs. I knew I would not see her in the morning, for I must leave before dawn. But in the emptiness left by her departure, I finally understood why Robert Dudley would have betrayed his own family for her love.

Given the opportunity, Elizabeth just might do the same for him.

Chapter Twenty-three

When did you say she'd arrive?" said Peregrine for what had to be the hundredth time.

"I didn't." I suppressed my own impatience as I peered through the ragged opening in the bushes, where I crouched with a crick in my back and my legs numb below the knee. The star-spattered sky displayed a sickle moon. A breeze rustled the woods behind us, where we'd tethered and muzzled the horses.

"She left her manor sometime yesterday. Seeing as she didn't head to London, as she'd have been arrested by now, we can only hope she took this road. But she could be anywhere."

At my side, smothered in a heavy blue wool cloak that matched the one he'd brought me, Peregrine scowled. "Bite off my head. I was only asking. If I'd known you'd be such a grouse, I'd have gone to Hatfield with Mistress Stafford and Urian."

I forced out a chuckle. "Sorry. Camping in a trench at the side of a road isn't my idea of fun, either. I'd rather be with Kate and Urian, as well."

"I should think so. I saw how you looked at her. You love her, don't you?"

The discordant blend of envy and longing in his voice gave me pause. He had been nothing if not resourceful, not to mention tenacious.

I now knew that while we'd crept into Edward's chamber, Peregrine had slunk past several manned guards in order to reach the stables, where he then avoided the night watch to saddle, bridle, and lead three somnambulant horses, and a dog, out to the gate. There he had waited, feeding the beasts tidbits of those crabapples he seemed to grow in his pockets, keeping them quiet until Elizabeth, Kate, and Barnaby arrived. According to Kate, when they heard the pistol and saw the duke's retainers racing out, Barnaby had to haul Peregrine onto Cinnabar. As soon as they reached the house, the boy demanded they turn back to search for me. He would have gone then and there, were it not for fear the duke had sent troops after them. As it was, Peregrine did not stop pacing the room where they hid. When Mistress Ashley and the men sent by Cecil arrived to spirit the princess away, he had exclaimed with relief that now he could go find me.

This same unwavering devotion had prompted his refusal to let me undertake my latest mission without him. He'd cited, not unreasonably, that as I had a penchant for tripping into disaster, it would be best if I had a friend. I had made the mistake, however, of treating him as he wanted me to, forgetting he was still a lad. Now, as I saw the trepidation in his eyes, I said, "Yes, I love her. But you will always have a place with us. I promise you."

Peregrine kneaded his cloak. "You do?"

"I do." I reached over to rustle his hair when I heard the rumble coming toward us.

We froze. I unsheathed my new dagger, having entrusted the sword to Kate rather than risk losing it again. Peregrine pulled out his knife.

The clangor of iron-shod hooves striking the road turned to muted thunder. I whispered, "Remember, we don't show ourselves until we know for certain it's her. The duke could have sent out a hundred decoys to flush out her supporters."

His eyes were wide. It sounded as if an infantry were upon us, yet when I looked out, I saw only a small company of horsemen, their lathered mounts flinging up clumps of dirt. Dark cloaks billowed about the riders. They had no torches, but as they galloped past, the leader glanced at the bushes where we lurked. Under his unadorned black cap, I recognized him.

My heart leapt into my throat. I half expected him to yell a halt and turn on us. When the contingent continued down the road, I sagged onto my haunches. "That was Lord Robert."

Peregrine stared. "*The* Lord Robert?"

"The same." I sprang to my feet. "Come!"

We raced to the woods. Cinnabar and Peregrine's mount (which had the odd name of Deacon) snorted as we leapt onto the saddles and yanked them about. "We'll ride parallel with the road," I said. "Hopefully we can find a quicker route."

The night was lifting. Though still a few hours away, dawn approached. Cantering at the forest edge, using the trees as camouflage, evading or jumping fallen trunks that could snap a horse's leg, I was grateful for the scarce moon. I couldn't see very far ahead, which was unfortunate, but it also meant Lord Robert and his men might not see us. I knew that if we were spotted we'd be hard pressed to make an escape.

How had Robert caught the scent so fast? We had expected the duke to send him after Mary, but her manor was miles from here. Somehow Robert had discovered she was on her way north and had determined to run her to ground, employing the same ruthless purpose he'd shown in pursuit of Elizabeth. Only this time he carried a warrant, not a ring.

Peregrine broke into my thoughts. "They're stopping."

I slowed Cinnabar, straining my eyes to a fork in the road. "Go farther," I said, "and wait there. If something should happen, don't be a hero. Ride back to Hatfield. I mean it."

I picked my way toward the group. Cinnabar had a light step, but even that couldn't stop the occasional crack of twigs underfoot or jiggle of harness. At every sound, no matter how subtle, I cringed. I'd hunted with the Dudleys in our youth, before the cruelty of the sport turned my stomach. I had seen the delight Robert took in tracking prey. How much more would he enjoy hunting the squire who had betrayed his trust?

But no one heard me, probably because they were too engrossed in their own vociferous debate. Sliding from my saddle, I continued on foot, drawing close enough to overhear but not so close that I wouldn't have a fighting chance if I were seen.

I counted nine; among the clash of voices Robert's was the loudest.

"Because I say so! God's teeth, am I not the leader here? Is it not my head that stands to roll if we fail to capture that papist witch?"

"Begging your pardon," retorted a gruff voice, "but we all stand to lose here, my lord. None of us wants to see a Catholic queen set the Inquisition over us, which is why we shouldn't have left our soldiers behind to wait for us. What if she has more retainers than we think?"

Robert scoffed. "You heard her steward at Hoddesdon. At the most, she travels with six: her treasurer, secretary, chamberlain, and three matrons. We don't need a host of soldiers to catch her. They'll only slow us down."

I had to smile. Out in the middle of a road, in the middle of nowhere, and still they trembled in their boots over what one embattled spinster might achieve. It was good to hear that, like her younger sister, Mary Tudor had a reputation.

Then my entire being went cold as I heard a voice drawl, "Perhaps we should come to an agreement, gentlemen, before she sets sail for Flanders and returns with an imperial army at her back. We'll need more than soldiers then, I can assure you."

Stokes. He was here, among Robert's men.

Robert conceded. "Yes, we can't afford to waste more time. She fled Hoddesdon and has been riding nonstop. All the signs indicate she's on her way to Yarmouth. She has to take refuge somewhere, if only to rest her horses. Most likely she'll seek out a sympathizer. I ask you, how hard can it be to track down one old woman and her servants on their way to Norfolk?"

"Hard enough," said the gruff voice. "Considering we've not seen hide nor hair of them. I still say we should head east. There are plenty of papists sympathizers there, too."

"And I say I've had enough of your bloody dissension!" Robert slammed his fist on his thigh, but I knew him well; I detected an unwitting fear in his voice. My former master was scared, and that gave me hope. "You've set us by our ears since we started out," he snarled, "and I for one am starting to wonder at your purpose. Are you with or against us, Master Durot?"

I watched this Durot swing about on his horse, a large muscular figure clad in a quilted doublet and oversized cap, equipped with sword, short bow, and quiver of arrows. "If you're questioning my loyalty," he said "and by implication that of my master Lord Arundel, I can always head back to London to report on

your progress. I feel no pressing need to continue on this particular goose chase."

Robert glared. "You might not, but your master the earl has
every need. He's made a fortune off pillaging the abbeys. I don't
think he'll appreciate having to explain himself to Queen Mary
and her friars," he added sarcastically. "So I suggest you follow
my orders, lest you'd rather see your master hang from a gibbet."

Durot didn't respond. Robert swerved to the others. "Anyone
else have cause for complaint? Best speak now. I'll not tolerate it
later." When none spoke, he said, "We'll head east. This area is
infested with Catholic landowners. She could be hiding with
any one of them. If we have to search house by house, we will."
He flung his next words at Durot. "Lest we forget, she doesn't
have the brains to fool us, even if she tried."

No one argued the point. Digging spurs into horse flanks,
they charged off.

I slipped back to Cinnabar. Peregrine waited at the crest. "To
Suffolk," I told him.

We rode at an unflagging pace, hours slipping past as dawn
drenched the sky in mauve. Though I had trusted my gut, as the
countryside emerged from night into a placid vista of rolling
vales and hills, I began to wonder if I had relied too much on it
and not enough on harsh reality.

Could Mary have gotten this far? Or was she at this very moment being marched out of her hiding place at the tip of a
Dudley sword, bound for the Tower? Rather than chasing her,
shouldn't I be rushing to Hatfield to warn Elizabeth and beloved
Kate, and making for the nearest port before the duke arrested
us all?

I wiped a hand across my chin. My beard itched. Tugging off my cap, I let my matted hair tumble to my shoulders, glancing over at Peregrine. The boy drowsed on his saddle. We had to stop soon. Even if the horses held out, we couldn't.

A half hour later I spied a manor ahead, nestled among orchards, a veil of bluish smoke hovering over chimney and courtyard. From this distance, it almost looked deserted.

"Peregrine, wake up. I think we've found her."

The boy started, raised bewildered eyes. "How do you know?"

"Look at the courtyard. There are horses tethered there—seven, to be exact."

We rode into the courtyard with our cloaks thrown over our shoulders to expose the sheathed blades at our belts, our hands free and heads uncovered. I instructed Peregrine to remember my new name and refrain from appearing perturbed, while I in turn feigned a calm I did not feel, as servants preparing the mounts froze in midbuckle of stirrups. One of three men overseeing the operation lifted a firearm. The other two advanced. Both were in their middle years, dressed in yeomen garb, their bearded faces haggard.

The elder of the two—who held himself with the dignity of a steward despite his attempt to appear common—barked, "Who are you? What is your business here?"

"Who I am doesn't matter," I said. "My business is a missive for the queen."

"Queen? What queen?" The man guffawed. "I see no queen here."

"Her Majesty Queen Mary. The missive is from the council."

The men exchanged terse looks. "Find Lord Huddleston,"

the older one directed, and the other ran off. "Jerningham, keep that musket aimed," he ordered the man with the firearm. The servants didn't shift an inch. "Dismount," ordered the man. Peregrine and I obeyed.

A moment later, a harried portly gentleman I assumed was the aforementioned Huddleston bustled out. "I advised her not to, Master Rochester," he said in a worried tone, "but she says she'll see them in the hall, providing they are unarmed."

The man Rochester turned a stern eye on me. "Your lad stays here."

Detecting the lingering scent of roast as I was escorted into the manor, my stomach rumbled. Rochester was at my side, the armed Jerningham at my back, and Huddleston ahead. At the entrance, Jerningham backed into the shadows, from where I had no doubt he would continue to aim his weapon at me. Rochester and Huddleston led me forth.

A slim figure clad in bucolic dress stood before a table. The men bowed. Dropping to one knee, I glimpsed a map on the table, alongside quill and paper, flagon and goblet.

A surprisingly brusque voice said, "Rise."

I came to my feet before Mary Tudor.

She did not look anything like Elizabeth. She more closely resembled their cousin, Jane Grey—short and too thin, with a hint of red-gold in the graying hair parted under her coif. Unlike Jane, Mary's age and her sufferings were written on her face, etched in the crevices of her brow, the webs cradling her lips, and the slackness at her chin. Her thickened hands were clenched at her girdle, each of her long fingers ringed. Only in her eyes could be discerned that indomitable Tudor strength—forceful

gray-blue eyes rimmed in shadow, meeting mine with a direct-
ness that imparted she was a superior being.

I recalled Elizabeth's words: *She has always believed the worst
of people, never the best. Some say it is the Spaniard in her. But I say
it is our father.*

Her voice came at me with strident force. "I'm told you bring
a missive." She thrust out her hand. "I would see it."

I removed the envelope from my interior pocket. Turning to
the light, she tore it open and peered. Her frown deepened. She
looked back at me. "Is this true?"

"I believe so, Your Majesty."

"You *believe*? Have you read it, then?"

"I would not be much of a messenger if I failed to memorize
so important a missive. Such letters, if fallen into the wrong
hands, can prove dangerous."

She gave me an appraising stare. Then she paced to the
table with brisk steps. "This dangerous letter," she declared,
with a hint of asperity, "is from none other than my lords Arundel, Paget, Sussex, and Pembroke, all of whom served my brother
and who now inform me that while they've no desire to see me
deprived of my throne, their hands are tied. The duke's hold, it
seems, is too powerful to resist. They fear they must uphold my
cousin's claim, though Jane has expressed no desire to rule." She
paused. "What say you?"

Her request took me aback. Though she hid it well, I sensed
her trepidation. Thrust into notice after years of obscurity, forced
to flee within her own realm, Lady Mary had been hunted before,
too many times, in fact, for her to trust anyone's promises, written
or otherwise.

I'd not heard anything positive about her, from anyone; indeed, the very possibility of her accession was rife with tumult.

Yet in that moment I felt only empathy for her. She was at an age when most women had wed, borne children, settled for better or worse into the rest of their lives. Instead she stood in someone else's manor, a fugitive marked for death.

"Well?" she said. "Will you not answer? You were hired by them, were you not?"

"Your Majesty, if you'll pardon my insolence, I would prefer to answer in private."

"Absolutely not," said Rochester. "The queen does not entertain strangers. You're lucky we haven't thrown you into a dungeon for conspiring with her enemies."

"Dungeon?" I repeated, before I could stop myself. "Here?"

There was stunned silence before Mary's gravelly laughter rang out. "At least he doesn't mince his words!" She clapped her hands. "Leave us."

Rochester marched to where the shadowy man with the firearm lurked; Huddleston followed behind. Mary motioned to her flagon. "You must be thirsty. It's a long ride from London."

"Thank you, Your Majesty," I said. Her terse smile revealed bad teeth. *She's not had much occasion to smile in her life,* I thought, as I drank deeply of the warm ale.

She waited.

I said, "Your Majesty, my companion . . . he is just a boy. I trust he'll not be harmed?"

"Of course not." She faced me now without trepidation. "Tell me honestly: Is my brother King Edward dead?"

I met her stalwart gaze. "Yes."

She was quiet, as if she contemplated something she had already accepted. Then she said, "And this letter from the council: Is it a ruse, or can I trust what these lords say?"

I measured my response. "I haven't been at court long, but I would say, no, you should not trust them." As her face tightened, I added, "However, you can trust their letter. Lady Jane Grey is indeed the duke's pawn. She'd not have assumed your throne given the choice."

She snorted. "I find that hard to believe. She did marry Northumberland's brat."

"Your Majesty can believe in her innocence, if you believe nothing else. The duke has devised this situation to secure his own power. He is the perpetrator. He—"

"He should be drawn and quartered, his head stuck on a pike," she blared. "How dare he contrive to steal my realm, which is mine by divine right! He'll soon learn that I am not a queen to be trifled with—he and every other lord who dares to exalt my cousin over me."

The fervor of her declaration animated her person. She might not possess her sister's charismatic appeal, but she was still Henry VIII's daughter.

"I gather Your Majesty intends to fight for your crown," I said.

"To the death, if need be. My grandmother Isabella of Castile led armies against the infidel to unite her kingdom. Nothing less can be expected of me."

"Then Your Majesty has answered your own question. The council's offer to support you is trustworthy only as much as you make it so. If you forgive their past transgressions, then you will have their loyalty."

Her eyes turned cold. "I see you've mastered their art of double-talk."

I felt a prickle of fear in my belly. Her face was drawn, closed. Elizabeth had warned me to be careful. I was struggling to find the right response, when Rochester strode in. "Your Majesty, we found this cur lurking outside!" He stepped aside, revealing three others dragging another man between them. As they threw him facedown on the floor, his cap slipped off his head. Mary prodded him with her foot. "Your name."

I could not contain my relief when the man lifted his face.

"Some call me Durot, Your Majesty, but you would know me as Fitzpatrick."

Chapter Twenty-four

Mary said, "Barnaby Fitzpatrick, my brother's servant?" From behind her I interjected, "Your Majesty, he's been working to keep the duke's son Lord Robert away from you. Whatever news he brings must be important."

Barnaby came to his feet. Streaks of his natural hair color showed through his walnut-juice stained mop. At Mary's nod, he said, "Robert Dudley and his men are fast closing in. I was sent ahead as a scout, because a local sheepherder swears he spotted you riding in this direction. Your Majesty has less than an hour to make your escape."

Rochester said, "Where is your proof?"

"My lord steward," said Mary, before Barnaby could reply, "Master Fitzpatrick served my late brother loyally for many years. He was often whipped for Edward's transgressions. I don't require further proof."

She returned to the table, Huddleston at her heels. She gathered her map and papers, thrust them at him. "We ride for Framlingham Castle. It's a Howard seat, and they revere the True Faith. If God is with me, I'll gather my supporters there. Otherwise, it's not far to the coast. My lord Huddleston, you must come with us. Your house is no longer safe for you."

White as the papers he clutched, Huddleston hastened after Rochester and the other men, who bolted from the hall shouting orders. As the manor erupted in pandemonium, Mary called out, "Clarencieux, Finch!" and two women emerged from the hall's recesses, bearing a cloak and a small valise. "These are my faithful servants," said Mary, as the women draped the cloak about her. "You must defend them with your lives."

She did not ask us how we felt about being entrusted with this duty. Crowned already in her mind, she merely assumed we would obey.

We followed her into the courtyard, where servants stuffed saddlebags with last-minute articles. Peregrine held our horses. His eyes snapped wide as he saw Barnaby dart around the side of the manor and return on his cob. While Rochester assisted the queen and her ladies to their mounts, Huddleston and Mary's other manservants jumped onto theirs.

Barnaby mumbled to Peregrine and me, "We may need someone to defend us before this day is done."

"Or maybe not," I said. "Lord Robert looked none too fresh last I saw him."

Barnaby chortled. "I thought I heard a rat in the brush. By the way, the beard suits you."

"A precaution of my new trade. In case anyone should ask, my name is Daniel Beecham, of Lincolnshire." I reached over to thump his back. "That was quite a voice you used, Durot. And the hair coloring is an accomplishment. How did you get yourself into Dudley's company?"

"Let's just say I was accosted by a certain earl who offered me the opportunity to avenge my king. The rest was easy. I made myself Robert's bane from the start. If I had said she was in France, he'd have gone looking for her in Brussels. He was only too pleased to send me off ahead. He probably hoped some papist sniper would rid him of me for good."

"You are bold. And you've helped save me twice now. I shan't forget it."

"Just pray you don't need a third." Barnaby's expression turned somber as he looked up. He lifted his voice. "Your Majesty, the hour isn't getting any longer."

Swiveling in the saddle, a sickening lurch went through me. Horsemen rode down a distant hill, coming straight toward the manor.

"This way," Barnaby shouted. Sandwiched between her servants, Mary galloped onto the road, hard after him as he led us to a ridge. Robert Dudley and his men were still too far off to pose an immediate threat, but as we climbed the path single file, the sun wringing sweat from our brows, we discovered we weren't moving fast enough.

A gasp escaped the women. Behind us rose a plume of thick black smoke. The manor we had left was being torched.

At Mary's side, Huddleston went white. "Let it burn," she told him. "I'll build you a finer house. You have my word as your queen."

Huddleston's dismayed look indicated he wasn't taking her promise to heart.

I motioned Barnaby aside. "We're too easy a target. We have to divide their pursuit."

Barnaby assented. "What do you suggest?"

"You proceed with Her Majesty and three of her people. Let Peregrine take the others along a different route. That way,

Robert and his men will have to separate. The less there are after her, the better her chances are of reaching Framlingham."

"Good plan." He paused. "What are you going to do?"

I gave him a cold smile. "I've an overdue appointment. I'll need your bow."

Peregrine kicked up a storm before he was convinced of the necessity of sacrificing personal preference in order to serve his queen. To my surprise, Rochester supported my proposition. Mary also agreed, insisting I come to her once I'd scouted the lay of the land, which I cited as my reason for staying behind. The two parties galloped off in opposite directions, the queen's escort headed farther into the hills, Peregrine's party turning to the road toward Essex.

As I scrambled up an incline and set Cinnabar loose to graze, I offered up a prayer for their safety, especially the queen, whom I found I admired more than my employer might prefer.

I located a cluster of boulders to hide behind and turned my focus to the winding path, notching an arrow in anticipation.

It didn't take long. As an influx of scudding clouds smothered the sun, four men came charging up the path, soot faced and sweat soaked. Robert wasn't among them. I soon found out why. The men dismounted a stone's throw from my hiding place, unhooked wineskins from their saddles, and proceeded to resume an argument that evidently had been transpiring for some time.

"He's as full of the devil's pride as his father," one of the men groused. "I've had enough of those Dudley upstarts lording it over us. Why didn't he just let someone else go back for the soldiers,

I ask you? Because he doesn't want to sully his hands, lest Mary wins the day and he finds himself at her mercy. Well, I say leave him to it. Papist or not, bastard or legitimate, she's still our rightful queen, no matter what Northumberland says. Remember, old Henry beheaded the duke's own father for treason. Treachery runs in their blood."

The other two grunted their agreement, glancing at the trim figure standing apart from them, sniffing the air as if he might scent the way Mary had gone.

"What say you, Stokes?" asked one.

The duchess's man turned with a swirl of his velvet cloak, revealing a glimpse of scarlet lining. "I think we must each act as our conscience dictates, Master Hengate. But I'll wager you're not the first these days to question the Dudleys' authority."

Hidden behind the boulder, I had to smile. Trust him to ensure his mistress's neutrality. The duchess was Mary's paternal cousin, and her daughter was about to don Mary's crown. Lady Suffolk stood to lose a great deal should Mary triumph, including her head.

Hengate stared at Stokes. "And you? What would you do if we decide to return to our homes and wait to see how this all ends?"

Stokes shrugged. "I'd go home myself and inform my lady that the duke needs a new hound. The one he sent has obviously lost its skill."

The men guffawed. Hengate hesitated before he went to his horse and swung into the saddle. He swerved to Stokes. "If you betray us, you should know my master Lord Pembroke's arm is long. He will find you, no matter whose skirts you hide behind."

"I'm not an informant," Stokes retorted. "I've no stake in what befalls the Dudleys. Neither does my lady, I can assure you."

"Good," said Hengate, as his accomplices mounted. "In times like these, it's the pliant man who survives." Digging heels into his horse, he and the others thundered off, leaving Stokes to wave a fastidious gauntleted hand before his nose, as if to dispel a noxious smell.

He started to move to his own idling steed when my arrow hissed over his head. He whirled about and froze, glaring toward the boulders with more arrogance that I would have expected from a man in his position.

I stepped out, extracted another arrow from the quiver strapped to my back, and fitted it to the bow. It was one of the first times in my life I had the chance to put my years of weaponry practice to action. I wasn't disappointed in Stokes's wary recoil.

"What do you want?" he said. "Money?" He unhooked a purse from his belt and flung it on the road between us. "That should be enough."

I pushed back my cap. "Don't you recognize me? It hasn't been that long."

He stared. "It . . . it can't be."

I adjusted the bow, aiming the arrow between his legs. "I'm thinking if I shoot you there, it will take you a few hours to die." I leveled the bow upward. "Or I could just shoot you between the eyes. Or you can start talking. Your choice."

He snarled, yanked his sword from the scabbard at his waist.

I let the arrow soar. It struck Stokes in the thigh, brought him howling to his knees. He grasped the protruding shaft, blanching with shock. There was little blood. I walked to him and pulled the bow taut again, ignoring the flare in my shoulder from the ball wound.

As I took aim, Stokes reared a vicious face. "Whoreson! You'd kill a defenseless man in cold blood!"

I paused. "Now, there's a start. A whore's son: Is that what I am?"

"A murderer is what you are. I'm going to bleed to death!"

"Not if you let that arrow be. You need an experienced surgeon to extract it; the tip is barbed. Without proper care, the wound will corrupt. Still, you've a better chance of survival than you gave me." I lowered the bow. "Back to my question: Was my mother a whore?"

"I don't know," he retorted, but he was quivering.

"I think you do." I squatted in front of him. "The duchess seemed to know. She saw the birthmark on my hip and was willing to kill me. Why does she want me dead? Who does she think I am?"

"Exactly?" he said, and he flew at me without warning, bowling me back and crushing the quiver of arrows under our combined weight. My head struck the path. For a second, the world melted. I rammed my knees into his ribs, clawing at the arrow shaft. His scream and the ensuing gush of blood were enough. I rolled, throwing Stokes off. I sprang up, kicked the bow out of reach. Unsheathing my blade, I leapt onto Stokes's back and pinned him in the dust. I pressed my blade against his throat, pushing the side of his face into the dirt.

"Shall I do it?" I hissed. "Shall I cut you here and now, and leave you to bleed to death? Or will you tell me what I want to know?"

"No! No! Please!"

I released him. Stokes panted, blood seeping from his maimed leg.

I yanked him over onto his back. Positioning the dagger at the site where the arrow protruded, I said, "I promise you, this will hurt. When I start cutting out that shaft, it will hurt more than you can imagine. But it might hurt less if you *don't hold your breath*."

I punctuated the words with an icy smile. Dark rage erupted in my heart, a sudden uncontrollable thirst for vengeance. In my soul's eye, I saw again a slash of steel, the slow terrible crumpling of a mutilated form. I stood swiftly, went and retrieved the bow.

Stokes was staring at me in horror when I located an intact arrow, fitted it, and wheeled about. I shot with precision. The arrow sang through the air and thumped into the cloak rumpled about his head, missing his ear by a hair's breadth.

He writhed and tore at the cloak, trying to get away from the arrow that held him fast. "You win!" he shrieked. "I'll tell you anything you want. Just cut me loose, damn you to hell!"

"Answer my question."

He suddenly let out a feral giggle. "You fool. You've no idea, do you? We were going to drown you, toss your body into the river, and you would never have known why."

I clenched my jaw. "You're going to tell me. Now."

"Very well." Pure malice gleamed in his sloe-eyed look. "You are the last child of Mary of Suffolk, Henry the Eighth's youngest sister, also known to her family as the Tudor Rose. That mark you bear—it is one her babe inherited, a mark she too carried. The only ones who would have known of it are those who were intimate with the late duchess's person."

My breath came in stifled bursts. A roar drowned out the sounds around me. I stared at the man before me and recalled in mind-chilling procession all the events that had led me to this unthinkable moment.

I tasted bile in my throat. "Are you saying the duchess thinks . . . ?" I faltered. I couldn't say the words.

Stokes sneered. "I've told you what you wanted. Now let me go."

Feeling as if I tumbled into an endless void, I raised my fingers to my lips and whistled. Cinnabar trotted down the hill. From my saddlebag, I removed Kate's salve and the linen she'd packed for my shoulder. I tore back his bloodied breeches, cut the arrow at the hilt, applied the salve, and dressed the wound. Then I wrenched the second arrow from his cloak.

I looked at his ashen face. "You'll still need a surgeon to remove the tip. See that you get to one as soon as possible. Otherwise, the wound will fester." I held out my hand. "Come. I'll help you onto your horse."

He gaped. "You lie in wait to shoot arrows at me, and now you want to help me onto my horse? It must be true. You must be one of them. You're mad as old Henry himself."

"Don't. Not another word." I took hold of him, yanked him up. He yelped as I held his stirrup and hoisted him onto his saddle. He gathered his reins, hauled his horse's head upward.

He swiveled about. I met his malicious regard, knowing he prepared to inflict a far deeper wound than any arrow of mine could deliver.

"Your mother," he said, in undeniable glee, "*her* mother—she delivered you in secrecy before she died of childbed fever. She never told anyone but her trusted eldest daughter that she was with child. She was mad with fear; she begged her daughter to keep it a secret. She hid her pregnancy from everyone, even her husband, who was by that time estranged from her, living almost full-time at court. But something happened in those last hours; Mary of Suffolk must have confided in the midwife, said something that fostered her mistrust, because my lady was told you were stillborn. She was at court at the time, so she ordered your body disposed of, the birth covered up. Had she known you in fact had survived, she'd have ridden from Whitehall that very night and strangled you herself. You see, you could take everything from her—the estate and title, her place at court and in the succession. You are the son that Charles Brandon had longed for, the heir to the Suffolk earldom. Think of that next time you muck out a stable."

My reply was passionless. "Next time, I give no quarter."

"Neither do I," he replied. "If I were you, I'd make sure there is no next time. Because should she ever find out you're still alive, it'll be far worse for you than for me."

He whirled about, galloping away.

Left alone on a road splattered with blood, I sank to my knees.

Chapter Twenty-five

Every man, no matter how humble, should know from whence he came.

Cecil's words echoed in my head as I rode in silence. By nightfall I had to pause to give Cinnabar time to rest. I chose a clearing in a forest, beside a shallow stream. Removing the saddle and bridle, I rubbed him down with a cloth from my saddlebag and set him loose to graze. "At ease, my friend. You've earned it."

I crouched in the bracken, opened my saddlebag, and brought out the ruby-tipped jewel Mistress Alice had given me. I almost couldn't look at it, knowing now its significance, the reason she'd hidden it all these years. I wanted to throw it away, forget it existed, though in my soul I knew I could not afford to delude myself anymore.

For if what Stokes had told me was true, there was no forgetting, no turning away. I had to uncover the truth, come to terms with something that was so vast, so far-reaching, it defied acceptance. I owed it to myself, to the many times I'd wondered as a child; more importantly, I owed it to the woman who had saved me—to Mistress Alice, who had somehow known who I was and preserved my life from my own murderous sister.

In the palm of my hand, the gold shimmered.

A Tudor.

I was one of them, born of the younger sister of Henry VIII; brother to the bestial Duchess of Suffolk, uncle to Jane Grey, and cousin to Queen Mary.

And Elizabeth. She and I: We shared the same blood. . . .

Tears burned in my eyes. What had she looked like, this mother I had never known? Had she been beautiful? Did I have her eyes, her nose, her mouth? Why had she borne me in secrecy? What had she feared, that she'd never let her pregnancy be known?

And what would my life have been like had she lived?

The Tudor Rose . . . the mark of the rose.

I arched my arm over my head. I should fling the petal away, never speak of this to another living person. Better to be a common stable hand, a bastard and foundling, rather than some being borne in secrecy and consigned to oblivion—condemned always to shadows and the fear of discovery, to a lifetime of hiding and of keeping others always from the truth.

My fingers would not release it, though. The petal had a truth of its own now, inextricably entwined with my own. God help me, it was a part of me I could not surrender, not until I had discovered everything there was to know.

I returned it to Kate's scented handkerchief and put it back in my bag. As I did, my fingers brushed the thin volume of psalms I had taken from the Dudley library, bringing a momentary smile to my lips. I carried another memory of Mistress Alice with me, as well, one that made me think of her as she had been.

After I finished the last of the stale bread and cheese I'd

packed, I lay down on the forest floor and closed my eyes. But I couldn't sleep. I kept seeing a shriveled hand on mine, setting in my palm a gift of unimaginable import.

When dawn finally broke over the horizon, I mounted once more to ride through fields dotted with faded golden irises. I tried not to think of anything until I reached the River Orr.

There, rearing on the other side of the banks atop its mound, was Framlingham Castle.

Its thirteen towers and immense ramparts overshadowed three moats. In the hunting park glittered an ocean of steel. As I forded the river and approached, I gleaned hundreds of men hauling cannon and firearms, stockpiling boulders, felling and stripping trees. I gave rein to Cinnabar's eager canter, for he sensed stables, oats, and a well-deserved respite.

Guards stopped me on the road. After a rough barrage of questions, I was obliged to dismount, give my name, and wait under their watch before word came that Rochester bid me to the castle. Shouldering my bag, I took Cinnabar by the reins and trudged to the looming edifice, which swallowed half the sky. Few men paused to mark my passage, the majority engrossed in labor, their ribaldry interspersed with barking dogs and the lowing of livestock, tended by urchins and women.

Despite everything, I felt my spirits lighten. A makeshift city had sprung up around Framlingham practically overnight, composed of ordinary people and retainers of local lords who had come to defend their rightful monarch. In less than seventy-two hours, Queen Mary had amassed her army. At least here, things were as they should be.

The main bailey was thronged with men and animals. Rochester strode to me, sweating profusely but otherwise looking like a completely changed man. He clamped my hand in his.

"Master Beecham! I failed to recognize the name. You're fortunate your friends informed me of it. Leave your horse to the grooms and come. Her Majesty wishes to see you."

Looking past Rochester, I had to laugh. Peregrine and Barnaby, both stripped to the waist and as filthy as they could be, waved at me before they returned to the arduous task of pushing a cannon into a forger's shed for repairs. I returned my gaze to Rochester.

"I'm pleased to find you all safe," I said with genuine relief.

"We might not be, had it not been for you. We owe you much. After we separated, Robert Dudley's men chased the others for miles before he realized his error. He then turned and came after us. Praise God he's since been apprehended."

My smile slipped. "Apprehended?"

"Yes. But of course you wouldn't know." Rochester steered me toward an incongruous red brick manor flanked by timber lodgings, all situated inside the castle's curtain wall. "It seems that when he discovered where we were headed, Lord Robert decided to seek reinforcements. He must have thought we'd have no means of defending the castle once he returned to set siege."

Rochester chuckled. "To be honest, we never expected to find old Norfolk's son waiting here with his retainers. But here he was, and by nightfall another five thousand had arrived. Word of Her Majesty's plight has swept before her, a call to arms has gone out. Men are arriving from all over England. It's as if God Himself watches over her."

"Indeed," I said quietly. "You were saying about Lord Robert?" As I spoke I thought of Elizabeth, standing in that anonymous room. *I do not want him harmed,* she had said. All of a sudden, to my disconcertment, I realized neither did I. Perhaps because he had been the closest thing I'd ever had to a sibling;

or maybe because while a Dudley to his very marrow, she was right: In truth, Robert was a victim of his upbringing.

"He made it as far as King's Lynn," said Rochester. "By then, several of his men had deserted him. When he got there, his soldiers also deserted, and he was forced to flee. He sought refuge in Bury Saint Edmunds and sent urgent word to London. His messenger got away, but he didn't. Baron Derby arrested him shortly after, in the queen's name. Fitting justice, you might say. He's being held in the ruins of the very abbey that his father helped destroy."

"And . . . what will happen to him?"

Rochester sniffed. "Her Majesty will decide his fate once she takes her throne. It shan't be enviable, I would think. At best, a cell in the Tower for the rest of his days; at worst, the ax, along with the rest of his traitorous kind. I vote for the ax, myself. Ah, but Her Majesty will be pleased to see you. She's asked about you several times."

The last of my brief exultation faded. Like Rochester, I should have been rejoicing in this blow to the Dudley cause. Without Robert, the task of apprehending Mary became all that more difficult. Yet all I felt was fatigue falling over me like a mantle. I wanted only a hot bath, solitude, a cot, and to shut out the world for a time.

I did not want to think of how I would tell Elizabeth.

We entered the manor, climbed a staircase to a rustic upper hall. Mary waited there, dressed in a plain black gown and gable headdress that looked too heavy for her thin shoulders. She paced back and forth as if its weight were of no account, dictating in a stern voice to a harried secretary whose quill couldn't possibly scratch fast enough to record the torrent of words issuing from her lips.

"Wherefore, my lords, we require and charge you, as your rightful sovereign, that for your honor and the surety of your persons, you employ yourselves forthwith upon receipt of this letter to proclaim us queen in our capital city of London. For we have not fled our realm nor do we intend to do so, but will die fighting for that which God has called upon us to defend."

Rochester cleared his throat. I bowed low. "Your Majesty."

She swirled about in her abrupt manner, peering at me. She was, apparently, severely nearsighted, for she blinked several times, her brow furrowed in perplexity before she exclaimed, "Ah, it is my mysterious friend," and motioned with her hands. "Rise, rise! You're just in time. We're about to declare war on Northumberland."

"Your Majesty, that is indeed good news." As I righted myself, I took note that despite her vigor, which must in no small measure be instilled by the spontaneous demonstration of loyalty she'd received, Mary looked strained about the eyes and mouth, and too gaunt. She had the look of someone who has not eaten well or rested in weeks.

"Good? It is more than good!" Her laughter was curt, derisive. "Our proud duke is not so proud now. Tell him, Waldegrave."

She swerved to her secretary, her ringed hands clasped, beaming like a school teacher as the man recited: "Six cities garrisoned by the duke have vowed allegiance to Her Majesty, offering artillery, food, and men. Her Majesty has also sent a proclamation to the council, demanding—"

Mary couldn't stop herself from interrupting. ". . . Demanding to know why they have yet to acknowledge me as their lawful sovereign in London. I also demanded an explanation as to why they dared to bestow my crown on my cousin. Do you know what they replied?" She grabbed a paper from the table. "They say my brother authorized a change to the succession before his death, denying my claim to the throne because of serious doubts concerning my legitimacy."

She flung the paper aside. "Serious doubts!" This time, her laughter was tinged with a darkness that stirred the hair on my nape. "They'll soon see how well I take to such. Heretics and traitors are what they are, to a man, and thus shall I deal with them when the time comes."

Silence followed her outburst. Her eyes shifted from face to face before fixating on mine. "Well? You are the council's courier, yes? Have you no opinion to impart?"

It was a similar inquiry to the one I'd faced in Huddleston's manor, only this time I felt sure Barnaby would not be dragged in. As though in confirmation, Rochester took a prudent step back. A pit opened in my belly. It seemed impossible that after everything that had occurred, I might still have to prove my loyalty. But then, how could she know where my ultimate allegiance might lie? How could she begin to trust a stranger, after what she had been through?

"Your Majesty," I said, "may I have your leave to examine this letter?"

At her gesture, I retrieved the paper, scanned down to the appended signatures and seals. I met her stare. "Those lords whose letter I first conveyed, are they represented here?"

"They are not, as you can see." Though her voice remained terse, her rigid posture eased somewhat. She moved to me, saying over her shoulder to the others, "Leave us. I would speak alone with our friend."

I had passed her test, though it did not ease my apprehension. The council had persecuted Mary without mercy because of her religious faith. My association with them, however tenuous, had put me at a perilous disadvantage.

She paused at the table. "I'm starting to wonder about you. You come out of nowhere and neglect to give us a name. Then you risk your life to help us escape. You're considered reliable enough to carry confidential letters yet feign ignorance of matters you should, in fact, know a great deal about. I would know exactly whom it is I am dealing with."

I swallowed against my dry throat, measuring my words: "Your Majesty, I assure you I am of no importance. I did what I was paid to do. As for my risking my life, you should know that Lord Robert's men had already decided to abandon him. And you must know by now that my name is Daniel Beecham."

"I do, though not by you." She fingered a quill. "Why were you chosen to deliver the council's missive? There are surely others they might have sent, men I would know personally."

I heard Elizabeth in my head: *I love my sister, but she is not a trusting woman. Life has made her that way.*

I mustered a smile. "Your Majesty must know how such matters go. I'd done a few errands in the past and was offered a fee, the lords being disinclined to travel. In addition, should anything have befallen me on the road . . . well, I'm not easily linked to any one in particular."

She snorted. "In other words, you are expendable—a man for hire?"

"Aren't most men, Your Majesty?" I replied, and she stared straight into my eyes.

"I've little experience with men, Master Beecham. What little I do possess tells me there's more to you than you care to let on. Life has taught me a thing or two about hidden motives." She held up a hand. "But, there is no need to say anything else.

I will not query further. Barnaby Fitzpatrick speaks highly of you, and you've proven your fealty. You will, of course, be welcome at my court once I'm proclaimed queen. For make no mistake, queen I shall be. Not even the duke can prevail against those whom God has ordained."

"I pray it will be so," I said. I believed her conviction. No matter what else she might be, Mary Tudor was no coward. Dudley had underestimated more than one princess, it seemed.

With a brittle smile, she retreated to a chair, putting more than mere distance between us. Her next words were spoken with the remoteness of a woman who has more important concerns to attend to. "As I'm sure you can appreciate, I'm not in the position to reward you at this time. However, you have my solemn word that you will be compensated as soon as I secure my throne. Until then, if you require anything, you must let Rochester know."

I bowed, resisting the sudden urge to retreat. I might never have another chance.

"I expect no reward for having served my queen," I heard myself say, and I marveled at the calm in my voice, for my heart had quickened. "But there is something I would ask of Your Majesty, if I might be so bold?"

"Oh?" She set her hands on her lap, her head tilted in curiosity.

"A few questions, is all; an indulgence." I paused. Though I knew it wasn't visible, I could feel myself start to tremble. "Your father King Henry the Eighth, he had two sisters. The Duchess Mary of Suffolk—was she the youngest?"

"She was. Margaret Douglas, dowager of Scotland, was the eldest."

"I see. Your Majesty, I don't mean to pry, but was your late aunt, Mary of Suffolk, also known as the Tudor Rose?"

She regarded me with that unwavering stare I now knew stemmed less from an innate perspicacity, such as Elizabeth commanded, and more from a basic goodness of nature tainted by years of corrosive betrayals. At length she nodded. "It's not widely known, but yes, thus was she called within the family. How is it you came to know of this?"

My throat knotted. I wet my parched lips. "I heard it once, at court, in idle talk."

"Talk, you say? Yes, well, my Aunt Mary always did lend herself to talk." She went still, her eyes turning distant. "I was named after her. She was like an angel, both to look at and in her heart. I adored her. So did my father. It was he who called her the Rose."

The sorrow flooded my chest. An angel, beautiful to look at, inside and out . . .

"This interest in our history," she said. "I find it unusual for one of your class."

Despite the chasm within me, the lie rolled off my lips as if I'd practiced it a thousand times. "An amateur enthusiasm, Your Majesty. Royal genealogy is an interest of mine."

Her smile was infused with warmth. "I commend it. You may proceed."

"I know of the late duchess's surviving daughter, of course," I heard myself say, and it was as though I stood apart, listening to someone else. "Did she ever have a son?"

"She did, indeed. She had two sons, both named Henry. One died in 1522, the other in 1534, a year after her. It was a tragedy for his father. Only a few years later, Suffolk lost both his sons of his subsequent marriage before his own death in 1545."

"How did his other sons die?" I asked, and an icy shiver crept up my spine.

She paused, considering. "I believe it was the sweat, though children are apt to die of so many things." She sighed. "I seem to recall my cousin Frances helped care for them during their illness. She'd had the sweat before; she was immune to contagion. Their deaths must have been hard on her. To lose one's brothers is a terrible burden."

I clamped down on my horrified burst of laughter. The Suffolk male heirs had all perished in childhood. This was how the duchess had inherited her estate! And somehow, everyone thought this was a coincidence?

"And Mary of Suffolk . . . ?" I asked. For regardless of the answer, I had to know. I had to be sure, no matter how much pain it might cause. "How did she die?"

"Of a fever, I was told, though she'd been ill for some time. The swelling sickness, other ailments . . . She was not old, however, nearly the same age as I am. We hadn't seen each other in so much time. She deplored the state in which my father had chosen to live and retired from court to her manor in East Anglia." Her face tightened. "Few took the time to mourn her. It was June; everyone awaited the outcome of that woman Boleyn's pregnancy."

She went silent. Though she didn't say it aloud, the struggle within her was apparent. Here then lay that seed of discord between her and her younger sister.

Then she added, "I remember the details because a few weeks after Charles of Suffolk's funeral, his squire came to see me. A stalwart man—very proper. He had a terrible scar running from his temple to his cheek. I asked him about it. He said he had served in the Scottish wars. Poor man; he seemed most affected by his master's death. But what I most recall is that he brought me a piece of a jewel that apparently Mary had left me in her will but was never sent to me. I still have it. One of the leaves from a golden artichoke given to her by that rogue King Francis the First, who conspired to wed her to Charles Brandon after her first husband Louis of France died." '

I felt my knees start to buckle under me, as if I were disintegrating from within.

Mary chuckled. "That jewel meant a lot to her; it was almost all she had when she was finally allowed to return to England. It turned out well enough in the end, but for a time my father threatened to throw both Mary and Brandon in the Tower for their presumption. He also exacted a stiff fine that they never succeeded in paying off entirely, even though she pawned her jewels. But not that one; she once told me that artichoke represented the best and the worst in her life, the sorrow and the joy. She would not part with it." Mary leaned forward suddenly. "Master Beecham, are you not well? You've gone quite pale."

"I'm tired, is all," I managed to utter. "Thank you for indulging me. I cannot begin to tell Your Majesty how much it has meant."

"Oh, I enjoyed it. It has been far too long since I thought of my late aunt. Perhaps one day you'll consider penning a family history for me. I'd happily commission it." She wagged her finger. "I daresay it would keep you from less-reputable sources of income."

"I would be honored." I forced out a smile, glad of the dimness in the room. "I should like to retire awhile, by your gracious leave."

"Of course." She held out her hand. As I bowed low she said, "I believe I owe your current employers an answer. Come back tomorrow, and let's see if I can arrange one."

"Your Majesty." I kissed her dry, bejeweled fingers.

Rochester led me to a building off the bailey. There was a trough in the quadrangle where I could bathe and a room up-stairs with the essentials. I stripped to my hose, careful to keep them above my hips as I washed in the mossy water, then went up and closed the door.

A cold meal waited on the table. I had no appetite, won-dered if I ever would again. Still, I tied back my damp hair and ate my fill. The needs of the body rarely care about the desola-tion in the heart.

After eating, I sat on the edge of the straw-filled cot and re-moved the jewel from my bag again. It shone like a fragment of a star. I marveled that I could have mistaken it for anything else. I ran a fingertip along a sculpted vein, as if it were alive, knowing now how far it had traveled to reach me, across the Channel from France, through a cherished lifetime. I looked down to my concave groin, and to the left, to the hip which bore my own mother's birthmark.

The only ones who would have known of it are those who were intimate with the late duchess's person. . . .

Charles of Suffolk's . . . squire came to see me. A stalwart man . . .

I closed my eyes. I had to rest. I slid the jewel into my cloak lining and pulled the coarse linen bedsheet over me.

As I drifted off to sleep, I thought Kate would be as surprised as me when she learned the jewel was not a petal, but a leaf.

Chapter Twenty-six

I dreamed of angels. To the echo of a soaring chorus, I opened my eyes and found the room submerged in night. A fiery glow flickered from the open window. I sat upright. The singing came from outside. Then I saw the figure in the room with me.

"Barnaby? Is that you?"

"Yes. I hope you don't mind. I let myself in." He stood with arms wrapped about his chest, staring out. "Did you make your appointment?" he asked, without looking around to me.

"Yes. I brought your bow back." I paused. "Where's Peregrine?"

"Fast asleep. He eats like the famished and drops like a stone. Come, look at this."

Pulling on my breeches, I padded barefoot to the window.

Indigo sky canopied the castle. An improvised altar had been set up in the bailey, draped in faded crimson sporting threadbare gold crucifixes. Before it stood a white-robed figure, holding aloft a chalice; banked about the altar were beeswax tapers, their wavering flames casting incandescent light upon the uplifted faces of men and women who kneeled in rapt silence. Perfumed smoke gusted from censers. The refrains of a hymn rose upward from a choir of children assembled on crates.

I saw Mary seated on a chair, a garnet rosary twined in her hands. The gems captured the candlelight, scattered it like blood drops across her dress.

"By God, she is secure of her victory," said Barnaby. "We can only hope this is all she'll make us suffer of her papist rites."

Mesmerized by the scene's eerie strangeness, I said, "I've never seen the old ways before. They're quite beautiful, in truth."

"For you, perhaps. To those of us who've seen heretics burn in France and Spain, it's not so pretty a sight." Barnaby turned into the room. There were no shutters or panes on the window, so I could only turn about as well and watch him pace.

"I don't like it," he said. "I want to do her honor as my queen, but already she brings out altars and burns incense, just as they warned us she would." He looked at me. "Word came tonight that the duke assembles an army against her. If he fails, her way to the throne is open."

"As it should be," I replied. "It is, after all, her throne."

"I know that. But what if . . . ?" He glanced at the door, lowered his voice to a whisper. "What if we're wrong? What if her devotion to Rome proves more compelling than her duty to England? Edward was terrified of this very thing. He sought to alter the succession because he believed she would bring us back into superstition and idolatry, overturn everything that their father and he had tried to achieve."

I started. "Philip Sidney said something to that effect, the night we were in the king's rooms. But he said Edward had been forced to sign something. And earlier today, Her Majesty told me the council had said she'd been disinherited because of doubts about her legitimacy." I paused, looking at him. "What do you know that you haven't told me?"

He did not hesitate. "The doubts about her legitimacy were the excuse. In truth, Edward didn't think Mary was a bastard; he believed all his father's marriages were legal. But he also never thought she should become queen. When he signed that addendum barring her from the throne, he did it willingly. But I thought you knew this already."

"No." My mind worked fast to absorb this unexpected development. "I thought the duke had forced Edward to sign it so he could name Jane Grey as heir. Are you saying Edward had plans of his own, before he fell ill?"

"Yes. He wanted Elizabeth to rule. He was going to tell her himself. That's why Northumberland went to such lengths to refuse her leave to visit. He didn't want Edward and her to meet and hatch a plot against him."

It all made sense now. There was far more to this tangle of half-truths and lies.

"And how do you know this?" I asked quietly.

Barnaby frowned. "How else? Master Cecil told me. He approached me shortly after Edward suffered his first collapse. He said the king and I were like brothers, and therefore I would understand his concern."

Again, I felt that sharp twist in my gut. "Concern about what?"

"That the duke aimed to safeguard his own power, regardless of Edward's desires." He went to the lone stool in the room and perched. Clasping his hands, he regarded me thoughtfully.

"Edward had been ill for three years; he was losing weight, suffering fevers. . . . He knew he might not live long enough to ever marry and sire an heir. By right of succession, Mary stood next in line to the throne. Edward was against any rapprochement with Rome, so he invited Mary to court to sound her out. Her refusal to accept the Reformed Faith convinced him of her unworthiness. According to Cecil, he decided to disinherit Mary in favor of Elizabeth. He told Cecil as much, asked him to help draft the necessary documents so he could present his decision to the council. But he developed a terrible rash and soon thereafter fell gravely ill. The duke took over his care. That was the last anyone of the council ever saw of him."

"Wait a minute." I held up a hand, the seemingly disjointed final pieces of the puzzle falling like knives into place. "Edward wanted to present his decision *without* the duke knowing of it beforehand? Why? Northumberland must have shared his concerns about Mary. Why hide it from him?"

Barnaby shrugged. "Edward could be tight-lipped when the occasion warranted. Once he decided against someone, he rarely changed his mind. I think he took a dislike to the duke when he realized how much control Northumberland had over him. In any event, after his collapse, he was denied access to anyone without the duke's leave, including Cecil."

"Which is when Cecil came to you." Had I not been so outraged, I might have admired the sheer audacity. Our master secretary had been far busier than any of us had imagined.

"That's right." Barnaby looked confused. "He told me he feared the duke might hasten the king to his death and turn the ax on anyone who tried to expose him."

"And you believed him." As I spoke, I recalled that dapper figure with its modulated voice, which could exude such sincerity. . . .

"I had no reason to doubt." Barnaby spread his big hands. "Cecil wanted me to watch over the king and report anything unusual. He didn't know the duke would dismiss me from service. I kept watch all the same, though, especially after I discovered Northumberland had also dismissed all of Edward's physicians."

I found it suddenly difficult to draw breath.

Barnaby went on, his voice edging with suspicion. "You're acting like you don't know any of this. But you work for Cecil. When you helped Her Grace, it was by his orders. That's what Peregrine told me. It's why I agreed to help you."

I made myself move from the window. I felt cold, numb. "Half-truths and omissions," I breathed, "that's how he functions." I looked up. "He knew everything, all the time."

Barnaby stared. "Who?"

"Cecil. He knew everything that was happening to Edward."

"He knew what the Dudleys were doing?"

"I think so." Implacable fury rose in me. "Without Edward to protect him, Cecil stood alone. If the duke succeeded in his own plots, he wouldn't survive. He knew too much, and Northumberland had grown too powerful. Even if a lone assassin could do the deed, there were still the duke's sons and his wife to contend with. That's why Cecil had to do more than just bring down Northumberland. He had to destroy the entire Dudley family."

I drew a shuddering breath. "I just never saw it. I never would have, had we not spoken tonight, though it was staring me in the face from the moment he asked me to spy for him."

Barnaby stood. "But if Cecil was going to destroy the Dudleys, why didn't he warn Her Grace away? All he had to do was tell her Edward was dying. Why risk her life?"

"I don't know." I retrieved my shirt from the floor. "But I intend to find out."

"I wish he were here!" He hit his fist into his palm. "I'd make him explain it, the snake."

I met his gaze, shook my head. "We've been cruelly used, my friend. None more so than you, whose devotion to your king became fodder for Cecil's game." I took a moment. "I have one more question. Did you tell Cecil about the herbalist?"

He averted his eyes. "Yes. It seemed odd. Why would Northumberland dismiss the royal doctors only to bring in some herb witch? When Sidney saw Lady Dudley in Edward's room one evening, giving the herbalist orders, I recalled Cecil saying he feared the duke might hasten Edward to his death. What better way than poison? It seemed right to tell him."

My heart felt as if a giant hand gripped it in a vise. I made myself draw a steadying breath, put on my jerkin and boots, and took up my battered cap.

"Where are you going?" asked Barnaby, as I fastened my bag's straps and shouldered it.

"To ask the queen for leave. If she grants it, I've business in London." I looked at him. "Promise me you'll look after Peregrine. I don't want him to think I've abandoned him, but I can't bring him with me. I can't risk them finding out what he means to me."

"By them, you mean Cecil."

"Among others."

"Let me come with you. I've a score of my own to settle with him."

I clasped his stolid hand. "I'd like nothing better. But you'll be helping me more if you keep Peregrine safe and support the queen. She may not share your faith, but it could be that with men like you at her side she can learn to rule with temperance."

We embraced as friends. Then I drew back and slipped away.

* * *

I had Cinnabar saddled by the time her summons came. Rising from my crouch in the shadows to follow Rochester, I made certain my expression conveyed only dutiful concern. My sudden bid for departure was bound to incite her suspicion.

She waited in the hall, her thinning hair in a net at her nape. Without her headdress, she looked tiny. The rosary hung at her waist, its scarlet stones muted against the array of rings on her fingers. She seemed in all other respects impervious to vanity, and I found her fondness for jewelry inexplicably disturbing.

"Rochester tells me you wish to leave," she said, before I had righted from my genuflection. "Why? Are our accommodations not to your liking?"

"Your Majesty, I assure you I've no wish to return to the road so soon, but I understand the duke plans to march against you. I think it best if I conveyed your reply to the lords sooner rather than later—that is, if Your Majesty still wishes to reply."

I held my breath as Mary shifted her gaze to Rochester, who gave a slight nod.

"I do," she said. "I need all the support I can get, even from your treacherous lords."

The bite in her remark carried a warning. She wasn't an easy woman to know, nor, it seemed, to please. What she had endured in her youth had marked her for life, warped her personality in some irreconcilable way. Elizabeth, it appeared, knew her well.

"Your Majesty," I ventured, "with the duke about to take the field against you, the lords will be even better disposed to your cause."

"I don't care what their disposition is. They'd be wise to do as

I say if they wish to keep their heads." She went to her table, thrust two folded and sealed parchments at me.

"The sealed one is in cipher. Anyone with experience will know the key. Tell your lords they're to follow it without deviation. The other is a letter for my cousin Jane Grey. Memorize it. It's a private message meant for her ears alone, so if you can't find a trustworthy way to convey it to her, destroy it. I don't want it falling into the wrong hands."

"Yes, Your Majesty." It was of course far more than I'd hoped to perform. Getting one letter into the proper hands would prove dangerous enough, much less two.

"I don't expect a reply from either one," she informed me. "I should be in London soon enough. But if you uncover any news that might influence my course, favorable or otherwise, I expect to be told. Your loyalty to those who've hired you should not supplant your allegiance to your queen. Do you understand?"

"Of course." I started to bow over her hand. She withdrew it. Glancing up, I found her looking at me as if she no longer recognized me. "Give my regards to Master Cecil," she said coldly. "Though it's not in my instructions, tell him from me that he knows what he must do."

I pocketed the letters and backed from her presence without a word.

Chapter Twenty-seven

Mist wreathing off the Thames formed a wavering veil. The day already promised to be hot, the midmorning sun casting a luminescent chimera upon the thrust and sprawl of London.

It had been a short ride, a mere day and a half. I'd not taken much rest. I avoided the main thoroughfares and skirted all townships. A few discreet inquiries of passersby had revealed that every town was jammed to the rooftops with the queen's supporters, gates shut and manned in anticipation of the duke. As with any situation that might result in anarchy, the streets were also teeming with riffraff. A lone man on a horse was an easy target, so I sought refuge in the woods, awakening before dawn to resume my ride.

I now sat atop a hill, a vantage spot from which to view the place where it had all started. Was it only eleven days ago that I had beheld this same city with the awestruck eyes of a boy eager to cull his fortune? Now, it made me feel hollow inside. All of my life, I had longed to know who I was and where I came from. Now a part of me longed to turn about and lose myself in an ordinary life, to forget a world where sons born to royal women were forsaken and men sacrificed kings to sate their ambitions. I knew now that whatever answers I had come to London to find would not reveal anything I wanted to hear.

Fortune often smiles on those least favored.

I gave a humorless chuckle. It seemed fortune had a sense of humor, for I, the least favored, had more than my share of responsibilities; and one of them drew near me even as I sat in the stillness, contemplating becoming a fugitive from my own truth.

I waited until I heard the telltale rustle, then said without looking about, "No use hiding anymore. I've known you were behind me since Bury Saint Edmunds."

A muffled clop of hoof preceded Peregrine's wary approach. He wore his hooded cloak. I took in the strips of homespun fettering his horse's hooves, and reins, bridle, and stirrups, even his dagger in its scabbard—in short, anything that might make a sound. The lad had more tricks up his sleeve than a relic peddler.

"You can't have known," he said, eyeing me. "I made sure to stay at least fifteen paces behind you at all times, and Deacon has a light step."

"Yes, but you forget that horses, especially those who've ridden together, make all sorts of signals when they sense the other near. Cinnabar practically bolted away last night toward that glen where you were hiding. You should have joined me. I had rabbit for supper."

"Aye, and with that fire you made you're lucky every poacher in the county didn't drop by to sample it," retorted Peregrine. He paused. "You're not mad at me?"

I sighed. "Only frustrated. I asked Barnaby to watch over you."

"Don't blame him. He did his best. He told me that under no

circumstances was I to follow you. He said you had private business to attend to and we must honor your decision."

"I'm glad you paid such close attention." I raised my hand to
my brow, scanning the road. "I'm surprised he isn't behind you.
You two must think I'm incapable of tying my own points, what
with the way you fuss and fret."

"I wasn't going to let you leave me behind again." Peregrine
squared his narrow shoulders. "You need all the help you can
get. I told you before we left Greenwich: You're no good on your
own. You only get into trouble."

"Is that what Barnaby thinks, as well?"

Peregrine nodded. "He was going to be the one to come after
you. I convinced him to let me come, instead. No one would
miss me, while Barnaby would have had to ask leave of Rochester, who isn't about to let a brawny lad like him get away from
the queen's service, not with the duke hot on her trail."

"True. But you should have heeded him anyway. You've no
idea what you risk."

"I don't care." Peregrine's eyes were earnest in his grimy face.
"I'm your body servant, remember? I go where you go, no matter
what. I must earn my keep."

I couldn't keep the smile from my face. "By God, you're stubborn as a pit bear and smell almost as bad. How did I end up with
such a tenacious mite?"

Peregrine scowled, about to retort, when a startled flock of
pigeons caught my eye. I turned back to the city. When I saw a
cloud of dust snaking toward us, I hissed, "To cover!" and we
spurred our mounts into the nearby fringe of bushes and beech.

We slid from our saddles and held the horses close, hands on
bridles, barely breathing. A militant thunder came closer and
closer. It reminded me of the night we'd sat at the roadside and

watched Robert Dudley and his men gallop past. Only this time the noise was like that of some great lumbering creature, composed of hundreds of metallic hooves striking the road. Its approach vibrated the air around us, sent the dust rising in gusts.

The standard bearers appeared first, carrying banners emblazoned with the Dudley bear and staff. The cavalry followed on leather-caparisoned horses, swords and bows strapped to saddles. Then marched the foot soldiers, line after line in chain mail, interspersed with oxen and mule-drawn carts; I detected the bulk of cannon under tarps and assumed those carts also contained a supply of equally lethal weaponry.

Then I saw the mounted lords. Each wore quilted battle gear and rode behind the duke, who, defiant at their head, was distinguished by his audacious crimson cloak. He wore no cap, his dark hair framing his granite face, which, even from my distance, appeared to have aged years in a matter of days.

At his sides were three of his sons—Henry, Jack, and Ambrose, outfitted in martial splendor. For the first time in all the years I'd known them, the brothers I had feared and hated, envied for their camaraderie, were not laughing. Like Robert before them, they understood they confronted the ultimate challenge, one that would end in triumph or tragedy for their family.

In tense formation they rode past, this army assembled to defeat Mary Tudor. I waited in silence long after they'd disappeared down the road, grappling with unexpected remorse. The Dudleys had never cared a fig for anyone but themselves. They'd gladly see both princesses, and all who tried to help them, to their deaths. There could be no room for pity in my heart, even if the duke and his sons were innocent of the one crime I most burned to avenge. And with Northumberland gone from the city, I had an opportunity I could not ignore.

I mounted Cinnabar and spurred him back onto the road, where the dust wafted in the air like tattered veils.

"Where are we going?" Peregrine asked as we cantered to-ward London.

"To see an old friend," I said. "By the way, do you know how we can get inside the Tower?"

"The Tower!" Peregrine exclaimed, as soon as we cleared the checkpoint at Aldgate, which had required distribution of most of the gold angels from the purse Walsingham had given me. "Are you insane? We can't get inside there. It's a royal fortress, in case you hadn't noticed."

"I'd heard, yes. But I really must get inside. I've a letter to deliver."

Peregrine blew air out of the side of his mouth. "The stron-gest fortress in England, and you have a letter to deliver? Why don't we just knock on the gates? It'll have the same result. Or haven't you heard the saying 'Once in, only your head comes out'? I'm beginning to think you're as much of a unicorn as Kate says."

I paused. "A what?"

"A unicorn. A fabled beast. A lunacy."

I threw back my head and laughed with genuine belly-heaving mirth. I suddenly felt much better. "I've never heard that before. I like it."

"I wager you'll like it less if you end up trussed in a dungeon with your horn cut off. We can't get inside the Tower without proper identification and leave, so forget about even trying. Any other wretched place you'd like us to try for instead?"

"No. But you've given me an idea." My smile lingered as we rode into Cheapside. The streets were eerily quiet, shuttered windows converting taverns into bastions. Except for one lone beggar too physically wasted to crawl away from the doorway where she huddled, there were no people to be seen. All of London cowered behind closed doors, as if to await a calamity.

"We should stable the horses and take to the river," said Peregrine. "We're too obvious. There's no one around but us. We'll be arrested if a patrol happens to see us."

"You'll have to excuse my aversion to water at the moment," I replied as we rode single file above the riverbank, where we might better avoid the conduits and refuse heaps, if not the ubiquitous sewage.

When I spied Whitehall's turrets in the distance, I reined to a halt. "Which way to Cecil's house?"

Peregrine looked leery. "Do you think he'll still be there?"

"He's there." My voice hardened. "Now listen to me: I want you to do exactly as I say from now on. Do I make myself clear? If you make a nuisance of yourself, I'll truss you up. This is not a game, Peregrine. One mistake and we could both end up dead."

"I understand." He gave a servile whirl of his hand. "This way, my lord and master."

He led us back into the labyrinth of crooked streets. The feeling of impending disaster was palpable, stalking the dark pockets where the houses staggered into each other like drunkards. I was glad when we emerged onto a wider street that ran through the palace, though even here it was astounding how deserted everything was, like a kingdom in some romantic fable, frozen in time by a spell.

When we neared our destination, I left Peregrine with the horses and strict orders, and proceeded alone. A high wall enclosed the house's exterior. I tried the postern gate first and found it unlocked. Moving toward the front entrance, I unsheathed my dagger. It would serve me little in a pitched confrontation, but the bow Barnaby had left strapped to Cinnabar's saddle was too cumbersome for indoor fighting.

I glanced up at the windows. The house appeared as uninhabited as the rest of the city. A small gate opened to the side. I vaulted it, landing on soft turf. I stood in the garden, which sloped toward a private landing quay screened by willows. As I suspected, a barge was moored there, the boatman hunched at the fore, swigging from an ale skin.

I turned to creep around the house. I found a coffer propping the back door open, as if someone had been coming and going in haste. Beyond was the mullioned window of Cecil's study. Flat against the wall, I inched forth and craned my head upward to peer within.

When I spied the figure inside, taking ledgers from the desk and stuffing them into a valise, I returned to the door and slipped into the house.

Gloom submerged the interior. I eased toward the far, open doorway with caution, looking to either side. The wood floor creaked under my feet. I froze, anticipating thugs to come lunging at me with knives and fists. Then, when nothing happened, I inched forth again until I was close enough to look inside the study.

Cecil stood with his back to the door, wearing his black breeches and doublet. A traveling cloak was tossed over his chair; he had the valise on the desk, about to close it when he went still. Without looking around, he said, "Now, this is a surprise."

I stepped over the threshold.

He turned, glanced at the dagger in my fist. "Have you come to kill me, Squire Prescott?"

"I should," I said. Now that I was face-to-face with the man who had played and outmaneuvered everyone with the skill of an expert puppeteer, my heart beat impossibly loud in my ears. I looked about the room. "Are you alone? Or do I have to deal with your assassin first?"

He gave me a thin smile. "If you're referring to Walsingham, I assure you the situation has become far too precarious for a man of his staunch persuasions. I imagine he's on his way to Dover by now, to book passage to the continent. I'd have gone with him myself, had I not my family's welfare to consider."

"What, is Queen Mary getting too close for comfort?"

His smile did not waver. "Entirely. In fact, I was about to take my barge to the bridge and hire a mount to Hertfordshire. It's not far from Her Grace's manor at Hatfield." He paused. "Would you care to join me? She'll be happy to receive you, I'm told, after everything you've done for her."

My anger, held too long under check, blazed. "Don't you play with me, not after everything *you* have done."

He regarded me without a single hint that I had perturbed him. "It seems you've a bone to pick. Come, let us sit and discuss it like gentlemen." He leaned to his valise, as if to shift it aside.

I didn't hesitate. Leaping forth, I pressed my dagger to his ribs, hard enough to be felt through his doublet. "I'd be careful if I were you. I don't need another reason to make you regret ever having met me."

He went still. "I would never regret that. May I at least sit? I have a touch of gout; my leg pains me today."

Despite everything, I had to admire his restraint. I even

found myself hoping I wouldn't be forced to act. Truth be told, I wasn't certain I could carry out my threat, particularly now that my initial blinding rage had started to ebb into something more manageable. I wasn't like him. I didn't relish the elaborate subterfuges, the coils within coils. And I needed his cooperation, if I was to discover the final reason for why he and I found ourselves like this.

"I'm not sure what I've done to offend you," he began, his hands draped on the armrests as if he addressed an inopportune guest. "I am no more a traitor than any other councilor obliged to support the duke against the queen."

I met his cool appraising eyes, which had been my first indoctrination into his perfidious world. "My business with you is private. I'll leave Her Majesty to ordain whatever punishment she deems best."

"Ah. I must say, you stay remarkably true to character. You believe Mary has been wronged and that I had a hand in it."

"Would you deny that you provided the duke with the information they needed to pursue her? Or was it coincidence that Lord Robert happened to be on the same road as me, at almost the same time?"

Cecil leaned back, crossing his trim legs in their dun-colored hose. "I won't deny that I nudged him in the right direction. However, I also did not lift protest when I heard Lord Arundel had Durot—or rather, our brave Fitzpatrick—infiltrate Lord Robert's company, though I knew he could confound the chase. You see, I'm not entirely Mary's enemy."

I likened his voice to a siren song—soothing, melodic, and all too convincing. A few days ago, I would have been lulled.

"You're lying. Mary is the last person you want on the throne. You've worked against her almost as avidly as you've worked against the duke. You wanted her taken on the road or, better yet, killed as she fled. It's what you planned. Fortunately for her, she proved less gullible than you thought."

"I've never hidden where my ultimate allegiance rests." He eyed my hand as it tightened on my dagger. "You should know that regardless of what you may think, Her Grace will have more need of me than ever before. She and Mary are not close, not as sisters should be."

He reached again for his valise. I snapped, "Stay away from that."

He paused. "I shall need my spectacles and cipher wheel. I assume the letter you bring is written in her usual code? You must have impressed her. She never entrusts her private missives to strangers."

He *knew* I brought a letter. I had the unsettling sensation that I was dueling with someone who exceeded any ability I had to thwart him. I struggled to make sense of what I felt, of what I saw and heard; to pry it apart and examine it for unspoken meaning. When I finally did, I nearly laughed aloud at my own naïveté: that I ever could have believed I'd found out everything there was to know about this subtle, lethal man!

"It was *you*. I overheard Lady Dudley telling Robert someone at court was feeding Mary information; Walsingham implied the same. You warned Mary away. You let Robert go after her, but you protected yourself first by sending her advance notice. She told me at Framlingham that you would know what must be done. I thought it was a threat, but it's not, is it? She will spare you because she thinks you helped save her from the duke."

Amusement laced Cecil's voice. "I can hardly take all the credit. I understand her cousin the duchess of Suffolk also sent her a communiqué, detailing all types of sordid goings-on at court. It seems Madame Suffolk had her own ax to grind against the Dudleys."

I was not surprised to hear of the duchess's involvement. She had vowed vengeance. What better way to achieve it than to feign compliance with the Dudleys while secretly inciting her royal cousin to action?

But there was of course the other matter involving her, the primary reason for my being here. I watched Cecil closely as he added, "As I've said, I'm not entirely her enemy. Oh, and she always uses the same cipher. I've advised her numerous times to devise a new one, but she never listens. One of the few qualities she does share with her sister."

He reached again to his valise and drew out a pair of silver-framed glasses. He held out his hand. "The missive, please?"

I gave it to him. Cold certainty began to seep through my veins. He was indeed a master of opportunism, an expert in games of deceit. Whatever I thought he had done or was about to do only revealed another layer underneath.

He read Mary's letter in silence, glancing now and then at the key wheel in his other hand. When he was done, he removed his glasses, set the paper and wheel aside.

"Well?" I said. I felt a subtle shift in the air.

"She too stays true to character." He raised weary eyes. "She orders that before the council even thinks of asking for her clemency, they must see that she's proclaimed queen to the exclusion of all other claimants. She also warns that those who failed to offer her support should remove themselves at once. Those who stay must show proof of their constancy by taking the duke and his sons into custody, as well as Jane Grey. She promises the usual array of punishments if she is disobeyed. Not that she will be; everyone knows the die is cast."

"You'll be safe enough," I said, but I had no satisfaction in the barb. There was an awful tingle in my belly, a growing awareness I had made an error in my assessment of him.

"Do you truly believe that?" He gave a rueful shake of his head. "I may have helped her stay one step ahead of the duke, but don't think for an instant that she's forgotten that I served the man. There'll be no place for me at her court." He sighed. "No matter. Country life suits me well enough, and it is time I got away from all this."

"She's banishing you?" I experienced keen disappointment. Cecil was not someone a wise monarch should disdain. If nothing else, his facility for spying made him an asset or a liability, depending on the circumstances.

"Not in so many words, but she knows I have no other choice. She'll never trust any of those who served the duke or her brother. I should be grateful that unlike these others, I needn't soil my hands by putting my former master in prison."

And those hands, I noticed, had changed. The ink stains under the nails were faded, as if he had already started to slough away the skin of his prior role.

Cecil went on: "Had it gone differently, we'd have seen her to the same prison quick enough. To be banished is fortunate indeed, considering not a few heads will roll before this matter is concluded."

His play for empathy was a mistake. I smiled. I had been wrong. She had not disdained him. She had seen through him. The time had come to cast my own die.

"But not your head. You made sure of that. No one knows the extent of your involvement."

This time, I was pleased to see the skin about his mouth tighten.

"Unless you've been filling Mary's ears with nonsense, yes," he replied.

"I would never stoop so low. Difficult as it may be for you to imagine, Her Majesty is an innocent when it comes to men like you."

"You shouldn't let her air of virginal righteousness blind you. She's an enemy to our faith, and her accession is a tragedy to those who've labored to bring greater glory to England."

"To England?" I asked. "Or to Cecil? Or are they one and the same to you?"

"I assure you, I've sought only to serve Her Grace."

Without warning, my anger resurged, virulent as fever. Lies and more lies—with him, they never stopped. No doubt, he would lie his way to his very grave.

No more. I would make him speak the truth, damn him to hell.

"Is that why you let her come to court?" I advanced on his chair. "Though you knew she risked her life? Is that why you failed to warn her away, because you sought to serve her?"

There was no mistaking the change in the air. He might have actually recoiled in his seat, had he the reflexes of a normal man, unused to guarding his reactions at every moment.

"You forget that I did advise her to leave," he said, in a measured tone. "I warned her several times of the danger, but she did not listen." Still, he didn't move, did not rise in alarm, though I stood so close I could have stabbed him before he had time to cry out.

"You didn't warn her," I said. "You manipulated her. You manipulated her just as you manipulated me. You've been playing a game with all of us from the beginning."

He smiled. Actually *smiled*. "And what, pray, did this game of mine entail?"

I had to step back, lest I went too far and didn't stop until he lay in a bloodied sprawl at my feet. It had all become crystalline clear, the truth surfacing as if a cloth had been wiped across the tarnished glass of my mind.

Everything was more horribly real than I had imagined.

"To see Elizabeth made queen instead of her sister—that was your game. The duke's time had run out. After years of watching him exercise control over Edward, you decided never would the likes of Northumberland and his clan rule again. When the time came, they would fall, all of them, no matter the cost. And they would take Mary with them." I met his stare. "But something happened. Something you didn't anticipate."

"Is that so?" He folded his hands at his chin. "Do go on. I find this all . . . fascinating."

"Jane Grey happened. You had no idea what the duke planned, did you, that night Elizabeth arrived at court? All you knew for certain was that the king was dying and Northumberland wanted the princess for himself. By the time the duke announced Jane Grey's marriage to his son and you realized just how far he was willing to go to keep his grip on the throne, it was too late. So you put Elizabeth to the test, because if all went as planned, she herself would help you dispose of your rival."

His expression revealed nothing.

My voice rose despite myself. I flung my next words at him as if they could humiliate, bruise, maim. "Northumberland posed no threat; you knew she would never have him. But Robert Dudley was another story. Only he had a claim on her more powerful than your own. Only he might have curtailed your influence over her. And it was that, more than anything else, which you could not bear."

"Careful, my friend," he said softly. "You may go too far."

I'd finally struck a nerve. I should indeed be careful, for the only thing more dangerous than his friendship was his enmity. In that moment, however, I no longer cared.

"Not as far as you. You knew the moment the king died, the duke would put an end to you because of what you knew. His Majesty had told you he wanted Elizabeth as his heir. Putting Jane Grey on the throne might prove a deadly error, but it was possible the duke would still succeed, that Mary might escape, or the lure of power would prove too great and Elizabeth would succumb to Robert. If any of these occurred, you could disavow yourself completely."

I paused. His pale eyes were now fixed on me.

"You were willing to abandon her, to turn coat and feign support of whoever won—including Mary, though in your heart you loathe and fear her more than the duke himself."

At this, Cecil raked his fingers across the chair arms. "You insult me. You dare insinuate that I would betray my own princess?"

"I do. But no one will ever know, will they? No matter what, your hide is safe."

He came to his feet. Though he was not a tall man, he seemed to fill the room with his presence. "You should be an actor. The profession would benefit from your flair for the dramatic. I should warn you, however, that before you even think of entertaining Her Grace with this preposterous tale, you should consider she'll require more than unsubstantiated charges."

My every muscle tensed. I was right, and the revelation stunned me. I had not thought to be so taken aback, so shocked, by what I had discovered. In some part of me, I had held on to the desperate hope that none of it was true.

"She is no fool," I told him. "It's clear to me, as it will be to her, that you let her and her sister walk into a quagmire of lies, completely unprepared for what might befall them."

An odd light flickered in his eyes. The violence I had glimpsed had vanished, replaced by disturbing levity. Uncoiling his hands, Cecil started to clap. The sound was rhythmic, reverberating against the oak-paneled study. "Bravo. You have exceeded my highest expectations. You are everything I had hoped you would be."

I stared. "What . . . what do you mean by that?"

His regard was all encompassing, merciless. "In a moment. First, let me say you've a rare gift for deciphering intrigue. For you are correct: I did want Mary dead and Elizabeth on the throne. She is our last hope, the only one of Henry the Eighth's children worthy to inherit his crown. I may have failed in my goal, but it is an untimely delay of the inevitable. She was born to rule, you see. And when her day comes, nothing—*nothing*—will be able to compete with her destiny."

"Not even her happiness?" I said. A hard lump filled my throat. "Not even love?"

"Especially not love." His voice was matter-of-fact, as if he spoke of a color she must never wear. "That, above all, would be disastrous. She may have been born the wrong sex, but in every-thing else she is the prince that her father longed for. Only she has his strength, his courage, his drive to conquer any obstacle thrown in her path. She must not give in to the weakness in her blood—a weakness she inherited from her mother, who was ever one to indulge herself. I'll not see her sacrifice her future for Dudley, whose ambition is his overriding vice."

"She loves him!" I yelled. "She's loved him since they were children! You knew that, and you deliberately set out to destroy it. Who are you to dictate her fate? Who are you to say where she may or may not give her heart?"

"Her friend," was his reply, "the only one with the stomach to save her from herself. Robert Dudley was her downfall. Now she need never be tempted. Even if he can survive Mary's wrath, which is most unlikely, he's lost Elizabeth forever. She'll never trust him completely again. It is a reward which, in my estimation, more than compensates her suffering."

"You're a monster." My breath came in stifled bursts. "Did you ever stop to think that in your grandiose plan to put a crown on her head you might break her spirit? Or that Jane Grey, who never wanted any part of this, could lose her life because of it?"

Cecil's gaze riveted me to my spot. "Elizabeth is more resilient than you think. As for Jane Grey, it wasn't my idea to make her queen. I merely sought to benefit from it."

I wanted to leave him there, with his papers and his machinations. Nothing he could tell me now would bring me anything other than revulsion, despair.

And yet I stayed, transfixed.

His smile was like slivered steel. "Have you nothing to say? We've reached the crux of the matter, the reason why you are here. So go on. Ask me. Ask what else I've been hiding from you. Ask me about the herbalist and the reason Frances of Suffolk had to surrender her claim to the throne to her daughter."

He let out a small sigh. "Ask me, Brendan Prescott, who you are."

Chapter Twenty-eight

You know," I whispered. "You have known from the start."

"Not from the start," Cecil said, with an air of reprove. "I only heard a rumor years ago, when I was younger than you are now—one of many scandals overheard in passing, like so much at court. I wouldn't have paid it any mind had it not concerned Henry the Eighth's beloved younger sister, whom so many knew as the French Queen—that headstrong princess who created an international uproar when she wed Charles of Suffolk, yet whose death at age thirty-seven caused nary a ripple."

"It was June," I said. A bone-deep chill enveloped me, as if I would never be warm again.

"Yes, June 1533, to be exact. King Henry had crowned Anne Boleyn in her sixth month of pregnancy, proof that God approved their union and the turmoil they'd wrought on England. Little did they know the child they awaited would be the beginning of Anne's downfall."

Cecil paced to the window. He stood staring out into his garden. Silence descended, laden like the pause before the opening of a well-thumbed book. Then he said quietly, "I was thirteen years old, serving as an apprentice clerk—another ambitious lad among hundreds, working my fingers to the quick. I got around; I was nimble and I knew how to keep my ears open and my mouth shut. Thus, I often heard a great deal more than my appearance suggested."

He smiled faintly. "I was a bit like you, in fact—diligent, well-intentioned, eager to seek my advantage. When I heard the rumor, it struck me as a sign of the times that the king's own sister had died alone, after months of seclusion in her manor at Westhorpe, allegedly having lived in terror that Anne Boleyn might discover her secret."

The chill infiltrated my veins. I heard Stokes's words in my head:

She was mad with fear; she begged her daughter to keep it a secret. . . .

"What secret?" I said, in a near-inaudible voice.

"That she was with child, of course." Cecil turned back to me. "You must remember that many actually believed Anne Boleyn had bewitched the king. She was a strong-willed woman, with strong opinions. The common people detested her; so did most of the nobles. She had destroyed Katherine of Aragon, threatened to send Henry's own daughter Mary to the block. Several of Henry's oldest friends had fallen into disgrace or lost their heads because of his infatuation with her. Anne Boleyn had staked her entire future on the fact that the king's first marriage was not valid and he had no legitimate heir. But until she gave him one, his sister's children were next in line to the throne."

"And Mary of Suffolk hated Anne Boleyn. . . ." I heard myself say.

"Indeed. She'd been vocal in her horror over Henry's break with Rome and remained a staunch ally of Queen Katherine, who, while imprisoned under house arrest, was still very much alive. Mary had already given birth to two sons and two daughters; any living child of hers posed a threat, but one born in those precarious months while Anne awaited hers—well, let us say she had reason to fear Anne's enmity. It was why she stayed away from court. Or it was the excuse she wanted everyone to believe."

My hands hung limp at my sides, my dagger pointed at the floor.

"Then she died," I said, without inflection.

"According to the rumor I heard, she died shortly after giving birth. She'd hidden her pregnancy from everyone, allegedly because she feared Anne would poison her. She was buried in haste, without ceremony. Henry didn't display much grief; he was too excited about his queen's impending confinement, as was everyone else. By the time Elizabeth was born, few remembered Mary of Suffolk had existed. In the next three years, her widower Charles Brandon—a man who embraced self-preservation— married his pubescent ward and sired two sons before his own demise. By then, Anne Boleyn had gone to the block and Henry had wed and lost Jane Seymour, his third wife, who gave him Edward, his coveted son. The king of course went on to wed three more times. In our world, nothing is as quickly forgotten as the dead."

"And Mary's last child?" I asked thickly. "What became of it?"

"Some said it was stillborn; others that it was hidden away at her dying request. Certainly, Charles of Suffolk never mentioned it—which he would have, had he known. His remaining son by Mary died the year after her; all he had left were daughters."

"So he would have welcomed another son . . . ?"

Cecil nodded. "Indeed. But he was abroad for most of the time before his wife's demise, and by all accounts he and Mary were on difficult terms. Suffolk had supported the king's quest to rid himself of Queen Katherine and marry Anne; Mary opposed it. Still, theirs was reputedly a love match, and he must have tried; she wasn't so old that she could not conceive. . . . In any event, she hid her last pregnancy from him, giving out instead that she suffered from the swelling sickness. He probably never even suspected. It does beg the question of what was going through the unfortunate lady's mind that she'd keep a child from her own husband."

"You said she was afraid of Anne Boleyn," I said, and I heard him step to me, so close we might have embraced. His face looked ancient, the marks of worry, of ceaseless statecraft and insomniac nights, engraved into his flesh.

"Maybe Anne wasn't the only reason," he said, and he started to reach out. Before he could touch me, I shifted away, though it felt more like lurching, so leaden were my limbs. The chamber closed in around us, shot through with random afternoon light and stark long shadows.

"How did you find out about me?" I asked abruptly.

"Entirely by coincidence." His response was certain, subdued. "As I said, Henry the Eighth's testament decreed that after his children and their heirs, his sister Mary's issue stood next in line to the throne. So when I learned that the duchess had renounced her claim in favor of her daughter Jane Grey, I was surprised. Frances of Suffolk never renounced anything willingly in her life. Northumberland informed me she had done so in exchange for Guilford as a spouse for Jane, but not even he seemed convinced. I decided to investigate. It wasn't long before I learned that Lady Dudley had threatened Frances with something altogether more interesting."

I gave him a hollow smile. "Me."

"Yes," he said, "though I didn't know exactly who you were at that time. I didn't begin to put it together until I learned Lady Dudley had presented you to the duchess in the hall, where she whispered a comment about the mark of the rose. Now, *that* caught my attention: The Rose was Henry the Eighth's affectionate nickname for his younger sister. You of course had already told me when we met that you were a foundling, but you also spoke of a woman you'd lost, who cared for you. I knew from Fitzpatrick of the herbalist Lady Dudley had brought to treat Edward, and so I started to put the pieces into place. It still took me time to figure it all out, but the conclusion, once I recognized it, was irresistible."

I was floundering, fighting against the unraveling of my own self.

"And it was . . . ?" I managed to utter. Silence ensued. For the first time, Cecil wavered, as if he debated whether or not to continue.

The cruelty of the game finally unhinged me.

"TELL ME!" My dagger clattered to the floor as I grabbed him by the doublet and rammed him hard against the wall. "Tell me this instant!"

In a low voice Cecil said, "You are the last son of Mary of Suffolk. The herbalist, Mistress Alice—the Suffolk household accounts show she had been in service to the late duchess; she attended her at Westhorpe in June of 1533. And years before, Lady Dudley had attended her as well, in France when Mary went to wed King Louis. These three women knew each other, and each was connected to you, the foundling whom Lady Dudley had brought to court to use against Frances of Suffolk."

With a strangled sound that was part moan, part sob, I released him. I staggered back, plunged back to that day years ago when Lady Dudley had taken the book of psalms from me. I saw its frontispiece in my mind, the handwritten dedication in French in that elegant feminine script. I had not understood, though it too had been with me, all along.

A mon amie, de votre amie, Marie.

That book I had stolen and carried with me in my saddlebag belonged to my mother. She had bequeathed it to a favored attendant—a lady who accompanied her during her brief time as queen of France, a lady she must have trusted, one she had called friend.

Lady Dudley. She had betrayed my mother's memory to further her own terrible ends.

Grabbing hold of the nearest chair, I threw it across the room. I wanted to tear the roof down about our ears, scour the walls to ashes, rip off my own skin. I spun back to him, enraged, my fists clenched and held before me.

He didn't shift a muscle. "Strike me if you must. But it won't return what was taken from you. I may be guilty of many things, but I did not do this. I did not steal your birthright. Lady Dudley did; *she* concealed it. She used and murdered your Mistress Alice for it."

I was beyond reason. An abyss opened beneath my feet, full of horrors I did not want to see. Of Lady Dudley, I could believe anything, including this monstrous deed. But my poor Alice . . . How could she have left me in ignorance, all these years? How could she have not realized that, in the end, what I did not know might be the one thing used against me?

"Alice cared for me," I heard myself whisper, as if I needed to convince myself. "She kept me safe. . . . They mangled her, tethered her like a beast, only to kill her in the end."

"Yes," he said quietly. "They did. And she endured it, out of love for you."

I looked at him. "Is that what it was? Love?"

"Never doubt it. Mistress Alice gave her life to you. She took you from your dying mother, from the sister who wanted you dead, and brought you to the one place where she thought you'd be safe. She couldn't have known what would occur; no one could have foreseen it, all those years ago. But she must have suspected enough about Lady Dudley to take steps to protect you. Your name alone proves it."

I thrust out a hand. "No more. Please. I—I cannot bear it."

"You must." He shifted from the wall. "You must accept the treachery and the lies, and you must overcome them. Otherwise, it will be *your* undoing." He paused. "She named you Brendan not because of her reverence for the saint but because it is the Latin form of the Irish name Bréanainn, which is derived from 'prince' in ancient Welsh. Mistress Alice gave you your legacy from the start. It has been with you all this time."

"Then why?" Desperation edged my voice. "If Mistress Alice knew who I was, why didn't Lady Dudley kill her the moment she brought me to her? Why did she wait so long?"

He went quiet for a moment before he said, "I can't say. All I can think of is that she depended on Alice's complicity. Any servant could raise you as one belonging to the lower class, and that was the illusion Lady Dudley had to create, that you belonged to no one. But servants gossip; word could get out about you. We can assume Lady Dudley knew you had to be hidden from Frances of Suffolk, and she needed someone to care for you whom she could trust. Alice would do both, so Lady Dudley took the risk that one day she might tell you the truth. At the time, there was no pressing need to do otherwise. You were still a babe; you could die, as many do. Nobody knew how the succession would resolve itself, but a secret like you could prove invaluable.

Absolute silence was required—silence and the patience to wait."

He paused, watching me. My heart pounded in my ears. There was more; I could feel it uncoiling just beneath the surface, shedding its brittle false skin.

Then Cecil added, "Of course, there is another possibility. Perhaps Lady Dudley did not kill Mistress Alice at first because she knew Alice had confided in someone else; someone who would reveal your existence should anything happen to her. If so, then between Alice and this other person, Lady Dudley found herself cornered; she did not dare act impulsively, at least not until she found her opportunity when King Edward fell ill." He paused. "Is there anyone you can think of whom your Mistress Alice might have trusted with so dangerous a secret?"

I went still, recalling Stokes's words: *But something happened in those last hours; Mary of Suffolk must have confided in the midwife, said something that fostered her mistrust. . . .*

And then Mary Tudor's: *Charles of Suffolk's . . . squire came to see me. A stalwart man . . .*

I wanted to bolt from the room, run as far as I could. I didn't want to know anymore. There would be no peace for me, no hiding. I'd be condemned to search until the end of my days.

But it was already too late. I knew how Alice had protected herself: with my birthmark, which another servant caring for me would see. And I also knew whom she had confided in. Like everything else, it had been there all along, waiting for me to learn enough to see it.

I shook my head in response to Cecil's question. "No, I don't. And it doesn't matter. Mistress Alice is dead." I hardened my voice. "But I know this much: You have no proof. There is no proof. I intend to keep it that way." I met his eyes. "If you ever tell another soul, I will kill you."

He chuckled. "I'm relieved to hear it." He adjusted his doublet, walked past the broken chair to his valise as if we'd been discussing the weather. "Because the revelation of your birth could create complications that would be most unfortunate for all concerned— especially you."

Raw laughter burst from me. "Is that why Walsingham was on the leads with a dagger? Given the uncertainty surrounding the succession, I must have presented a terrible hindrance!"

"You were never a hindrance." Cecil draped his cloak about his shoulders. "I underestimated your ingenuity perhaps, but I had no intention of letting you die, in my service or otherwise." The gravity in his tone took me aback. "If you consider the events, you'll see that when you first arrived here, all I had was an unfounded rumor and knowledge of an herbalist who had once served Mary of Suffolk. I couldn't possibly have known everything beforehand."

As if I were back in Whitehall the night of Elizabeth's arrival, I heard that cryptic whisper: *Il porte la marque de la rose.*

I couldn't rage anymore. I couldn't fight. "Not until someone confirmed it for you," I said. "That's why you had Walsingham follow me, isn't it? To see if he could catch me undressed. The mark on my skin, the mark called the rose—it would have proven everything."

He inclined his head as though I'd offered him a compliment. "I have no further secrets from you. Now, we can work together toward a cause greater than both of us—the cause of Elizabeth, who, I assure you, will soon face a challenge far worse than any Dudley."

"I didn't say I wanted anything more to do with you," I replied.

He smiled knowingly. "Then why, my dear boy, are you still here?"

Chapter Twenty-nine

𝕴t was late afternoon when we emerged from the house. Having never been on a barge before, I had to concede it was the preferable way to travel when in London. Though the river surface was peppered with flotsam I didn't care to examine too closely, exuding an acrid aroma that clung to one's clothes, the periodic tides that washed in ensured the Thames remained cleaner than any city street and far more navigable. I was amazed by the speed with which the hired boatman, half drunk as he was, propelled us toward that great stone bridge spanning the river, over which ran the main road from Canterbury and Dover.

The cakelike structure was perched on twenty cramped piers, ornamented with a southern gatehouse and roofed with teetering tenements. As I gazed up, Cecil said, "Some people are born, live, and die on that bridge without ever leaving it. When the tide is full, 'shooting the bridge' can be quite an experience, if you survive it."

The boatman grunted, displaying a toothless grin, and catapulted the barge with nauseating force through one of the bridge's narrow vaulted arches. I gripped the edge of the wood seat, my belly in my throat. Catching a churning swell on the other side, the barge reared up and down like a leaf caught in a maelstrom. I tasted vomit.

I would stick to my horse henceforth.

We entered steady water, sailing toward a breathtaking view of a mirror-still tidal pool, where anchored galleons swayed against the lowering sky. The Tower brooded at the far end, guarding the city approach. Though I couldn't see them, I was certain cannons protected every inch of those river-lapped walls. In the waning sunlight, the Tower's weathered stone was tinted with a rusty hue like blood, confirming its repute as a foreboding place no one should willingly enter.

Cecil said, "You needn't do this in person. There are many ways to deliver a letter."

I stared at the central keep mortared in white, its four turrets tipped with standards. "No. She deserves this much, and you owe it to me."

Cecil sighed. "Ingenious *and* headstrong. I hope you understand we can't overstay our welcome. I've no idea what to expect after I relay the queen's orders; regardless, in a few hours, curfew will be upon us and the Tower gates will close. Whoever gets locked inside, stays inside."

The barge docked. Cecil stood. "Pull down your cap. Whatever you do, don't speak unless you have to. The less they see and hear of you, the better."

"You'll get no argument from me," I muttered.

We mounted the water steps, turned past an open field to a gatehouse, where an alarming number of guards patrolled the entry into the Tower. I heard the muted roar of lions, lifted my hooded gaze to the edifice rising before me. Crenellated battlements studded with barbicans thrust into the sky, shielding the white keep.

A guard stepped forth. Cecil pushed back his hood to reveal his face. The guard paused. "Sir William?"

"Good day to you, Harry. I trust your wife is doing better." Cecil's voice was as smooth as the tidal pool shimmering below us. I hunched my shoulders, watching the guard from under my cap, which I'd yanked down about my ears. I was glad for once for my slim build and modest height. Dressed in my worn traveling gear, I looked like any other servant accompanying his master.

"She's on the mend," the guard said, with evident relief. "I do thank you for asking. Those herbs your lady wife sent served us in good stead. We are indebted to Lady Mildred and you for your kindness."

I had to smile, despite my mistrust of Cecil and his wiles. Trust him to have sowed a debt where it most mattered by offering medical assistance to a Tower guard's wife in need.

I heard him say, "Absolutely not. Lady Mildred will be pleased to hear her panaceas worked. She's ever tinkering with her recipes. By the way, Harry, I forgot to collect some papers when I was here yesterday." He motioned to me. I bowed. "This is an apprentice clerk of mine. Would you mind letting us through? We'll only be a moment."

Harry looked discomforted. "I'm afraid I can't, Sir William." He glanced over his shoulder at his companions, who were engrossed in a game of dice. "My lords Pembroke and Arundel gave strict orders to let no one in without their express leave." He moved closer to Cecil in confidence, his voice lowering to a whisper. "A missive from the Lady Mary arrived this morning. My lords left at once for the earl of Pembroke's house. Rumor has it, she's threatened to send the lot to the block if they don't declare for her by tonight."

"Indeed?" said Cecil, as if the news were of no particular account. "Rumors say so many things these days; one hardly knows who or what to believe anymore."

Harry chuckled uneasily. "Aye, it's like a gander of goodwives around here lately. Still, what with all this talk of mutiny at Yarmouth and the duke's army up and deserting him, a man need be careful with what he does, if you understand my drift?"

"I do, most certainly," replied Cecil, and he remained quiet, a subtle smile on his lips, his manner so disconcerting in its tranquility that it prompted Harry to blurt, "Before they left, the lords even ordered Lady Jane and Lord Guilford confined to their apartments for their own safety. Lady Dudley was beside herself. She threatened Lord Arundel with a dire end when her husband returns. My lord wasn't exactly civil in return, if you get my meaning."

He paused, searching Cecil's expression. "Some say his lordship of Northumberland cannot win. I'm not one for gossip, Sir William, but if it's true, I'd appreciate fair warning. I've my own to see to, as you know, and truth be told, I only follow orders. I rightly don't mind who sits the throne as long as I can feed my wife and children."

"Naturally." Cecil set a hand on Harry's arm, a gesture so imbued with understanding for a lackey's circumstances that Harry visibly started. "I don't think we should be discussing this in the open," Cecil added, and he drew Harry into the gatehouse shadow, where they conversed out of my hearing. I saw him slip Harry one of his ubiquitous pouches.

When Cecil returned, I hissed, "What is he talking about? What missive? The queen entrusted me with her letter, and I gave it to you less than an hour ago."

"It appears yours wasn't the only one she sent." He smiled

thinly. "I had to bribe Harry for more information and to let us through, so save your questions for later."

He walked forward briskly, nodding to the other guards, forcing me to hasten after him like the menial I was supposed to be. We passed under the iron portcullis, into the outer ward.

Cecil halted, pretending to adjust his sleeve, his valise clutched in one hand. In a hushed tone he said, "Mary has learned a thing or two, after all. She dispatched a duplicate of her orders via another courier, along with the news that she's amassed thousands to her cause. She prepares to march on London. The more sensible lords on the council have retreated to debate her reception; Suffolk went with them. More telling, his wife the duchess has departed for their country manor. It seems all those involved save for Lady Dudley have abandoned Jane and Guilford. Both are here, in the same rooms where they were scheduled to await their coronation."

He looked about, drew a quick breath. Again, I was struck by the turns and twists of these past few days, that I must now rely on the very man whom I'd considered my foe only hours ago.

"I believe the council will declare for Mary by this evening at the latest," he said. "As soon as they do, anyone still inside these gates will most likely not leave until she deigns it. Are you certain you still want to proceed? I for one would rather not take the chance. The Tower is no place for an extended stay."

I regarded him. "You sound afraid. I didn't think you capable of it."

"You'd be afraid, as well, if you had an ounce of sense," he retorted. He squared his shoulders, assuming his suave aura of invincibility as if it were a well-worn coat. "Come, then. Let's get this over with."

We strode onward toward the keep.

* * *

I barely had time to reflect on the fact that I was in the infamous Tower of London. The murmur of the Thames at the water gates echoed through the inner ward, magnified by the breadth of unrelenting stone walls. Guards, pages, and functionaries rushed to and fro, attending to their business without a smile to be seen among them, adding to the claustrophobic air.

Cecil didn't acknowledge anyone. In his unadorned hooded cloak and flat velvet cap, he could have been any one of the numerous clerks looking for their shifts to end. Indeed, any of said clerks could have been other than what they appeared. I scanned the ward. For a heart-stopping moment I thought I glimpsed a slim figure pause to mark us. When I focused, however, there was no one there.

The hair on the back of my neck prickled. It couldn't possibly have been Stokes; he'd be with the duchess on her way to her country manor, seeking to put as much distance between her hapless daughter Jane and herself as she could. I must be more tired than I'd thought. I was letting fatigue get the best of me. And I was beginning to think I must be mad to have insisted on this errand. Impregnable walls closed in around me; under my feet unraveled miles of pits and dungeons, where men suffered the most agonizing of torments. Death on the scaffold was considered a mercy compared to the array of devices inflicted on those imprisoned here, some of which were so horrific many never made it to the scaffold.

Fear rooted in the pit of my stomach. I concentrated on keeping my expression impassive when we were detained again at the keep's entrance. Once more Cecil parlayed his credentials and astonishing recollection for first names and familial details, not to mention a discreet use of coin, to earn us admittance.

Inside, torches on the walls gurgled flame. The hall we traversed was damp, cold; the sun never penetrated here. We climbed a turnpike staircase to a second floor roofed in timber, where two stern-faced yeomen in uniform, with snub-nosed dags at their belts, stopped us.

"Master Cecil, I regret to say no one is allowed in," a burly fellow informed us, though not without an apologetic note in his voice. Did Cecil know every guard of import in the Tower?

Evidently, for Cecil smiled. "Ah, yes, Tom. I was told the lords had ordered the lady confined for her own protection." He removed Mary's letter to the council from his pocket, the broken seal showing. "However, this man brings news from Lady Mary. I don't think we should interfere with Tudor family business, do you?" His tone was light, almost amiable. "We might soon find ourselves having to explain our own rather insignificant roles in this unfortunate affair, and I for one would prefer to say I did what was right. Besides, he needs only a moment. "

Good guard Tom didn't need to be told twice. Motioning brusquely to the other, he had the door unlocked. I waited for Cecil to move forward. Instead he stepped aside. "I actually do have some papers to fetch," he told me. "You've a few minutes. That is all."

I stepped inside.

Though small, the room was not unpleasant; it looked like any lady's bower, hung with tapestries, fresh rushes strewn on the plank-wood flooring. She sat in a chair positioned at the casement window, which offered a circumscribed view of the city.

Without looking around Jane Grey said, "I'm not hungry, and I am not going to sign anything, so put whatever you have on the table and go."

"My lady." I bowed low. She stood, her anxiety showing in her quick movement. She wore a fustian gown, her ginger-colored hair loose over her thin shoulders. In the gloom of the chamber, where premature dusk already began to settle, she seemed tiny, a child in adult garb.

Her voice caught in her throat. "I . . . I know you."

"Yes, my lady. I am Squire Prescott. We met at Whitehall. I am honored you remember."

"Whitehall," she repeated, and I saw her shudder. "That horrible place . . ."

I wanted to take her in my arms and hold her close. She looked as if she hadn't known an hour of peace in years, as if nothing except tragedy would ever touch her again.

"I've little time," I told her, and I took a step closer. "I've come to tell you not to despair." I removed Mary's second letter from within my cloak. "Her Majesty sends you this."

She recoiled, as if she'd been struck. "Her Majesty? Is it over, then?"

"It will be soon. By tonight, the council must declare for her; they can do nothing else. The duke's army has deserted him. It is a matter of time before he surrenders or is captured."

She gnawed at her lip, glancing at the letter in my hand. "God knows in His Wisdom, I never desired this," she said. "The duke and his wife, my parents and the council . . . they forced this on me. They made me marry Guilford and do their bidding. Thus shall I tell Mary, if she ever finds it in her heart to forgive me."

"She already has. Her Majesty knows how grievously you've been used."

Her voice was as firm as the hand she held up. "Pray, do not seek to lighten my burden. I've committed treason. There is no other-remedy than to suffer the punishment. I will not shirk my duty, not even for my life."

I felt tears perilously close. I extended the letter to her. "Her Majesty won't let you suffer anything. As soon as she's seen to the true culprits in this affair, she will release you. You will go home, my lady, back to your studies and your books."

"My books . . ." Her voice caught, and I couldn't resist anymore. I strode to her, engulfed her in my arms. She sagged against my chest. Though she didn't utter a sound, I felt her weep.

Ebbing light slanted through the window. In that moment, I wanted to tell her everything I had discovered, so that she would know she was not alone, so that she would always find in me an uncle who cared for her.

But the words stuck in my throat. I could never tell her the truth; it was too dangerous. It would only darken the terrible burden she already carried. Though I might one day come to understand why the Dudleys had done what they had, I knew in that instant that I would never forgive them for the devastation they had wrought on this fifteen-year-old girl.

She drew back. She was composed, the wetness on her cheeks fading as she took the crushed letter from me and slipped it into her gown pocket. "I'll read it later," she said, and she was about to say something else when she was interrupted by the sudden disquieting toll of bells.

"You must leave," she said. "You cannot be found here. It wouldn't bode well for you."

"My lady," I said to her, "if you ever find need of me you have only to send word."

She smiled. "Not even you can save me from the path God has ordained."

I bowed again, went to the door. I glanced over my shoulder. She had returned to her vigil at the window, twilight gathering itself about her.

Cecil rose from a stool in the passage. Thanking Tom, who locked the door once more, he took me by the arm. "I was about to come in after you. Did you hear the bells? We must leave at once. In an hour at most, the gates shall close in Mary's name. This will be her prison."

I shook his hand away. "God speed, then. I still have unfinished business."

He stared at me. "No. I know what you're thinking, and it is madness. She is not a prisoner. She's free to move about, tell anyone she pleases that you are alive and well."

"She won't. She's too busy trying to save her precious son. Besides, there was never any proof. Alice is dead. I'm no longer a threat, if indeed I ever was."

"Be that as it may," he said, and for the first time since we'd met I sensed genuine concern in his voice. "Would you put your life in her hands? Think before you do this. I will not be held responsible for whatever may befall you."

"I never expected you to. I've asked Peregrine to wait for me in the fields outside the city with our horses. If I'm not there by nightfall, he's to go to Hatfield. You can meet him and ride off to be with your family. But I must stay. She has something I need."

Cecil's jaw tensed under his beard. He stood silent for a long moment before he drew his cloak about him and tightened his hold on his valise. "May you find what you seek," he said tersely, and he went down the staircase without a backward glance.

I resisted the claw of fear in my belly. Turning to meet the guards' curious stares, I said, "If one of you might indicate the way to Lord Guilford's room . . . ?"

The yeoman Tom said, "I'll take you to him."

Chapter Thirty

𝕴 climbed worn stone flags to the uppermost story, Tom ahead of me. Despite my icy bravura, I dreaded the upcoming moment more than I'd admit.

We came to a narrow door. As Tom spoke with the guards there, I almost turned and fled. I could still catch up with Cecil, who was another kind of monster, yes, but one I'd prefer to deal with any day. I could meet Peregrine in the fields; by tonight I could be with Kate and Elizabeth in the safety of the princess's manor. I could live out the rest of my days in ignorance and most likely be the better for it. Whatever lay beyond that door would only bring me more suffering.

Even as I thought this, my fingers strayed to the inner pocket in my cloak, seeking the almost intangible object I'd secreted there. The feel of it strengthened my faltering resolve. I had to do this, for Mistress Alice, if nothing else.

"Five minutes." Tom handed me his weapon. "Be careful. She's rabid as a dog, that one."

He unbolted and pulled open the door. Shoving the pistol in my belt, I stepped inside.

A large leather coffer was in the middle of the room, heaped with clothing. Upon the floor were piled papers and books. Two figures labored in a corner, hauling a wooden chest from the wall. Near-identical shades of fair hair mingled damply, the lean bodies under sweat-stained clothing molded of the same rib and bone.

At the sound of the door opening, she reared around to face the intruder. At her side Guilford likewise looked up. He froze.

"It's about time you deigned to—" she began. She stiffened. "Who are you? How dare you intrude on us!" She meant to sound commanding, but her voice was strained, her appearance so unlike the impeccable unforgiving matron I'd always known that I couldn't formulate a word.

Then I remembered. I had a beard. I wore a cap.

I removed the cap. "I thought you'd recognize me, of all people, my lady."

Guilford yelped. Hissing breath through her bared teeth, Lady Dudley stalked to me, her unbound hair showing streaks of silver, framing her gaunt, infuriated features.

"*You*. You are supposed to be dead."

I met her empty eyes. I could see now that she was ill. She'd been ill for years, both in mind and spirit. She'd kept it hidden under her glacial facade, against which nothing had seemed to penetrate, but all the while it had consumed her, her husband's betrayal after years of dutiful marriage exposing the raw, desperate creature she had become. Faced with abandonment after a lifetime of self-sacrifice, she had lashed out with all the cunning at her disposal. Lethal as she was, in the final say she had acted out of unbearable grief. And grief was something I understood, even if the realization brought no comfort.

"I'm glad to disappoint you," I said.

Her mouth twisted. "You always did enjoy making a nuisance

out of yourself." She reached up a hand in a phantom echo of her previous elegance, pushed back tendrils of hair from her brow. "How tedious. I'd thought myself well rid of you by now."

"Oh, you will be—as soon as you answer my questions."

She paused. Behind her Guilford cried, "You—you stay away from us!"

"Be quiet." She did not take her gaze from me. "Let him ask whatever he likes. It costs us nothing to hear him waste his breath."

I flipped back my cloak, revealing Tom's dag. Her eyes widened. "I may not be the best shot," I said, "but in such a small room I'm bound to hit something. Or someone."

She stepped before me. "Leave my son alone. He knows nothing. Ask your miserable questions and be gone. I've more pressing matters to attend to."

For once she spoke the truth. When the bells had begun to toll, she'd been in the middle of packing valuables. Like Jane, she understood what those bells signified; she knew the end approached. So she and Guilford had started dragging that coffer to the door in a futile attempt to block it, to gain time before they were both officially declared prisoners. She knew the council would soon come to put him under arrest—Guilford, her most beloved child, the only one she'd ever cared for. Her hunger for revenge was equaled only by her feral devotion to the one soul she had molded entirely to her will.

She was human, after all. She could love. And hate.

"You cannot save him," I told her. "Those bells ring for Queen Mary. You've lost. Guilford Dudley will never wear a crown. In fact, he'll be lucky to keep his head."

"I'll tear you to pieces, bloody cur," snarled Guilford.

Lady Dudley's laugh was a blade ripping through skin. "You're still not nearly as clever as you think. I never wanted a crown for him. It's my husband who will lose his head for this, not Guilford. I will save him, even if I have to beg for his life on my knees. Mary is a woman; she knows what loss is. She will understand that no child should pay for his father's crimes."

She took a step closer to me, her breath acrid. "But *you*—you have lost everything. Mistress Alice is dead, and you'll get nothing more from me. You don't exist. You never did."

I took her measure. "I know about Master Shelton."

She went utterly still.

"Archibald Shelton," I went on, "your devoted steward. I know he was the one who shot at me that night in Greenwich. I thought he displayed rather poor aim for a man considered an expert marksman during the Scottish wars. But now I know he wasn't really trying to kill me. He was trying to spare me when he aimed at the wall. The ball just happened to ricochet."

"Fool," she spat. "Shelton took the gun, yes, but it was dark. He couldn't see. Had there been better light he would killed you. He despises you for everything you've done."

"Oh, I don't believe that," I said, and then I paused, suddenly realizing what had eluded me. "But you didn't know, did you? He never told you. You never knew he was the one Mistress Alice had confided in. You only knew someone else had been told, someone who could reveal who I was if you ever harmed me or her—as eventually you did when you killed Mistress Alice. Master Shelton thought she'd died on the way to the fair; he believed the lie you told, just as I did, but then he came into the king's room that night with your sons and he saw her. He knew how far you had gone. You thought he'd do anything to serve you, but in truth his ultimate loyalty lay in protecting me—the son of his former master, Charles of Suffolk."

She threw herself at me, keening like an animal. Her attack

threw me off balance. As I fended her nails from my face, the door flung open and the guards charged in. They grabbed hold of her, hauled her off me as she flailed and screamed obscenities.

"No!" I yelled. "Wait. Leave her. I have to . . ."

It was too late. Two of the guards dragged her away, her shrieks rebounding against the walls. I knew then, as I'd known little else, that it would be a long time before I stopped hearing that unearthly sound in my nightmares.

The echo faded to silence. Tom stood on the threshold. "It's time you left. They're shutting the gates by the council's order. You don't want to spend the night in here."

I nodded numbly, moving toward the door, when I heard a muffled sob. I looked over my shoulder. Guilford sat crumpled on the floor, his face in his hands. I tried to feel some compassion. It saddened me that all I could muster was disgust.

"Where is he?" I asked.

Guilford raised tear-filled eyes. "Who?" he quavered.

"Master Shelton. Where is he?"

Fresh tears choked Guilford's voice. "He—he went to fetch our horses."

Wheeling about, I bolted from the room.

Night had fallen. In the bailey, torches exuded smoky light, limning the stone walls. Bells rang out in discordant spontaneity, as more than one local pastor took to his steeple in an excess of joy. Outside the Tower walls, all of London had emerged in celebration for their rightful queen, while inside, pandemonium erupted, as those still loyal to the duke recognized their folly and sought to escape, even as ramparts were manned and gates bolted shut.

Rushing down the stairs out of the keep, I came to a halt. My heart pounded in my ears. I could scarcely draw breath as I scanned the crowded bailey for that figure I'd seen earlier, which I now knew had not been a figment of my overwrought imagination.

It had been Master Shelton in a black cloak. Master Shelton: who'd been abetting Lady Dudley and Guilford in their escape and saw Cecil and me going into the keep. He had to be near. Lady Dudley was expecting him, and he wouldn't abandon her until he determined there was nothing more he could do. Master Shelton was nothing if not reliable; he fulfilled his duty, no matter what.

But I now knew he had been doing something more. He had served Charles of Suffolk before he came to the Dudley household, and Mistress Alice must have known him from that time; unbeknownst to Lady Dudley, she'd entrusted him with the truth of my birth. I knew he had mourned my mother, brought the piece of her broken jewel to Mary Tudor. I knew he had spared my life at Greenwich. What I did not know was how deep his bond with my mother ran, if he was in fact the very reason she had hid her pregnancy. I had called myself Suffolk's son to disarm Lady Dudley, but deep inside something was still missing, an elusive key I did not possess, which, if found, would unlock the final secret.

He held that key. Only he could tell me if he was my father.

I cursed, peering into a flickering darkness in which cloaked figures rushed about like shades. I'd never find him in this mess. I should give up, make my escape while I still could, before they locked the gates and I was trapped inside.

I started to turn toward where the majority of those in the bailey headed. As I did, I caught sight of a shadow at the wall opposite me, where the night crept thick as ink.

A hood shielded its face. It stood still as a column. I paused, every nerve on alert; it lifted its head. For an electrifying instant our eyes met. I sprang to him, just as Master Shelton whirled about and ran, pounding on powerful legs, into the crowd that plunged like stampeding cattle from the ward.

I crashed headlong into the onslaught, wedging my way forward. Master Shelton was ahead, distinguished by the bullish width of his shoulders. The cobbled causeway narrowed, forcing the fleeing officials and menials into a bottleneck. The portcullis was shut, a maw of teeth impeding escape. From behind us, the clangor of hooves signaled the arrival of mounted patrols on steeds, accompanied by scores of guards in helmets and breastplates.

I watched in horror as the soldiers began pulling men with apparent randomness from the throng, their staccato question— "Whom do you serve? Queen or duke?"—accompanied by the sickening thrust of pikes rupturing skin. Within seconds, the stench of urine and blood thickened the air. At the portcullis, men clawed at each other in frenzy, scrambling over heads, shoulders, ribs, breaking and crushing flesh and bone.

Master Shelton was trying to pull back, to fight his way out of the panic that had erupted. If a guard or someone else identified him as a Dudley servant, in this madness he'd be killed.

A blood-flecked guard on a massive bay approached, forcing the crowd to part. Several unfortunates flew off the causeway into the churning moat, where others swam or drowned. I rammed forward with my shoulders, as hard as I could, pushing those behind Master Shelton. The steward whipped his head about, the puckered scar across his face starkly visible.

He glared when he saw the guard coming toward him. I started to shout a warning just as the crowd lurched into motion, swallowing him from view. The portcullis had been forced up. There was chaos, men tearing up hands and knees as they sought to crawl under it, desperate to escape certain arrest or death.

Master Shelton had vanished. I started shoving and elbowing, battling to stay standing. I staggered over the inert bodies of those who'd fallen underfoot and been trampled. As I was dislodged along with the rest of the horde onto a landing quay, I looked about.

No sign of him anywhere.

Behind me I could hear the charge of the guards on horseback, followed by those with pikes. Scattering in terror, many of the men began leaping off the quay into the river, preferring to risk the tide than be caught and skewered alive.

"NO!" I roared, even as I too ran forward. "NOOO!"

I kept roaring as I plunged into the tide-swollen Thames.

Hours later, dripping and reeking of sewage, I reached the fields outside the city. Above me a bonfire-lit sky blazed. Behind me London reverberated with clanging bells.

I had managed to paddle my way to a set of crumbling water steps on the south side, avoiding the river depths, where whirlpools churned the surface. I also avoided the sight of those sucked under by the pools' vortexes and those clambering back onto the quay like drenched cats, only to find the soldiers waiting. I could only wonder how many would die tonight for having served the duke, even in the most minor capacity, and if Cecil had gotten out. No doubt, he had. The master secretary possessed a knack for survival.

I tried not to think of Shelton, whom I doubted had ever learned to swim.

Even more painful was the thought of Jane Grey, who as of this hour had become a captive of the state, dependent on the queen's mercy. Instead, I focused on putting one sloshing foot in front of the next, dragging the sodden length of my cloak behind me as I slogged to the road. I had no idea how far it was to Hatfield. Maybe I could hitch a ride on a passing cart after I dried off enough to not resemble a vagabond.

When I thought I'd reached a safe enough distance, I sank to the ground to search my cloak. I extracted the gold leaf in its drenched cloth, moved it to my jerkin. I was squeezing the excess water from my cloak and rolling it into a bundle to carry on my back when hoofbeats sounded, galloping toward me.

I crouched near a hawthorn bush, which of course offered little cover. Fortunately the night was dark, moonless. Maybe whoever it was would be too intent on their own escape to notice me. I huddled as close to the ground as I could get, holding my breath as two horsemen neared, both in caps and cloaks. When one came to a halt, I cursed my luck.

"It's about time," said a familiar voice.

With a weary smile, I stood.

Cecil looked me up and down. He rode Deacon. At his side, on Cinnabar, was Peregrine. The boy exclaimed, "Finally! We've been searching for you for over an hour, wondering what kind of trouble you'd gotten yourself into this time." He chuckled. "Looks like another dip in the river. Are you quite sure you're not part fish?"

I gave him a sullen stare.

Cecil said quietly: "Did you find what you were looking for?"

"Almost." Tying my half-bundled cloak to the saddle, I swung up in front of Peregrine. "It wasn't a pleasant experience."

"I never thought it would be." Cecil followed my gaze back to the silhouette of the Tower. "The rabble's gone wild," he said. "They clamor in the streets for Northumberland's blood. Let us pray Queen Mary proves worthy of it." He returned his regard to me. I met his eyes in tacit understanding. Enemies we should have been; indeed, should have remained. But the times demanded more of us.

"To Hatfield, then," said Cecil.

We parted ways many hours later, as dawn spilled over the horizon. Cecil's manor lay a few miles away. He gave me detailed directions to Hatfield; there was an awkward moment when I uttered my gratitude that he'd stayed behind to help Peregrine. "Though I did tell the rascal not to wait for me," I admonished.

Cecil inclined his head. "I was happy to oblige. It's a relief to know there is still something to be redeemed in me. Please, give my regards to Her Grace and to Mistress Stafford, of course." He jolted me with a knowing sparkle in his cool eyes before he cantered off.

I looked after him. Too much had gone between us for friendship to ever develop, but if Elizabeth must have an amoral champion, she'd find none better than William Cecil.

Peregrine slouched behind me, half asleep. "Hold tight," I said. "We're not stopping till we get there."

I spurred forth under a lightening sheet of a sky, over summer meadows and through copses of beech, until we came upon the red-brick manor nestled amidst towering oaks, the floury scent of baking bread rising warm in the morning air.

I slowed Cinnabar to an amble. As we neared, I saw that Hatfield was a working manor, with an enclosed pasture for livestock, fruit trees, orchards, dairies, and other outbuildings. I knew, without seeing them, that the gardens would be lovely yet slightly wild, like their mistress.

Solace stole over me. This looked like a place where I might heal.

When I saw the figure running from the house onto the road, her auburn hair tumbling about her shoulders, I lifted my hand to wave, in joy and relief.

I was home, at long last.

Chapter Thirty-one

did not dream.

Awakening to the chamber where Kate had brought me in a state of mind-emptying exhaustion, I lay under rumpled linen, absorbing the scent of lavender coming from a wreath on the wall, which mingled with the linseed polish of the chair, the clothes press, and the table.

I stretched my aching bruised limbs and rose. Stepping past a pewter pitcher and basin, I looked out the mullioned window to the parkland surrounding the manor. I did not know how long I had slept, but I felt refreshed, almost whole. I turned back to the room and began searching for my clothes, which I seemed to recall Kate peeling off my inert body as I dropped into bed.

Without so much as a knock, the door banged open.

Mistress Ashley bustled in, carrying a tray. "Breakfast," she announced, "though in truth it should be supper. You've slept away most of the day. So has your dirty friend. He's in the kitchen devouring a lamb."

I gasped, my hands shooting down to cover myself.

She chortled. "Oh, don't mind me. I have seen a man in his

skin. I may seem a bit long in the tooth to you, but I'll have you know I'm a married woman."

"My—my clothes?" I was stunned. The last time I'd seen Mistress Ashley, she'd scoured me with her eyes. I barely recognized this stout partridge with her cheery voice and convivial manner.

"Your clothes are being laundered." She whipped the linen off the tray to reveal a platter of manchet bread, cheese, fruit, and salted meat. "There's a fresh shirt, a jerkin, and breeches in the press. We tried to match your weight and height to one of the grooms. Nothing fancy, mind you, but they'll do until we have you properly fitted."

She eyed me matter-of-factly. "You needn't fret. Mistress Stafford found your things in the lining and has them safe. She's in the garden now, picking herbs. It's down the stairs, through the hall, and out the doors to your left. You can meet her there once you've eaten and washed." She paused. "You're too slight for a beard. There's water in the ewer and lye soap in the basin. We make the soap ourselves. It's as good as any you'll find, including that silly perfumed stuff from France they charge a king's ransom for in London."

She marched to the door. Then she stopped, as if she'd forgotten something. Turning back to me as I whipped the rumpled sheet from the bed and flung it around my waist, she said, "We owe you our thanks. Mistress Stafford told us how you helped Her Grace visit with His Majesty her brother, God rest his soul, and then escape the duke's clutches. Were it not for you, who knows where she might have ended up? Northumberland never wished anything but harm on her. I warned her not to leave this house, but she didn't listen to me. She never listens to me. She never listens to anyone. She thinks she's invincible. It'll be her undoing one day, mark my words."

She babbled like a brook! Who would have guessed?

I lowered my head. "I was honored to be of service," I mumbled.

"Yes, well." She snorted. "Serving her is no charm, you'll see. I should know; I've been with her since she was this high, and you never met a more contentious soul, even in her leading strings. Always did have to have her way. Still, all of us in this household couldn't love her more. She has this way of stealing into your heart. You can't help it. And before you know it, she has you wrapped about her pretty finger." She wagged her finger. "*That's* when you have to be careful. She can be canny as a cat when the mood takes her."

She smiled. "Well, I'll be off, then. You've the two of them waiting on you, and I'm hard-pressed to say which of the two is less demanding. Wash yourself well. Her Grace has a nose like a blood-hound. Nothing she hates more than sweat or too much perfume."

The door closed. I descended on the fare with gusto. After I'd eaten my fill, I bathed and took out the clothes from the press. I was glad to find my saddlebag there. Gently, I removed the leather-bound volume, which was more battered for the wear. I opened it to that front page and the handwritten inscription in faded blue ink.

Votre amie, Marie.

I caressed the slanted writing, penned by a beloved hand I'd never felt. I set the book on the bedside table. Later, I would read Mistress Alice's favorite psalm. And remember.

I was able to shave using lather from the soap, my knife, and a sliver of cracked mirror from my bag. Though I couldn't see myself well in its fractured reflection, what I did glimpse as I washed away the hair-flecked spumes brought me to a halt.

The face looking back at me was bruised, pale, more angular than I recalled, its youth tempered by hard-earned and sudden maturity. It was a face not yet twenty-one years of age; a face I had lived with all my life, and it belonged to someone I did not know. But in time, I would come to know the stranger I had become. I would make myself his master. I would learn everything I needed to survive in this new world, and I would stake my place.

And I would not rest until I found Master Shelton.

For he knew far more about me than he had ever let on, of that I was sure. He had served the late Charles Brandon, duke of Suffolk, and mourned the duke's wife, my mother. Had he also known that the golden leaf he'd conveyed to Mary Tudor was from the same jewel whose other leaf had ended up hidden among Dame Alice's possessions? And if so, did he know Dame Alice had been entrusted with it, and why? I had so many questions that only he could answer.

I turned away to dress. The clothes were a remarkably close fit.

Passing through the great hall with its impressive hammer-beamed ceiling and Flemish tapestries, I proceeded to the open oak doors and into a lingering summer evening that drifted over eglantine and willow like a velvet rain.

Kate stood ankle-deep in an herb patch, a straw hat on her head as she bundled fresh-picked thyme into a basket. She glanced up at my approach, the hat slipping off to dangle on ribbons at her back. Gathering her in my arms, I indulged my starved senses.

"I assume you slept well," she whispered at length, against my lips.

"I'd have slept better if you'd been with me," I said, my hands running down her waist.

She laughed. "Any better and you'd have needed a shroud." Her laughter turned husky. "Don't you think to tempt me. I'll not give in to any old tomcat that decides to wander home."

"Yes, I like that about you," I growled. We kissed, after which she drew me to a bench. We held hands, gazing at the diminishing sky.

Presently Kate said, "I have these." From her skirt pocket, she brought out the leaf and, to my surprise, Robert Dudley's silver-and-onyx ring.

"I'd forgotten about this," I murmured as I slipped the ring on my finger. It was too big.

"Do you know what's happened?" she asked.

"Last I had heard, the duke started to march on Framlingham when his army deserted."

She nodded. "Word came today. He never reached it. The moment the council proclaimed Mary queen, Arundel and the others rushed to grovel at her feet. Arundel then went to arrest Northumberland, Lord Robert, and his other sons. They're being taken to the Tower, where Guilford is already imprisoned." She paused. "It's said Mary will order them executed."

My fingers closed over the ring. "Who can blame her?" I said softly, and as I spoke, my memory flew back to a time long past, when a bewildered boy crouched in an attic, fearing discovery and envying the tribe of sons who would never accept him.

I felt Kate's hand on mine. "Do you want to talk about it? You still have the petal. Did you find out what it means?"

The memory faded.

"It's a leaf." I met her gaze. Opening her palm, I set the golden leaf in her hand. "I want to tell you everything. Only, I need some more time to sort it out. And she is expecting me. Mistress Ashley said she is waiting on me."

I noticed the subtle stiffening of her posture. I knew she couldn't help it, and it was something we'd have to learn to deal with if we were to build a life together. Elizabeth had become too much a part of both of us.

"She is," said Kate. "She had another of her headaches this afternoon, which is why I came out to gather these herbs for her evening draft; but she did ask to see you as soon as you were ready. I can bring you to her, if you like. She's taking her exercise in the gallery."

She started to rise. I pressed her hand to my lips. "Sweet Kate, my heart is yours."

She looked at our twined hands. "You say that now, but you do not know her as I do. A more loyal mistress cannot be found, but she requires undying devotion in return."

"She has it already. But that is all." I stood, cupped her chin, and kissed her lips. "Keep that leaf close. It's yours now, a symbol of our troth. I'd match it with a ring, if you'll have me."

I was warmed by the luster in her eyes. I had time enough later to prove nothing would interfere with the love I wanted to share with her—a love far from the tumult of these days and the malice of court, a love in which the secret of my past could finally be put to rest.

I followed her back to the manor. At the entrance to the gallery, I paused. The slim figure with Urian at her side appeared taller, arresting in its solitude. I drew a quick breath to ease the sudden tightness in my chest, then stepped forth and bowed.

With an elated bark of recognition Urian bounded to me.

Elizabeth stood silhouetted in the diffused sun that slipped through the embrasure, her pale mauve gown catching the light like water. Her red-gold hair was unbound, loose about her shoulders. She looked like a startled fawn caught in a clearing, until she strode toward me with that determination that was more of the hunter than the prey. As she neared, I noted a parchment clutched in her hand.

I met her amber gaze. "I am overjoyed to see Your Grace safe."

"And in good health, don't forget that," she teased. "And you, my friend?"

"I too am well," I said softly.

She smiled, waved me to the window seat, the worn uphol-stery and stack of teetering books to one side indicating it was a favored spot. I perched on the edge, taking the time I needed to readjust to her presence. Urian sniffed my legs and then curled at my feet.

Elizabeth sat beside me, close but not too much so, her ta-pered fingers fussing with the parchment. Remembering how those pampered hands had wielded a stone against a guard's head, I marveled at her mercurial duality, which was as much a part of her as her coloring.

It was only then that the reality of our situation struck me. I hadn't considered how she might react when I told her. Would she welcome me as a long-lost member of the family? Or would she, like her formidable cousin the duchess of Suffolk, see me as a threat? I might be, after all; if Charles Brandon was my father, I most certainly could be, in her eyes. She might never under-stand that regardless of the Tudor blood in my veins, I had no aspirations to a throne.

As if she could sense my thoughts, she said, "You are comely." She spoke as if she hadn't noticed it before. "So lean, with your light gray eyes and hair the color of barley. . . . It's no wonder Jane thought you looked familiar. You resemble my brother Edward, or what he may have looked like had he lived to be your age."

Emotion welled in me.

Whether or not she could accept me as kin seemed not to matter in that moment, though I had decided this was not the time to confess. I still had to feel my way into this new world I inhabited. For no matter how true I was to Kate—and I was true, and would be to the death—I had no doubt I was also in love with this princess. How could I not be? Only, mine wasn't the earthly obsession of a Dudley, and I was glad of it. To love Elizabeth Tudor would indeed demand more than it could ever give; it condemned one to eternal limbo, yearning for what could never be. In this respect, I felt pity for Lord Robert, whose physical chains could never equal those she'd forged about his heart.

"Where have you drifted, squire?" I heard her ask, and I pulled myself to attention.

"Forgive me, Your Grace. I was just thinking of everything that has transpired."

"Indeed." She regarded me with unwavering focus.

I removed the loose ring from my finger. "I believe this belongs to you. Lord Robert gave it to me that night he sent me to you. I think he'd want you to have it."

Her hand trembled as she reached out. "You risked much in order to get this to me, I know. Some might say too much."

"Some might, Your Grace."

"But not you." She raised her eyes. "Was it worth it, everything that transpired?" As she waited for my answer, her regality faded. She reverted to what she was at heart—an achingly young woman, vulnerable and uncertain.

"Yes," I said. "Every moment. I'd risk it all again to serve you."

She gave me a tremulous smile. "You might find reason to regret those words." She unfolded her other hand to reveal the crumpled parchment she held. "This is my sister's summons to London," she said. "Or rather, a summons from her new lord chamberlain. I'm expected to join her at court to celebrate her victory."

She paused. When she next spoke, her voice was barely above a whisper. "I will have need of your keen eyes. Mary and I . . . we are not like other sisters. There's too much pain in our past, too much loss. She doesn't know how to forget, though all I've ever done against her was be the daughter of her mother's rival."

I wanted to touch her. But I did not. "I am here," I said. "So are others. We will see to it that you are kept from harm."

She nodded, slipped Robert's ring into her bodice. The letter drifted from her fingers to the floor. We sat in silence for a long moment before she glanced at me, and without warning she let out a clarion laugh. "So somber! Do you know how to dance, Brendan Prescott?"

I started. "Dance? No. I . . . I never learned."

"Never learned?" She leapt to her feet, Urian springing up beside her. "We must remedy that. How do you expect to enjoy, much less excel, at court if you don't know how to dance? It's the weapon of choice for every well-heeled gentleman. Much more has been done on the dance floor to save a kingdom than in any council room or battlefield."

I felt my grin emerge, lopsided, as her sudden clap brought Kate and Peregrine into the gallery. My suspicion that they'd been lurking close by, awaiting her cue, was confirmed by the lute in Kate's hands.

Jaunting at her side, Peregrine was another boy altogether, scrubbed to shiny perfection, his lithe form in a suit of jade velvet that matched the hue of his eyes. His smile looked to split his face in two when Elizabeth ordered him to beat time on one of her books: "Slowly, as if it were a kettledrum or the hindquarters of an ill-tempered steed. And Kate, play that pavane we learned together last week—the French one, with the long measure."

Strumming the corresponding chords, Kate gave me a mischievous smile.

With a look that warned I would take my sweet revenge later, I surrendered to Elizabeth as she took me by the hand and led me into the dance.

AUTHOR'S NOTE

*I*t is important to note that this is a work of fiction. It takes as its premise: *What if?* and interweaves fact and fiction, rumor, deduction, and imagination to tell a story. While I've strived to remain true to the historical period and limit conjecture to a circumscribed realm of possibilities, I have made certain adjustments to create my narrative.

The most obvious, of course, is that history makes no mention of Elizabeth Tudor visiting the court during the days leading up to Edward VI's demise. There is also no definitive proof that the young king was poisoned to extend his life. Nevertheless, the historical events I describe surrounding the nine-day reign of Jane Grey and Northumberland's fall are true. The duke did in fact seek to supplant Mary Tudor with his new daughter-in-law, and his army did desert him in favor of Mary. Likewise, Robert Dudley was sent after the embattled Mary to capture her; had he succeeded, there is little doubt that Elizabeth's arrest would have followed.

Kate Stafford, Peregrine, Archie Shelton, and Mistress Alice are fictional characters based on servants from the Tudor era.

Mary of Suffolk, Henry VIII's younger sister, did in fact oppose her brother's break with Rome and his marriage to Anne Boleyn. Mary refused to acknowledge Anne as queen and stayed far from court in the months before her death. Nevertheless, the supposition that Mary hid a pregnancy is fictional, as is Brendan Prescott—though the idea of a secret Tudor does fascinate.

Because writing by its nature is a solitary obsession and by profession a creative collaboration, I owe a debt of immense gratitude to my agent, Jennifer Weltz, who has championed my work with boundless enthusiasm. She and her colleagues at the Jean V. Naggar Literary Agency are my touchstones in an often unpredictable business. My editor, Charles Spicer, has been a longtime supporter of my writing, and I'm privileged to be working with him and his assistant editor, Allison Caplin, as well as my copy editor, Kate Davis. Everyone on the publishing team at St. Martin's Press, from publicity to marketing to creative, are phenomenal, and I thank them for giving this book their all.

On a personal level, my partner has stood by me with humor and sagacity as I struggled to make the transition from unpublished writer to author. I must also thank our beloved corgi, Paris, for showing me every day how to live with joy. My brother and his wife provided early feedback. My friend Linda read the manuscript several times. Fellow aficionado Paula jammed with me for inspiration. The two Jeans—Billy and LuAnn—and Jack of the Sunset Writers Group gave me laughter and encouragement. Sarah Johnson of the Historical Novel Society is a special friend, indeed, both for her tireless support of the genre and support of this book in its previous incarnations. My dog-walking friends in McLaren Park kept me humble, and my late friend Marie H., with whom I took long walks while this book was written, provided me with tea and wisdom. I miss her and remember her often.

I also must thank all the bookstores, sales reps, fellow writers, and the many bloggers who continue to champion the importance of books in our increasingly frenetic culture.

I wish to thank my mother, who gave me my first historical novel and ignited a spark in me that has never faded, and my father, who encouraged me to write. Though he did not live long enough to see my books published, he would have been proud.

Last, but never least, I thank you, my reader, because without you, books only exist as pages between covers. Your eyes bring my words to life. I am humbled to be one of your storytellers and sincerely hope to entertain you for many years to come.

For more information about my work, including scheduling book-group chats and features on my upcoming novels, please visit me at www.cwgortner.com.

Reading
Group
Gold

THE TUDOR SECRET
by C. W. Gortner

About the Author
- A Conversation with C. W. Gortner

Behind the Novel
- Historical Timeline
- "Elizabeth I: An Endless Fascination"
  An Original Essay by the Author

Keep on Reading
- Recommended Reading
- Reading Group Questions

*A
Reading
Group Gold
Selection*

For more reading group suggestions,
visit www.readinggroupgold.com

 ST. MARTIN'S GRIFFIN

📖 A Conversation with C. W. Gortner

Tell us about your background and how you decided to become a writer.

I grew up in southern Spain; my mother is Spanish and my father was American. For as long as I can remember, I've been fascinated by history. A ruined summer castle that once belonged to Isabella and Ferdinand was a stone's throw from where I lived; I was raised not only reading history but seeing it all around me. My mother tells me that I was always writing stories in my notebooks and illustrating them; indeed, even while pursuing other careers, I kept writing. I began to seriously contemplate becoming a published novelist in my mid-twenties. It took almost another twenty years before that actually happened!

Who are some of your favorite authors?

Too many to cite here; I have wide-ranging and eclectic taste. Growing up, I was influenced by classic writers in the genre—Alexandre Dumas, Rafael Sabatini, Daphne du Maurier, Jean Plaidy, and Margaret Campbell Barnes, among others. Ms. du Maurier in particular was so skilled in her ability to transcend barriers; she proved as easily at home with epic historical tales such as *The Glass-Blowers* as with psychological suspense, like my favorite of hers, *My Cousin Rachel,* or her international bestseller, *Rebecca.* Today, there are many wonderful historical fiction writers who acknowledge their debt to our past writers, while forging new ground. Historical fiction is more popular than ever, mainly because so many gifted writers have chosen to work in the genre.

Are there any historical figures you feel a particular affinity toward?

I hold a lifelong love for Anne Boleyn, and hold great affection for her daughter, Elizabeth. I'm also rather fond of the historical women I've written about in my

previous novels, the courageous Juana of Castile and the formidable Catherine de Medici. The Tudor court, however, is an especially interesting and dynamic place to explore, in that within a relatively short span of time so much happened politically and socially. The drama, intrigue, and tumult of the Tudors have, for good reason, captured generation after generation of readers; it seems there's always something new to discover about them.

What was the inspiration for _The Tudor Secret_ and its hero, Brendan Prescott?

Years ago, I read a fascinating book titled _The Elizabethan Secret Services_ by Alan Haynes. I had known through my other readings that William Cecil and Francis Walsingham developed one of the most sophisticated systems of intelligence in the world on behalf of the embattled queen, who faced enemies both in England and abroad for much of her long reign. But I'd never really stopped to consider the details, such as what the nascent seed of that service might have looked like before Elizabeth took the throne or how an innately skilled but otherwise common person such as Brendan Prescott might have ended up working for her. I thought to myself, _Hmm. This has promise._ Within a few days, after a conversation with a friend who's also a Tudor aficionado, I began to draft the outline for the novel you've just read, featuring a spy who becomes the secret confidant and protector of Elizabeth, rousing the enmity of her lover, Robert Dudley, even as the spy uncovers the key to his past—a key that threatens the kingdom's future.

Do you adhere to historical fact in your novels or do you take liberties if the story can benefit from the change? To what extent did you stick to facts in writing *The Tudor Secret*?

While I believe historical novelists should adhere to historical facts whenever possible, even as we spin a tale that is by and large a fictional re-creation of past events, history can be complicated and even inconvenient, particularly for the novelist. We often walk a delicate line in balancing the factual requisites of our story with the obligation to entertain our reader. It's not an easy feat, by any means. Nonfiction writers have the luxury of saying: "This and that happened, but we don't know why or how," but the fiction writer must make a determination. It should be an informed one, naturally, but still conclusions must be drawn. This is where historical fiction is so interesting to work in and why I think some nonfiction historians are drawn to it themselves: You paint in the empty spaces, the gaps where facts contradict each other or are simply not clear.

In *The Tudor Secret,* I weave three separate threads into the plotline: The first thread involves the events surrounding the demise of Edward VI in July 1553 and the Duke of Northumberland's plot to raise Jane Grey to the throne. I have not so much altered the facts in this case as reexamined them from another perspective, conjecturing what Northumberland's ultimate goal may have been. In the second thread, I deviate from the facts in that I speculate what may have occurred had Elizabeth decided to follow in her sister Mary's footsteps and visit the court during those tension-filled days leading to Edward's death. Historical accounts tell us that the princess in fact did not go to court, that she remained in Hatfield; however, it is not outside the realm of possibility that she undertook a secret trip, and that is my premise. I do not alter what is known about Elizabeth's character

or motivation. In the third thread, I create a purely fictional plotline that intersects with the above, involving Brendan, who is brought to court to serve Robert Dudley and is thrust into the drama surrounding the princess. While nothing in *The Tudor Secret* contradicts the known facts of what happened in the summer of 1553, I do mix things up and seek to reveal what might have been transpiring behind the scenes. This is, after all, a book about secrets—the secrets we carry; the secrets we use as weapons; the secrets we use to seek truth.

**In your research, what was the most interesting/
surprising/shocking thing you learned?**

I was actually surprised to discover how truly ruthless people at court were. We tend to see the court as a glamorous place of gorgeous costumes, minstrels, and rumors—and it was. But there was a much darker and more lethal side to it; proximity to the monarch promised riches or ruin, and fortunes rose and fell on a whim. Success was most often determined by how far you were willing to go to win, and at court people went very far, indeed.

Take, for example, Robert Dudley. I'd always seen him as a romantic figure—the forlorn and long-suffering suitor for a fickle Elizabeth's hand. After all, she was a survivor, scarred by the past; she cannot have been easy to love. However, as I researched Robert's youth and his actions in the days I describe in *The Tudor Secret,* I began to see a less sympathetic edge to him, one of callous disregard, of determination and ambition that mirrored his father. I think he learned the hard way that he had to bend his pride but I also think he's more complex than he's been popularly seen. To me, that makes him more interesting and fun to write. Likewise, William Cecil emerged as a much tougher character; he was not so much the benevolent paternal figure who guided Elizabeth to glory as a manipulative genius. But all this is what makes researching and writing historical fiction so engaging; you begin with an idea that sparks your imagination, you plunge into research, and that idea is transformed as if by alchemy into something entirely new and unforeseen.

Why do you think readers are so drawn to historical fiction?

I believe historical fiction helps us fill in spaces in history—we can know the facts by heart but what we crave is to experience the emotion, the inner lives, to share the trajectories and worlds of these people we feel so connected to. I write historical fiction because for me, it offers the ideal medium for bringing these long-gone people into our present, in a way that is immediate, visceral, and relevant. While they of course reflect the imaginary constraints and preferences of the author, that in and of itself makes the genre exciting. My vision of Elizabeth may differ wildly from another novelist's; in this way the past remains alive, constantly reexamined and reinvented.

Are you currently working on another book? If so, what—or who—is your subject?

The Tudor Secret is the first in a series about the rise of Brendan Prescott as a secret spymaster for Elizabeth I. I'm currently working on the second book in the series, in which Brendan is drawn back to his guise as a spy, this time in the court of Mary I.

Do you have a Web site or blog where readers can find out more about you?

Readers can always visit me at www.cwgortner.com and at historicalboys.blogspot.com. I enjoy talking to book groups and can easily chat with groups via speaker phone or Skype; to schedule a time with me, just visit the Book Groups link on my Web site.

 # Historical Timeline

Reading
Group
Gold

January 28, 1547	Henry VIII dies; his nine-year-old son succeeds him as Edward VI.
March 1547	Edward Seymour, Lord Protector, assumes power.
Summer 1548	Catherine Parr discovers Elizabeth's dalliance with her husband, Thomas Seymour; Elizabeth is sent away to Hatfield.
March 20, 1549	Thomas Seymour is beheaded for treason.
January 1552	Edward Seymour is executed; John Dudley, later Duke of Northumberland, seizes power.
1552	Edward VI approves the Second Act of Uniformity; Princess Mary is harassed for her adherence to Catholicism by Dudley.
January 1553	Edward VI falls gravely ill; rumors sweep the court that he is dying.
February 1553	Princess Mary visits Edward; their reunion is antagonistic because of Mary's resolve to remain Catholic.

*Behind the
Novel*

May 1533	Guilford Dudley, youngest son of Northumberland, marries Jane Grey.
June 1553	Edward alters his succession, coerced by Northumberland.
July 1, 1553	Edward VI makes his final public appearance.
July 6, 1553	Edward dies in Greenwich Palace. Soon after, Northumberland issues an arrest order for Mary, who, informed by an anonymous informant of her brother's demise, flees north to garner support.
July 10, 1553	Jane Grey is proclaimed queen of England.
July 19, 1553	Mary gathers an army of nearly twenty thousand and marches on London. She is proclaimed queen by popular acclaim; Jane Grey becomes a prisoner.

An Original Essay by the Author

Elizabeth I: An Endless Fascination

Elizabeth Tudor, known as Elizabeth I, has exerted an endless fascination over our imaginations, even in looking at her life before she took the throne in 1558. She was the only surviving child of the glamorous, ill-fated Anne Boleyn, whose passionate liaison with Henry VIII shattered his twenty-four year marriage to Catherine of Aragon and set off a cataclysmic upheaval that changed England forever. Elizabeth's parents believed that the child Anne carried was the long-awaited prince Henry had been denied; Anne staked her claim, and her unborn child's legitimacy, on the fact that Henry and Catherine's marriage had been incestuous due to Catherine's previous marriage to Henry's deceased brother, Arthur—a marriage which Catherine steadfastly proclaimed had never been consummated. Yet the child Anne bore was not a boy but a girl—a child of controversy, destroyed hopes, and disappointment, of chaos and uncertainty. Elizabeth came into the world with what seemed to be a curse already writ into her fate. Within three years, Henry would send her mother to the sword and remarry four more times; she would gain a younger brother, Edward, as well as an older sister Mary, with whom she would engage in a near-lethal collision of wills; she would face a daunting fight for her life that would test her mettle to its core; and she would, if the legend is true, fall madly, impossibly in love with the one man she would never fully have.

Elizabeth's struggle for survival in one of the most treacherous courts in history and the glorious, often turbulent forty-four year reign that ensued upon her accession have become fodder for our entertainment for centuries. In many ways, this brittle red-haired princess with the enigmatic eyes and spidery fingers—

so reminiscent of her mother—personifies our loftiest ideals of emancipation: Elizabeth refused to marry and never bore children (despite numerous rumors to the contrary), sacrificing her body and her heart for her country; she was arguably as alluring as Anne Boleyn yet never fell prey to the pitfalls that Anne paid for in blood; she displayed the fickle, silver-tongued wit that catapulted her mother to fame, coupled with the cruel, sometimes tyrannical temperament that transformed her father into a monstrous figure. Yet unlike Anne, whose tragic destiny overshadows her intense joie de vivre, or Henry, whose golden splendor is muted by the horrors of his later years, we tend to forgive Elizabeth's foibles and her mistakes, indeed even her bloodiest blunders; we forget her carcinogenic eccentricities and look past her capricious excesses, because we recognize in her a nobility of purpose, a single-minded drive to succeed, no matter the odds. We feel that we know her, intimately.

Elizabeth excelled in a time when few women could. Though she owed a debt to those who paved the way before her—such as the formidable Isabella of Castile and the flint-hearted Eleanor of Aquitaine—and she shared her stage with such unforgettable ladies as the embattled Catherine de Medici, queen-mother of France, and her own cousin, the flighty, irresistible Mary Stuart, Queen of Scots, Elizabeth transcended even these legends to become a mythical heroine in her own right, a figure apart from the porous mortality of her contemporaries—autonomous, instantly recognizable, inimitable, and uniquely unforgettable.

 **Recommended Reading**

 Reading
Group
Gold

Stephen Budiansky
*Her Majesty's Spymaster: Elizabeth I, Francis
Walsingham, and the Birth of Modern Espionage*

Antonia Fraser
The Wives of Henry VIII

Joan Glasheen
*The Secret People of the Palaces: The Royal Household
from the Plantagenets to Queen Victoria*

Alan Haynes
The Elizabethan Secret Services

Eric Ives
Anne Boleyn

Lady Jane Grey: A Tudor Mystery

Mary M. Luke
A Crown for Elizabeth

Liza Picard
*Elizabeth's London: Everyday Life in
Elizabethan London*

Alison Plowden
The House of Tudor

The Young Elizabeth

Chris Skidmore
Edward VI: The Lost King of England

Derek Wilson
*The Uncrowned Kings of England: The Black History of
the Dudleys and the Tudor Throne*

Tudor England

Sir Francis Walsingham: A Courtier in an Age of Terror

**Keep on
Reading**

Reading Group Questions

1. *The Tudor Secret* takes place during the succession crisis of 1553. What did you discover about England at this time? Who were the major players and what were their motivations?

2. Religion plays a crucial role in the story's conflicts. What were the main issues between Catholics and Protestants? Were their conflicts based on actual religious differences or larger political power struggles? Do you see any parallels to today's religious divides?

3. Brendan Prescott is a fictional character with a secret. Like many servants of the time, he is entrusted with his master's private information. What were some of the possible repercussions he could have suffered for his actions? If you had been in his place, what might you have done?

4. The jewel featured in the book is based on an actual jewel shown in a painting of Henry VIII's younger sister, Mary Tudor, Duchess of Suffolk, and her husband, Charles Brandon, the Duke of Suffolk. Both Mary Tudor and Mistress Alice end up with different pieces of this jewel; why do you think the jewel was broken into pieces? If it was done at Mary's request, what message do you think she was trying to send?

5. Lady Dudley hides secrets of her own. What are they? Did you understand her reasons for doing what she did? What does her character tell us about the role of noblemen's wives in the sixteenth century?

6. Brendan carries a clue to his past with him all along. Why doesn't he understand its significance until the end? What part of his past does he fail to solve?

7. The death of Edward VI remains shrouded in mystery. Do you find the author's hypothesis plausible? If not, why?

8. Elizabeth Tudor is one of history's most popular figures. Why do you think she continues to exert such fascination, so many years after her life?

9. Who was your favorite character in the book, and why?

*Keep on
Reading*

Want to learn more?
You'll find the author's "Historical Boys" blog,
behind-the-scenes features, book trailers,
and other secrets at www.cwgortner.com.